Vision Speak

Eden Remme Watt

PublishAmerica
Baltimore

© 2010 by Eden Remme Watt.
All rights reserved. No part of this book may be reproduced, stored in a retrieval system or transmitted in any form or by any means without the prior written permission of the publishers, except by a reviewer who may quote brief passages in a review to be printed in a newspaper, magazine or journal.

First printing

All characters in this book are fictitious, and any resemblance to real persons, living or dead, is coincidental.

PublishAmerica has allowed this work to remain exactly as the author intended, verbatim, without editorial input.

ISBN: 978-1-61582-324-6 (softcover)
ISBN: 978-1-4489-9491-5 (hardcover)
PUBLISHED BY PUBLISHAMERICA, LLLP
www.publishamerica.com
Baltimore

Printed in the United States of America

Dedication

This book is dedicated to all the children who left us too soon,
And especially to two young people who touched me
on their passage through,
Madeleine, a dancer, artist and lover of life,
who wanted to make a difference — and did,
Taylor, a kind-hearted young man and team player
whose competitive spirit lingers still,
They will never be forgotten.

Acknowledgements

Dreams are so much easier to attain when people believe in you. I've been blessed with family and friends who offer encouragement and support.

To my first readers, my husband Doug and son Jordan, parents Ola and Camille, sister Rebecca, brother-in-law Bill, aunts and uncles, especially Patti, Jane, Suzie and Aub who all read early drafts of my manuscript and provided feedback and encouragement. This project would never have crossed the finish line without your help.

Finally, thank you to Jennifer Knoch who is a brilliant young editor on her way.

Chapter 1

"As any change must begin somewhere, it is the single individual who will experience it and carry it through. The change must indeed begin with an individual; it might be any one of us."

Carl Jung

Someone was angry. The experience flooded the nineteen year old without warning, jolting her out of a snooze on the airbus. Wondering who it was, she scanned the other passengers but saw no outward signs. She'd always been sensitive, more aware of the interplay of emotions around her than most but that was nothing compared to what she could sense now.

It was April in the year 345 of PURE or by the archaic calendar, 2453 AD. Willow was a loyal citizen of the Republic with a promising future but, in three short months, her world had been turned upside down. If the authorities had known then what was happening with her, they probably would have taken action. If they'd had any idea of what she would become, they definitely would have.

Her new path began on the day her great grandmother whispered in her ear: "Visit me tomorrow—alone". Before that, she'd been immersed in scholastic activities and a busy social life. Now her class standing was slipping and she'd been avoiding friends and family, everyone except

Great Bet. It was as if Willow's life was spinning off its axis. Just this morning, after the matriarch called, she'd skipped class again, cancelled lunch with Sophie, and, worst of all sins, ignored her mother's call—again.

But Great Bet had insisted. She said they were running out of time. So now Willow's heart hammered in her chest after sprinting non-stop from the airbus tower. The stone walkway, trailing through manicured gardens, passed quickly under her feet. Finally, she landed on Great Bet's doorway, gasping for air. She wiped the sweat from her forehead, pushing back her dirty blonde hair, oblivious to the tangled strands protruding at odd angles.

She pressed her hand against the sensor lock on the front door and scurried inside when it slid open. Stepping into the alcove of her great-grandmother's small home in the Upper Elder Community, she searched for the old woman. The matriarch wasn't waiting in her usual lounge chair by the patio windows. The living area and kitchen were empty.

"Great Bet?" The silence shrieked in her ears. Louder, she called again. "Great Bet."

"In here." It was a croak but definitely a sign of life. Willow rushed into the bedroom to see the old lady tucked into her bed, her white head propped up on puffy pillows. The young woman stood in the doorway while her heart rate settled, watching her great grandmother appraise her. "What in the name of Marrisha is wrong with you? You look like you've seen a ghost."

"Oh." Willow released the breath she'd been holding. "I'm sorry, Great Bet. I was worried when I didn't see you."

"Relax, my dear. I'm not dead yet." Elzabeth McGregor, former agent to the Republic and matriarch of the Tyler line, had always had a prickly tongue. Willow and her cousins called her Great Bet but non-family members would address her only with the highest respect. Advisory Agent McGregor, she'd heard them say.

"That's a relief. I've already had a stressful day."

An ancient chuckle resonated from the bed. "Alright, child, come over here." She motioned towards the chair at her bedside. "Let's get started."

"Great Bet, you really did frighten me when you sent that urgent message." Willow took the seat by the bed. "I was just here yesterday, and two days before that. You know everyone's starting to ask me what I've been doing and where I've been lately. My mother, in particular…"

"Tell that busybody Joley that you're a grown woman and it's none of her business." Great Bet interrupted, her voice rasping. "We must continue, Willow. You're advancing so fast. I was astonished yesterday."

Willow suppressed a smile at the description of her mother. "Oh, it was unbelievable, Great Bet. I can't stop thinking about it but I'm nervous too."

"Nervous? You should feel more relaxed. Don't you feel peaceful afterwards?"

"Oh, yes, I do but then after a while, my mind starts spinning. Everything seems so different now."

"That's exactly right. Everything is different. You're changing inside, your inner senses are awakening."

Willow shook her head. "I will keep working at it, Great Bet, I promise but are we really violating the Spiritual Contract?"

A mottled, blue-veined hand reached out from the sheets, demanding company. Willow placed her hand in Elzabeth's. The loose skin was surprisingly soft and warm; the grip, strong. "Willow, trust me. You must keep quiet about this. I wouldn't put you in this position if I didn't think it was important." Elzabeth gazed out the window sightlessly. "The truth is that I'm breaking vows, on two fronts, that I spent my life enforcing—but it doesn't matter anymore. Not to me. My only concern is for you. For your own safety, my dear, you must keep this to yourself."

Willow pulled her hand back, suppressing a sigh. She respected her great grandmother too much to disobey. "Great Bet, I'm confused but you know I will do as you say."

The old woman grunted her approval. "Okay, good girl. Now, I'll help you get ready. Settle back in your chair and close your eyes."

After that, time swept away. Despite her agitated morning, Willow reached the state quickly, effortlessly—with minimal guidance from her mentor. It seemed to go faster every time. Within minutes, she became immersed in a waking dream, a trance-like existence where she was still aware, still conscious of her surroundings and yet her inner being was animated and exposed as never before. The old matriarch and her young descendant interacted with visions and feelings, thought-pictures and senses. It was like an inner voice, a connection of directed, shared dreams. Great Bet called it Vision Speak. The two women were oblivious to the absolute silence in the room. To them, their surroundings were vibrantly alive.

Finally they stopped. Willow sensed that her great grandmother was growing weary. Returning her attention to the physical world, she gawked at the time display. Two hours had passed. She resigned herself to missing her Experimental Art class too, yet it didn't seem important anymore. The room, its occupants, the outside world—everything—had a fresh glow. The world was transforming before her eyes. It all coalesced unlike ever before.

Elizabeth had sunk deeper into her pillows, her eyes glazed. Concerned, Willow bounded out of her chair, energy pulsing through her. She leaned over her great grandmother, smoothing back her silvery-white halo. "Great Bet. Are you okay?"

Deep wrinkles and lips curved upward. "I'm wonderful, so wonderful thanks to you." Her voice was barely above a whisper. Willow leaned in closer. "Oh, my dear, why didn't I teach you long ago? I didn't sense the possibility until I saw you again at my birthday party. It struck me that day so clearly that you were open but even then, I had no idea what you would be capable of. The others will be shocked when they experience your abilities."

"You must tell me about the others. Who are they?"

"I meant the Vision Speak group at the Center, especially Jill, Aaron, and Simon. But, you can't meet them yet. I don't know how I'm going to explain this." Her eyelids fluttered but she continued. "I'll sort this out before I'm gone, my dear. I promise." Her words trailed off at the end so that Willow had to strain to hear.

Leaning forward, she kissed the wrinkled forehead and pulled the covers up. "I'd better go now, Great Bet. You need to rest."

"Wait." Elizabeth's eyes shot open and she gripped the young hand. "I forgot to tell you something."

"What is it?"

"When I die…"

"Shh—no, don't say that."

"Don't be foolish." The frail woman snapped. "I'm dying soon and it's long past due so don't waste my remaining time with platitudes."

"Okay, sorry." She mumbled. "Please continue."

"I want you to know that I've changed my will. I've made you my Protector."

Willow gasped. To be the keeper and protector of memories was a privilege, usually entrusted to someone more mature, someone who had known the departed for many years. This meant that she, and she alone, would be responsible for Elzabeth's Life Journals.

"Oh, I'm honoured, Great Bet. Really I am, but what will Grandma Sybil say? What will my mother say?" Her voice raised a decibel when she mentioned her mother. Willow sank back down into the chair, chewing on her fingernails.

"I don't give a donkey's ass what they say. I'm tired now, Willow, we'll talk more later. You should know that before I found you, I wasn't entrusting my journals to anyone in the family. And now that I've discovered you, now that I see what you can do, this is the only way. But, I know the legacy I'm leaving you…it won't be easy. There may be, uh, interference."

"What do you mean?"

The old woman closed her eyes again. She was silent for seconds that stretched out like minutes. She never answered Willow's question but she did whisper one more instruction. "Please be careful. Keep the journals secret, even with the family—at least until you're ready." She smiled weakly. "I'll explain more next time."

But there never was a next time.

Chapter 2

"The truth is: you don't have a life, you are life. The One Life, the one consciousness that pervades the entire universe and takes temporary form to experience itself as a stone or blade of grass, as an animal, a person, a star or a galaxy."*

Eckhart Tolle

Elzabeth's heart pounded as she gazed out the window beside her bed, marveling at the golden glow of the setting sun. Just like her, it was nearing the end of a brilliant cycle before disappearing into the dark night.

"Do you understand me, Simon?" She pushed herself forward, using her elbows to prop herself up further on the inclined bed. She stared into the small camera on her portal screen and continued her recording. "I had no choice. She is gifted beyond anyone we've ever encountered at the Center. When I realized this, I had to work with her alone. There was no time to involve the group, to follow protocol. Already, she's more powerful than I've ever been, even though she doesn't realize it yet. I can only imagine where she'll go next—and where she might lead us."

---

* From the book *Stillness Speaks* Copyright 2003 by Eckhart Tolle. Reprinted with permission of New World Library, Novato, CA. www.newworldlibrary.com.

The care worker would return soon to force feed her dinner. Her hand, blue-veined and wrinkled, gripped the remote control device under the covers as she continued her recording. "I sense danger in her future." She wheezed on her out breath. "She could be a catalyst that will draw unwanted attention both to herself and to our group."

The worry lines around her eyes deepened into ridges. "Her abilities will be threatening to the Republic and even to the Cult." She closed her eyes, pondering the challenges before them. "The People's United Republic of Earth was designed to stop us from destroying ourselves again, to prevent another near-Armageddon." The old woman inched her face forward to glare into the screen. "In the end, I question the laws I enforced my entire career. If we've really discovered a universal truth—one that could unite us all—how do we reach for it under such rigid control? It may have been necessary once but now we're like teenagers in a playpen, repressed, unable to grow."

She unleashed a deep sigh, oblivious to the raspy breathing that escaped into the microphone. She was wasting her last breaths preaching to one of her protégés, a young man who already shared her concerns. "Simon, I'm afraid for her. I agonize over what I've started now that I won't be around to protect her. People disappear if they don't follow the PURE tenets. I know this only too well after my days on the job and what we had to do to my poor, misguided boy."

Her anxiety fueled her, the strength that had sustained her for over a century returning briefly. "You'll receive this message after I'm gone. I still have high security access to the PURE systems so I've triggered this to be sent once they've taken certain actions. I can't allow them to harm my great-granddaughter as they did my son." Despite her weakened state, a note of arrogance crept into her voice, her eyes glinting with her trademark bravado. "Even now, they have no idea of what I can do."

"Willow will have my journals and her incredible gift. Still, I'm counting on you and the rest of the Vision Speak council, Jill and Aaron, to lead her, to watch over her, and to protect her. The instructions that I'm about to outline must be followed explicitly if the World Governors take action."

When she'd finished issuing her instructions, she used the last remnants of her strength to finalize the set-up of the delayed message and send it before she closed down her portal unit. Simon would get the message when it was time but not until then. No one would know she had sent it. Even the CRKA wouldn't know. Her personal mission accomplished, she collapsed into the bed.

In a near catatonic state, she gazed at the setting sun, reminiscing over her long life—the mistakes she'd made, the losses she'd suffered. And then she thought only of the wondrous gifts: the people she'd loved, her unique experiences, the differences she'd made. The spectacular landscape of her life shimmered before her. Finally, in her twilight years, she'd found the answer. She was sure of it.

"But my time has run out." She thought. "It's up to Willow and her generation now."

She watched a distant light source as it crept gradually closer. The family was coming to visit her tonight but it would be too late.

Elzabeth's portal unit crashed to the floor, the sound echoing in the otherwise silent, still room. It alerted the woman who was preparing soup in the small kitchen.

Approaching the bed, the care worker discovered that the old woman had stopped breathing.

She pulled her personal portal unit from her hip pouch and selected the Notification Center, rapidly pronouncing her message. "Elzabeth Tyler MacGregor, Matriarch of the Tyler line, former Agent to the Republic, Gold Citizen, has passed on. Send the team to her quarters."

Chapter 3

"After your death you will be what you were before your birth."

Arthur Schopenhauer

Willow sat alone in a sea of people. It was a solitude she'd sought her entire life yet now, thanks to Great Bet, it was shifting, expanding.

Hundreds of people had come to pay their respects to the matriarch. She tried to ignore them. She wished they would ignore her as people had always done but something indefinable had changed. With her emerging abilities, she actually felt their presence, sensed some of their emotions. She was alone even while she was becoming part of something much greater.

Camouflaged by her stillness, she watched them stream into the room. She stopped nibbling on her finger tips just long enough to wipe the moisture from her cheeks.

The auditorium on the seventy-third floor of the House of Records was filling quickly. It was the largest closure ceremony Willow had ever attended. All the family seats were pre-assigned to the centre and right of the stage. A special section was roped off for VIPs to the front left. The remaining guests sat in the sections along the back.

Willow had been one of the first to take her seat. Always uncomfortable in crowds, today especially, she preferred to be alone with her memories. No one in her family would understand her agony. For most of the other attendees, it was a time of celebration. A great matriarch had surpassed a century and lived an admirable life, a noble citizen of the Republic. This was an occasion to rejoice in her life contributions.

Attendants were in the VIP section, opening the hidden, separate door at the front of the room for their entrance. She'd been so distracted that she hadn't even reviewed the guest list, but now she remembered that Great Bet had joked about it. "You won't believe the dignitaries that will venture from their ivory towers for my closure ceremony." She'd laughed, "Oh, yes. They'll be there, alright, especially now that I've invited them."

Crazy Great Bet. Willow couldn't imagine sending out invitations to your own closure ceremony. If anyone would do such a thing, though, it would be her great grandmother.

"Hey, where've you been lately?" The whisper on the back of her neck launched her forward in her seat. She suppressed a screech. Whirling around, she saw her cousin Sophie, adorned in a purple, red, and gold patterned jumpsuit, skintight as usual. She was even outrageous for the current fashion which was hard to do. By comparison, Willow's clothing was pale and hung loosely on her slender frame. No doubt Sophie would say Willow's outfit was boring.

Willow frowned. "Sophie, shh. We're supposed to keep quiet until after the ceremony. Have some respect, will you?"

"Oh, puleease! It's a stupid rule." Sophie waved her hand, showing off chunky, red and glittery-gold bracelets. "Great Bet always said we could ignore the really stupid rules, remember?"

Willow did remember and almost laughed out loud. Instead, she maintained a stern expression, biting her lips together. At her silent regard, Sophie continued. "Hey, did you see who's here?"

Unable to resist, Willow whispered back. "Who?"

"The regional World Governors are here. Sharon and Craig. I heard their security team talking in the lobby. Yep, you just wait and see. They'll be taking their seats in a minute." Her black and white streaks bobbed as she nodded her head with emphasis. "In the name of Marrisha, I had no idea Great Bet was so important." Sophie's whisper was quickly transforming into an excited squeal.

Her cheeks burning at the attention Sophie was attracting, Willow watched with relief as Sophie's mother—Willow's Aunt Careena—put a hand on her daughter's shoulder, motioning for her to sit back and be quiet. Sophie scowled even as she sat back obediently.

Facing forward again, Willow was paralyzed by Sophie's news about the World Governors. Would they be watching when she was called to the stage?

Leaning back in her seat, she focused on her breathing while she admired the effects of the auditorium. When she'd first sat down, the ceiling and three walls of the room had been glowing with hazy sky blue and white cloud formations, hints of shimmering gold on the edges of the clouds. Juxtaposed with the artificial sky, the large floor to ceiling windows against the back wall, overlooking the magnificent city, admitted the true sunshine.

She turned slightly to watch the newcomers. Again, she jumped when Sophie's breath was in her ear. "Hey, check that group out. Do you know them?"

Willow watched a group of ten take their seats in the back row. They were an odd mix of young and old although not a family that she recognized.

"I wonder if that could be the Vision Speak group." She whispered, more to herself than to Sophie.

"What did you say?" Sophie had leaned forward again, her head an inch from Willow's shoulder.

"Uh, nothing. Do you recognize any of them?"

"No, but I'd like to meet that one." Sophie pointed at the man in the center. He was definitely the type of guy Sophie, and Willow's sister Claire, would go for. Nice hair—light brown with gentle waves. He carried himself with self-assurance, unlike anyone that Willow had ever dated.

"He is cute, Sophie, but a bit old for you, don't you think?"

"Too old? Are you kidding me?" She tugged on her cousin's long wavy hair. "How about you? I could see you with a steamer like that."

"Stop it. Not my type, way too pretty. I couldn't compete. Really,

Sophie, you're impossible. Great Bet's Viewing of Life is going to start soon. Please, I'm begging you, sit back and we'll talk after." Despite her protests, she continued to see his face long after she'd turned away.

While she waited for the proceedings to start, Willow's stomach twisted uncomfortably at the prospect of being named the Protector. The next group to attract her attention only added to the painful somersaults in her abdomen.

Over by the entranceway, an immaculately groomed threesome paused to gaze about the room before continuing towards the family seating area. The man was tall and fair, his lean figure erect; the women, with elaborate, crimson hairdos, were noticed by many as they stepped into the auditorium. The older woman had a wide black streak down the left side of her coiffure.

Willow watched her parents and sister parade down the aisle. They'd spotted her and were now headed in her direction. Her mother's eyes, wreathed in shadows, seemed to be descending upon her, their intensity unsettling. Willow gulped down her momentary panic—did Joley know about the journals?

Chapter 4

*"There is not one way to a spiritual life.
The roads are plentiful.
The means are infinite.
All ways are honourable."*

Marrisha and Kamon

Two men from the brotherhood stood in the square facing the Spiritual Center, their long robes flowing in the wind. One was short and stout; the other, tall and sinewy. The shorter man hissed with an authoritative air, pointing towards the entrance, beckoning the taller, younger man to follow.

They'd walked outside along the streets, staring up at the towering infrastructure of the city. The glass walkways that joined all the major buildings formed a perpendicular web of crystal glinting in the sunlight, with figures gliding along the fast moving walkways. They were among few people who had chosen to walk outdoors that day. The cool, early spring weather encouraged most to traverse the buildings via the enclosed glass walkways three stories above.

The Square was enormous, with stone seating carved into the center pit, like an inverse pyramid with a flat bottom stage, where ceremonies and rituals were conducted in the warmer months. The Festival of All

Faiths, on the summer solstice, initiated the weekly celebrations every year.

Statues inlaid with bronze commemorated the founding leaders of the People's United Republic of Earth on all four corners. Each of the statues showed the pairs, Mother and Father, their arms linked together lovingly in the center, their outer arms spread wide in benevolence and caring. They all faced inward toward the center, their forms and outstretched arms rounding out the edges of the Square.

In ornate bronze lettering, thirty feet in the air, the label "Centre of Enlightenment and Spiritual Freedom" was emblazoned, suspended in front of the skyscraper that stretched high into the sky. Gold mirror-plated glass interspersed with coloured windows to form intricate designs, revealing images only from a distance but mesmerizing to the eyes both near and far. An archway enticed visitors into the terraced entranceway, which ran the length of the building, its height just below that of the glass walkways surrounding the city. The archway had the words "Sanctuary of Peace and Tolerance" inscribed along the curve.

Glancing at the words, the shorter man snorted. "How revolting," he muttered. "In the name of the one true God, Master of the Holy Annihilation, it's time to put an end to this." With nostrils flaring, his wide nose upturned, and bushy eyebrows over piercing black slits, he resembled a snarling bulldog. "Our messiah will lead the way."

His companion noticed a group approaching in their direction and touched a finger to his lips. He shuffled inside the arch, motioning for the other man to join him. They stopped under the covered walkway, standing to the side of the magnificent golden doors. They scanned the plaque that graced all such Centers around the world: "The Spiritual Contract, ensuring everyone's right to Tolerance, Freedom and Choice."

The four guiding principles lunged out at them. They pretended to read the familiar words outlining the contract. Everyone, even in the remote country towns, had memorized this in school and signed it when they reached adulthood.

1   I am free to practice any religion, philosophy, or spiritual quest of my choice so long as it is a sanctioned offering of the Spiritual Centers.

2   I will never speak against a sanctioned Spiritual Offering nor of a citizen's choice to follow an offering.

3   Exclusivity is forbidden. There are, and have always been, many alternate paths to enlightenment. I will never declare any offering to be the only way.

4   Religious rituals, sermons, and formal gatherings are forbidden outside of the Spiritual Centers. I will participate in these traditions only within the confines of the Spiritual Centers.

As their eyes traced along the words, they murmured to each other, mentally preparing to enter the Center.

"Okay, let's go in now. Today we have only one mission. It should be easy. Are your hand covers and lenses in place?" The short man asked, emphasizing his question with a sharp glance. The young man's features were more attractive, his brown eyes shimmering from the lenses. At the moment he appeared childlike as he glanced nervously at his hands. His thick lips framed straight white teeth. His skin was a creamy mocha shade, accentuated by a full head of black, curly hair.

He stretched his hands out, brought them together and intertwined his fingers, ensuring the covers were as snug as the second skin they were intended to be. "Yup, fits perfect. They said they've never had any problems so no worries, right?"

Grabbing his partner's arm, the shorter man led him to the entrance. "That's right. Now, let's enter the Sanctuary of Tolerance." With the whispered sarcasm dripping from his tone, the plain face became harsh, almost ugly. "And remember, from this point on, we're the brothers Hanniwell. Let's go Charlie."

Chapter 5

"At fifteen, I set my heart on learning.
At thirty, I was firmly established.
At forty, I had no more doubts.
At fifty, I knew the will of heaven.
At sixty, I was ready to listen to it.
At seventy, I could follow my heart's desire without transgressing what was right."

Confucian Analects, 2:4

At the back of the auditorium, Aaron sat with the Vision Speak group. Each member was centered in his or her seat along one row. Their feet were placed squarely on the floor, as if organized in military fashion, evenly spaced. They breathed deeply, in and out, rhythmically. Their heads were lowered so no one could see their closed eyes.

In anticipation of the ceremony, shades descended over the windows so that they appeared as a fourth wall. Ceiling lights dimmed while the four walls gradually changed colour and brightness. The scenes of evening skies surrounded them, with darkness and twinkling silver stars.

The seating, which had been unfolded from the floor for the ceremony, was arranged in a semi-circle around the front stage. There was a gradual incline from the back to the front.

Security forces ushered in the final guests. Aaron recognized the

PURE Governors for their Region—the current reigning couple: the honourable Sharon and Craig—together with the past leaders. He hadn't realized how important Elzabeth had been.

Once the dignitaries were seated, the lights dimmed further and the large screen on the stage was lowered for the Viewing of Life. The room was silent, everyone in rapt attention to pay homage to the great woman. Elzabeth's image was lifelike, leaping from the screen, grinning down at her audience. Her face was young and unlined as the video of her life streamed before them. After short episodes from her childhood, the image showed her accepting her diploma from the Institute of Record Keepers. Aaron found it hard to reconcile the blossoming beauty of the red-head on the screen with the craggy, leathery-skinned woman with winter white hair whom he had come to know.

Scenes from Evan and Elzabeth's marriage revealed a loving couple. The images of a life well spent flowed across the screen: the birth of their two children—Roland (who had been gone for many years) and Sybil (who sat in the front row, in the place of honour, the closest living relative)—and their parenting years, followed by family events, marriages, grandchildren, and footage of Elzabeth's public appearances during her long career with the Central Record Keeping Agency (CRKA).

At each stage of life, selected Summary Entries from *Elzabeth Tyler MacGregor's Journals* were read in her voice, sections that she had recorded and chosen during her lifetime, to share publicly with those celebrating her life when the time came.

"Sybil always had a fascination with the Grooming and Pampering Centers," Elzabeth remarked with fondness while images of Sybil curtsying in a new dress danced across the screen. "Even as a young child, she was always primping. For her birthdays, I would give her all my grooming credits so perhaps she got used to a privileged life early on." Chuckles could be heard from the front row, in the family seats. "But she always made our house a home. She was a better meal designer than I was by the time she was ten. She had a knack for making every dinner an occasion with her creative touches."

Elzabeth spoke about her immediate family and the many blessings of her fifty-three year marriage as the pictorial life images continued. The room erupted in laughter when scenes from the Family Games were shown. The MacGregors had enjoyed a hearty rivalry with two other families, in particular. Many of them were in attendance. No one missed that Elzabeth had selected images primarily depicting the MacGregor wins, and none of their defeats.

Family pictures continued to roll as events and gatherings were recalled with precise details, triggering laughter and tears amongst the audience members. People who'd worked with her, some many years her junior, whom she had trained, smiled as she related the changes she had seen over the course of her career. Friends, including many who were already gone, were remembered with the unique insights that were characteristic of the great matriarch.

Finally it was time for her closing words. It was customary on New Year's Day, a time of introspection, for everyone to record their closure summary in their journals, to summarize their life's impressions and experiences, final messages that they would want to impart if their time were up. If one were to depart during the year, then the words from the past New Year's were used, unless something more recent had been saved.

In Elzabeth's case, not only had she written her words just days before her death but she had recorded them in her own voice, as well.

"My wonderful family, my friends, my colleagues, my spiritual partners, my many loved ones…" Elzabeth's voice croaked, the advanced years showing in her voice, while the face on the screen showed her at a much younger age, seventy maybe. "I have been blessed. My life has been full, my experience all the richer for your many contributions. I married a man that I loved; we had our quota of two children. Although we experienced the heartbreak of losing our son, a pain that I take with me to my final breath—we lived to see our grandchildren thrive and grow, and I have even had the pleasure of knowing and loving my great grandchildren. I have outlived many of my peers, beloved friends and coworkers, and so was able to honour their lives, as you are honouring mine now, to say goodbye to them as they went on their way. The Republic places the utmost importance on the Family Unit, and this I believe to be right. Family history, family relationships and nurturing—

this legacy must be the ultimate inspiration. Our open path to spiritual freedom—this too I know to be good, although at times it may seem overly structured and bureaucratic. They tell us that the world before us had terrible conflict and unnecessary death over differing beliefs. I've always thought that if bureaucracy and control can save us from that fate, then so be it.

"In my final quest, I have spent time searching and learning, enraptured with the wealth of these years when I can immerse myself in wisdom, in the lessons of humanity. Finally, I've had the time and freedom to meditate on all that is, was, and might be. After retiring, I started a fledgling spiritual offering where I've experienced unimaginable growth at a time when I thought that I would spend my twilight years watching the tele-stories." Inadvertent guffaws escaped at this point, as no one could imagine Elzabeth sitting around watching tele-stories no matter if she lived to be two hundred. "I encourage all of you who are still searching to seek out Vision Speak on your next cycle. We are on the verge of great things, a new exploration into the mind and spirit of humanity, an exhilarating experience with endless possibilities. This has been a lost art to humankind but found again, now, at a time when peace is prevalent in the world and our species is ready to soar. I hope that my dear friends from Vision Speak are here for you to meet." Heads turned, eyes searching the room to try and identify the unknown group.

In the back row, Aaron and the others sat up straight, alert, wondering what more Elzabeth was going to say. Openly recruiting for any spiritual offering was strongly discouraged, practically an unwritten rule of the Contract. Of course, many departed broke any number of the societal mores and rules in their closing words. Those who knew the woman and her strong character might not think twice about her endorsement. Still, the group was sensitive about the reputation of Vision Speak. Their offering was an unusual one and they preferred to keep a low profile. Aaron knew that Elzabeth had reached a level far beyond the others. Was there something deliberate in these final words? Had she meant to cause a reaction?

After a pause, Elzabeth's tone lowered, her voice softer. "In my final months, I have spent a great deal of time with one of my descendants, a young lady who I have grown quite fond of and with whom I have shared many intimate details of my life and of my quest. This young lady is of the highest character and I expect she will show herself to be a valuable member of the Family, of the Community, of the State, and of the Republic as she moves through the stages of her life."

"It is to this young lady that I leave my memories, my thoughts and experiences, my life story. Many of the details of my younger life are open for all to see; however, I have chosen to lock certain entries, particularly in my twilight years, and there are portions of my Journal that have been marked either Secret or Sealed." After a series of audible gasps, the room was silent. Secret entries would be locked for ten years, unless released by the Protector, whereas Sealed entries could remain locked for as long as fifty years. What could Elzabeth be trying to hide?

"So, now, I must say good bye. I love you all, with my whole heart, and I thank you for making my life the joy it has been. I am still here amongst you and will live on in so many ways, some of which you cannot yet fathom."

Elizabeth took a breath, loud enough for those to hear who were holding theirs. "Finally, to be the Keeper and Protector of my Journals, I name Willow Tyler Olsen."

As the lighting came back on and the screen rose, the master of ceremonies stepped forward and spoke into the microphone: "Willow, please come to the stage and acknowledge your acceptance of this responsibility."

The astonishment in the room was a palpable, living organism, with no power of speech. There was silence as all eyes centered on the third row and the fair-haired young woman who had not yet arisen, her slender form frozen in her seat.

Chapter 6

"All religions, arts and sciences are branches of the same tree. All these aspirations are directed toward ennobling man's life, lifting it from the sphere of mere physical existence and leading the individual towards freedom."

Albert Einstein

    The lobby inside the Spiritual Center was grand, with fifty-foot high ceilings and third floor balconies surrounding the entrance. Three decorative multi-coloured walls rose up, ending at the balconies. The walls were adorned with gigantic holographic moving images of world, state, and regional leaders both past and present. There were numerous kiosks to choose from, all along the sides of the room. The Center was not busy so the two men sat in two adjacent stations with no one on either side.
    A portal on the back wall in the center of the great room—with the caption "Honouring the Great Traditions"—cycled images of ceremonial events from past festivals, as well as religious art over the ages. The final pictures in the slide show depicted Marrisha and Kamon at the Great Debate. The moving images on all the walls gave a vibrant, multi-dimensional feeling to the building, and visitors claimed to feel inspired upon entering. These two men, however, blinked as if adjusting to a blinding light. They paused before the kiosks, finally gazing about,

absorbing the myriad of reflections. They had to remind themselves that they were just computer animations and not real. The holographs were larger than any they had seen before.

The shorter man slid his hand into the handprint identifier and positioned his left eye in front of the retina scanner. After a moment, he was greeted with the automated, "Welcome Jakob Hanniwell". The screen showed the standard listing of the offering categories:

Ancient Philosophies and Mythology
Traditional Western Religions
Eastern Philosophies and Religious Studies
Variants from the Technology Age
Pagan Tribal Beliefs
Mysticism
Psychology
Personal Development

On the left side of the screen where Jakob's current offerings and schedule would usually be shown was a bold message, indicating that he needed to select his path for the next cycle.

His partner performed the same action at his kiosk and after being greeted by, "Welcome Charlie Hanniwell" his screen showed a similar interface, with the message that he needed to choose his path for the coming cycle. The counter showed they were five days from being investigated for absence. One could miss up to two cycles in a row before being sought out and encouraged to rejoin the citizen's spiritual quest.

"Perfect. We both passed." Jakob arranged his mottled lips into a smile as he wiped his brow. Although outwardly cool, he'd been prepared to bolt if it didn't work. "As always, our leader's instructions were flawless. Let's get enrolled and then we can go find our lodgings in the city."

Chapter 7

"Be nothing first! And then you will exist:
You cannot live whilst life and self persist—
Till you reach Nothingness you cannot see
The Life you long for in eternity."

The Conference of Birds (Mantiq atTair), Sufi poems

Willow slipped into the reception hall unnoticed. By then, the party was well underway. She scanned the room, recognizing various groups huddled together, sipping their drinks, deep in conversation. The VIP's had one corner blocked off with their security team. Great Bet's screen presentation was running again in silent mode on a smaller portal in another corner. People at that end of the room were idly watching the pictures again as they talked. Along all the walls of the great reception were digital images that represented a gallery of her life. There were both family pictures and portraits of Great Bet, interspersed with awards and diplomas she'd received over the years.

At the end of the ceremony, when her name was called, all her worst fears had been realized. She'd felt the eyes of the audience, but most especially of her family, boring into her from all directions. To aggravate this, she could actually sense her mother's agitation in the seat next to her, this new ability she was only just starting to understand adding to the tension. It had taken several moments before she forced herself to rise and make her way to the podium to accept the symbolic golden sphere, holo-engraved with Elzabeth's image. Although she could have spoken to the group at length had she wished, she couldn't find the words, her courage faltering.

She held the golden ball in her hands and addressed the audience for only a moment, speaking softly into the microphone. "I'm honoured and humbled by this responsibility. Great Bet was a woman of remarkable resources and talents; a matriarch that will never be forgotten. I will make it one of my life missions to respect her memories and her wishes." Brushing aside tears that rose unbidden in her eyes, she turned around and joined the keeper who was waiting for her. She followed him off the stage so that he could match her handprint and retina scan, and set her up as the Protector of Great Bet's Journal.

Once the job was accomplished, the keeper left her alone to review the instructions. She lingered in the Records Room, breathing in and out, taking herself to a peaceful place where she might find her center of strength again. She would need it before facing the crowd. Her visions were chaotic. It took some time but she was able to calm her personal angst far more effectively than in her conscious state. As she neared completion, ready to return to regular consciousness, she sensed an unexpected presence, one she had never encountered before. The shock of it jolted her out of her trance. As she walked into the reception hall now, she wondered about the experience, wondered if the person was in the room.

"Willow, we thought you'd never get here." Sophie grabbed her arm from behind. Cousins Triska and Michael and Willow's sister Claire were with her.

The artist in Willow had always admired her sister Claire's features, the angular profile of her jaw line and nose, congruent forms in a flawless complexion. She glanced at her to gage her reaction, always sensitive to her big sister's moods. Claire's cat-like green eyes were focused on her, all right, but her expression was unreadable. In contrast, her cousins would be light and easy company. Willow smiled, relieved to face the younger family members first.

Sophie continued. "Well—that was quite a shocker! Great Bet bequeathed her journal to you. We were stunned. Now talk, tell us how this came to be before all the parental units get their hands on you."

Laughing, Willow replied. "Well good to see you too, Soph. I've been fine, thanks for asking. School's okay although…"

Triska cut her off. "Okay, Willow-tree, we'd love to hear all about your studies, your friends, any new love interests…but that will have to wait. You've got to know we're absolutely dying of curiosity. Your name was the last one we expected to hear. In fact, I think everyone assumed it would be either Grandma Sybil, or maybe even my mother, being the eldest granddaughter." Triska's hair was the same fashionable crimson shade as Claire's and Joley's. Willow wondered sarcastically if they'd gotten a group deal at the Hair Pampering Center.

"Come on, Willow, we don't mean to give you a hard time, honestly, but how did you and Great Bet get so close?" Michael was Triska's younger brother. He and Willow had spent a lot of time in their youth, confiding in each other and avoiding their sisters, so his earnest, direct manner had a more potent effect on her than the others.

"Okay, I'll tell you." Better to just get her story out. If she told it to these four, perhaps they could disseminate it and save her having to repeat herself all night long. "It would be nice to have a drink first, though." She raised her left eyebrow inquisitively. Claire and Triska crossed their arms. Sophie and Michael gently shook their heads. Apparently not. She sighed, "Well, alright but there's not that much to tell, really. Great Bet loved all of her descendants and I always spent time with her over the years, at the gatherings, as did all of you." They nodded, waiting. "Then, a few months ago, at her birthday party, she asked me to come see her the next day. After that, she kept asking me to come back. So Great Bet and I had a lot of one-on-one time to talk about things we'd never really talked about before." Willow paused, planning her next words carefully.

"What kinds of things?" Michael asked, watching her closely, his serious brown eyes matching his short hair and suit. Of the group, he would be the hardest one to fool. He knew her too well.

"Oh, lots of stuff—her life, my life, our family, the meaning of life and death, the Republic, and, of course, her spiritual quest which she was absolutely passionate about."

"Oh, is that all?"

"Funny, Sophie." As she spoke, their mothers joined the group. The three daughters of Sybil were intimidating at the best of times. Mela, the oldest, was Michael and Triska's mother; Joley, mother of Willow and Claire; and, finally, the youngest by minutes, Joley's identical twin sister: Careena. She just had Sophie, which was enough. The sisters were decked out in the latest fashions, their grooming immaculate and oddly coordinated, their colouring dramatic.

Inclining her head in greeting, Willow continued. "She knew she was in the final months of her life and she wanted the company, saying she had many things to share before she departed. I felt privileged to be asked by such a great woman. So, I made the time and as it turned out, we saw each other several times a week over these past months. It was hard to manage sometimes but I have no regrets. I learned so much…"

Aunt Mela bustled into the conversation. "Willow, are you saying that you visited two or three days every week with Elzabeth, for the last several months?"

Actually, it was more like four or five once they got going, Willow thought, but that would be even harder to explain, so she just nodded.

"And you never said a word to me?" Her mother's eyes opened wide, black eyeliner, her red cheeks and cocked head enhancing the intensity of her expression.

Willow stepped back, unconsciously looking for a means of escape, as she stammered: "I-I'm sorry, I couldn't… Great Bet insisted I not say a word to anyone. I felt uncomfortable about it but I also felt that I should honour her wishes."

Seven pairs of familiar eyes stared at her, momentarily speechless. She decided to make her escape before the silence ended with a fresh batch of questions. "Uh, you know, I think I'll just go grab a drink…. a bit parched, you know," she gripped her throat as she turned around and walked away.

Willow could imagine the outrage that would be voiced at her rapid departure but she didn't care. It would be bad enough when the reception was over and she had to go home to her parents' house.

She squirmed through the crowd, avoiding eye contact with anyone, intent on making it to the bar. A large group was gathered around the gas bar to her right, enjoying the selection of oxygen, nitrous oxide, and helium. Brushing aside a momentary thought of joining in, she moved past and decided on a liquid diversion instead.

It was hard to believe that mere months had passed since Great Bet first confided in her. There were four generations of women in the Tyler line—at least there had been until Great Bet passed on. Willow had always felt so different, like an outsider. The other women in her family spent so much time on their appearance, going in for the latest treatments and hair colours. They were all striking. Willow felt drab and boring by comparison but she just couldn't be bothered with any of it, despite her mother's constant pestering. Her mind was always busy in other areas, most often absorbed with her art. During those visits with Great Bet, she had finally found a kindred spirit in the family. It had been like striking gold.

At the bar, she made a successful acquisition, a lime green concoction with a high concentration of numbing fluids. She was just wondering where she might be able to hide from her family, when someone tapped on her shoulder.

Whirling around, she found herself face to face with Sophie's 'steamer' from the ceremony. He was only a couple of inches taller than Willow but broad shouldered and even more attractive up close. She approved of his attire. His clothes didn't stand out and announce his presence—which was a relief. They were simple, earthy tones, gently hugged his body, woven in a soft, comfortable fabric. Too many of the people at the party, even the men, wore clothes with the in-vogue garishly bright colours.

"Ms. Olsen?" He extended his hand. "My name is Aaron Braxton. I knew your great grandmother well."

Willow took his hand, gripping it in the customary fashion, her eyes locked with his. "Nice to meet you, Mr. Braxton." She left the conversational ball in his court; her social finesse was unpracticed at the best of times but today, with this man, she felt completely inept.

"Please, call me Aaron." His easy smile triggered an immediate response. "Is it okay if I call you Willow?"

"Sure, of course."

"Did Elzabeth ever mention me, Willow?"

"Uh, not really. I mean, I think she mentioned your name. How did you know her?" As she spoke, Willow felt watched. Glancing sideways, she noticed the group of VIP's in their roped-off corner. Were the World Governors and their entourage staring at her? Maybe she was getting paranoid.

"We met at the Spiritual Center, in the Vision Speak sessions. I've known her for a long time, around ten years. She and my mother were close."

"Oh, right." She peered at his face a little closer. She guessed his age to be around thirty.

Aaron laughed. "I can see you're not quite as talkative as the rest of your family. Are you always this reserved?" He took a sip of his drink, eyebrows raised in inquiry.

She gulped her green brew. "I'm sorry, Mr., ur, I mean Aaron." Self-conscious, she reached up and smoothed her long hair back. "To tell you the truth, I'm a little overwhelmed at the moment. In fact, I'm trying to avoid that very talkative family you just mentioned." Taking another sip of her drink, she asked, "Do you know the rest of my family?"

"Well, I don't know about all of your family. I suspect that could be quite a large number. However, I did have the distinct pleasure of meeting your parents, your sister Claire, an Aunt Mela and Sophie. We shared Elzabeth stories at the buffet table a short while ago. I got the sense that they were waiting for you, though. More than once, they commented on how long you were taking. They sure seemed anxious to see you." Irony dripped from his tone. "Have you always been this popular or has your stature suddenly changed in the family?"

Although his words were meant to be light, the mild ache in her abdomen multiplied, eclipsing the easy conversation. She focused on her breathing, willing the pangs over her family to subside. "Yes, they are all somewhat, uh, surprised that Great Bet left me her journal. It will be dreadful for a while, I think, as they're going to be asking endless questions, not to mention pestering me to open the sealed entries for their review."

"Oh, you mustn't do that." Aaron exclaimed. "No, you can't—Elzabeth wouldn't like that at all."

"Really. And how do you know that?" Her emerald eyes widened, enhancing the narrow brownish-blonde curve of her eyebrows.

"Well, I just do and I suspect that you know that very well for yourself or else she would never have entrusted you with her journal, would she?" Aaron's steady gaze and even smile took the edge out of his words.

She shrugged. "No, she wouldn't have. Don't worry, I have no intention of breaking my word to Great Bet but it won't be easy. They're a hard bunch to say no to…but perhaps you've already noticed?"

"Maybe so—but you strike me as someone who will stick to her convictions regardless of how much pressure might be applied." She was graced with a partial wink and a glimpse of one perfect dimple before he continued. "Actually, Willow, your great grandmother got in touch with us shortly before she died and asked that I contact you…bring you into the fold as she put it."

"She told you about me? You're kidding…er, what exactly did she tell you?" Her voice lowered to a whisper. She glanced at the groups nearby but they appeared to all be engaged in boisterous conversations. She caught sight of her mother and aunts, watching her from across the room. It was only a matter of time before they came over if she stayed in one place for too long.

Aaron observed the furtive look she directed towards her family. "Why don't we take a walk and get away from this crowd? Then we can talk more freely." He held out his elbow, motioning for her take hold of it. "Do you want to go up to the terrace level for some fresh air?"

Relief at the idea of escape outweighed her need for immediate information. She grasped his arm as if it were a lifeline. "Yes, Aaron… I would love to go to the Terrace level with you. But, then I expect some answers."

Chapter 8

"...it is not, so much, that we are human beings having a spiritual experience; rather, we are spiritual beings having a human experience..."

Dr. Wayne Dyer

With her arm in his, they pushed through the crowded reception hall, nodding greetings where necessary. On the outer fringe of the room, they came face to face with some of Aaron's companions from the ceremony. He hesitated for a moment, perhaps considering whether or not to make introductions. Instead he let them know that he would find his own way home, gave a dazzling blonde a peck on the cheek as he whispered something in her ear, and then led Willow away. Except for Aaron's friend and a skinny young man with purple streaks in his hair, the others in the group were older. She'd noticed two men and three women who'd all regarded Willow with mild, friendly curiosity, unlike the intensity of the younger woman who continued to stare at her as they walked away.

The hallway was busy so they remained silent as they waited for an elevator and then ascended to the 110th floor.

Willow remembered Great Bet's explanation of Vision Speak, when they first started their private sessions. She'd questioned her great grandmother, eager for details of what it was all about.

"Willow," she'd replied, "I'll tell you what I've learned when I feel you're ready, but my beliefs go beyond what you'll hear at the Center... In fact, there's a great deal I haven't shared with the group. My experience, both on my own and in the past before I created this offering at the Spiritual Center, has reached other levels..."

"Do you mean there are other world groups? Are they conferenced in to your meetings?" It was not uncommon when a region first adopted a new offering that had been popularized elsewhere, to have the speaker and other participants connected via remote portal. "Where did this first start?"

"N-no," she'd stammered, "thus far, as a group, we have had no contact or collaboration with the others." She continued, but seemed reluctant, offering minimal details. "I know about some other, similar endeavours, from my research with the Record Keepers and I have personally, um, interacted with some of them."

The question forming on Willow's lips had been interrupted then, as Great Bet moved back to the original discussion, outlining the standard Vision Speak doctrine. "When you do attend the sessions at the Center—and I hope you will—they will tell you that Vision Speak explores the depths of the human mind and spirit, within ourselves, which ultimately connects all of us at an unconscious level."

"Unconscious? You mean when we're sleeping?"

"Well, yes, and a basic understanding of dreams and myths, imagery and symbolism will help you to understand the language of visions. But beyond that we can, with training—initially through deep meditation—and with practice, reach that level in our waking state, or maybe even at will, and in so doing, transcend into realms that cannot be described with our traditional languages and logic...but only for those that are ready, and open. Although the possibility exists within everyone, there are some that are more able to make this leap now. Perhaps someday, it will be easier for everyone...as it was so very long ago..."

The elevator reached its destination and the doors opened so smoothly that Willow, lost in her thoughts, didn't even notice until Aaron placed his hand in the small of her back, guiding her forward. His touch was slight yet triggered a tingling sensation. As she moved in the direction he indicated, he removed his hand, leaving behind a chill where there had just been warmth.

Catching herself, she wondered at her reaction to this man, especially on this day of all days—her great grandmother's closure ceremony. Her sexual edification was complete and she was well versed in the art of physical pleasures but this man seemed entirely unsuitable. He was probably outside of the recommended age range and, judging by the blonde's reaction, might even be close to a commitment. At that point he would be completely off limits.

Breaking the silence, she asked: "Who were the people that you were speaking with? Were they all from Vision Speak?" She glanced at him sideways as they walked along the stone walkway, their steps in harmony.

The terrace was covered with greenery, encased in glass so the sky was visible above them, the sunset in the distance was an enormous orange ball being swallowed up by the horizon of the city line. Although there were in fact over fifty people on the garden rooftop at that time, the small groups found privacy in pockets of gardens and shrubbery. Aaron led her to a secluded bench down a narrow pathway where a lilac branch dangled. They both breathed the scent in deeply, in harmony.

"Yes, they were all from Vision Speak but one of them also happened to be my mother." He grinned at her. "I apologize for not introducing you but I figured you would meet them soon enough and if we'd stopped to chat, you may not have made your escape in time."

"Oh, your mother. That's right. I assume everyone there knew my great grandmother?"

He nodded. "Yes, they all knew her and everyone respected her although the feeling was not completely mutual." The dimple returned at his last words. "As I'm sure you're aware, your grandmother was quite opinionated and there were some she didn't have much time for…"

"Ha! Not surprising…except, I thought Vision Speak was supposed to connect people at a deeper level, so we could eliminate misunderstandings and conflicts?"

"Well, yes, but some of them couldn't relate at Elzabeth's level and she was just as sharp with her mind as she was with her tongue!" Their eyes locked when she returned his grin. To Willow, in that instant, their private garden intensified in colour and fragrance. She inhaled deeply, savoring it, gathering up her courage.

"And how about that gorgeous blonde woman? Was it my imagination or did she seem threatened by your departure with a less than threatening companion?"

His flush betrayed that her question had taken him off guard. Aaron replied, "Oh, you mean Jericho? She's a friend." At her pointed look, he acquiesced. "Okay, we've dated a bit but it's not serious. I'm sure she wouldn't have cared about us leaving together. She's just a tad intense at times." Leaning back, he squinted at her, appraising her long, lean form and her flowing dark-blonde hair with glints of gold catching in the light. "But, I wouldn't say you were non-threatening. A bit young, for sure, but I'd say you're, uh, very enticing in that slinky, violet dress. How old are you, anyway?"

"I've been nineteen for several months now." Sitting up straighter, her shoulders back, she held her head high.

"For several months now—really? That old." He chuckled.

She glared at him for a moment, pretending indignation. "And how old are you, then?"

"I'm sorry, Willow… I couldn't resist. Let's just say I'm too old to be flirting with such a beautiful young woman." An unexpected, fluttering sensation spun about in her stomach at the word beautiful. But then he shuffled back into the far corner of the bench, distancing himself, observing her for a moment before he continued. "I guess we'd better get back on topic before one of your crazy relatives tracks you down. It caused quite a stir when you were named the Protector of Memories in the ceremony. Did you know it was coming?"

"Uh, well, yes—just between us, I did know. However, as instructed by that most domineering and beloved old woman, I hadn't said a word to anyone." Shaking her head, she grinned. "I guess if I can remove myself from the situation, my family's reaction is amusing…" Her grin receded as she remembered that she had to go home shortly, where she lived with her parents still. "Okay, so tell me, what did Great Bet tell you about me? When did she contact you?"

"Well, she didn't exactly tell me anything specific about you—or even your name." Aaron looked up through the glass ceiling to the sky above, as if tabulating the time in his mind. "Just last week, she arranged for a secure meeting with my mother, Jill, and I on the videoconference portal. We offered to come for a visit but she said she wasn't well and preferred to meet remotely. Said she wanted to save us the trip."

"She was getting weak," Willow volunteered, "and I visited her so often these last months, she probably wanted to conserve her strength…"

"Yes," he conceded. "No doubt that was part of the reason. As it turned out, she passed on two days later. It also seemed to us that she wanted complete control over the meeting even in her weakened state. After she'd explained her reason for meeting, we expressed our concerns, tried to question her. She avoided our questions. Finally, claiming to be tired, she ended the connection rather abruptly. If we'd been face to face that would have been harder for her to do."

"Hmm…so she had something she wanted to tell you…but didn't want to give you the opportunity to draw anything else from her?"

"Yes, something like that…" Aaron held up three fingers to emphasize his next words. "She said she had three things she wanted to share with us." He paused as a young couple wandered down their pathway, apparently seeking the bench they were sharing. The man grunted his disappointment when they spied Aaron and Willow already comfortably situated there. Then the two of them stood inside the pathway for a moment, taking a moment to breathe in the lilac aroma while the man reached into the tree, eventually pulling out a flower for the woman. After the twosome had wandered away, he continued. "Well, they looked happy to see us," Aaron quipped. "I wonder what they had in mind to do in this little alcove?"

Willow chuckled and gave him a slap on the arm. "Enough of that. You were about to tell me the three things she said?"

"Right, well the first thing was that she was dying. She didn't seem upset about it at all, very matter of fact…almost as if she were going on vacation or moving."

"I know what you're saying but perhaps if you reach the age of one hundred and one, you might get used to the idea."

"You may have a point. Because she was dying, she wanted us to replace her as an official representative for Vision Speak. It had been she, my mother Jill, and I who formed the inner council—she told us to name Simon LaChance as her successor."

"Simon LaChance? Who is he?" Willow asked.

"Oh, you'll meet him soon enough. He's a bit of odd fellow, actually."

"Odd, how so?"

"Uh, well, it's partly the way he looks: kinda gangly with big eyes, weird purpley streaks in his hair. You definitely would notice him."

"Purple?" Willow groaned. "I'm getting so sick of purple these days."

"Yeah, I hear you." Aaron laughed. "But for this guy, it's not about the fashion. Purple was his thing before it was in with everyone else."

"Okay." Willow grinned. "So, why would Great Bet want him named as her successor on your council?"

"I don't know their past connection but she brought him in years ago, seems they've known each other forever." He paused. "Actually, I got the impression that he was an old friend of the family. You don't know him?"

Willow shook her head. "Name doesn't sound familiar."

"Anyway, he's very committed, one of the fastest to learn so he's already climbed to the top level. She always trusted him, that's for sure." He shrugged his shoulders. "He's really a decent guy. I shouldn't give you the wrong impression. He's just, uh, well, as I said, different." Leaning forward, he moved his face closer to her. "We didn't really question why she wanted Simon as her successor. We accepted it as we did just about everything Elzabeth directed. He is now our third representative."

"Okay, so what was the second thing?"

"Well I suspect you're the second thing, actually." The creases in his eyes indicated he smiled frequently. "She said she'd been spending time with someone very special to her. She'd been training this person in Vision Speak outside the Center. She was very excited about the potential of this young woman, said she had tremendous natural ability beyond Elzabeth's own capability. She insisted we keep this information private for the moment and to reach out to her protégé after she passed on."

"She didn't tell you who it was?"

"No, she was very secretive on that topic—presumably so we would have to wait. We, of course, admonished her and tried to find out more details. All she'd say was it would become obvious who this person was later. In fact, she was right on one count, anyway—it was obvious who you were by the end of the ceremony."

"Okay," she grinned, "...sounds rather cloak and dagger to me. So what was the third thing?"

"It was about her journal. She said she had documented details of her experiences with Vision Speak that would be of interest to the group, but probably not understood or taken seriously by those outside of it." Breaking eye contact, he focused on a blossom hanging between them, mesmerized. "She promised that she'd sealed entries that might be sensitive. Her hope was that her shared experiences would eventually become the common knowledge for anyone committed to the Vision Speak doctrines. She suggested they would be of great benefit to us all."

"Really?"

She still remembered the last time she'd seen Great Bet when she'd told her to keep the journals secret. She gazed at Aaron, noticing he'd averted his eyes, suddenly suspicious of his assertion.

Willow sat up straighter, her intense gaze forcing him to turn back. She asked him. "Did she give you any details on which entries? I've had a quick review of her instructions when I became the Protector and didn't see anything about passing this information on..."

"You're kidding. Nothing was mentioned? I was afraid of that." He shook his head and his forehead crinkled. "We tried to pry. Tried to find out the identity of the Protector but all she'd say was that it would be someone who was knowledgeable in the art of Vision Speak and who would understand what needed to be done. To be honest, we hoped that it might be one of us. Our greatest fear was that she might be referring to this mysterious, new protégé of hers."

"Hmm..." Willow was at a loss. She was surprised that her great grandmother had shared so much with these people. Great Bet had been reticent about divulging many details about the actual group of people at Vision Speak. She'd have to read the journals to find out more.

"I take it that means you aren't quite ready to reveal the required entries to us?" His smile was engaging, it was that impossible dimple.

Her return smile was unintentional. "Not quite." Although her initial instincts had been to trust this man, she wasn't sure how much of that was influenced by his obvious charm. She knew she would need to spend time both with the journals and with the Vision Speak group before she could even consider his implied request. While he portrayed lightheartedness, she sensed that his humor was veiling something more intense.

He laughed, shifting the mood. "Listen, this is a lot to absorb in one day. Let's first make sure that you're signed up for our twice weekly meetings. This is the last week of the cycle to sign up. Would I be correct in assuming that you haven't done anything yet?"

"Oh my. You know I haven't yet. I didn't do anything last cycle either because I was so busy between Great Bet and my studies." She glanced at the time on her portal unit where it was hanging from the belt on her hip. "I'll go to the Center tomorrow to register."

Aaron rose and reached out a hand to help her up. "We should get back before they send a search party after you. Can I make one request?"

"Okay." She stood, facing him in the narrow pathway, close enough to feel the warmth of his breath on her cheek.

"You may not be ready to share anything in the journal with us yet, Willow, but I assume you'll also refrain from revealing anything Elzabeth may have documented, particularly about Vision Speak, to anyone else." His voice had an edge unlike the lightness of a few moments before.

"Aaron, that's probably a safe assumption but I'm not ready to promise anything to anyone—except the promise I made to Great Bet…"

"Understood." He nodded and then turned to leave, motioning for her to go first.

As they exited the pathway into the main gardens, Willow was surprised to see the couple still lingering just outside where they had been sitting. When they walked out, the couple moved away nonchalantly, wandering in the opposite direction.

"So, I guess I'll see you on Wednesday night?" Aaron turned to her, as they waited for the elevator doors to open.

"Uh, okay, sure..." They stepped into the elevator along with others who were leaving the terrace garden.

As the lift sped silently down, uneasy sensations crept into her consciousness. Something had struck her as untrue. She wasn't sure what it was that was bothering her: the way Aaron had tried to get access to the journals or that couple hanging around just outside of their view. Perhaps it wasn't so much a lie as it was something unsaid, some missing piece of information. She searched her mind, running over their conversation again.

Had he been deceiving her in some way—could that be it? She liked Aaron, had liked him immediately, and yet it was entirely possible that she'd been blinded by her attraction to him. Maybe it was just the stress of the evening but Great Bet had taught her to trust her instincts.

She resolved to watch him more closely at their next encounter.

Chapter 9

*"Our philosophy conquers our past and future problems.
Our present problems conquer our philosophy."*

Francois, Duc de la Rochefoucauld

The Worldwide Conference went on longer than planned so they agreed to continue with their meetings on the following day. As World Governors Sharon and Craig were escorted out of the Council of Earth Conferencing Hall, they whispered to their assistant, Burton that he was to arrange an impromptu update from the Watchers either in person or via their secured office channel to the CRKA. Burton pulled on his cape and scurried ahead to make the arrangements.

They exited the Oval Conference room with the wall to ceiling holographic portals. During conferences, the walls displayed attendees as if they were gathered around the massive table when a meeting was in progress. With the meetings over, they made their way through a series of corridors until they reached the Great Hall.

The Great Hall was awe-inspiring—even to those who saw it every day—with a circular glass ceiling showcasing the skyscrapers that surrounded the main entrance as their glimmering masses towered into the sky. All government buildings were accessible via this Great Hall, with their elevator banks tucked away out of sight in the octagonal-situated corridors. The walls of the great room were alive with moving images and holographs, and touch screen interactive directories and check-in centers.

There was an entire building dedicated to the Central Record Keeping Agency, who maintained records on all citizens, including access to their full DNA make-up and medical records from Health Services, their family history and status, any and all crimes or demerits, rewarded credits or honours bestowed upon them, details on their education and vocational path, and up-to-date locations. The justice and security departments, all video portal surveillance teams, and the LifeJournal system, although private for each citizen, were managed by the CRKA.

With the stringent controls put in place by the People's United Republic of Earth (PURE), violent crimes and crimes against the Republic were not tolerated. With CRKA's advanced records and investigative techniques, guilty parties could easily be found and guilt proven beyond a doubt without need for lengthy trials or juries. Smaller crimes and rule breaking were punished via the demerit system. Credits were dispensed to all citizens based on contribution to the community and via their assigned occupation but they could be taken away for bad behaviour. All luxury items and services were accessible only via the credits managed by the CRKA.

By the time the leaders reached their suite of offices, Burton had already arranged a secure line with the CRKA Watch Team. They were standing by, waiting to give their leaders an update.

Burton cleared out the administrative staff, ensuring they had privacy. The massive, gold desk in the centre of the room glittered in the streaming rays from the setting sun. Chocolate and cream-coloured leather furniture, with bronze finishing, and high, ornate ceilings, established a rich, comfortable setting for the World Governors and VIP's that frequently visited.

Burton activated the connection with the team at CRKA. Although he was practiced at staying in the background and being as unobtrusive as possible, to those who were unaccustomed to his appearance, Burton had a startling effect. He was short and stocky, in his mid-forties, with slanted eyes indicating ancestry from Asia, however, his hair was white, his eyes an unusual pale blue, and his skin pale, the absence of pigmentation causing him to glow in the light from the setting sun which filtered into the office from the grand windows. When he was accompanying his superiors outside, typically he covered himself with a hood and dark glasses, but in the comfort of their home offices, he was more open.

"Tell us what you've found out about Elzabeth's Protector. Has she talked to anyone about the journals? Have you been following her?" Craig barked out his series of questions, anxious to get the report underway.

There were three people at the other end—the lead inspector for this investigation, Ramona Markel, and a young man and woman. Ramona spoke, glancing down at a device in her hand from time to time while the others stood silently on either side of her.

"Willow Tyler MacGregor, age 19, in second year at Institute of Higher Ed and final year of living with her parents; has a sister, Claire, who is following in the father's footsteps and just starting her vocation within the CRKA umbrella, working in the DEFJ—Department Ensuring Fair Justice. Willow has demonstrated exceptional artistic ability and has applied for the Arts Community. Our sources indicate that she will get in." Ramona looked up from her report to ensure they had all absorbed that. Only the exceptionally talented were permitted to pursue a vocation in the arts. "Currently unattached, she commenced normal sexual relations in the expected timeframe, just over two years ago. Her first long term amorous relationship, with a," Ramona squinted at the name on her report, "Benjamin Walinski, ended two months ago and since that time, there has been very little social activity. She's the great-granddaughter of Elzabeth through the maternal line. Apparently she's been visiting Elzabeth for the past several months, and somehow pursuing spiritual studies outside the Center, at Elzabeth's request, an offering called Vision Speak. We could probably charge her with breach of the Spiritual Contract, if that would help at all."

"Really? Do you have any details on when they met and what exactly they were doing?" Sharon was intrigued.

"No, not really…so far it's just been 'hearsay', overheard conversations and the like." She glanced at her young associates as she said this.

"Well, see if you can get any definitive details but we'll just keep that as possible leverage in the future, for the moment. What else do you have?"

"Several family members appear disgruntled that she has been named the Protector. None of them were aware of her meeting with the old lady. Although Willow has never taken the Vision Speak offering before, she just signed up for it with the assistance of Aaron Braxton, the gentleman who made her acquaintance at the closure ceremony. They appeared quite cozy. Incidentally, he, along with his mother, also had some communication with Elizabeth shortly before she passed on."

"Hmmm..." Sharon leaned over and whispered into Craig's ear. They sat side by side behind their glimmering monstrosity of a desk. Looking back up at Ramona's boxy, androgynous features on the screen, she ordered. "I'd like background on the Braxton family as well." Ramona nodded.

Craig continued with the questions. "Do you know if she's read much of the journals yet? Has anything been revealed about the sealed entries?"

"We don't think so. She seems to be intent on honouring her great grandmother's wish for secrecy. We'll keep watching but so far, we don't believe she's had any further conversations about the journals, except to tell people she doesn't want to talk about it."

"Okay, keep watching her. Now what about the spiritual offering—Vision Speak—that Elzabeth was so involved with? Have we had anyone attending sessions?"

"Yes, we've been monitoring this group for some time, sir."

"What do you make of Elzabeth's statements? Do you think she's shared classified information with anyone in this group? Are they following the rules of the contract?"

"We're going to summon their leaders for interrogation. We have a few questions on that regard although nothing for you to be alarmed about, at this point."

Craig and Sharon looked at each other, their silent language understood only by each other. Apparently, they'd decided it was time to end the meeting.

Craig turned back to the portal. "Okay, we'll expect another report afterwards. Keep watching her and inform us immediately if anything changes," he commanded before motioning for Burton to sever the connection.

Chapter 10

*"The goal of life is to make your heartbeat match
the beat of the universe, to match your nature with Nature."*

Joseph Campbell

Willow was captivated by Great Bet's journals. In the evenings, rather than focus on her assignments or go out with friends or watch tele-stories with her family, she would close herself into the privacy of her room, surrounded by her art projects, and immerse herself in Great Bet's journals, sometimes with a sketch pad on her lap. Some sections were text-based only; others were recorded by voice; occasionally there were pictures or streaming video clips to accompany the anecdotes and stories. There was so much—Great Bet had been a prolific and entertaining writer—that Willow felt guilty at times that it was hers, and hers alone, to enjoy for the present.

After the first evening, when her mother had quizzed her unashamedly upon her return home, with Willow repeating the same information over and over, her parents had left her alone. They knew their child well enough to realize that they were not going to break through. Although quiet and unassuming on the surface, she'd been known to demonstrate stubbornness unequaled by even Joley, so they'd backed off for the moment.

She'd had so little time to review the journals herself—she'd barely read anything yet. In her current searches, Willow avoided the entries about Great Bet's official history and even the family memories. For now, she was curious about Vision Speak and Great Bet's early experiences. She felt an even deeper kinship with her great grandmother after she read the Summary Entry of her early connections, recognizing the parallels with her own experience.

Great Bet's journal—Sealed Summary Entry

I felt the contact for the first time when I was in a deep meditation, during my undercover work, before we even called it Vision Speak. When I tried to explain my experiences to Evan using words later, it came out sounding crazy. Perhaps that's how this passage will sound as well. How does one verbalize something like this? Even now I struggle.

It was both frightening and exhilarating. Every day, I longed to get back, to find that place again. I wanted to keep going; I was on fire— but then circumstances prevented my continuing for so long, for far too long…

When I was finally able to pull the group together, to get it established at the Spiritual Center and attend in my retirement, I was thrilled to finally be able to pursue it openly.

The visions, dreamlike images and events, made little sense. In our sessions, I sometimes connected with the others, at random, with little control or understanding. Other times, I found another presence entirely but it took a long time to decipher this, to even realize what was happening. It was a connection, a kind of conversation unlike anything imaginable, and yet it was all, most definitely, being controlled by someone or something else. Of this I became certain. But who, or what, was on the other side, I could not ascertain.

I would do my deep breathing, focus deep inside myself, turning off the random thoughts that cluttered one's consciousness. I know some people would spend hours getting to this state but I had learned to get there within a few minutes if I had absolute quiet. I even started doing it outside of the sessions, although I knew this was against the rules. It became so much a part of my new nature that I couldn't help myself. It was how I relaxed and I eventually found that I could reach new levels when alone, without the distractions of the other vision speak followers and their random images intruding into my sub-consciousness.

Sometimes, on my own, I would reach that stage and there would be no visitor. Images would flow in and out, but I knew they were mine. I had gotten so practiced in the art of visual thinking that this became a new form of reflection for me.

Other times, though, I would feel the presence, always with the common form of greeting. I would be on a bench by a river, with trees and wildflowers surrounding me. A dove would swoop down and settle onto a nearby branch. The eyes of this dove were unlike any bird I had ever seen and they were trained on me, gazing at me, inside me...and then I knew that I had made contact. It did not matter where I was or what time it was. I could not predict when the visitor would come, but it was a regular, blessed occurrence. And when it was time to say goodbye, always the dove would come back into focus, having been on that branch the whole time apparently, invisible, staring, and it would silently flap its wings, rise straight above me, hovering for a moment—with a benevolent, kindly expression—and then turn away, flying higher and higher, out of sight.

But, it was what happened in between the dove's visits that were most incredible and so very difficult to put into words.

Willow smiled, picturing the eyes of that dove but remembering that for her, having made her early journeys along with Great Bet, there had been two birds, not just the one. Since Great Bet had passed on, she had not yet gone there on her own, although she had been reaching the state easily in the weeks prior to her demise.

Leaning back, Willow resolved to find her way again, relaxing her mind and body in the way she had been taught, focusing inwards.

Chapter 11

"At least two thirds of our miseries spring from human stupidity, human malice and those great motivators and justifiers of malice and stupidity: idealism, dogmatism and proselytizing zeal on behalf of religious or political idols."

Aldous Huxley

Charlie leaned on the railing of the terrace from their unit on the 43rd floor of Labour Tower 19, gazing out at the immense city. The skyscrapers glimmered in the setting sun and even the country boy, full of disdain for city life, was in awe of the magnificence of the structures. Beyond the edge of the city, in the distance, he could just catch sight of the Ruins of the Old City. The outer ruins had been preserved and were frequented by school groups and tourists, but the inner area of the ruins was restricted and most people had little desire to go there, an inexplicable taboo about visiting the original hypocenter of the nuclear blast.

Charlie had no such phobia and his anticipation grew daily, knowing that he would soon be there in the deep of night, at the most holy of all ceremonies. They would meet in the center of the ruins for midnight mass, commemorating the anniversary of the Ancient Cataclysm. As he envisioned the ritual, performed in the open air at one of the original sites, he could feel the exhilaration already.

For a brief moment, he thought of his parents and his sister, wishing they could be with him, and wondered if he would see them again. The path he had chosen was not in his hands anymore. He had committed to follow their leader, come what may, knowing that he might not return. His father had known that too, but the pride in his eyes when he said goodbye would be with him in the end, if it came to that. The time had come to make the world listen regardless of the consequences.

Jakob burst onto the terrace, exclaiming: "A communication has just been received by the leader on the secure channel."

"What does it say?"

"Come and read it for yourself and then we must delete it."

The two of them leaned over their small portal unit to read the leader's communication in silence.

To the loyal followers of the Cult of Armageddon who have entered the ministry, devoting their lives to taking mankind forward to the ultimate destiny, I commend you all. I give you my assurance that we are closer than ever before to achieving our mission.

Our quest that began at the dawn of this new age, as predicted in the Holy Journals of our Trial, is fast approaching the crossroads.

We will now initiate the stages of descent, to bring this Republic to its knees and show them the way to the true Judgment Day.

Each of you will have a role to play in this and will receive your specific orders following the Cataclysm Ceremony.

Afterwards, Jakob removed all traces of the message. They sat at their table by the window, gazing outwards, enraptured by the words of their leader.

Charlie's expression was soft, gentle curves on a face absent of wrinkles, eyes filled with emotion. The certainty of his convictions and the heartfelt belief that he was following a noble, higher path gave him an aura of serenity that contrasted sharply with Jakob's harsher profile. Charlie glanced at the man that he had been partnered with for this special task and noted the throbbing pulse in his temple, wondered at the grim set of his jaw, his intense stare at the skyline.

"Jake, do you know what will happen next? I'm so excited. I don't know how I will sleep tonight." He placed his hands down on the table, gazing across at his partner. "Aren't you as excited as I am about our mission?" Charlie spoke quietly, despite his heightened emotions, careful not to intrude into the other man's thoughts too abruptly. He'd only known Jakob for a couple of weeks but he watched the older man with the blind trust that a young child might bestow upon his father, secure in the knowledge of his infallibility and benevolence.

Jakob felt a rush of impatience but held it back; knowing this juvenile devotion would serve both him and their cause well. Instead he forced his eyes away from the window and looked steadily back into the deep pools of brown liquid that were trained on him, feeling the tension ease from his body, as he responded. "Charlie, I don't know what comes next but like you, I anticipate that our leader will understand best how to guide us all to our glorious destiny—and, I will follow unflinchingly to the end."

Chapter 12

"...even in dreams, we do not experience what earlier peoples saw when awake."

Friedrich Nietzsche

Willow barely slept the night before her first "Introductory" Vision Speak session, worrying about how it would go, what would happen. As it turned out, she hadn't imagined all the possibilities.

Her plan had been to slip into the room quietly and sit unnoticed at the back of the room, as she had been accustomed to doing for most of her life. It was not possible with this crowd. It soon became apparent that almost everyone there knew who she was—and, to add to her discomfort, they seemed to have an unnatural interest in her. If they weren't staring from across the room, they were surrounding her and making a point of introducing themselves to her directly.

Once she discovered that she wasn't going to have the luxury of easing herself slowly into this group, she managed as best she could. After the fifth group introduction in the space of ten minutes, her friendly smile was wearing down.

The next surprise came a few minutes before they got started. Her cousins Michael and Sophie, along with her Aunt Careena had all enrolled. Suppressing a groan, Willow greeted them warmly, hugging her aunt, and smiling at her cousins. "I had no idea you were involved here.

Have you guys been holding out on me, now?" She winked at Michael.

Careena, always so spookily similar to her mother in appearance, dress, and manner, answered first. "After Great Bet's recommendation at the closure ceremony, I couldn't stop thinking about it. I guess we all felt we owed it to her memory to come and share in her final passion." At the word "all", Careena waved her hand to encompass Michael and Sophie.

Before taking a seat, Michael whispered in her ear. "I'll give you one guess at why we're really here." His raised eyes as he walked away spoke volumes.

Sophie stayed to chat after her mother and Michael moved away. "Hope you don't mind us joining you, Will but, you know, the parental units thought it would be a good thing given the emphasis Great Bet placed on it and, well, I have to confess that I was a bit curious..." Sophie's eyes were scanning the room while she talked, conducting her typical search for "potential candidates" as she called them. Suddenly, her eyes froze and she exclaimed, "Whoa, who is that? He looks adorable—so dark and exotic."

All told, there were over fifty people in the room, and Willow estimated she'd met most of them by the time they settled down, although she wouldn't remember many names. As she followed Sophie's line of sight, she easily picked out the young man that had aroused her cousin's interest, realizing that he was one of the few people that she hadn't met. Laughing, she replied, "You don't waste any time do you?" Sophie's only response was a slow shake of her head, long strands of black and white hair swinging, as she kept her eyes locked on her target.

"I'm afraid I haven't met the gentleman in question but, you're right, he is cute. Do you think I should go over and say hi?" Willow's question was met with a territorial glare back from her cousin.

Just before they got started, the strawberry blonde beauty that she'd noticed with Aaron sauntered over for formal introductions. Jericho was one name she would not forget. Friendly in a guarded way, Willow displayed her frozen smile again, while watching Sophie greet the man/boy across the room. *The poor guy doesn't stand a chance*, she thought to herself. Despite Sophie's outlandish appearance, she was gorgeous. When she turned her charm on full, most guys couldn't resist.

Aaron led the session on that first evening. Before starting, he spoke about Elzbeth to the group, expressing their respect and admiration for the matriarch to the members of her family that were now joining the group. He turned to look directly at Willow as he spoke. "For us, she was a pioneer and a leader," he stated, "who inspired many of us to continue despite our many setbacks. My mother has asked that I share this entry from her own journal about Elzabeth." He nodded in the direction of his mother, a small woman with smooth skin, and silver hair. Jill's eyes spoke of her pride in her son.

Aaron read from the screen in front of him, sharing his mother's words with the group: "My early days with Vision Speak were incomprehensible in many ways. I didn't really understand what I was embarking upon. Looking back, many of the images were repetitive and simple, linking back to stories and myths that have been embedded in our psyches from the early days of our species. Now I understand this to be an intricate component of our thought patterns but I didn't see this then. I grew frustrated. Elzabeth somehow sensed this. At the time, I didn't understand how she knew but she drew me aside, spent time with me, shared her vision and understanding in a way that inspired me to go on. She had educated herself on ancient societies and stories, the archetypes that repeat themselves over and over. She told me that the vision source was a collective consciousness that connected mankind from the beginning—but that we had not been ready to embrace until now. Many world religions found their beginnings from this same place.

"And so, for the longest time, I continued, watching the images as if I were an observer viewing a tele-story in a foreign language, until something wondrous happened and I sensed the outside contact, experienced the heady rush of being a part of that symbiotic, spiritual realm.

"Yet my nerves were jumpy, and I inadvertently broke contact, my logical side intervening, trying to make sense of what was happening. After the third time this occurred, I was blocked and the possibility that I might never progress or even return, left me in mourning, desperate to find my way again. Once again, Elzabeth was there for me and I soon came to understand that I had been overly anxious and upset—feelings that made it impossible to achieve the state of serenity that I had previously attained, and which was a fundamental requirement. She helped me in so many ways that I cannot even describe. She mentally joined with me, to transcend to new depths, the likes of which I had never been able to reach without her. Finally, her gentle coaching brought me back to where I had been and taught me so that ultimately I could make the journey on my own. I will forever love her for this."

The expressions in the room at the end of this recitation were mixed. Some had tears in their eyes, apparently moved; some even looked envious, while others appeared puzzled and a few, probably the newer members, seemed to be wondering what they had gotten themselves into.

At last, it was time to start so they all got settled into loungers—soft, comfortable chairs that were embedded in the floors, and could be closed back down under, to allow for smooth, open floor space when needed.

With everyone relaxed in their loungers, eyes closed, Aaron began, his deep voice soothing over the soft, musical background sounds, as he talked them into a deep trance-like state

Willow assumed she'd have trouble reaching her state with so many strange people in such close quarters but it had been unexpectedly easy—and so different than her experiences with Great Bet.

In that first group experience, and in the subsequent weeks, she found herself floating, making random connections. The depth of her previous experiences with Great Bet and the unmistakable presence of some greater life force had been much more intense but she reserved those experiences for her alone time.

She enjoyed the lightness of these encounters as she slowly got to know the group, engaging in an intimate level of unconscious conversation of which many of them were oblivious.

Willow's approach with her passage into Vision Speak was similar to the one she'd planned to take with her physical attendance: unobtrusive, quietly watching, preferring not to announce herself. And through this gentle exploration, she learned a great deal.

For one thing, she realized that her abilities were advancing rapidly.

She had yet to encounter anyone who seemed to have the level of control that she did—or at least that was how it seemed. The sessions were organized into two weekly meetings. Once per week they got together with the entire group and in the other session, they broke out into their different levels.

Willow was terribly bored in the novice group where she was automatically assigned. Even in the larger group, she felt more adept than the others. She wondered if some of them had advanced beyond her current understanding and were masking themselves—for she'd encountered a few enigmas. She couldn't be absolutely certain.

Tentatively at first, but then with a boldness foreign to her presence in the physical realm, she reached out to Aaron. Generally, she got further with him when he was participating, rather than leading the sessions. The three leaders—Aaron, Jill, and Simon—along with three others from the highest level took turns running the sessions. When Aaron was leading, his conscious mind was too busy so she focused elsewhere.

In those early, gentle connections, he didn't seem to be aware of her but she would flirt with him nonetheless, sending playful images. She'd chosen a beautiful, iridescent unicorn, swiftly moving, when she wanted to join with him. Usually he would be receptive, following her lead, although she suspected that he did not truly understand who he was following.

Afterwards, she'd chastise herself for keeping at him. She barely knew the man and, watching him in the group interactions, she definitely sensed something going on between him and Jericho. Not to mention, he was at least ten years older. It was unusual at her age to date outside of her peer group.

One evening, a couple of weeks after her first session, she found the courage to speak to him again.

Aaron smiled as she approached. "So, how's it going so far?" His eyes were sleepy, his soft brown hair thick and chaotically wavy.

"Interesting. I'm really enjoying it, actually." She hooked her thumbs in her pants pockets, peering up at him, strands of golden locks streaming around her eyes. "I have so many, uh, questions." Taking a breath, she pushed forward, willing herself not to blush. "um, Aaron, I was wondering if…" But, unfortunately, she couldn't finish her sentence. Just as often occurred with her family life, she was interrupted by Jericho.

The blonde beauty had, of course, chosen that moment to join their conversation, speaking even before she'd stepped into the middle of it. "Willow, how's it going?" She kept her eyes on Willow as she reached blindly beside her, tucking her arm into Aaron's elbow possessively.

"Uh, okay." She stammered. "You?"

"Fabulous." Jericho grinned up at Aaron, her eyes breezing over his face, before she returned her attention to Willow. "So, is the process what you expected? Did your great-grandmother tell you much about it?"

"Uh, well, not too much, really." Willow started to back away. "I, uh, should probably…"

"Oh, don't rush off on my account," Jericho insisted. "In fact, Aaron and I were going to head out and grab a drink. Perhaps you'd like to join us?" She hugged Aaron's elbow closer, gazing up at him. "You wouldn't mind, would you, Aaron?"

He didn't look happy. The physical signs were there—a rush of colour to his cheeks, rigid jawline, eyes hard—but Willow thought she could also sense a sudden tension. He forced a smile at Willow. "No, of course I don't mind. Willow, you would certainly be welcome to come out for a drink with us."

"Oh, no, no, I wouldn't dream of intruding." She moved a step further back. "I have to go. Have a nice evening."

"Willow, wait." Aaron reached out and grabbed her arm as he released himself from Jericho's hold. With his hand still on Willow, he turned back to the other woman. "Jericho, can I meet you outside, please? We were just in the middle of something when you interrupted."

Jericho was tall. With her blonde hair pulled back, her profile was exquisite—a long, lovely neck leading up to a perfectly shaped chin. Her full lips parted in surprise. "Wait outside? Uh, sure."

"No!" Willow's outburst was louder than she'd intended. "No, please." She pulled her arm gently back and smiled up at Aaron. "It was nothing, really and my cousins are waiting for me, anyway. I'll see you next time." Anxious to get away from them, she scurried over to catch up with Sophie and Michael who were already out the door.

She took a last glance back just before the exit and saw that he was watching her, an inscrutable expression on his face.

Chapter 13

"I say to mankind, Be not curious about God. For I, who am curious about each, am not curious about God—I hear and behold God in every object, yet understand God not in the least."

Walt Whitman

The summons was unexpected.

Aaron Braxton, his mother Jill Carson Braxton, and Simon LaChance had all been summoned to the CRKA Interrogation Center.

Many spiritual offerings had official representation by a traditional leader with the full time vocation of running the sessions and educating people in that belief system. Newer offerings, without the history of a committed congregation, were managed by the members in addition to their primary vocations. In the case of Vision Speak, Aaron, Jill, and Simon were the official contacts listed.

They had been summoned without warning and ushered directly into the interrogation room so there'd been no time to talk beforehand, but this eventuality had certainly been anticipated in the past. Elzabeth's coaching had prepared them.

As the three of them sat in the room along one side of the table, waiting for the interrogation to begin, Aaron began his deep breathing, quietly signaling for the others to do so as well. They quickly sensed that they were being watched as they sat there, easing themselves out of their tension, and into a calm space where they would be able to deal with the interrogator more effectively.

Jill sat between the two young men and reached under the table to hold each of their hands for a moment. Squeezing gently, she let them know that there was nothing to worry about. Her only concern was Simon. She knew there was nothing the interrogators could throw at her or her son that they couldn't handle but Simon was more of an unknown. She wondered, not for the first time, at the wisdom of choosing him to step into Elzabeth's vacant position. Certainly he'd shown promise from the start, and rapidly ascended the levels, but there were several others with more maturity and longevity within the group, that had seemed suitable. Yet, Elzabeth had insisted that he was the one.

Sensing his nervousness, she glanced over at him. There were fresh purple streaks on his neatly trimmed beard to match the streaks overpowering his brown hair. Simon's eyes were large and round in a small bony face, today they were almost bulging.

When she released their hands, they all set them, evenly spaced, on the table and coordinated their breathing, the synchronicity of the soft in and out sounds aiding them in their goal. Jill, herself, was already the picture of serenity with her silver hair pulled back smoothly into a knot, her slight form comfortably ensconced in a flowing, peach floor length dress. Her unlined face was a testament to the life of calm introspection she led and not the result of any anti-aging treatments.

Hidden away with the team who were secretly watching the threesome in the interrogation room, the woman noticed Aaron begin his breathing ritual. Her eyes traced his appearance. Usually he would style his hair straight and back, his clothing simple and appropriate. Today, his brown locks were a little wild and he looked uncomfortable—she detected sweat on his brow and observed his rolled up sleeves. She had an unexpected urge to reach out and touch him, taming those natural brown waves as she stroked her hand through his hair. Mentally refocusing, she forced herself to behave in her official capacity. Perhaps later, if they got through this early enough, she'd call and see if he wanted to get together.

She nudged the leader and suggested she go in soon, before they'd had time to prepare themselves. Ramona was surprised. Usually people became more nervous the longer they sat alone in the room waiting but, observing this group, she realized that the opposite was occurring.

When Ramona entered, the three representatives from Vision Speak smiled at her with peaceful, glazed expressions. Even Simon's eyeballs weren't bulging so much anymore.

She stood before them, assessing the situation, her stocky figure and black uniform imposing, her stance aggressive. She had short spiky black hair. Arched eyebrows and dark eyeliner surrounded sharp, green-grey eyes that stared at each of them in turn. Her demeanor had intimidated many in the past but did not seem to be fazing these three. "Jill Carson Braxton?" She focused on the woman in the centre. "I understand you are the leader for Vision Speak?"

Nodding, Jill touched Aaron's hand on the table. "My son is second." Sharpening her gaze, she demanded. "Why have you summoned us here on such short notice? We were all busy in our primary vocations, serving the Republic," glancing at the tag on the woman's uniform, she finished by referencing her first name, "Ramona."

Ramona took a step back. Apparently, she shouldn't underestimate this diminutive, silver-haired woman who, in dress and appearance, had seemed passive, even meek. She pulled the chair out, carelessly scraping the floor. She sat down across from the trio. "You've been summoned here because we have concerns that the offering that you are managing—Vision Speak—may be in breach of the Spiritual Contract."

"What? That is absolutely absurd. Which clause are you suggesting we might be breaching?" Jill spoke slowly, with careful disdain.

The women let silence hang in the air for a full minute as they stared at each other. The young men were still, gazing pleasantly at the inquisitor.

Ramona broke the silence. "Tell me the basic doctrine and beliefs associated with your Spiritual Offering."

"Surely you have already reviewed this from the records?"

"I'd like to hear you explain it, if you don't mind?" Ramona smiled sweetly.

Jill easily recited from memory. "Vision Speak is a personal exploration of human spiritual potential. Through deep meditation and training, participants may experience an enlightenment achieved by reaching into the unconscious mind and ultimately, the symbiotic spiritual realm to which we are all connected. Those who have followed Eastern Philosophies and Religions should find it consistent with those teachings."

"Hmm…seems that you've memorized your catalog entry." Ramona grimaced. "Sounds interesting but I'm wondering, do you recruit people to join your group?"

"Of course not. Aside from the fact that we would consider that distasteful and a waste of time, as you know, it's strongly discouraged. Is this where you think we have breached the contract?"

Ignoring the question, Ramona continued. "It's a little unusual for a group to grow as fast as yours seems to be. This last cycle, you had a 30% increase, didn't you?"

"We did but we're a relatively small group so 30% of our number is nothing compared to some of the more established traditions. We certainly didn't do anything to recruit them."

"Still, that's a big jump and at this rate, you'll be able to apply for absolute sanctioning and a full time leader soon. Why do you think so many new members have suddenly joined?"

They shrugged their shoulders in unison.

"Perhaps it has something to do with Elzabeth Tyler MacGregor's words at the Closure ceremony?"

"Well, actually, several of the new people are her family members so no doubt her passing has influenced them, or made them curious, to check it out. So, yes, that could have had an effect."

Ramona reached down and removed her portal unit from the holder on her hip. After flipping it open and selecting an item, she read aloud: "I encourage all of you, who are still searching, to seek out Vision Speak on your next cycle. We have been on the verge of great things, a new exploration into the mind and spirit of humanity…Do these words sound familiar? Doesn't that sound like recruiting to you?"

Jill, Aaron and Simon glanced at each other and, following Jill's lead, chuckled. Shaking her head, Jill explained: "Elzabeth was over 100 years old, you know, and quite unpredictable. Surely, you're not going to hold us responsible for what she said in her closure ceremony? Besides, there's not actually any rule against encouraging others to follow your spiritual path… Surely, this statement of Elzabeth's is not why you have summoned us here, is it?" Arching her charcoal-grey eyebrow, she gazed at the inspector, waiting to hear what else she had.

"Actually, there were other statements that she had set up for her parting words that the CRKA removed."

"Removed!? You tampered with Elzabeth's closure ceremony?" At this unexpected admission from the interrogator, Jill's composure wavered for the first time. Shifting in her seat, she straightened her back. When she finally spoke again, her expression matched her incredulous tone. "That breaches the Citizen's Code. Surely, you're not serious?"

"Ahh, but if the closing presentation contains material that threatens the Republic's basic precepts, then we can override that law. It's why the CRKA is allowed to preview all closure ceremonies in advance of the showing."

"You couldn't possibly view all of them?"

"No," she conceded, "but we did view this one."

"And what on earth did it say that would cause you to tamper with Elzabeth's parting words to her family and the community? I'm surprised you didn't remove the statement you just read us, if you were going to those lengths."

"That statement was harmless compared to this one so we left it." Glancing at her portal, Ramona opened another entry. Pointing at the wall portal at the back of the room, she held her unit in the air above the table and launched the actual video for everyone to watch, on the big screen. Elzabeth's voice was loud and clear: "…When the truth is finally revealed—a truth that can unite and liberate all our disparate faiths—how do we resolve this within the bureaucracy and elaborate safeguards that we have constructed to protect us from such an eventuality? How can we separate this from all the lunatics and religious zealots through the ages that have insisted that their vision, their way, is the only way? Alas, this is the challenge we must face in the coming years. For the truth is upon us—

indeed it is—but only the enlightened will see this." She tapped her portal to end the video and stared at the group expectantly.

They were all silent, considering how to handle the situation. Aaron felt the soothing hum of his mother's mental pictures in his head. There was only one way out. They had to distance themselves from Elizabeth's words.

Finally Ramona spoke again. "Surely you must realize that implicit in these last words is a violation of both the tolerance and exclusivity clauses of the Spiritual Contract?"

Jill cleared her throat and looked steadily into Ramona's piercing eyes. "No doubt, you are reading more into these words than Elizabeth intended. Surely, her reference to religious zealots related back to the time of despair, before Marrisha and Kamon?"

"Do you think so?" The inspector's words had a sarcastic ring to them.

"I do think so, Ramona." Jill's use of the inspector's first name was deliberate, refusing to address her with her formal title. "And, anyway, isn't there a regulation, in the Personal Records section of the Citizen's Code, which prohibits use of closure ceremony material against any individual or group? As I have already stated, Elizabeth was over one hundred and had been spending more and more time on her own, her health failing. The Vision Speak group cannot take responsibility for what she chose to say in her parting words."

Sitting up a little straighter and setting the portal on the table in front of them, Ramona's face darkened in colour. "You seem to have a very strong grasp of the contractual laws of the People's United Republic of Earth for a teacher of literature. Do you have the entire Citizen's Code memorized?"

Smiling, Jill waved her hand. "No, I'm just familiar with the basics, really."

"Well then, tell me something. Do you think that your offering, this Vision Speak, contains a truth which will bridge the gap between the many different religions and spiritual beliefs throughout the ages? In essence, do you believe that you have the one true path to enlightenment?"

"My goodness, of course not, Ramona." Jill proceeded to quote the axiom: "There is not one way to a spiritual life. The roads are plentiful."

The inspector interrupted, "Yes, the means are infinite—I know, I didn't ask you to quote Marrisha and Kamon. So, you're saying that your Vision Speak principles are consistent with this?"

"Absolutely."

"And I assume you two would corroborate this?" Glancing at Aaron and Simon, her raised eyeballs duplicated the cynicism that resonated in her tone.

"Yes, Ramona, I would echo my mother. We believe wholeheartedly in the original intent of Marrisha and Kamon's words." Aaron responded as Simon nodded quietly.

"Okay, then Jill, let's concentrate on your own words from a recent session then." Clicking on her handheld portal again, Ramona read aloud: "…the vision source was a collective consciousness that connected mankind from the beginning but that we had not been ready to embrace, until now. Many world religions found their beginnings from this same place…"

Jill interjected. "I'm not sure of your concern as this reference does not exclude any other belief system or claim superiority. Our premise is simple. Although mankind had tapped into this vision source, and it guided us at key stages in our development, we were too unsophisticated, too early in our development to fully grasp the significance." Placing both of her hands on the table, she raised herself slightly, her eyes piercing into Ramona. "We followed blindly, we believed blindly and in many ways, this made us much more open and connected but superstitions and fear interfered, as with a child who is rushed into a next stage of development." Jill relaxed and leaned back into the chair. She smiled at the woman interrogating them. "Do you have any children, Ramona?"

"Uh, no…no, I don't…" Ramona shook her head. Her brow was stitched into angles of perplexity.

"Well, I can tell you that my boy here had his share of mishaps whenever he learned something new. I think he still has some scars from his first year of walking." She reached over and brushed aside his bangs, looking for invisible marks. Aaron grinned and pushed her hand out of his hair. "But, alas, as mankind's focus changed with the advent of agriculture, industry, civilization, writing, we progressed rapidly on our logical side. Millennia were spent advancing in mathematics, science, and technology. We even employed our reasoning minds to evolve our philosophies, religions and spiritual theories but in the process, we lost something precious—but not forever. Finally, in this time of peace and tolerance where ideas are permitted to flourish, there exists a potential for the dawning of a new age for the human spirit."

"Are you saying that Vision Speak is a new religion that will provide our civilization with the only way for us to reach this new age?" Ramona perched forward in her seat.

Jill shook her head. "No, I do not consider it a religion, nor does it replace any religious traditions. It is simply a part of us, another sense, both deep inside and an element of some universal life force which I cannot explain to you with mere words. Perhaps some would call this god but it is not an external, all powerful entity who sits in judgment—it is a life force, or psychic energy field, of which we are all intrinsically, divinely, a part. In this realm, all living creatures on this planet, and even beyond, are connected: cognizant beings such as humans and proto-humans, even animals at some level."

"Proto-humans?" Ramona's furrowed brow and low forehead reminded Jill of the distant ancestors she referenced. She held back her involuntary smirk, picturing Ramona in animal skins, pounding her club.

Jill continued her explanation. "Religion and spirituality have been in existence on our planet for hundreds of thousands of years—in fact, they predate our species, Homo sapiens. Evidence of spirituality and ritual burials has been traced to our distant relatives, the Neanderthals, who roamed Europe over a hundred thousand years before our Cro-Magnon ancestors, and evolved separately. So, even at the dawn of man, in our primitive state, we had a connection, an understanding of something beyond our physical presence. Why did we leave the warm climate of Africa to go straight north in the middle of an Ice Age? Why did we not only survive the harsher environment but actually thrive and evolve because of it? The Neanderthals and other humanoid species became extinct, whereas we survived. What was different with Homo sapiens?"

When Jill finished, Ramona responded to her rhetorical question. "I don't know—bigger brains, better tools, luck… Are you suggesting that our ancient ancestors had some connection, akin to your Vision Speak, which gave them an advantage somehow?"

"There have always been special people, in the history of our species, with unique insights into the mysteries of the universe. Many of the offerings at the Spiritual Center originated from their life work. At key stages in our development, wise men have had revelations, sparks of genius and invention, or messages from their gods that led mankind in new directions. Our history books are full of this but there are also many gaps, before there were written records, upon which we can only speculate—that is, if we only look for answers in the material world or in our writings. In truth, all of our history, all of our past, is still here, right in front of us, at all times. It is still embedded and alive within each of us—and so much more."

As Jill spoke, Aaron sat back in his seat, observing both the slight form of his mother and the intimidating physical presence of Ramona. He sensed that his mother was starting to lose the interrogator, which no doubt had been her plan, and that Ramona was going to have trouble getting the discussion back to where she'd been heading. Even without his inner sense, there were physical signs: her brows were drawn together in a deep frown and she was angrily tapping her fingers on the table. The tapping was increasing in intensity.

As Jill continued to lead Ramona towards an unsatisfactory end to the interrogation, Aaron's mind wandered to a conversation between his mother, Elzabeth, and himself on this very topic. He felt a rush of frustration that she'd bequeathed her journals to Willow. When he and Jill met with Elzabeth before her passing, she hinted that she'd found a solution to their worries.

Still, she'd been cryptic and refused to share details. Now he was certain that answer lay within her journals. Journals were supposed to be safe from any prying eyes, even the CRKA, unless allowed by the Protector. But Aaron felt uneasy based on Ramona's revelation that they'd been able to tamper with Elzabeth's closure ceremony. If they could do that, a logical thought was that they might also be able to find a loophole in the Protector Laws and systems. They might find a way to access the journals.

He had no idea what Elzabeth's mysterious solution was but he feared that if it fell into the wrong hands, it could spell disaster for them.

Determination set in as he straightened his back, teeth clenched. He resolved to do whatever it took to get Willow to relinquish control to him. If he couldn't reason with her directly, then he would find another way to penetrate her stubbornness.

Chapter 14

*"You can only apprehend the Infinite by a faculty superior to reason,
by entering into a state in which you are your finite self no longer,
in which the Divine Essence is communicated to you. This is Ecstasy.
It is the liberation of your mind from its finite consciousness."*

Plotinus

    The sun's rays caressed her skin, the mixture of heat and light radiating contentment through her nerve fibers. A gentle wind rustled the leaves and birds could be heard chirping, squirrels rummaging in the trees. Willow came to this place often, even on cloudy days, to escape the bustle of campus life. They called it the Hidden Sanctuary although it was just 100 meters from the Arts Center and everyone knew where it was. The noisy populous, although close by, were nothing but a distant hum. There was a limit on the number of people who could enter the gardens to maintain the serenity of the surroundings but Willow had never seen it get that busy away.
    Dropping her sketch pad and lying back, she let the outside sounds and smells fade into the background, enjoying the sensations of the sun, the grass, and the breeze. Her mind was drowsy and, yet, her psyche was alert. As she let herself drift, she sensed the presence of the others in the gardens. It was becoming easier all the time, like someone who had

removed ear plugs and suddenly could hear. Once where there had been random thought patterns and images approaching her from many directions, she was now starting to sense direction and gaze deeper into the source, really seeing inside the person, understanding their innermost emotions. Sometimes she wondered if she could even go beyond just seeing. Could she influence them? She hadn't dared to try yet.

As her mind roamed around the immediate vicinity, watching the images play about, some amusing, others silly or boring, she found herself fascinated with a woman who seemed to be on the other side of the stream. She could read this woman with such clarity that it took her by surprise. She sensed that the woman was with her lover and yet her being was fixated on another. The inner turmoil was enough to disturb Willow's peaceful state. She experimented, planting soothing images, trying to distract the woman from her obsession. The woman was a hard case but in the end, it worked and she seemed to relax.

Willow's pride of accomplishment was quickly overshadowed by guilt—like someone who had eavesdropped on a conversation by accident and then stuck around to listen to the whole thing. Thus far, no one had detected her presence. What she'd been doing was harmless, although she knew many would consider it intrusive. Still, she couldn't stop. She understood, not only from Great Bet, but from her own innate sense, that she was on the brink of something important. She could no more stop herself from this than she could avoid inhaling the scent of the lilies as she walked in the garden.

Wandering further a field, she was startled to see her own image among someone's thought pictures. She opened her eyes and sat up skimming the area but there was no one in sight except the couple across the pond.

The sound of footsteps on the pathway warned of people approaching and she stood up, grabbing her bag in anticipation of a quick exit.

"Willow—there you are. We figured we'd find you in here somewhere." Sophie's shrill voice was loud in the peaceful environment. She was with two mutual friends from college. The three of them sauntered over to join Willow.

"Sophie! You gave me a fright." Willow relaxed the tight hold on her bag that she'd clutched against her chest, letting it drop down beside her as she greeted her friends. "Katie, Benjamin—how's it going?" They were all enrolled in the Institute in different programs, and hung out frequently. In fact, she'd dated Benjamin for a while but it had ended shortly after she started visiting Great Bet. So much had happened since then that Willow had scarcely given him much thought.

"Willow, I haven't seen you around much lately. What have you been doing?" Benjamin's surreptitious eye contact and body language told her that he was uncomfortable but she was sensing more—he'd been hurting. Benjamin was tall and fair with a baby face, rosy cheeks, soft, puffy lips and eyes that belonged on a ten year old. She remembered the closeness they'd shared and for a moment, she was sorry, but then his anger reached her. The resentment she sensed just beneath the surface was so out of character from the boy she had known, or thought she had known, that she physically stepped back, temporarily speechless.

"Hey, are you okay, Willow?" Katie smiled quizzically.

"Uh, yeah, I'm great. Sorry, you guys caught me off guard. I think I was snoozing when you came down the pathway." She reached down to brush the grass off her skirt. "I've seen a lot of Sophie lately." She gave her cousin a sidelong glance, "but, I haven't had a chance to catch up with you guys in a while. How're you doing?"

Katie grimaced. "The usual, busy with projects. Actually, we've been looking for you because we're going to the 'Monkey and the Lizard' tonight and wanted to see if you could come."

"The Monkey and the Lizard, eh?" Turning to Sophie, Willow pointed at her outfit. "I'm assuming you're dressed as the Lizard?" Sophie's skintight, green jumpsuit was very stylish and, in Willow's opinion, a bit ugly but she would never say that directly to her cousin. Teasing her was more fun.

They all laughed, as they chatted for a few minutes about Sophie's clothes and then their heavy load of assignments with the school year winding down. Willow was stalling for time, searching for a good excuse. Clubbing was the last thing she felt like doing.

In the midst of their conversation, Katie interrupted with: "hey, what's this?" and reached down. She picked up Willow's sketchpad which she'd left by the tree.

"Oh, I forgot about that." The blood rushing up from her neck belied the nonchalant wave of her hand. "It's just a drawing I was working on." She tried to take it from Katie but the diminutive, freckle-faced girl was holding it tight with both hands, the bottom of the pad anchored against her belly as she looked down at it. Benjamin and Sophie gathered around, standing on either side of Katie while all three studied the drawing.

Sophie exclaimed, "Wow, that is so amazing, Willow! I wish I had your talent." Katie murmured her agreement. In the center of the picture was the face of a young man, dark-skinned, with heavy, thick eyebrows and large, deep pools of black eyes on a thin, bony face. His hair was long, tousled and shaggy, hanging around his cheeks and over his ears. His expression was intense, haunting, and so life-like. The eyes, in particular, were mesmerizing. Misty, dreamy images of forest and sky surrounded his detailed image.

"So, who's the guy?" Benjamin demanded.

Willow took advantage of their diversion to snatch the sketchpad from Katie. "He's no one, really," she stammered. "Just a face I imagined. I was working from images that were roaming around in my head." She stuffed the pad into her bag, averting her eyes from their curious stares.

"But, how can you imagine such detail in a face without him really existing? Come on, Willow, tell us who he is. You didn't really imagine him, did you?" Sophie's tone was skeptical.

"Well, I don't know what to tell you, Soph, but I just did," she insisted. Just then, her portal unit vibrated on her hip. Glancing down, she saw a new message. Relieved at the distraction, she pulled the unit from her holster and read it.

The message was brief and to the point: "Can we meet for dinner tonight? Aaron." A monkey, or maybe it was a lizard, did a somersault in her abdomen, her nerves suddenly aflutter. Now, this was an intriguing offer.

"Guys, you know, I'd love to go to the Monkey with you tonight, but I've got a dinner date and I really have to run. I'm sure you'll all manage to have some fun without me, though." She winked, remembering that these girls knew how to have a good time. She got a sullen glance from Benjamin, a pout from Sophie, and a grin from Katie, who she realized was happy to have Benjamin's attention without the presence of an ex-girlfriend.

"So who's the date with? I bet it's the guy in the picture, isn't it? Why don't you bring him along?" Sophie's curiosity was piqued.

"It's not the guy in the picture! I told you that he's just a figment of my imagination. As for tonight, he's just a friend, honestly, and I'm not sure if he'd be into the scene at the club. He's a bit older." Willow was having trouble picturing Aaron Braxton dancing at the Monkey and the Lizard and, anyway, she had no idea why he wanted to have dinner with her—no doubt, it was something to do with Vision Speak or her great grandmother.

"An older man? Really? That settles it. You have to bring him so I can check him out. It's the least I can do for the family." The smirk on Sophie's face had them all giggling—even Benjamin.

"Uh, yeah, sure... We'll be there. Just stand by the door and wait for us all night, okay?" Willow swung her bag over her shoulders and started walking. "Come on, let's get out of here. I have to go home and get changed."

As they walked out of the Sanctuary, Willow quickly replied to Aaron on her unit, "sure, what time and where?" and wondered to herself what the evening might hold. Suddenly, she was in a hurry to reach home and get ready.

Chapter 15

"When we blindly adopt a religion, political system, a literary dogma, we become automations. We cease to grow."

Anais Nin

World Governors Sharon and Craig sat side by side on the lush brown leather sofa in their office as Burton activated the connection with the CRKA.

Ramona and her team were waiting and ready to give their report.

"We understand you brought the Vision Speak representatives in today for questioning. Tell us how it went." Craig spoke first.

"Yes, sir, we brought in Jill Braxton, her son Aaron Braxton and Simon LaChance. I interrogated them for over an hour."

"Under what pretense did you bring them in?"

"We had enough to warrant questioning them about their offering and its adherence to the Spiritual Contract. In particular, we asked them to explain some of Elzabeth's closing words and a recent reading from a session. Both the possibility of recruiting and claims of exclusivity were suggested."

"How did they react to the line of questioning surrounding Elzabeth?"

"They responded appropriately, that she was in her elderly stages and her words should be taken in that vein. Jill Braxton, the current leader, was well versed in their rights with regards to the Citizen's Code. We had to let them go without any charges."

Sharon glanced behind Ramona to the three people standing at attention—two young women and a man. "Did your team witness the interrogation?"

"Yes, they did."

"What was the general consensus on the interrogation?"

"The woman was highly intelligent and confident, knew their material cold, and there was no doubt but that they believe in their quest completely. In fact, I would have to admit that the premise behind it was intriguing."

"One of your team members has been attending Vision Speak—is that agent present?"

The blonde woman on Ramona's left spoke up: "Yes, sir, I am. I have been attending sessions for almost a year now."

"Your name?"

"Agent Perkins."

"Did you encounter Elzabeth?"

"I knew her and she was well regarded at the center, although I have not yet reached the upper levels. They are a tight group so I'm afraid I was never taken into her confidence. I am continuing to get closer to those that were."

"You are aware that Elzabeth was once an agent of the CRKA, of very high rank?"

"Oh, yes."

"In that capacity, she was privy to many of our secrets, the ways that we operate. In fact, she was instrumental in developing our counter-intelligence strategy for the imposters. Unless this information is maintained in complete secrecy, it could jeopardize the tenuous hold we have on these dissidents."

"Yes, we understand and share your concerns, Governor Sharon-Lee."

"In her later years, Elzabeth became so convinced that Vision Speak could overcome our human tendencies towards dissension and conflict that she may have put the needs of this fledgling offering ahead of her obligation to the CRKA. We need to know if she divulged any classified information—either with this group or in her private journals."

"There was no indication, in our questioning today, of such a breach—although they were not likely to slip up. They were well prepared mentally and seemed quite able to handle themselves in an interrogation."

"Perhaps we should question them individually. I understand the woman did most of the talking. Might we get more out of the young men?"

Ramona shook her head. "At this point, I don't think so. Depending on how this investigation proceeds, we may exercise that option at a later date."

Craig continued with his inquiry while Sharon sat silently by his side. "What about the young woman, the Protector—Elzabeth's great-granddaughter? We understand that she's joined the group now. Agent Perkins: have you made her acquaintance?"

"Yes, but she's very reserved," Agent Perkins responded promptly. "She doesn't volunteer information and prefers to keep to herself. It will take time to get to know her."

"We don't have time. We need to know what's in the journals." Craig barked.

"Y-yes, sir, I understand. I'll step up my efforts with her." The young woman's face reddened but she stood in rigid obedience.

Sharon interjected, directing her attention back to the lead agent. "Thank-you for the report, Agent Markel. We look forward to your continued updates." Flicking a switch on her desk, she ended the meeting abruptly.

Craig turned to her, his left eyebrow raised in inquiry. The heavy, dark eyebrows, not yet turned grey like his hair, drew one's attention to his deep set eyes, accentuated by fine, feathery wrinkles. At the moment, he gazed steadily at his partner.

Sharon felt his unspoken questions. She stood up and crossed the room in silence. Finally she turned to Burton. "Can you please give us some privacy?" She noticed Burton's short, white hair stood straight up, giving him a startled appearance, as he nodded his agreement and walked swiftly out of the office.

The whoosh of the closing door came and went while the two stared at each other from across the room. With the distance between them, Craig couldn't help but admire the woman with whom he had pledged to share his life and career. She was stunningly attractive, even approaching sixty, with a soft voluptuous form, platinum hair immaculately coifed with wide, intelligent eyes. She had assistants who helped with hair and makeup to ensure her image to the world remained intact but even so—she was a natural.

He waited. Experience told him that she had something to say. She would say it when she was ready.

At last, she spoke. "They're going to recommend questioning the girl soon."

He nodded, "yes, I think they should. Do you want to do it this week?"

"I'm not sure. Craig, this journal of Elzabeth's, I mean of Former Agent MacGregor..." She paused, apparently searching for words, "well, I'm not certain what it might contain. Maybe this is all a big 'to-do' about nothing but..."

Craig got to his feet and walked over to her, surprised at the hesitancy he heard in her voice. He was used to her confidence, her authority. Sharon rarely flinched from anything, never had trouble making decisions. He reached his hands out, holding her shoulders, keeping her at arm's length. She raised her eyes slowly to meet his, allowing him to see the inner turmoil mirrored there. "Sharon, what is going on? I can't fathom what you can be so afraid of. Surely, this is not concern over Elzabeth having exposed the CRKA counter-intelligence strategy?"

"N-no, Craig, in fact the more I think about it the more I doubt that Elzabeth would have revealed those details in her journal. The CRKA are forbidden from sharing top secret information in their journals and she was a devoted agent." She shook her head, "no, not that information. I don't think so. However, there was a case that she worked on that became very personal for her...and, I fear that in this situation, she may have breached protocol."

"And what do you know of this case, Sharon? It seems that this may have been personal for you too?" His voice was incredulous, realizing that she must, indeed, have some secrets that she had never shared with him.

"I was very young, Craig. It was before we met, before I decided to pursue a political career but, yes, there were some things that, er, happened that…" She reached up and touched his face. "Let's just say that I'd done my best to forget, that I have some memories that I hoped to leave behind forever, okay?"

"Is that all you're going to say?"

She pulled away to stand by the windows. They were enormous, spreading across the whole back of the office, reaching from floor to ceiling. She pressed her hands against the glass, her back to him, her front facing the city they governed together. "I can tell you that it was during this mission that Agent MacGregor discovered what she later termed Vision Speak and eventually brought forward to institute as a sanctioned offering."

"Really?" He waited, again sensing that she had more to say but aware that he could not press her.

"Because she was so strong in her convictions about Vision Speak, I can't help but wonder if she'd feel this mission and the events surrounding it to be important enough to document in her journals." She leaned her forehead on the glass, her breath leaving a fog on the window. "Craig, for now, please, can we just focus on the present situation?"

He said nothing but she felt his eyes boring into her back.

She took a deep breath and whirled around to face him again. "I think you're right, Craig, we should bring her in for questioning soon, but I want to be there. I want to control the interrogation."

His response was dangerously monotone. "Okay, Sharon, fine but know that I will be there too." As he turned away from her, he delivered a final warning. "If there's anything—anything at all," he emphasized, "that you aren't telling me, I suggest you do so before then."

Just before he reached the door, she spoke to his back. "Craig, I was under oath not to talk about my activities when I was with the CRKA; but, you have clearance and in this case, you should be briefed. I'll dig out the records and we can review it together."

She heard him grunt and then the swoosh of the door closing when he walked out in silence, leaving her alone with the city.

Chapter 16

*"The meeting of two personalities is like the contact
of two chemical substances: if there is any reaction, both are transformed."*

Carl Jung

As Aaron walked along the path to the Olsen family residence, he admired the simple layout of the grounds. The pathways were concrete, not fancy, inlaid stone as in the upper levels; however, the gardens alongside were well designed with rocks and trees and wildflowers.

Approaching the entrance, he hoped that she would come to the door, ready to leave. Then he could dispense with the formalities of greeting her parents. It had been a long time since he'd had to worry about this when picking up a young woman. Most of the women he dated were well past the stage of living with their family.

As his foot touched down on the porch, he heard the bell ring. The front door slid open; a woman stood waiting in the entranceway. It was definitely not Willow.

"Good evening," he forced warmth into his greeting, his smile hiding clenched teeth.

"Good evening," she responded, stepping onto the porch and extending a hand with long scarlet nails. "I'm Willow's mother, Joley." As she moved closer, she squinted, studying his features. "You look familiar, have we met somewhere?" Before he could reply, she continued: "I know, wasn't it at the closure ceremony?"

"Indeed it was. Allow me to reintroduce myself—Aaron Braxton." He reached out his hand and held hers for a moment, remembering his own mother's advice to always be courteous to the girls' parents. He smiled, applying his charm, "We met at your grandmother's closure ceremony, during the reception. At the buffet table, I believe."

"Yes, of course. You and your mother knew Elzabeth from the Vision Speak group. I suppose that's how you met Willow?"

Just then Willow rushed out onto the porch and interrupted them. Following close behind her were two others, presumably her father and sister. "Hey, Aaron, nice to see you again." She clasped his hand in greeting and then quickly released it. Her face was flushed. "Thanks so much for coming to fetch me." She glanced back at her family. "We'd better get going. See you later."

"Hey, not so fast." Her father laughed while he reached out to shake hands, inviting Aaron to step inside their home for a few moments.

"Uh, sure, thanks." He responded, glancing down at his unit. "We've just got a few minutes though, or we'll be late for our reservation."

When he stepped into their main living space, he was struck by the array of visual art adorning the walls. It was brilliant, unlike anything he had ever seen before, particularly at a home in the middle levels. This artwork was clearly of a superior nature, the likes of which were usually reserved for the Top Contributors' homes or on display in public buildings. His eyes were drawn to the walls, mesmerized by the bold images and swirling vibrant colours. They were a mix of abstract and realism, with embedded faces and images so lifelike they appeared almost photographic.

"This display of art is absolutely incredible!" Aaron gazed about the room, his mouth gaping open. "How did you acquire such a collection?"

Beaming, his lean, serious face transformed, Arild Olsen reached for his youngest daughter, his hand on Willow's back. "It's all Willow's work. Isn't she talented? You know, she'll find out next month if she's going to be taken into the Arts Community."

Aaron's gaze shifted to Willow. He could see she was embarrassed but couldn't fathom why. "Willow, I had no idea. This is amazing, really. I'm very impressed." And he certainly meant it. Being chosen as a member of the Arts Community was a vocation that would be envied by many. Only the very best were permitted to pursue a lifelong creative path.

He was graced with a flicker of a smile and a quiet, "thank-you" before her sister, Claire, stepped into the conversation.

Grasping his right hand with both of her manicured ones, Claire inspected her sister's date unashamedly. "Aaron Braxton? Yes, I certainly remember you, so nice to see you again. So, you and my little sister are going out? Where are you off to?"

She knows how to adorn herself for maximum affect, he thought to himself, like a younger version of the perfectly-coifed and stunning mother. He glanced back at Willow and realized that she was quite different, seemed hard to believe that they were even related. She was more like her father, in appearance anyway, with his tall, lean figure, fair complexion and sandy blonde hair. Observing the frown forming on his date's brow, he thought it best to get on their way.

Easing himself out of Claire's grip and her analytical stare, he smiled, reaching over to gently clasp Willow's elbow and steer her out the door. "We do have a reservation, so we should be on our way. It was great to see you all again."

Having survived the family meeting, they chatted on the way to dinner. He was intrigued with her art, leading to questions about her studies and the creative process that she followed. Once he broke through her self-consciousness, she talked openly. He hadn't expected to enjoy her company so much. There was no pretense, just Willow. A few times, he thought he could detect her emotions directly, felt a connection inside that he would usually only be able to experience in a deep trance.

When the subject of her family came up, he asked about Claire. "It seemed like your sister was going to interrogate me."

Willow laughed. "Oh, probably," she said. "Claire is an investigator with the Justice Department, the perfect job for her. She's relentless, nosey, and not at all shy about asking personal questions." She nodded solemnly. "Oh yes, it was very astute of you to escape while you still could."

Aaron pulled into the parking facility, chuckling at her explanation.

When they entered the restaurant, she exclaimed: "Oh, it's so beautiful. I've never been to 'Constellations' before but I can see it's everything I've heard—and more." As they followed the host along the winding paths, amongst gardens and trees with white lights, to their private table in the darkly lit room, she gazed upwards. The images of twinkling stars on the distant ceiling were so lifelike—in fact clearer than the true evening sky. "Thank-you for taking me here," she made a direct hit with her smile.

He drew in a breath, adjusting to the impact of her unexpected charisma. She was wearing a slinky, cream-coloured dress with glimmers of gold, a perfect fit on her tall, slender frame. As he led her through the indoor gardens, he inhaled, breathing in her feminine scent. She had even applied color to her face—something he'd never noticed on her before. Yes, she was certainly attractive in a sweet, innocent kind of way. Although not typically his type, when she looked at him like that, he sensed trouble. It transformed the shy, pretty young girl into a dangerously sensual, ethereal beauty. Perhaps it's the lights and the atmosphere, he thought to himself but judging by the sudden ache in his abdomen, the throbbing around his groin area, he realized that he probably shouldn't have brought her to this place.

He kept the conversation light and friendly over dinner. There was no shortage of topics—her art and dreams for the future, his vocation in the health lab, some of the more interesting characters in the Vision Speak group, their families, even Elzabeth stories that they both enjoyed. He deftly avoided the heavier subjects. As much as he wanted to ask about Elzabeth's journals, he sensed that it would shut her down if he went there too fast.

"Your mother, she seems quite a remarkable woman and fairly advanced with Vision Speak. How long has she been involved?" Willow sipped on her wine, holding the stem of the traditional glass tenderly as she would a freshly picked flower. She drank it slowly, breathing in the aroma.

"Yes, she is quite advanced—not as much as Elzabeth but with her gone now," he smiled gently, "she's probably the most experienced person there. Mother has been involved since early days, within a year of when Elzabeth started it."

"Great Bet thought quite highly of your mother. I've read a few entries in her journal where she mentions Jill Carson Braxton with great affection."

"She mentioned her in the journals?"

"Well, yes, she mentions a lot of people—even you." Grinning, Willow continued, "Actually, on another topic, I'd like to share something that I recently came across in the journals, assuming I can trust you?"

"Of course, Willow. I hope you know that my interest in the journals has always been to protect any sensitive information and make sure it doesn't get widely distributed." As he spoke, he reached for his wine glass, the deep burgundy glowing in the dim light. He glanced away so he didn't reveal the anxiety that was starting to bubble up in his stomach. When he shifted his gaze to the bar, at the far end of the room, a woman caught his attention.

"Okay. For now, I'd be interested in your opinion on this particular entry as it kinda gave me a jolt. Hold on while I bring it up." She pulled her personal portal out and with a few, swift entries, had it in front of her. "Here, I'll read it to you…"

"Wait a minute." Alarmed, he glanced around, making a quick decision. Something had been nagging at the back of his mind and he wanted to check it out. He stood up, holding out his hand. "I need to dance with you."

She reached her free hand out to hold Aaron's, her frozen expression mirroring her bewilderment as he pulled her up. She stood directly in front of him. Before she could retreat, he wrapped his arm around her, drawing her body against his. He whispered in her ear, "Just come with me and I'll explain."

As they made their way to the center of the room, he kept his arm around her and at one point, again, leaned in close as he whispered, "try not to show that you're looking but do you see that couple sitting at the end of the bar? The woman with the pink and white hair. Do they look familiar to you?"

After a brief glimpse, she responded, "I don't think so. I'd remember that 'do…'"

"No, don't look at the hair, it's changed. Just look at their faces. Remember in the garden at the closure ceremony?"

As they reached the dance floor, she glanced over again. "Hmm…maybe, but that would be an odd coincidence? I'm not sure, Aaron, but they're coming this way."

Willow slid her portal unit into Aaron's jacket pocket and wrapped her arms around his neck as they moved slowly together to the music. The couple from the bar joined them on the dance floor. Aaron nuzzled his head against hers, his words soft in her ear, "I don't think it's a coincidence."

She stiffened at his words but kept moving. After a pause, she whispered back, "I need to focus for a few minutes and I'll try and find out. I'm just going to rest my head on your shoulder while I concentrate."

Her hair grazed his cheek, silky soft, as she leaned her head on his shoulder, facing inwards, and breathed silently, the warm air caressing his neck and ear. Suddenly, in the quiet of the moment, with her warm body swaying against his, chills coursed through his body. He was electrified by her closeness yet stunned by her suggestion that in a few moments of silence she would be able to probe these two. Was she actually using Vision Speak?

As they danced, he realized that her movements were slowing and she was becoming limp in his arms. He held her tighter, guiding her in the dance moves. In the middle of a public place while they were dancing, it seemed she had very quickly reached a deep trance. For the first time, he wondered if there was more to this great granddaughter of Elzabeth's and her rapid entrenchment into Vision Speak than he had realized.

As the song came to an end, she slowly lifted her head, opening her eyes wide and stared into his. She was silent for a full minute, apparently struggling to return to the world of spoken language.

"Aaron? It's the strangest thing. I just saw an image of you, your mother, and that other guy—Simon. Anyway, I saw you through a window, sitting at a table in a room. The three of you were sitting on one side—your mother in the middle—and there was a large dark haired woman facing you. It seemed like you were being questioned. And, these people were watching you. Does that make any sense?"

His head jolted back, her unexpected words triggering a physical reaction. "You just saw this now? What on earth…" He paused as the implications of her vision started to sink in.

"Aaron, what's going on?" She stared up at him, her eyes wide. "On top of that, I can tell you that, yes, they are definitely watching us." In her confusion, her whisper was louder than she had intended.

What's going on? That's what I'd like to know, he thought to himself. "Willow, let's get out of here and go somewhere that we can talk in private." He broke their embrace abruptly and led her back to the table.

Chapter 17

"All religions have always said: there's only our path, our saviour, our system, our beliefs, our rituals and only through those will you find salvation. This has been the constant of all religions."

Krishnamurti

The midnight sky cloaked them in darkness with only the sliver of a moon and hazy stars to guide their descent into the open cavern. The people streamed in steadily, camouflaged in their black robes, exposing an occasional glimmer of orange concealed underneath.

They came in small groups or alone, eyes staring straight ahead, fixated on the holographic image of their leader. He was wreathed in light, standing in the center of the circle. They may have been beside a friend, a family member, or even a foe but no one knew, no one cared, they simply gazed at the light, walking forward as if in a trance.

Thousands strong, the crowd gathered around the hypocenter—once Ground Zero of the Great Annihilation for this district. It was the anniversary of that most holy of times—350 years from the day that the first bomb was dropped—and this same ritual would be repeated around the world.

Charlie's heart was thumping as he found a place amongst the crowd. This was the first time he had actually stood on one of the ancient hypocenters. The Ruins were dust where he stood now but as they had weaved their way in to this center, through the secret tunnels, they could still see remnants of the original city buried underground. He shivered with blessed rapture as he brushed against these monuments—proof that the legends were true.

The crowd was assembled, waiting expectantly, motionless, when the leader began to speak. The voice boomed into the still night air.

"On this day, in our ancient past, our ancestors faced God's Judgment, the ultimate Trial, Armageddon." His booming voice vibrated that holy word, pausing while the crowd chanted "the day the bombs fell" on cue. Then a hush fell upon them, the hypocenter silent as a tomb, while they waited for the leader's next words.

"Our saviour, Samuel, was born from the ashes of the destruction. His parents, both sterile and diseased from the radiation sickness they endured, lived to record the Holy Journals of our Trial, and miraculously bore the strong, healthy son who went forward to found our brotherhood."

The leader's hands had been outstretched but now he pulled them inward, placing both hands on his heart as he appeared to scan the crowd, his eyes glowing in the light. He appeared to be a tall man as he floated above the crowd, his dark robes concealing his figure, as they billowed around him.

"Our society, cloaked in secrecy for centuries, was founded in the wreckage of the old world—and Samuel proclaimed in his sacred journals that a messiah would arise amongst us when the time was right, after the first Judgment Day." As he spoke, his hands actively punctuated his words, the holographic image rotating slowly so that he equally faced everyone in the crowd.

"The Messiah will lead us to glory!" A section of disciples, clothed in robes of the initiated, responded.

"We have been patient, biding our time, even as the People's United Republic of Earth arose out of that carnage, the leaders burying the truth, feeding the people on lies. They manipulate our lives, regulate our spiritual path, tell us what we can and cannot believe but—no more!"

"The Chosen One will show us the way." The crowd chanted in unison.

"Their manipulations may have averted God's will for a time but ultimately, our promised destiny will be fulfilled."

"Yes! It will happen again!" The shout was jubilant, immediate.

"It will happen and the time is coming closer. Tonight I unveil the greatest surprise, the most glorious gift to us all, something that you and your ancestors have been waiting for, for generations. I tell you tonight that the Chosen One, the spiritual descendant of Samuel, is amongst us, just as Samuel foretold. We have found him!"

The pronouncement triggered an audible gasp.

"Yes, we have truly found him. He is scarcely more than a child but rich with the wisdom of the one true Lord of the Universe, possessed with knowledge and foresight that will lead us to triumph." The holographic image continued to rotate, a beatific smile on the leader's face, holding his silence for a full minute while the crowd waited in anticipation to hear more.

Finally, a young voice, near the inner circle of the crowd, could bear the silence and the mystery no longer. He called out, "Your worship, please tell us more. When will we see this Messiah? Who is he? Where did you find him?"

After a few moments, the leader laughed aloud. "I hear questions from so many locations...and yet all the same." He lifted his arms high in the air, raising his eyes and hands to the heavens. "Loyal followers of the Cult of Armageddon, the chosen children of the Earth, your patience shall be rewarded. Tonight you shall behold your Messiah. We found him as a boy and now, on the brink of manhood, he is ready to face you, his followers, to lead us to our destiny." The leader's image gradually disappeared into darkness and then, after a few moments that felt like an eternity to Charlie, a teenage boy appeared with brown skin, shaggy black hair, and heavy dark eyebrows. He was cloaked in white robes in contrast to the black garments that the crowd, the leader, and disciples were all covered in. Even after the leader's image had faded away and transformed into the serene, still image of the young man, his words could be heard as if from a great distance. "This is your Messiah, the Chosen One, who possesses great powers and can see into the hearts and minds of men. He is in communion with the Lord—no secret can be hidden from him."

In moments, the crowd was on the ground kneeling, lowering and raising their heads to the earth. They rocked back and forth in worship. Random exclamations could be heard, "Halleluiah"; "He is here!"; "Son of Samuel"; "Praise the Lord", resulting in an excitable murmur. Yet, the image of their Messiah simply gazed forward, rotating slowly. His enormous black eyes were wide open, intense and, yet, somehow all-seeing. His silence and apparent indifference to their devotion gave him an otherworldly presence. Finally, there was quiet as they all rose, their eyes fixated on their new Messiah, wondering and waiting, hoping to hear his voice.

At last, he opened his mouth to speak but uttered only three simple words. The simplicity and clarity of his message echoed in the hypocenter. He said, "It is time," and raised his hands above his head, his eyes focused heavenward. Slowly his image faded away and was replaced again by the leader.

From his place amongst the crowd, watching the messiah as he disappeared from view, Charlie had goose bumps down his back, his heart exultant with the news that the Chosen One had come.

The leader returned with his arms reaching high. Gradually, he lowered them and spoke to the crowd. "Our Chosen One, Kalesh, is the son of Samuel, the spiritual being who has come to lead us to the final Judgment. With him, our place in the Great Galaxy can be assured but only for those who are brave enough to execute the plan. There can be no looking back once we take our first definitive steps forward."

The crowd replied, in unison, "The Chosen One will show us the way!"

"But, first, I must remind all of you who are here today, who share our common vision and know that we must meet that Trial once more. We will launch a series of events following the anniversary of the Great Annihilation. Ultimately we must again initiate for all mankind the final and true Judgment Day."

"Yes, it will happen again!"

"Yes, it will happen again and our rewards will be just. The sacred verses have been hidden for hundreds of years, containing the secret words of the one and only God. Finally, we are ready to expose this to the world. Once they were embedded in many holy books, leading mankind to necessary earthly conflict but they have all been tampered with, exploited. Public records of these holy scriptures were destroyed, desecrated by the PURE leaders so they can manipulate the people and maintain control. But, no longer. Finally, after generations of secrecy, we have a means to release these lost words of the prophets. We are ready. This revelation will mark the beginning."

"The beginning of the End!"

Again the leader's figure faded away however, this time, a very different image replaced him. Towering into the night sky, a tall cylindrical shape, wider in the middle than on the two rounded ends, gradually came into view. The metallic body had both silver and copper components with the bottom end rooted in a deep hole, just below the crowd's vision. A panel with small, flashing lights was exposed just below the middle of the device. Suddenly, the image exploded in an immense fiery glow which was replaced by a mushroom cloud, billowing and growing in size before their eyes.

A surge of exulted cries was heard as, in frenzy, the people dropped their robes and the crowd was transformed from a sea of faces with dark, immobile, shapeless bodies, into rapidly moving, bright, orange figures, wearing replicas of the jumpsuits of emergency workers from the past.

They quickly moved into their formations, performing their ritualistic dance, their bodies pounding to a primitive beat, while they chanted: "The day the bombs fell. Judgment Day. It will happen again!"

Chapter 18

"Love the animals, love the plants, love everything. If you love everything, you will perceive the divine mystery in things. Once you perceive it, you will begin to comprehend it better every day. And you will come at last to love the whole world with an all-embracing love."

Fyodor Dostoyevsky

They drove in silence, each locked in the caverns of their own thoughts.

At Willow's request, once they were sure they weren't followed, Aaron drove to the Hidden Sanctuary and she led him from the car to her special place, by the stream under the enormous willow tree. In daylight, the leaves were fluttery, glowing green but now, in the moonlight, the majestic branches lorded over them, cloaking them from the night sky. Aaron dropped a small blanket on the ground beneath the tree.

When they were seated, she kicked her shoes off and folded her legs in, smoothing her dress to cover her slender calves, her toes peaking out the edge. Then she held out her hand. He looked at her quizzically.

"My portal unit, please." Smiling tentatively, she kept her hand proffered.

"Oh, right, I forgot about that." Reluctantly he reached into his pocket and placed the unit into her hand. By now, it would have locked the screen anyway and she would be the only person who could bring the journal back up. "Why don't we start with what you were going to show me in Great Bet's journal that had you puzzled?"

Arching her left eyebrow, she regarded him for a moment, apparently trying to make a decision. "Hmm… I guess we can do that but I certainly hope we will follow with an explanation of what I saw. And why you never mentioned it?"

"Yes, absolutely, but I have a few questions of my own, Ms. Olsen, so don't think it ends there." He poked her gently in the arm, trying to keep the conversation light but in reality he was masking his true feelings, not wanting to scare her into silence. His inner mood was anything but light. In any case, after what he'd just witnessed on the dance floor, he wondered if he could hide anything from her.

"Okay, we'll start with Great Bet." Willow quickly got her portal unit screen back up, turning on the light so she could read it in the dark. "There are a few references to this incident from this time period forward but I'll just read you the section where it first happens. It was the last Vision Speak session that she ever attended. Her illness wasn't the only reason that she had stopped attending, did you know that?"

Aaron returned her inquiring gaze, a flicker of surprise in his deep blue eyes as he shook his head. Willow could tell it was genuine. She didn't try to penetrate to see what he was thinking. She could tell he had his guard up and respected his privacy. "Okay, here goes." Willow read softly from the entry in her great grandmother's journal, dated just four months before her parting:

> *Today, something happened and I am truly frightened for the first time since committing myself to this glorious path. I was in my trance at Vision Speak, sharing first with Jill who I can connect with easily. She's a kindred spirit; we know each other so intimately, beyond what had ever been possible with a friend before. Then, I moved about the room, gently exploring, guiding some of the others in their early endeavours. It was a peaceful session and up to that point, I hadn't reached further than the people who were in the immediate vicinity, had not tried to venture beyond that state.*

Suddenly, I felt a presence, unlike the otherworldly connection I had previously experienced on my own. This presence was powerful, intrusive and masked from me. I could not detect the source. I had never before encountered one with such control, who could invade my inner self with such force, without consensus or accord from me.

I broke from my trance, trying desperately to rid myself of this invasion. Searching the room with my eyes only, I saw no one that I thought could have performed this feat. Everyone there I had at some point connected with or coached along. I couldn't believe they could have hidden this power from me.

Looking back at what happened as I record this entry, I struggle to find the words to describe the actual encounter. What stands out in my mind is the power of the visitor. I cannot say what the intention was—the force of it took me by surprise and my only response was to flee, to sever the connection.

I am home now and for the first time, I question what this new evolution of the human spirit will bring. Have I been too naïve? I've been so convinced that once all humans could relate at this level, understand each other to the depths of their souls that senseless violence, misunderstandings and manipulations would cease to hinder mankind's progress.

But what if I am wrong? What if there are evil forces that will use this power for destructive means? I worry now that perhaps the cult has been resurrected. I thought we had disbanded them and their Sacred Trance sessions but now I don't know. I pray that I have not been wrong.

Willow finished the passage and turned her unit off, gazing at Aaron. She admired the contours of his face in shadow, his wavy, thick hair. Not for the first time that night, she had to contain an urge to reach out and touch him, stroking the wild hair down, running her fingers along his muscular arms and back.

"Whew—that's intense. I wasn't aware of this." Aaron looked off into the distance as he talked, searching his memory banks. "I'll ask my mother if Elzbeth shared this with her but I think she would have mentioned it. Do you know what she meant by the cult?"

Willow slipped the unit into her handbag, and set it down on the grass beside them. She stretched out her long legs, leaning back with her hands holding her weight behind her, gazing up at the majestic branches overhead. She knew Aaron's eyes followed her movements, first her legs then tracing his way along her body up to her throat and face. Could he really think that she didn't notice? Her long hair hung back behind her, almost touching the ground.

Softly she responded, careful not to disturb the currents that were humming between them. "No, I was hoping you might know." She looked into his eyes then. "Have you ever experienced anything like that?" It was dark, they could barely see each other but something snapped between them.

Although she stayed perfectly still, she drew him in. It was imperceptible—a slight arch of her hips, the staccato sound of her breathing, perhaps pheromones triggered by her intense longing. He responded as if on a string.

He leaned forward on the grass beside her, pulling her against him, his mouth covered hers, his free hand firmly around her shoulders, entangled in her silky hair. Moaning, her body on fire, she kissed him fiercely, wrapping her leg around his, pushing herself against him in a way that left no doubt as to what she wanted.

Soon she was lying down, half on the blanket and half on the grass. He was over her, their hands and mouths exploring each other. All her nerve endings were alive, pulsating. His hands caressed her breasts, traveled down. She gasped aloud, reaching to take his clothes off. In that moment, his logical mind almost had a vote but she smothered it, smothered him. He was incapable of stopping.

It was a collision course between two irresistible forces. When Aaron tried to slow it down, wanting to make use of all of his experience to give her pleasure, she wouldn't let him, couldn't let anything but instinct and passion propel them forward. Nothing was more important than driving to that ultimate end: the mating, the joining of their bodies in a heated, violent encounter.

When it was over, they were both completely nude, their clothes strewn around them, starlight glistening on their sweaty bodies. Breathing heavy and tingling, they lay side by side for a time, staring up at the sky, the edge of the great tree obscuring their view of the moon. They were oblivious to a couple of late night strollers who politely looked the other way as they passed. Sexual ardor between young lovers was encouraged; no one would intrude upon them.

Finally, Aaron rolled onto his side, smiled into her eyes, almost shy as he glanced down at her lithe figure. "My god, what happened there?"

She giggled. "I think lightening struck." Her hand reached up, smoothed away a lock of hair that dangled over his brow.

"Uh, yeah...wow. I, uh, honestly never planned—I mean, never meant to..."

"Aaron, it just happened, no one could plan that..." She ran her fingers along the side of his face while her eyes traced the contours in shadow, murmuring, "When something like that strikes, I think you just need to go with it, you know?" She dropped her hand, sensing that he was starting to retreat.

He leaned over, kissed her lightly, nuzzling for a moment. "You're a beautiful girl, Willow, do you know that?"

"You mean woman, right?" She eyed him threateningly.

"Yes, woman," he ran his forefinger along her hipbone ending with his hand under her arm, "definitely a woman." Giving her one last kiss, he sat up, reaching for his clothes. "Let's get dressed and walk a little bit." Glancing back at her, he checked to make sure she was okay. "I think I'm going to need a bit of time to process this."

She laughed, "I understand, believe me."

When they were dressed and had playfully brushed the grass off each other, Aaron threw the blanket over his shoulder and wrapped his arm around Willow. They strolled leisurely along the pathway, arm in arm. The skin that made contact felt more alive, along her back, the occasional touch at the side of her hip to his.

She drew in a deep breath, returning to their earlier conversation, "Okay, now where were we? Right, I was asking you if you had ever experienced anything like that before."

Aaron stopped in his tracks, grasped her shoulders in both hands.

"Never." He whispered the word and then kissed her again. Willow's heart thudded so loudly, she wondered if he could hear it.

She kissed him back, breathless, anticipation in the air again—but the moment was fleeting. She smoothed back her hair with trembling hands as they turned back to their stroll. After a few more heartbeats, he answered the original question. "I can't say I've ever experienced anything as scary as the journal described although I've had a few inexplicable encounters, where I was unsure of the source—once or twice it was a little frightening—but not like that. Elizabeth was always so completely dedicated to Vision Speak as the solution to the "basic human dilemma", as she called it, that I'm very surprised to hear these doubts. It's a little disconcerting, to be honest…"

They had been following the pathway and reached a small footbridge over the stream. It was too narrow for them to walk side by side, so he led her in front of him and they released their hold on each other.

Once they reached the other side, she casually linked her arm into the crook of his elbow and they continued along the path. She nodded. "Yes, I know what you're saying. She was not in the least negative nor did she falter in her convictions in these last months that I spent with her. This section that I've shared with you is the only instance I've seen of it, so far. As time went on, she returned to her optimistic view of the future in her entries—and Vision Speak's role in our ultimate evolution. She never figured out what had happened on that day, though. It's almost like she deliberately put it aside." She gazed up at his face, angled and mysterious in shadows. "Can you tell me what you've experienced?"

He shrugged. "It's hard to explain, it's been so random. Images of scenes or people that I don't recognize, that I believe are coming from somewhere else. They're mostly odd things but not the invasive type of experience that Elzabeth described. I've always felt that I could block it. Recently, there's been some harmless stuff—a beautiful white unicorn, a woman with long flowing blonde hair, soft and warm, fluffy stuff like that keeps creeping in but it's not triggered by my own mind, feels like it's coming from…" He stopped abruptly as Willow started to laugh. Staring at her incredulously, he suddenly realized the source. He halted in the pathway, turning her about to face him. "You! You've been doing this?"

She grinned at him, a blush creeping up her face. "Uh, yes, I'm afraid so… Sorry, I was just trying to reach out, I guess. Really didn't mean any harm…"

He just stared at her a moment and then led them back along the stone walkway into the garden area. There were benches. Another couple was sitting on the opposite side, apparently wrapped up in their own world. They walked in silence for a few minutes, leaving the gardens behind, back into the wooded area. Finally, she asked, "Aaron, are you upset about this?" She was trying her best not to find out for herself how he was feeling, knowing that this was a tenuous time in their new found relationship.

"Upset?" He looked over at her, seeking something in her eyes. "No, I'm not upset but I am confused. I have to confess that I assumed you were a novice in the art of Vision Speak and I'm starting to realize that you may have already reached beyond my own capabilities. Tell me what happened when we were dancing. Were you really able to reach into the minds of those two agents and extract that information, in a matter of minutes, without their involvement?"

"Y-yes…"

"Show me what you saw." He commanded. "Can you do that, right now, while we're standing here?"

She nodded, closing her eyes. He felt the invasion like a jolt. This was not the gentle, playful connection that she had triggered recently. He saw himself, Jill, and Simon sitting in the Interrogation Room, but not from his own memory of the events—he saw their images through a one-way window. They had been watched, alright. That was the room and there they were.

"Okay! Got it." She released her hold on him and he reached his hand up defensively, rubbing his head. "Clearly I've misjudged you, Willow. How did you learn to do that? I don't think even Elzbeth could have done what you just did, at least not without being in a deep trance and working with someone who was ready and receptive."

"I don't know, really, Aaron. Elizabeth tutored me in the beginning. She said that I was moving along faster than anyone she had seen but it's really only been these past weeks, since I've come to the sessions, that things seem to be changing. Every day I notice something more, find myself reaching further…"

"This is unbelievable." He shook his head. "We've speculated on the possibility of a new generation who would take to this more naturally than we have all done. I'm not sure whether I'm excited or afraid, to tell you the truth. So, what's the deal, Willow? Am I an open book to you? Can you completely see inside me, know my innermost thoughts and feelings?"

"No, well, I'm not sure." She hesitated, eying him sideways. "I mean, if I really pushed it, forced my way in per say…well, it's possible but I wouldn't do that. I'm trying very hard to respect your privacy. I can tell that you're guarded."

"Hmm, well I appreciate that." He grunted. "Okay, I'm going to send you a memory stream of the events in the Interrogation so you can understand everything that happened. Can you just focus on that and leave the rest of my measly images alone?"

Smiling, she concurred, "Yes, of course." They leaned their heads against each other, closing their eyes and concentrating. Aaron relived his experience in the Interrogation, remembering the questions and answers, everything he saw and heard. Willow experienced everything from Aaron's perspective. When he was done, he opened his eyes, holding his head and obviously dizzy. Willow sensed his disorientation immediately. Eyes wide open and alert, she led him to a nearby bench.

"Are you okay?" She wrapped her arm around his back, smoothing loose strands of hair away from his forehead with her other hand. "Just breathe deeply, in and out…that's it."

He leaned forward, elbows on his knees. He held his head, breathing loudly. "It's okay, just give me a minute."

Finally, he felt well enough to walk so they turned back towards the car. Before they drove home, he reached over and kissed her, whispering: "Willow, you have literally blown my mind tonight."

Chapter 19

*"I saw more than I can tell and I understood more than I saw;
For I was seeing in a sacred manner the shapes of all things in the spirit and the shape of all things as they must live together in one being..."*

Black Elk

Kalesh sat in the middle of the gardens, meditating, facing the rising sun. Every day, he would emerge from his trance with a deeper sense of the order of all things, comforted with the knowledge that everything was as it should be.

Today, however, he experienced an imbalance that had been brewing gradually but now seemed unavoidable. There was a precarious divide in the future. Along one path, he foresaw great tragedy. It was the path he was expected to take.

A crease formed in his brow, his heavy dark eyebrows furrowed over a lean, smooth face.

To that point, his instincts had led him safely along the chosen path but now, he gazed into the divide in the road ahead, his inner eyes squinting, trying to discern what must be done. He prayed he would have the fortitude to face the challenges ahead.

His eyes closed, his body still as the boulders at the edge of the stream, he felt the presence of the man before he saw him.

The leader was a tall man with thick, unruly, white hair. He stood silently in front of Kalesh, waiting, knowing that the boy would turn to him when he was ready. Although he could communicate with Kalesh non-verbally, the leader's abilities were insignificant in comparison. The small, slender figure of the man-boy who sat cross-legged on the grass in front of him was unmoving, in such communion with his surroundings—the vibrant gardens, trees, and flowing stream—that he may have been missed by a casual passer-by.

When finally the boy rose, he gazed steadily into the leader's eyes. The intensity of his silent regard would be unnerving to many, but not to this most authoritative and confident of men.

The man cleared his throat. "I understand that you wish to speak with me, Kalesh?"

His voice little more than a whisper, Kalesh responded, "Yes, father, I do. Can you please walk with me?"

Nodding, the man led the way forward. The retreat and grounds had been carefully architected so that the only place the not-so-distant cityscape could be seen was from the upper terraces of the sprawling, cedar and stone building which connected all of the services and facilities, as well as the staff and some of the guest residences. Others were housed in cottages around the island.

"Aren't you planning to attend your classes today, my son?" The man asked this without concern. They both knew it was merely a formality for Kalesh, his knowledge and abilities already soared far beyond the other students at the city school he attended by remote portal. Although his father had been strongly urged by the school administration to send him to the Institute for Gifted Students, he refused to let him leave the retreat.

Kalesh glanced up at the man that he'd called "father" for many years. Despite the leader's advanced age, he was tall and lean, his shoulders erect, his shaggy white head high and proud. There was no one else who could have summoned him, as Kalesh had done that morning, and expect such a prompt response.

"Father, I have some questions about the meeting last night." Their steps were in sync as they walked slowly and thoughtfully through the woods. A yellow-gold glow streamed through the trees just over the great body of water which fed the creek. The rush of water could be heard under their feet as they crossed over it on a makeshift wooden bridge. Kalesh spoke softly although he knew there were no other humans in close proximity who might overhear them.

The white head nodded. "I expected that you would have questions. This first exposure was probably a little overwhelming for you, Kalesh, but you'll have to get used to the adoration and trust that these people will be placing in you. You are the one. I felt it from the first moment I set eyes on you, and I know it to be true now."

Kalesh leaned his head down to avoid a low hanging branch as the path led into a less traveled area of the woods. "I wish to talk more about what that means, father, but first I must share with you my, uh, unease. I was wondering why you did not let me speak. Why did you limit my words?"

"I told you it would be so." His voice was an octave deeper, a hint of the stern, unflinching tone that Kalesh remembered from his younger days.

"Yes, you did," he responded. "I'm not suggesting otherwise but I must confess that until I actually was there, saw the crowds, and experienced what we were doing, I did not question your directives. Now, I must ask about this. I've been meditating on this all through the night, father." His voice rose in pitch as he struggled to communicate his thoughts. "I sense many forces out of alignment." Kalesh broke off, unable to express himself with words, instead he used his greater power to demonstrate his concerns.

The elderly man stopped in his tracks and turned to face the boy. The communication was swift and intense, causing the man to hold his head with both hands, helpless to do anything but absorb it.

When he was done, Kalesh proclaimed. "Do you not see what I have been trying to tell you? We must take these steps more cautiously or the effect could be unpredictable, disastrous."

They were both silent, staring at each other—wide gleaming green eyes, surrounded by winter white eyebrows, and a web of wrinkles contrasted sharply with the smooth, coffee-coloured skin and deep-set, black eyes framed by heavy, dark eyebrows.

Finally the man spoke, his voice soft and caressing, "Have I not taught you, my son, in the wisdom of Samuel, that disaster—death and destruction—may be the required event to bring results for the greater good of the masses, possibly even for the human race? Do not be hasty in judging this. You must let my experience lead you."

Turning away, Kalesh began walking again, moving aside branches for them. He led them up to a point where they could look down into the rushing water of the creek. Birds chirping in the early morning sun surrounded them. He stopped, his eyes averted to the distant scenery before he spoke again, "Father, when you found us we were lost and destitute. You took care of us—taught me how to read and write, showed me the world, but most importantly, led me on the path inward to the other-worldly realm where I have found great peace, a calling unlike anything I could have imagined."

"I did these things gladly." He reached his hand out, placing it on the young man's shoulder. "I truly cared for your mother and you. And beyond my personal feelings, I knew you to have great potential and felt it was my calling to do what I have done. When your mother passed on, she left you in my care and I take my promise to her very seriously."

Tears welled in the young man's eyes as he remembered his mother's dying words. She'd believed in this man who had rescued them from squalor in the labour camp and given them a life in this tranquil setting. He glanced upwards, captivated by the intensity in the man's eyes. "Father, in this journey we've taken together, you've taught me that I am special, showed me that I have powers and vision beyond other men. I feel it too, father, suddenly now more than ever. My purpose is becoming clearer everyday where it was once hazy and shrouded in mystery.

"Perhaps we have rushed my introduction—you know I had reservations—but having done so, you must now let me speak to these people who believe I have wisdom to share with them. You must understand, father, I feel a new responsibility has been placed on me now, and I must not let them down."

The man did not respond to his words but Kalesh watched the white, weathered face become absent of expression as the eyes turned to slits, glaring down at the water rushing over the rocks below. Careful not to pry, nevertheless, he sensed a wall descend over the mind beside him.

Respect and gratitude for his adopted father were deeply ingrained in Kalesh. The devotion his mother had felt for this man, remembrance of the squalor in the tropical wasteland where they had lived, knowing how he had helped them after his real father disappeared—so many memories, so much history, and all of it told him that this was a man that he should trust.

And yet, the sting in his chest and the visions in his head were triggering inner turmoil, questions with no answers. He shook his head, resolving to obey as he always had. His father knew best.

Chapter 20

"And so the mystery remains that we have sorrow so we can understand joy;
Failure so we can recognize success;
Pain, so we can relish pleasure.
Somehow built into the mystery of this duality in life is a blueprint for growth that has the potential for shaping us."

Antoinette Bosco

"What did Great Bet mean about that 'cult' and disbanding them?" Willow murmured to herself as she pulled on her robe and sat down in front of her wall portal. She quickly signed in and opened the journals.

It was early in the morning and the world around her was just beginning to stir, the sound of air-car traffic humming in the distance.

She'd slept restlessly; preoccupied with Aaron and the night they'd spent together. The early dreams had been pure fantasy, her young mind obsessed with the passionate experience—on the threshold between waking and sleeping, she'd dreamed of more encounters, his eyes always tender and loving with promises of a future together. She remembered lying awake for a time, her heart full when she eventually fell back into a peaceful slumber.

When she'd awoken again later, her memory of the dream visions were dark and lonely. She'd been searching for Aaron, lustful and eager. She'd found herself in the middle of a field, tall grass flowing in the wind, brilliant wildflowers everywhere. Admiring the gentle breeze and the images, she hadn't noticed him at first but he was there, in the distance. She started towards him, struggling to walk in the tall grass—but, she'd been stopped in her tracks. The glowing sun was covered by clouds. Mist blocked her view and she could barely make him out although he was still there, bathed in sunlight. The fog was only where she was. Then there was someone else in her way. It was the boy's face that she kept seeing in her dreams, the one she had sketched. He was wearing a long flowing robe and stood at the edge of a dark forest. She looked down and saw two pathways dividing in front of her. The path to the right opened widely surrounded by the tall grass and flowers, sun shone on the walkway in the distance highlighting a clear trail—and Aaron. The fork to the left quickly grew dark as it led into the forest, the trees thick and twisted.

She and the boy stared at each other in a timeless, stateless world. She was enthralled, sensing a world of unimaginable possibilities buried deep within him, but then she jerked away, remembering Aaron. She could still see him along the easy path but he didn't see her. She started towards him again but the boy grabbed her arm and she couldn't move. She saw a woman with long, shimmering gold hair approach Aaron; they embraced. The boy pulled her onto the thick, twisted path. They were hurling into the deep, dark forest, low hanging branches slapping against her face as she ran, the boy beside her.

Willow had jolted awake, sweating and agitated, wondering what it all meant and who the mysterious young man was. She could easily bring his image into her mind's eye. He was younger than her, maybe 16 or 17. His skin was brown, his eyes deep and dark, full of wisdom beyond his years, surrounded by heavy set eyebrows. She was sure she had never met him before but he was real. She was certain of that as well. So, why did she keep seeing him?

After tossing in bed restlessly for another hour, she pushed the dream from her mind, remembering the conversation she'd had with Aaron. Finally, she decided to forget about sleep and see if she could find out what Great Bet had meant about the cult.

After searching through the journals for a while, and pursuing various dead ends, she finally found what she was seeking. It was hidden well, in one of the most secured areas of the journal, dating back over 30 years ago, when Great Bet had still been working with the Central Record Keeping Agency.

Elzabeth's journal—Sealed Retrospective Entry

As I write this entry, the knots in my stomach remind me that I'm breaking my oath to the CRKA: an oath that I have upheld faithfully for 37 years. Yet, I am compelled to do this. The reason is clear to me: it is because this case, above all other cases that I have worked on, has affected me at a deeply personal level. I must record this life event but I will keep it sealed and be cautious not to disclose any of the names of agents or top secret internal CRKA operations unless they pertain specifically to the aspects of the case that I must share for my own personal history.

At the core of this case and my personal situation are both the greatest loss of my life and the beginnings of a new future. Losing a child is unbearable, even when that child is grown and you have reached the height of disillusion with respect to who they have become and where they are going. To have this loss occur at the same time as I have discovered this new human potential that I want to rename 'Vision Speak'—the spiritual path that I know will take me into my twilight years—is perhaps timely.

I am preparing my final report on this case, just months before my retirement from the CRKA, with a heavy heart. I find myself questioning, for the first time, my chosen career path. With these realizations came the necessity to record what happened in my personal journals.

The case began as many did: new intelligence indicating that a situation that we thought we had under control was starting to rise up again. For many years, we've tracked the activities of a particular "doomsday cult". There have been secret societies with variants of these ideas for thousands of years but since the Century of Despair and establishment of PURE, they've taken on a new intensity. For three centuries, it has been the job of my team and our predecessors to keep these dissidents from the public eye, contain them and ensure that they do not pollute the general populace with their radical ideas and blatant disregard for the Citizen's Code and the Spiritual Contract.

For fledgling groups, our approach might be to arrest and disband the group. For larger groups, this approach would be too disruptive and it could backfire. Giving groups with a large following this type of attention, could result in publicity, martyrdom, and ramifications that we weren't prepared to deal with. So, typically, we would plant agents within the group, have them rise to levels of influence and keep them contained by manipulation. Arrest or execution would only be used as a last resort and often in a guarded fashion, to select members at unobtrusive times. Occasionally we were given orders for the individuals to just disappear and we understood the greater good that necessitated these unpleasant tasks.

One might wonder why we had to worry about publicity since the Regional Leaders have control of the Media Centers and, if we insisted, could contain any unwanted news story on grounds that it would be disruptive to the Republic. This is true but to a point, and it's certainly not something we wanted to depend on, on a regular basis.

At any rate, we had managed this particular group in just such a fashion, for decades, since before even my time.

When my squad was reassigned the case, our intelligence indicated that new leadership had formed within the group. Some of the younger, more radical members had risen up the ranks to their high council. We were also told that they'd advanced with some unusual forms of mind control that warranted investigation.

Two of my assigned agents were close colleagues, people I had worked with for many years. I knew and respected their skills. I'll call them Agents X and Y. The third agent that was placed on my team was a new recruit. She was young and headstrong, ambitious and smart. Agent Z gave me worries right from the outset, a young woman of numerous talents but, unfortunately, I thought a little green for such a mission.

This organization followed some typical doctrines found among the extreme doomsday cults. They had romanticized our horrific past, describing the Century of Despair and the Great Annihilation as glorious. They referred to this terrible time in history as the first Judgment Day, decrying the People's United Republic of Earth and its practices. They insisted the PURE government suppressed mankind from following our destined and divine end. According to their beliefs, the end of Mankind through these violent means was the only way that we could ultimately ascend to heavenly heights and move on to the next great phase of our spirituality—or some nonsense like that.

For the mission, Agent Z and I were chosen to infiltrate the cult. We already had one agent on the inside but he needed help. They were expanding rapidly and dividing into sub-groups with congregations at different times, in between their larger gatherings.

Maintaining our anonymity was easy after the preliminary screening. Everyone wore camouflaging garments and hoods to the meetings and they were always after dark, in the hidden ruins and caverns at the edge of the city, in the ancient commercial center. Even by the time we had been initiated into the third level, we hadn't seen anything more than a glimpse of anyone's face. It took a long time and we continued to work on other cases while we infiltrated the cult. The early levels were repetitive, demanding regular attendance and behavior; essentially, they were testing grounds to ensure they had loyal followers who had all the basic doctrines firmly implanted. Many drifted away before moving up. Perhaps they were just curious, wanting to flirt with the danger of flaunting the rules but not really into pledging themselves to such a radical philosophy. Whatever it was, we were relieved to see the numbers diminish as we ascended the brotherhood.

When it was time to split into alternate paths, I was taken deeper into the Sacred Trance studies while Agent Z was to study the Holy Journals, a journey that could ultimately lead to the ministry of the cult. It was important that one of us was chosen for this opportunity.

While this was happening in my professional life, Evan and I were experiencing the heartache of Roland and his non-conformist ways which I've detailed in my daily journals. Roland had split with his wife after fourteen childless years of marriage and was dissatisfied with his *vocation as a research analyst at the Media Center. I offered to assist him in his application to change vocations but he resented my help, insisting it wasn't needed. He'd had minor infractions: refusing to attend the Spiritual Center, missing his work-day more than the allotted times, excessive use of spirits in a public place, and he was served with a number of demerits which meant that the bachelor home he received was small and limited in amenities. Roland's frustration was escalating and we felt like failures as parents as we watched him drift further away from us.*

Evan and I disagreed on how best to help Roland. He thought we should turn our backs on him and that he would eventually find his way on his own. I couldn't bear it. It seemed too late for this tactic with a child who was approaching forty. These were difficult times in our marriage. My solution to my heartache was to dive deeper into my work, immersing myself in the mind altering meditations that I was being taught. At the same time, Agent Z was learning more about the inner workings of the cult, attending some of the secret rituals of the higher order. So, as a team, we felt that we were making good progress.

We continued on this path for many months before the crisis hit. When it ultimately unraveled, I was completely unprepared for the personal aftermath that I had to face.

Willow was startled out of her absorption in Great Bet's words by her father pounding on the door as he called out: "Hey, are you awake in there? You've got fifteen minutes to get ready if you still want to share a ride."

Leaping out of bed, she reluctantly closed the journal and went about her morning preparations, promising herself she would continue reading this section when she returned home later that night.

Chapter 21

"Change your thoughts and you change your world."

Norman Vincent Peale

Jill gaped at him, her forkful of food suspended in midair. "This is unbelievable. You've got to be kidding me?"

"I wouldn't do that to you, mom." Aaron chewed his food as he talked; glancing at his unit to make sure he wouldn't be late getting back to work at the Health Center. "There's a lot more to her than we thought." Setting his cutlery down and reaching for his drink, he leaned back in the booth seat and grinned at her. "I guess Elzabeth had this one final surprise for us."

"Surprise? No, I can't believe that Elzabeth would keep something like that from me. It would serve no purpose." Shaking her head, Jill asked, "Are you sure you weren't tricked?" She set her fork on the plate and concentrated on their conversation, oblivious to the restaurant lunch crowd, buzzing around them. "For all we know, maybe she was there during our interrogation. Maybe she's an agent?"

"Mom, seriously, now you're kidding me!" His teasing grin was not returned. Her mood reached out to him—stone cold and concerned. He drew his head back, the grin disappearing. "You're serious?"

"Why not? It's no crazier than the story you're telling me." She leaned forward, whispering. "They're everywhere, you know."

"Okay, that may be so, but I can assure you—not in this case. I experienced her power firsthand." He looked away, unsure of how much he wanted to share with his mother. They had always been close but he was still trying to figure out what had happened himself. Gazing across the room, unseeing, he continued, murmuring, "she was really amazing." For a moment, he remembered the encounter under the willow tree. A deep throbbing began in his throat, spreading down his body. Not quick enough, he squelched the longing that he felt.

Something in his tone caught her attention. She jerked her head back, glaring at her son, her acute senses on high alert. He faced her intense stare. With the heat rising up his neck, he met her eyes without flinching.

Finally, she raised an eyebrow and asked: "So, what exactly happened between you two on this outing? I'm getting the impression that you haven't told me everything."

Fortunately, at that moment, the auto-waiter came to collect their lunch dishes and refill their waters. They slid their plates onto the robot's cart and then entered their requests for a hot drink.

"Mom, maybe you're right. I didn't tell you absolutely everything about our date. For the moment, I'd rather not. I'm sorry but some things are private between Willow and I."

"Really? Well, I think I can surmise what that means." Choosing her words carefully, Jill continued, "Aaron, you've been on your own for a long time now. I've never presumed to tell you who you should or should not bed before—but this one, well, my goodness, you could be playing with fire here. She's so young. On top of that, she's Elzbeth's Protector and to top it off, there's what you've just told me." She shook her head. "And, what about Jericho?"

"Mother, please! As you say, I am an adult now." He placed his hands on the table, his tone sharp, all traces of humour gone from his eyes. "Right now, I'm concerned about the pledge we made. With what I've just told you, don't you think this changes everything?"

Her teacup clattered in its saucer, drawing the attention of neighbouring diners. Smiling at them and mouthing an apology, she hid her reaction well but Aaron could read her. Her words, when they came, were spoken slowly and clearly so there could be no misunderstanding,

"The only thing that's changed is that we need to be more on our guard than ever. What you've just told me about Willow is frightening and goes against the precepts that we first set forward in our mission. Elizabeth was one of the founding members. We, who first established these guidelines, did so for the protection of Vision Speak, to ensure the integrity of our mission, and so that we would not be tarnished by our early beginnings."

"But, mother, you couldn't possibly have predicted or planned for something like this."

"No, son!" Her words were louder than she'd intended. Quieter but no less firmly, she continued, "The traditions set forth in our Guiding Principles are sound. We cannot possibly let anyone into that inner circle unless they have passed the tests. No one can leap through the levels without the required time and practice." Watching the determined set of her chin, Aaron recognized the expression setting in. He had his work cut out for him if he was going to sway her.

In this case, however, he wasn't going to back down. She hadn't experienced Willow's ability—he had. "But, if in fact she has already surpassed everyone that is at the upper level—what then? She may actually be able to lead us to new levels, new dimensions. Perhaps we will have to revisit everything—our mission, our Guiding Principles, everything."

"Aaron, stop. Have you completely lost your focus? Are you ready to abandon everything we believe in, everything we have worked so hard for? You made a pledge. And don't forget that until one has reached the final stage, the full history of our path must not be divulged." Jill's agitation spilled into her speech. Although she kept her tone down, she was practically hissing by the end.

"Of course I'm not abandoning anything, mom, but are you forgetting that she is the Protector? If Elzabeth recorded anything in her journals, they will be there for Willow to read. You can't stop her. And, even if you could, we must assume that Elzabeth knew what she was doing and respect that. I think the time for secrets may be over where she is concerned. One way or another, Willow will gain access to everything we know. I can almost guarantee it."

"No, I can't believe that. I won't." Jill was firm in her beliefs. "There is an explanation for this and I will find it. In the meantime, you would be wise to stay away from that girl." She placed her hands on top of his on the table, her eyes imploring him.

Aaron was silent as he gathered his thoughts. He decided to try another tactic. "There's more, mom." He spoke quietly.

"More? What now?"

"Willow showed me one of the sealed entries from the journal. Elzabeth experienced something—a violation, I think. Someone very powerful."

"A violation? Who was it?"

"That's the thing—she didn't know."

"Elzabeth didn't know?" Jill was stunned.

"No, and it scared her."

"She said that?"

"Yes."

Jill drummed her fingers on the table but was otherwise silent. She looked out the window, her expression dark and unreadable. Finally she turned back to her son. "Oo-kay, that is unexpected. So, what are you suggesting, Aaaron? I assume you think this means we need her?"

"Well, mom, this is what I think. Things are changing. When the Guiding Principles were first developed and formed, they were based on our understanding at the time. Right now, there are at least two anomalies out there, two people who have progressed, and will likely continue to, beyond our current comprehension. Our guidelines for how and when they will reach our upper levels are irrelevant because I suspect that they have already moved beyond."

"You're convinced of this? You're sure it wasn't an elaborate trick?"

"I'm sure. And, again, you must remember that where Willow is concerned, she has access to everything that Elzabeth left behind in terms of her recorded memories and thoughts."

Jill grimaced. "I don't know what Elzabeth was thinking. She was a wily old woman so I have to believe that her purpose will become clear. She must have known the danger she was putting us all in by placing her journals into inexperienced hands."

"Aside from that, remember, there's someone or maybe some others out there, that Elzabeth experienced. She mentioned the cult. If they're back then our only hope to try and understand what they are up to, may be with Willow's help." He grasped her hands. Holding them tight, he beseeched her. "Mother, I strongly suggest you test her, meet with her, and then decide. Don't just discount this because it breaks with our traditions, our Guiding Principles that were established when Vision Speak was in its infancy. The time may be upon us when we must abolish them."

Chapter 22

*"This we know...the earth does not belong to man, man belongs to the earth.
All things are connected like the blood which connects one family.
Whatever befalls the earth, befalls the children of the earth.
Man did not weave the web of life—he is merely a strand in it.
Whatever he does to the web, he does to himself."*

Chief Seattle, 1854

Kalesh sat from his position of height on the upper terrace. The murmuring of the priests of the brotherhood in the room below was a faraway sound in his ears. He gazed across the water at the deep gorge of the hypocenter and the ancient ruins surrounding it, in the distance. This city, CanTor, had been a thriving, multicultural metropolis—no one ever expected it to be the site of warfare. In the days of separate countries and governments, it belonged to a nation who had not threatened others on the world stage, one that had tried many times to avoid conflicts, had been instrumental in developing peacekeeping forces. It was really the close allegiances of the old country with the major superpowers of the west that had led to the near devastation in two of its cities and the complete destruction of its island city to the far west. In the years following, earthquakes and flooding continued to wreak heavy damage, with some oceanic coastal towns and cities disappearing worldwide by the end of the aftermath.

At the edge of the great lake, there had once stood an enormous tower. Now, still among the ruins, Kalesh remembered the sight of the remnants of that tower. Approximately 50 feet of its upper portion was still intact and tucked securely into the ground, standing erect like a giant phalanx symbol.

He could hear their voices. The debate had subsided for the moment as they recited verses from the Holy Journals. His father's voice, deep and booming above the rest, was the loudest. If Kalesh had not known the words by heart, he may not have understood what they were saying, but he did know them, had repeated them with his father since his infancy. He whispered the words, following quietly along with them. "These trials that we undergo, we must suffer them. We must revel in that suffering. Those that went before us were ready, were gloriously taken in the first Apocalyptic Act." Samuel had recorded these words so long ago. "For those of us that are left, now we must prepare ourselves and our ancestors for the next apocalypse, a holocaust of unprecedented proportions. We must lead them towards it with great anticipation. To expire in great numbers, together, this is the way to an unimaginable heaven, our ultimate incarnation."

Kalesh meditated on this past now, picturing that world in his mind's eye, as if it were yesterday. He could see the enormous refugee camps that had formed on the fringe of the desolated areas. By today's standards, it had been chaotic: people living like gypsies in abandoned and damaged homes, tents set up around the properties, bonfires in the streets, non-functioning cars at odd locations forming storage areas for clothing and kitchen items. Everywhere, there were the sick and injured, at first with terrible burns, later, for generations, with deformities and deadly diseases, plagues that killed thousands, but still many stayed, untreated. Some retreated to the country but for the vast majority, there was nowhere to go—this was their home.

Out of this devastation and chaos, Samuel had been born. His parents had recorded the first generation of the Holy Journals, Samuel had continued in their footsteps, his words and memory overshadowing theirs. While the surviving populations of the earth began to rebuild, creating the People's United Republic of Earth, their brotherhood had also been born and the seeds of their mission planted.

Now, it was up to Kalesh to take them forward, to fulfill the destiny that had been predicted so long ago, in those dark and gloomy days of post-nuclear warfare.

He saw what had come before like a distant memory viewed through another's eyes. He had no doubt that what he could see was authentic. In his most peaceful, meditative state, he could see this past at the same time as he connected with the present, understood the forces that he would need to manipulate to bring his people forward to their ultimate goal.

But, again today, as the misty images of possible future paths appeared before him, he shivered with a sense of the consequences their actions would cause.

Equally disturbing, in every direction he looked, down every path, he saw her. First he saw the eyes, glowing green like dew-covered leaves in the early morning sun. Her hair flowing, long and golden, her face pale and soft—there was something innately good, or humane, about her. On one path, he saw a glorious future with her, where warmth exuded from the green depths. There was love there and he reveled in it. He must not go there. He knew this. In the other direction, down the path he knew he was destined to follow, he saw her eyes, dark as the shadowed forest, turn to shock and disbelief, then to hatred.

He broke out of his trance, deeply distraught.

For a moment, just a moment, he'd lived in that other place, the one where she had loved him, where she had been one with him. A silly dreamlike place—this he knew. It was pure fantasy, a teenage fantasy—like the ancient story of Romeo and Juliet—one that would surely spell disaster for his brotherhood. With that path, the future was hazy. All he could discern was the love that he might share with this girl.

With the course that the leader, his father, had chosen, the future was clear. Once they set in motion a series of incidents, there remained only constant care and manipulation, to lead them to the next Judgment Day.

Earlier he had spoken privately with his father and one of his outside aides, an odd man, always huddled in his robes, his face glowing white from under the hood. They had been questioning Kalesh about his visions so he told them about the girl.

"You keep seeing a girl? What do you mean? Is she a woman of the order?" His father had demanded answers.

"N-no, I don't think so. I've never seen her before—at least, not in person. But, if I ever did, I would know her immediately." He paused as he saw her again, in his mind's eye. "She is lovely…gentle and kind. She represents something, I think, a new beginning perhaps…"

"New beginning? The beginning of the end, I hope!" The wrinkles formed stern angles in his father's brow.

"Uh, well, I'm not sure but it seems more like a new era, a new direction, like a rebirth. It's just a sense I have, I can't say why, really…"

"Are you saying that she, as a vision, represents this? Or is she, in fact, a real being of great power who will cause this?" Both men were standing in front of him now, twin sketches of anxiety etched into their frowns as they waited for his response.

"I don't know. Perhaps I have exaggerated the vision. It's more that she is a catalyst, I think, but I'm not at all certain." Kalesh rose from his seat, uncomfortable with the two men towering over him. He wandered to the window as he spoke, his voice thoughtful. "I sense her just at the edge of my reach. She seems real but I don't know who she is, or where she is. I cannot fully see her, nor understand her. I need to get closer."

"We will find her. If we bring her to you, will you be able to tell us more? Determine if she is a threat to our plans?"

Kalesh felt a somersault in his stomach, a frightful, full-out somersault. He wanted to see her but he dreaded anyone finding her. "Perhaps but I don't know who she is. She may be on the other side of the world for all I know."

His father walked over to him, and turned him forcibly around until they were eye to eye. "Show her to me. I want to see what you see."

Kalesh paused but only for a moment. Obedient as always, he closed his eyes and transmitted his vision, letting them both see the beauty of the young girl that haunted him.

When he was done, he opened his eyes and gazed at his father. What he saw there was surprising. "Do you recognize her, father?"

He nodded, his jaw tightened smugly, "Yes, I do, my son. I know exactly who she is..." He glanced over at his partner and they held eye contact, nodding in unison.

"But who is she? You must tell me. Show me what you know." Kalesh begged his father, grabbing hold of his sleeve.

"All in good time, my son, all in good time." He released his sleeve and turned to the door without another word, his companion following closely behind.

Kalesh watched them leave. He knew she was out there, he could sense her. Everyday, he sensed her more. Everyday, she was getting stronger. His father said he knew her but how could he? Who was she? For a moment, he was tempted to forcibly get the information he sought—but he couldn't. His father had strictly forbidden him from ever doing that.

Yet, he wondered about her. He realized that the time was coming rapidly when they would bring her to him. Part of him wanted this very much yet he also dreaded their impending encounter. It meant she would have to decide. She would either join with them completely—or they would destroy her. There was no other way.

He shivered despite the caress of the warm rays through the window.

Chapter 23

"...one of the main reasons we have incarnated is to grow in consciousness and one of the most important things we can do in life is to share those things that have helped us evolve in consciousness."

Meditation Society of America

Willow wasn't following Simon's instructions.

They were in one of the smaller rooms, everyone reclining on the floor on their mats. There were only twelve of them in the novice level so, with Careena, Michael, and Sophie there, Willow and her family made up almost half the room. Glancing around surreptitiously, she saw that they were all concentrating. She skimmed along their plains of consciousness, grinning inwardly as she touched on Sophie. She was so earnest and intent, her thoughts the loudest in the group. Even in calm, introspective, meditation, it was hard to ignore her.

The elementary exercises were trivial—absurd for Willow—but she had decided not to interfere with the group process. Instead, she retreated, leaving them to carry on.

At the beginning of the session, they'd all sat quietly in a lotus position while their instructor for this session, Simon LaChance, had discoursed on concepts and theory. He strove to make them understand what they were attempting to accomplish and the various levels they should aspire to reach. "To expand your consciousness," he had said, "you must first learn to quiet the mind."

Willow stifled a giggle. When Great Bet had said the same thing, she remembered laughing out loud. "But, it's not making any noise, is it?" At her great-grandmother's grimace, she had learned to refrain from silly remarks and focus. As she'd made strides quickly after that, she could still picture the satisfaction and pride that had emanated from her mentor, although, later, as her progress continued, there had been a time when pride had been replaced by bewilderment and something else—was it fear?

"Before you can make steps to reach out into the cosmic consciousness, to feel as one with the universal life force that pulses through all of our beings, you must have control over your mind. You must be able to soothe your random thoughts, your triggered responses and emotions, ignore them, and move beyond to the greater world that exists all around us. It is everywhere and yet most people are completely oblivious to it." Simon paused for breath, as he walked around the room, stealthy as a tiger, gentle as a lamb, his soft soled feet not making a sound as he moved. He placed his hand on everyone's shoulder as he walked by, seeking to transmit loving, connected signals to the group. "It will take time before you make those first steps—so be patient. Patience is critical, of course. Any anxiety or impatience will only hinder your progress. These are further examples of how you must gain control over the machine that we call your mind."

Back at the front of the room, he turned to face everyone, the purple streaks in his hair stark in the light, his voice elevated slightly. "Many of you have taken meditation sessions before, I know. These exercises we do in the first level will be similar to previous experiences if you have meditated before, and you may progress more rapidly. It's impossible to say for sure. Once you've reached a state where you have demonstrated that you are ready to move on, we will transfer you to the next level."

The lecture over, the group was now all lying down, in the early stages of reaching a relaxed, meditative state.

Simon spoke in a calm, clear voice, the background music soft and barely audible, "1…breathe…2…the essence of the universe is flowing into your body...4, now hold, 2, the world is still, 3, keep holding...4...and release, 1, gently, very carefully, 3, 4, 5..."

Closing her eyes, and leaving her arms limp along her side, Willow breathed rhythmically, pretending to follow along as she let herself drift.

Immediately, her thoughts focused on Aaron. She couldn't help it. Ever since that first night in the Sanctuary—under the moon and the stars, lying beneath her favourite tree, their limbs entangled, their passion ignited—she couldn't get him out of her mind. Since that first experience, she'd seen him again—three more unbelievable nights—and, each time, they'd ended up back at his place, irresistibly drawn to each other physically.

She relived their last night together, hazy images of messy curls matted with sweat, tendrils hanging over glowing blue eyes, smooth, muscular arms, swollen lips descending upon her. The way he touched her, gentle movements, soft caresses, her skin tingling, heat rising. Then, finally, as their fervor increased and they couldn't bear it any longer, tenderness had come to an abrupt end, replaced by violent, intense coupling.

As the images and emotions replayed in her mind, her body reacted. She felt the heavy beating of her heart, the aching in her loins, moisture seeping, her abdominal muscles clenching. For a moment, she almost let escape a loud moan, her memory of the experience too real, her desire overwhelming.

Like a cold shower, she opened her eyes, forcing her obsession away. *What is wrong with me?* She asked herself. *These fantasies are consuming me.*

She halted her thoughts at the sudden sensation of an intrusion. Jerking her head around, she met deep, black eyes that were trained intensely upon her. It was the young man that Sophie liked, lying beside her. Her momentary shock was interrupted by Simon who was walking towards them, after a loud clearing of his throat. Standing over them, he motioned for them both to close their eyes and continue with the breathing.

Returning back to her relaxed state within moments, she had a fleeting instant of realization that her physical obsession with Aaron was distracting her from her progress. She made a concerted effort to 'quiet her mind' and step beyond, into that other realm that brought her such peace.

It was just as they had completed their session and were getting up, mats in hand, that the object of her obsession walked into the room. Sucking in her breath, her earlier desire came flooding back. She gazed at him, hoping he had come to take her away, take her home. She was ready for him already.

They made eye contact and she saw that he read her, felt the need she pulsated across the room. For a brief moment she sensed his instinctive reaction but then he blinked and it was gone. He masked his face, stifled his response. Glancing behind him, she understood why. His mother was with him.

She watched as Aaron and Jill had a brief, quiet chat with Simon and then stood by the doorway waiting—for her apparently.

Chapter 24

*"With or without religion, good people can behave well and bad people can do evil...
But for good people to do evil—that takes Religion."*

Steven Weinberg

Sophie stood with her hands on her hips as she watched Willow exit the room with Aaron and Jill, without even a backwards glance.

"Hmmph!" she hissed to herself, "I guess we're not going out to the Chocolatta tonight, after all!" Her cheeks burned red, her array of emotions on display for all to see. Her mother, Careena, noticed something was amiss and sauntered over, Michael following closely behind.

"What's the matter, hon?" She quizzed, "Everyone else in the room appears relaxed and calm after that session but you look like you're going to explode."

"Huh? Oh, hi mom." She waved her hand in dismissal. "It's nothing really, just that Willow and I had plans to go out afterwards but it seems she's forgotten. Or maybe she has a better offer." She pointed towards the door. They all turned to see Willow disappear down the hallway.

"She does seem distracted lately, doesn't she?" Careena remarked.

"Distracted?" Sophie exclaimed. "I'd say she's in heat. Whenever that guy's around, sheez!" She raised her eyes to the roof.

Michael jumped to Willow's defense. "Oh, come on, Soph. You probably mentioned it in passing days ago and she just forgot. Between what's happened with Great Bet and her busy schedule at school, I guess you're just not at the top of her priority list." He grinned, teasing. "Hard to believe that anyone could possibly forget about you, isn't it, poor thing?"

Careena smiled at the interchange. "Actually, I'd hoped to catch her as well. Your Grandma Sybil is planning a Family Retreat and I want to see about you two sharing a cottage with Claire and Triska. We're hoping that Willow will prepare an intimate family sharing of Great Bet's Journal."

"That's the first I've heard of this," Michael responded. "I'd have expected my mother to say something."

Sophie interjected before Careena could respond. "When does Grandma want to do this?"

"Weekend after next. She just decided today. Anyway, I'm sure Joley will talk to her and no doubt your mother will be waiting for you when you get home, Michael." She put her hand on Sophie's elbow, raising an eyebrow in inquiry. "Well, I don't know if you want to hang out with your mother, but I'd go to the Chocolatta with you, if you want? Michael, you could come too. My treat."

Sophie grinned, an acceptance on the edge of her tongue but then she spied the young man packing up his bag in the corner. "Thanks, mom but you know, there's someone else over there that I've been planning to hang out with so I think I will take you up on that another time, okay?"

After her mother and Michael had left, Sophie adjusted her hair, the long black and white bands twisted into a knot at the nape of her neck. Today, she'd dressed simply, at least for her tastes. The skintight red and white jumpsuit showed off her curves, was comfortable for lounging or exercising but would also serve just fine for an impromptu date. Her face was still flushed and her confidence, as usual, was steady. She kept her eyes on her prey as she picked up her purse and wandered toward him. He was just starting for the door.

"Hey, how's it going?" She nudged him to ensure she got his attention.

He nearly dropped his bag when he jerked backwards. Turning around abruptly, his eyes opened wide as he responded, "uh, hey, uh, I'm fine." He backed up towards the wall, eyes scanning defensively side to side.

Sophie laughed. "Whoa, sorry! I guess I startled you."

He relaxed a touch and returned her smile, brilliant teeth gleaming white, surrounded by milk chocolate skin. "Yes, I guess I was in another world…still. Sorry." He gazed downwards, apparently shy, surreptitiously raising his eyes to take in her blinding beauty as he talked.

Sophie had approached him several times in recent weeks. He was always like this, timid, uncertain of himself. She thought he was adorable but enough was enough. Tonight she was determined to break through. "You know I just had some plans fall through and I was wondering if, uh…" Uncharacteristically, she faltered on the verge of her request.

He lifted his head and stared at her in surprise. "You were wondering?"

"Uh, yes, I was wondering if you have any plans right now?"

"No, not really. I was just going to go home."

"Okay, that means you can come out with me, then, right?" As she spoke, she saw his eyes glance at her figure, settling on her breasts. When he realized what he was doing, he averted his eyes, staring down at the floor. Smugly, she watched his body language, thinking *this is going to be easier than I expected. He is a man, after all.*

His smooth mocha skin deepened in colour, a blush creeping up from his neck to his eyes. "Go out with you? Uh, sure, I guess I could." At a loss for words, he stumbled onwards. "Where do you want to go?"

Giggling, she looped her arm inside his elbow and steered him towards the door. "Well, you just let me worry about that…now, what was your name again?"

He beamed at her. "My name is Charlie, Sophie. And I, at least, remember your name."

"Cool," she murmured, glancing sideways as they walked, treating him to her favourite provocative expression, the one she practiced in the mirror before she went to bed at night. "Let's get out of here, Charlie, and have some fun."

Chapter 25

"Concentrate on doing nothing and everything will turn out well."

The Tao Te Ching

Willow ended the trance abruptly and sat still in her seat, eyes riveted on the others as they slowly came back. The four of them were seated on chairs facing inwards on the corners of an imaginary square. They were crowded in close just in front of the desk in the center of the room, the walls of the small office surrounding them.

She watched Jill and Simon's expressions change from a dreamy, drowsy stupor to sharp-eyed bewilderment. Aaron, for his part, controlled his satisfied smile. He seemed on the verge of an "I told you so" but he held his tongue, waiting along with Willow for the others to react.

Speechless, Jill rose and moved towards the window—the only window in the room. They were on the fifth floor of the Center so the view was limited. She could see the Festival Square immediately below and to the right but otherwise her vision was cut short by the tall buildings across the square. They'd booked the room based on economy, not luxury. The view and room size were irrelevant to the purpose of their meeting.

Staring out the window, Jill breathed in and out deeply, regaining her composure before she spoke. Smoothing her hair back, she turned to face the three who were still sitting in their chairs, waiting. Finally, she broke the silence. "Well, I guess I misjudged you, my dear." She leveled her gaze at Willow, who thankfully, beamed back at her with her pleasant, non-confrontational demeanor. Her pale, freckled face smiled meekly at Jill with respect—yes, actual respect—still evident in her eyes. Hard to believe, looking at this young girl, that she had been so powerful, so far advanced beyond anything Jill had ever experienced. The innocence of a young tiger, she thought, who didn't fully comprehend her power, didn't yet know how to use it.

Simon expelled a loud whooshing sound from the back of his mouth. "In the name of Marisha, what on earth has happened? How could you have been advancing to this degree in my session and I never noticed?"

Willow giggled. "I'm sorry, I thought it would be rude to interfere with what you were doing so I backed off in your session. It was really Great Bet—I mean Elzabeth—that trained me in the beginning…" As she spoke, she glanced over at Aaron, basking in his pride. She saw it in his eyes, felt it humming along to her. Even as they had all joined together and she'd led them on the journey, she had sensed him more open to her than ever before.

Aaron winked at her, the intimacy they shared on display for an instant, for only her to see. Warm shivers slid down her belly. Would they be alone tonight? She felt her face burning and prayed no one could read her thoughts.

Simon was apparently oblivious to their undercurrents as he continued. "Now, as I sit here and look back, I wonder if I was dreaming. Did I imagine everything? But, of course, we were all there together, weren't we?" His puzzled expression surrounded by spikes of purple hair would probably have appeared comical at any other time.

"Yes, we were all there." Aaron nodded slowly, his nose just a little large and slightly crooked, making his profile unique. "We all experienced the same dream, the one that Willow led us along."

She smiled back at him. "What was that all about in the beginning? You know, those simple images and concepts that you instructed me to visualize?"

Aaron looked towards his petite mother, standing by the window. Jill's silver hair gleamed as the moonlight from the window caught it. She lifted her fine, dark eyebrows a touch, grimacing, as she answered. "That was a series of tests—to make sure that you would be ready to pass the early levels." She paused, adding an ironic twist to her voice. "Don't worry, you passed."

"It was very, uh, personal—almost intrusive, though, at one point." Simon added. "I mean, once we got past the preliminaries. I sensed that you were able to reach inside of me, read me, understand me even, beyond what I was opening up to you." He folded his arms together, leaning back slightly. "It was a little frightening, actually."

"Oh! I'm sorry. I thought you wanted me to demonstrate that I can connect with you all? Was that not the way you would do it?"

Aaron laughed and gave her a reassuring wink. "Willow, it's not at all the way we do it but perhaps it's just because we can't." At her wide-eyed gaze, he continued, trying to explain. "Generally, when we connect, it takes great meditation and concentration where each individual is focused on projecting themselves—or at least the thoughts and images that they want to share. First we must reach a state of unconscious thought where we can exist on the metaphysical plane—that inexplicable place outside of time and space that facilitates this type of communication, a connection of our spiritual selves. We are the most advanced here who have been able to accomplish this—or at least we thought we were." He shook his head. "We don't simply waltz into each other's inner beings and help ourselves as you seem able to do. We can sense other people's emotions at times but nothing like what you have demonstrated."

Willow stared at him, rethinking her experience now that she understood better what had been happening. Jill interrupted her reverie. "My dear, surely Elzabeth must have explained this to you? What was her reaction when you started jumping in and out of her head like a puppet master?"

The young girl at the center of their collective attention, appeared thoughtful, her speech slow as if she were deciding on each word as she spoke. "You know, I guess I wasn't quite doing that when she was first

training me. She told me that she was amazed at my progress and I have since read a passage of her journal where she confesses to being jealous of my ability at such a young age." They all grinned at that—no doubt, she had been. "But, it wasn't until after the closure ceremony, when I first joined the group that I started to expand even further. Everyday, I discover something new, understand a little more...but, truthfully, there is so much more that I am starting to encounter that I cannot fathom at all." She stammered a little. "I don't know how to explain. I-It's not just the motifs and visions—the rush of emotions from others, like yourselves, that I connect with. How do I explain? I, uh, I'm starting to see people, events, things that I don't think are just symbolic. I think they are real or maybe in the future? I'm not really sure."

"Willow, remember when you showed me in Elzabeth's journal that she had encountered someone else? That she had been frightened?" Aaron asked. When she simply nodded, he continued. "Have you encountered anyone like this? Do you know what—or who—she might have been referring to?"

"Uh, yes, I have, for sure, but..." She licked her lips, eyes roaming to stare into an inner distance. "I'm not sure where to begin or even how to describe everything in words. I've felt other groups, like ours, but I'm not sure where they are. Perhaps Elizabeth had inadvertently tapped into them." Shaking her head, she returned her gaze back to Aaron. "But, I have also felt the presence of some individuals, at your level at least but one in particular who is very strong, beyond anyone I've ever encountered. In fact, I've seen him."

"You've seen him? What do you mean, at the Center?"

"N-no, I've seen him in my head. A lot, actually."

"Do you know who he is—or where?"

"I don't—but, there's someone else, too, and I wonder if this is the person Great Bet sensed. He is more, um, frightening, I guess you could say...although not as powerful as the younger one."

Aaron stood up and strode over to the window, standing in front of Jill. "So, what do you think?"

She cleared her throat, holding her head high as she spoke. "You were correct to have brought this to our attention. We must explore this further and changes could result, however," she paused for a moment before she continued, choosing her words carefully, "breaking our Guiding Principles cannot be done without careful consideration for the consequences. They are the foundation for what we teach, how we grow spiritually within this group. And that's not all. They actually form the basis for our contract with the Spiritual Center. Elizabeth worked diligently to negotiate them many years ago and they are a condition of our existence here."

"I understand that, mother, but what's happening with Willow could have a major impact on us, on everything. It's not just about our procedures. She may be on the cusp of a metamorphosis of consciousness. We must learn from her. We must discover what more is possible."

Simon interrupted. "Section 12 of the Guiding Principles instructs us to report any anomalies, such as this." He waved his arm in Willow's direction. "What do you suggest we do about that?"

Aaron's colour deepened as he moved to stand threateningly in front of Simon. "Are you crazy? You want to report her?"

Jill stepped between them. "No! Of course not. Simon is simply raising a good point. We need to move forward cautiously." Glancing down at the young girl who was watching their interaction with a pale face and wide eyes, she spoke gently but with authority. "Willow, my dear, I thank-you for sharing your gift with us—and, make no mistake about it, you are gifted." She reached out her arm to lead Willow to the door. "The three of us need to discuss this further, if you don't mind, so please excuse us. We will come back together with a plan at the next session, okay?"

"Uh, sure, okay." Willow swallowed her disappointment. It seemed she would have to leave without Aaron.

She had her hand on the door when Jill called out. "One more thing, Willow. It's in your, and our, best interests if we all keep this quiet for now, okay? No need for you to flaunt these special abilities of yours just yet." Nodding her head in agreement, Willow rushed out of the room.

Chapter 26

"All art intuitively apprehends coming changes in the collective unconsciousness."

Carl Jung

Joley and Arild stood waiting in the entranceway as the sliding door swished closed behind Willow. Startled, their daughter stepped back, almost colliding into the door. "Oh, uh, hi," she stuttered. "What are you doing, er, are you waiting for me?"

"Yes, dear. When we heard the air car service was bringing you home, we wanted to make sure we caught you before you retired to your room. You've been so busy lately that we've hardly talked at all. Can you come and chat with us for a few moments? Your father is just making some tea." Joley smiled sweetly as she reached for her daughter's bag and stowed it away. Arild put his arm on her back and led her into their living space.

"Sure…" Swallowing back her frustration, Willow's shoulders slumped as she meekly took the seat that her father indicated, instead of escaping to the solitude she had been so eager to reach. The room was still vivid, even with the darkness of night because of Willow's artwork surrounding them. The special lights that always displayed them to their best advantage were on. Her parents had spared no expense on that—and the furniture was a good setting for the vivacity of the room, the sofa was soft cream, almost white, with clear, plexi-glass tables. She took a deep breath, and let the expressions of her art restore her peace of mind.

Her parents fussed over her, making sure she had a cushion to lean back on, setting up her tea and offering her a treat from a tray they had set up. She relaxed, enjoying the pampering regardless of the motives.

Joley took a sip of her tea, her fingers elegantly curved around the cup. The long, scarlet nails were startling against the white porcelain. "So, how was the session tonight, hon?"

"It was good, uh, interesting." A lame answer, she knew, but what could she say?

"Interesting? Hmm...well that tells us a lot." Joley laughed good-naturedly. "What is it about teenagers and their verbose explanations?" She asked no one in particular.

Willow grunted and took a bite of her cookie. Her father smiled at her, a secret smile that told her he understood. The tea warmed her hands.

Joley continued. "Did you see your Aunt Careena this evening?"

"Yep, she was there. So were Soph and Mike."

"So, you know about the plans for the Retreat?"

"Huh? What retreat?" Willow's eyes darted away from the plate of snacks over to her mother, a crease forming in her brow.

"I thought you said you talked to her?"

"I said I saw her. I, uh, had to run out with some people afterwards and didn't actually talk to Aunt Careena. Oops!" Willow suddenly remembered she'd told Sophie she would get together with her after the session. Her mother's sculpted eyebrow lifted inquiringly. Willow waved her hand. "It's nothing. I just forgot to tell Sophie something, that's all. So, what's this about a retreat?"

"Well, it's apparently something that Great Bet set up for us, before she moved on."

"What?"

"Yes, your Grandma Sybil received information about this just last week. You know, the Island Retreat and Spa that's located on the City Islands? It's so exclusive that we've never saved enough luxury credits to go there ourselves."

"Well, that's because you spend them as soon as we get them, my dear." Arild responded, winking at his daughter. His mirth was contagious. Grinning, she glanced at his fair hair and unlined face, reminded that her father was still a young man.

Willow snorted. "That's right, mother." Then she sobered, returning to the mystery of this planned family retreat. "So, you're going with your sisters?"

"Well, yes, but we're all going. My sisters and mother, really the whole Tyler line—husbands and kids included. It should be a very special time for us. I've blocked off everyone's calendar for this special event—so you shouldn't have any conflicts. It's the weekend after next." Joley rattled off their plans succinctly, leaving no room for objections.

"But." Willow's mind searched for a way out. The last thing she wanted to do was go away on a family retreat. She had too much going on. There was Aaron—it meant she wouldn't be able to see him for a whole weekend. Plus her inner world of Vision Speak and the journey of Great Bet's journals—she needed time alone to sort through it all. On top of that, there was the constant struggle to keep everything to herself. She knew her family would make it harder.

"But, what?"

"Well, it's just not a good time for me. Can't we wait until school is over?"

"You're only going to miss one half day of school and I have already checked the schedule. It's not going to cause you any trouble. We're booked. It's happening, Willow, and your presence is required."

"Sounds like you've got it all figured out then." Willow squirmed in her seat, adjusting the cushion. "Tell me again how this came about? I can't imagine that Great Bet could have really set this up. There's no mention of it in her journals or her instructions. This makes no sense to me."

Her mother's eyes were ice, her face firm and unflinching. "It may make no sense to you but we are going as a family. The director of the retreat contacted my mother personally, indicating that Elzbeth had already covered the expense and left instructions. This is very important to your Grandma Sybil. Willow, you have no idea how hard this has all been on her. Surely, you must realize that she expected to be named the

Protector? How do you think she felt when she was shut out and you were named instead?"

"Uh, I guess I didn't think about it too much." A lump of guilt formed at the base of her throat. "I'm sorry, mom, but what do you expect me to do? It was Great Bet's decision and all I'm doing is honouring her final wishes."

"Yes, I realize that, but your grandmother is very distraught and it's about more than just the naming of the Protector. She's been talking about Uncle Roland a lot lately."

"Uncle Roland?"

Her father's soft green eyes were trained on her. "You wouldn't remember him, of course, Willow. He was gone long before you were born."

"Yes, I know. I still remember the surprise of finding out there had been someone there, someone important in the family and he was gone. When I was younger, I used to wonder if the family would be different, somehow, if he had, uh, survived, had children of his own…" Her words trailed off, and they were silent for a moment, wondering at what might have been.

Joley spoke first. "I was only a young girl when it happened but it was quite a shock."

"Whenever I asked about him as a kid, everyone was so vague."

"Well, your grandmother knows the details but apparently things had been going downhill with your Uncle Roland for some time. I remember my parents speaking in hushed tones, concerned about his behaviour. He seemed to be getting in a lot of trouble, minor infractions, blow-ups at work. Around that time, at the Annual Family Games, he got into a terrible argument with some of his cousins during the feast. I didn't understand what he was saying but apparently he had strong, political views, against many of the policies and procedures that we live by. Radical and destructive views, according to my mother and, for her mother—your Great Bet—it was extremely difficult. At that time she was a high ranking official in the CRKA. For him to speak out against the Republic, the Spiritual Center, our leaders, and even the CRKA, in such a public fashion—well, let's just say it must have caused her a great deal of embarrassment. He made quite a scene that day. I'd never seen anything like it before. One of my uncles tried to pull him aside and quiet him down and he punched him. It was frightening." She set her teacup on the table and leaned forward on the sofa. "His wife, Emma, was a lovely woman. Very tiny, pretty, soft-spoken—the whole family loved her. That day was simply horrid for her, I'm sure. And, as the story goes, she'd been having trouble conceiving. I think they tried for many years."

"Poor thing," murmured Arild. "But, there are so many children that need to be placed. Surely, they could have acquired a new baby?"

"Yes, and I believe she was in the process of arranging it." Joley agreed. "Except that, for some reason, Uncle Roland was becoming increasingly difficult and was getting demerit points all over the place. By the time their union started to fall apart, the adoption had been put on hold indefinitely. I'm sure that was part of the reason that they did ultimately apply for dissolution." She shook her head in regret. "It was sad, really. In these times when we have so much, when the world is at peace, and we have complete freedom to follow the spiritual path of our choice, how did he end up so angry, so unhappy?"

Arild leaned forward and placed his hand on hers. "It's hard to understand, Jo dear, but it happens sometimes. Did you ever see your Aunt Emma again? I remember you speaking fondly of her from your childhood years."

"No, I never saw her again but my mother says she did eventually remarry, never was able to have children, though." The room hummed around them, distant outside sounds harmonious with their thoughtful silence.

"I remember wanting to read about him when I was younger. There are no journals in the Family Records for your Uncle Roland. No journals, no closure ceremony to review, some pictures and memories from his younger years but very little is in the memorial documentation for him. Do you know what happened to him, mom?" Willow probed, curious to hear what the family knew.

"Well, honey, from your Grandmother Sybil's perspective, she's always had trouble understanding what happened, never was able to find closure. She hadn't seen Roland in almost two months, not since that horrible scene at the Family Games, and then her mother came to see her one day—to tell her the news."

"What did she say?" Willow asked, holding her breath.

"She said he'd died in an accident. There had recently been an explosion at a plant at the edge of the city, somewhere that Roland would have no reason to be and yet, he was there. Great Bet said she had sent him there, trying to help him. His job was not working out and he was considering a change in vocation, reviewing the possible career options in working at this plant, apparently. It was a freak accident, she'd said."

"This story is familiar. I think you told me about it when I was very young—how horrible for Grandma to lose her brother like that." Willow didn't know what to say, especially since she now knew that this last bit of family history was simply not true.

"Yes—and then to have no closure ceremony. It just isn't done. My mother hounded her mother but she wouldn't do it. She said that Roland's ending time with us had been so tormented that she just couldn't bring herself to rehash it all. Sybil said they could focus on the good times, his younger years but she still refused." Joley released her hands from her husband's gentle touch, standing up abruptly. She paced the room. Finally, she stopped on the other side of the coffee table from her daughter, her hands on her hips. "Don't you see, Willow? Now that Great Bet is gone and she's made her journals so secretive, your Grandma Sybil is having nightmares about Roland. She's feeling the anguish of his loss anew and can't help but wonder if there's something in the journals that will explain what happened to her brother. You must tell me—have you come across anything about this?"

She'd been gnawing on her fingernails when her mother stood up, fearing what would come next and, of course, it had. Now her mother came to tower directly above her, waiting for her response. Joley had the advantage—she was the authority figure here, not to mention, she had played the guilt card well with Willow, who was fond of Grandma Sybil. Although, she had never bonded with her to the same extent as Great Bet, she admired her. What to do, what to say? She struggled inwardly.

She pulled her fingers from her mouth, choosing her words as she answered her mother. "I've come across some, uh, references to Uncle

Roland, yes. Not all the details that you've described but, yes, some information, very limited, about the end of his time here. It's not a coherent story yet. I'm still piecing it together from different journal entries."

"Tell me what you've learned, please Willow."

It was the first time she'd ever heard that pleading tone from her mother which made it all the harder to refuse. "Mom, I can't yet. It's fragmented knowledge and it's in a sealed area. I need to understand all the implications before I divulge anything." At her mother's angry snort, she stood up and went to her. Willow held her mother's arms and adopted her own pleading tone. "I'm really sorry. Honestly. I understand what you're saying, how important it is to Grandma Sybil. I'll try to figure out a way to help but you have to be patient. There's a lot more going on here than you can imagine and I just can't tell you about it, not right now anyway."

Arild came to join them and he spoke to his wife on his daughter's behalf. "Honey, we have to respect what she's saying. Great Bet, whatever her reasons, placed a great deal of trust in our daughter. In that context, she is behaving appropriately, honourably even." He pulled Willow to him, hugging her tightly. "I'm very proud of you, my dear. I believe that you'll do the right thing, however," and he released her, eying them both with a wry expression, "you do need to be mindful of the torment that this is placing on others in the family."

Joley's features relaxed but she had one more request. "Willow, your grandmother Sybil is planning to dedicate some time at our Family Retreat to do a small closure ceremony for her brother, Roland." As Willow began to protest, she raised her hand to silence her. "No, don't say anything. We tried to debate this with her but she's insistent. She needs to do this. Our expectation is that you can be prepared by then, to tell us what you've learned about Roland. I respect what you are saying, honey but, please, pull your fragments together by then and plan to do this for us, okay?"

Reluctantly, Willow nodded, promising to do her best. At the same time, she wondered what she should really do. She wished she understood what Great Bet would have wanted.

Chapter 27

*"Men never do evil so completely and cheerfully
as when they do it from religious conviction"*

Blaise Pascal

Charlie's heart pounded against his chest as he returned her embrace, his lips following her lead. She had her hands inside his jacket, stroking his back, her body pressed against him. Unsure of what to do or how he should react, nevertheless his body was responding without the benefit of his mind's command. Never before, in his young life, had he experienced a woman like Sophie. A yearning grew deep inside, a desire for physical pleasures that he'd wondered at but never experienced. Would it be so wrong? he wondered. What harm could it do?

They'd been at a nightclub she frequented where he met some of her college friends. All evening, he'd been tongue-tied but she'd kept him laughing. She shocked him sometimes—so brazen and confident, outrageous in her speech—yet, all night he'd felt this desire building between them. She'd made him dance even after he told her he couldn't, didn't know how. She'd shown him some moves, then. Oh yes, she'd really shown him. When the club was closing, he'd been helpless, knowing it was all up to her. Tonight he would simply do as she asked, go where she desired.

Ironically, they were now in the City Center, having wandered the streets arm in arm, stopping to kiss, pressed up against the memorial to Marrisha and Kamon. There was a small alcove between one of the statues and the memorial screen. She pulled him into the shadows, just out of view and they lay down there, locked in a passionate embrace, his breathing out of control. The bulge in his pants was straining hard against the material. The blood that had rushed in was pumping steadily, desperate for release. She touched him. He groaned, his hands finally reaching for her in places he had not dared before. All reason was gone for the moment.

"Oh, Charlie, you're so hard." She rubbed her hand along him. "I want you so much. Oh, Charlie, do you think we should?" Even as she asked the question, she was undoing his pants and he felt the cool breeze of the evening air on his skin.

"Sophie, I don't know but I want to." He could barely breathe. "I want to so much." He pulled open her jumper. It released easily, a miracle garment that looked like a second skin but seemed to be made for easy removal. He saw her breasts and gasped, reaching his hands out in wonder.

They were on hard pavement and it was a cool, dark night but he was oblivious to this. Before long, she had taken charge again, and he experienced the exquisite sensations of her hot, moist movements on him. He couldn't control himself and exploded in ecstasy, screaming her name. "Sophie, oh my god, Sophie!"

When it was over, she was efficient, dressing herself and then helping him, snuggling for a moment. "Charlie," she finally murmured, "there were a few moments where I had the distinct impression that you had never done this before…"

He was glad his face was hidden. He buried his burning cheeks in her wild hair. "Uh, well, that's true. You were amazing, Sophie. I hope I, uh, did it right." He gulped down his embarrassment.

It seemed that she was actually speechless. Back on their feet, they kissed again, warm throbbing sensations lingered from their lovemaking. Finally, they reluctantly broke apart and picked up their bags, preparing to leave.

Charlie looked up, curious at the monument that had been witness to this monumental occurrence in his life. "Now, what does this say?" He asked out loud.

They both turned to read the story that scrolled continuously down the screen with the two great statues on either side.

The end of despair and the beginning of hope— Establishment of the People's United Republic of Earth

By the end of the Century of Despair, after hundreds of millions of men had died violent deaths, there were few alive who could remember the source of the conflict. Only the hatred that had been bred in them remained alive, fueling further racial tensions and religious conflicts; acts of terrorism and retaliatory attacks that seemed to have no end.

At that time, the Enlightened Ones roamed the Earth, speaking to the people, imploring the World Leaders to stop, but their voices were not heard in the din of War. Marrisha and Kamon were among these voices, although, coming from opposite ends of the earth, they knew each other only by reputation in the time before the Annihilation.

Religious leaders, men, women, and children everywhere despaired and watched helplessly.

Finally, the Week of Annihilation brought the world to its knees. Mushroom clouds hung over twelve major cities and the death toll approached 500 million, doubling, in just one week, the casualties that the wars and conflicts had brought in the previous century.

During the hush following the shockwave of unprecedented human carnage, when rage turned inwards and people tallied their dead, religious zealots declared it to be Judgment Day, warning that the End of the World was upon them all. They said that only the chosen would be saved but as time carried forward, their prophecies proved false.

In the resulting confusion, the Enlightened Ones stepped forward.

For the ultimate judgment was Man's and the wise leaders of economic, social, and religious structures that had survived, came together with a common vision for harmony. Finally the world was ready to listen. Seeing the devastation that man had wrought upon man, people everywhere understood that drastic measures would need to be taken, and common beliefs set aside.

The Republic sought to establish a worldwide society where all religions, philosophies, and traditions were tolerated and brought together, where the wisdom of the ages was shared for the common good. In the new order, more focus was to be placed on the family unit and building ancestral histories to replace reliance on ancient histories and traditions which had become the source of political agendas, violence, and propaganda.

At the Council for Earth's Children, twelve men and twelve women were chosen to represent disparate faiths and peoples from around the globe. They were secluded for 30 days and 30 nights, tasked with solving the most difficult of problems—finding a middle ground: a spiritual path, common politics and a world community, that could bridge the exclusivity and embittered battles that existed between the races and the different faiths.

The story was sobering for Charlie and as he read it, he was reminded of the society he was in and his mission. "Ridiculous." He scoffed, under his breath.

"What did you say?" Sophie's head reared back. "Surely, you are familiar with the story of Marrisha and Kamon, the PURE beginning?"

He recovered. "Yes, I've heard it before."

"You've heard it before? Didn't you memorize this in school every year?"

"No, not quite."

"Where on earth are you from?" Sophie turned to face him, her hands on her hips.

"I'm from the country. We don't do things quite the same." He tried to make light of the situation, not wanting her to know that even for a boy from the country, he was unusual. His family had sheltered him from the Republic school system.

Their conversation was stilted after that and they both turned away to walk to the transport area, each lost in their thoughts. Charlie was swallowing down spasms of guilt. He knew that he must report his indiscretion immediately.

Chapter 28

"The world is simply a dream that we have agreed to experience together. The dream disappears when we withdraw our awareness from it."

Joseph Campbell

Sharon left the conference early and headed straight for her private suite. She needed solitude before they interrogated the girl—time to think, reflect, prepare. Craig could finish without her. She'd given him a signal, innocuous to anyone else in the room but he'd understood the request, nodding imperceptibly, touching her hand gently under the table.

Having dismissed the attendants, she closed the door softly and sank into the air-cushioned lounger, her arms spread out, hands dangling off the sides, head thrown back. The chair molded to her body. The suite's amenities were luxurious. A well stocked snack and drink area and a professional station for fixing her make-up and hair were at opposite ends of the large room. Right now, neither of these interested her, nor did she want to watch the enormous flat screen portal unit with the latest news and entertainment. All she wanted was silence—and to be completely still.

She breathed deeply, letting her thoughts drift, traveling down memory paths that had been blocked for years. In order to be chosen for the Leader Society, to be a member of that elite group with a chance to become a World Governor—there were enormous challenges to overcome. Experience in senior jobs with at least five government divisions, achieving champion status in all of them, and, finally, to be selected out of the entire Society—it was a great achievement, a rare accomplishment. After all those years of hard work and dedication, she'd proven herself, leading with competence and honour, a respected member of the Council of Earth. Usually, she felt proud of what she'd accomplished but not today. Instead she was remembering her first stage on the journey to lead. Elzabeth had delivered that glowing recommendation during her tenure at the CRKA after the mission they'd worked on together. She'd even helped her to clean up the mess; the mess that could have ended her career at the very beginning. It could have been so different but Elzabeth had chosen to help her that way. Why?

She shook her head, this mystery from her past alive again, unsolvable. She'd asked her then but Elzabeth had told her nothing, just helped her on her way, leaving behind a commendation for Sharon. She figured that Elzabeth had felt guilty, somehow responsible for what had happened but Sharon knew the risks she'd been taking. For Elzabeth to help her so much, to even cover up what had happened—that was beyond what most agents would do, even with a guilty conscience. As a result, Sharon had moved on and focused exclusively on her career, leaving the pain behind, replacing it with a renewed drive to succeed.

And now, decades later, her original mentor was gone, with a great-granddaughter who might hold the keys to this enigma. Yet, this was a mystery that needed to stay buried—this she knew—but the burning question for Sharon was: had Elzabeth revealed anything in her journal?

The buzz from her unit startled her, eyes flying open, her hand reaching mechanically down to allow the communication to come through. "Madame Governor? The girl is here. Do you still want to join us for the interrogation?"

Sharon was on her feet in an instant. "Yes," she said in her most authoritative voice, "I'm on my way. Do not start without me." As she walked out of the suite, her waiting security team followed.

When they had all assembled in the viewing gallery, they stared at the young girl sitting in the interrogation room below, unable to hear or see them.

Sharon had left her security team outside in the hallway so there were just five of them in the room. Craig had not been able to escape from the conference in time to join. Secretly, Sharon was relieved at his absence. In addition to Sharon, there was Agent Ramona Markel and her three agents. To her left sat the brawny young man with auburn hair, Agent Jackson, and his female partner in surveillance, Agent Sorbara. The most striking of the group, was the tall blonde woman who had been attending Vision Speak, Agent Perkins. She contrasted sharply with Ramona's dark, masculine looks beside her, both seated to Sharon's right.

Ramona led the discussion with the group on her planned approach to the questioning. Sharon noticed that the CRKA Team Leader seemed fidgety. Probably, this would be the first time that a World Governor had watched one of her interrogations.

They debated on the approach—should she ask her outright about the journals or focus on accusatory comments related to her Vision Speak training with her great-grandmother and subsequent breaking of the Spiritual Contract? The hope with the latter approach was that she would become frightened and perhaps reveal more in her wish to defend herself.

Ramona wanted to go on the offensive but Sharon intervened. "Look at her, Agent Markel. She is little more than a child." While gazing down at her in the room below, they witnessed a transformation. A few moments ago, she'd been biting her nails, anxiously darting her glance from the door to the portal screen in front of her but her demeanor had changed. Similar to the others of her group, she was now sitting still in her chair, eyes closed, apparently meditating, breathing deeply. "I would prefer that we not threaten her."

Agent Perkins spoke up. "Yes, she appears young and innocent, I agree; however, I assure you that she is every bit a woman." A bitter twist at the end of her words had them all waiting for her to continue. She realized her show of emotion and evened her tone with her next words. "I'm sorry. It's just that I've been starting to detect a lot more to this girl than her childlike manner might indicate. She's been spending a lot of time with Aaron—one of the leaders of the group. He is the one that I was originally assigned to watch."

Sharon's right eyebrow rose a fraction as she glanced at the young agent's superior, Agent Markel. The young agent noticed the interchange. With burning cheeks, she continued rapidly. "I-it's not just that. In addition to whatever is going on between the two of them, Aaron and the other leaders seem to be having special sessions with her. They've already graduated her up several levels. It's very unusual."

"In an extreme situation, Madame Governor," Ramona turned to Sharon, "we can administer the probe to force the information out that we need. Usually that's reserved for criminals, however, if this is important to you..."

"No! Please, that will not be necessary." Sharon did not want them mistreating Elzabeth's young descendant; she did not want this interrogation to get out of control before she knew what they were dealing with. She returned her attention to the girl. "Look at her. Is she even awake? Agent Markel, perhaps, you'd better go down and see what she's doing. Just go carefully with your questions. I would prefer if you could hold off on anything threatening unless it's absolutely necessary."

It was while Agent Ramona Markel was on her way down to the Interrogation Room that Sharon began to sense something unusual. She may not have noticed it, or understood it, had it not been for her experience of so many years ago.

She felt herself relaxing, in an almost meditative state herself—in fact, the whole room quieted down, everyone apparently lost in their own thoughts. An internal humming, a peaceful, connected sensation absorbed her. She closed her eyes, her mind and spirit drifted; somehow, open, listening. Her past and present, inner thoughts and feelings were exposed, suddenly out there, secrets she had guarded, kept to herself. She had been desperate for so long to ensure they were not revealed, to the point where she didn't even let her mind wander down those paths often. It was odd, like there was another presence guiding her—and yet, she did not feel threatened, only comforted by an inexplicable human closeness or bond. Suddenly, the message came to her, as clear as if someone had spoken to her in the room. "I know what happened. I know about the lost child." It said. "Don't worry, I won't say anything."

Sharon heard, from a great distance, Ramona's voice as she entered the interrogation room, sat across the table from the girl and spoke to her. Ramona was asking questions and the girl was answering slowly, quietly, in monosyllables.

Forcing herself into a conscious state, she opened her eyes, a sudden realization of what had occurred and where she had been came upon her. Glancing at the others in the room, she saw their eyes were glazed. Clearly they were oblivious to what had happened, what was still happening. The girl below was both conscious and unconscious, able to discourse with Ramona, while she watched inwardly, connected with them all. Sharon saw this and wondered at her powers. How had she done this? Never before had she encountered someone with such control, not even the cult leaders. Having been away from it for so long, she had dismissed this ability, forgotten the potential she had once gleaned.

The girl was apparently starting to focus more on her conversation with Ramona. Sharon listened as she thought through the implications of what she'd just discovered.

"Miss Olsen—may I call you Willow?"

"Sure, that is my name after all." She smiled, softening the sarcasm.

Ramon ignored it. "Willow, we've recently met with the representatives of your new group at the Center, Vision Speak. We understand that you joined recently. We shared our concerns about some of your great grandmother's comments in her closure ceremony, related to Vision Speak. Perhaps they have mentioned this to you?"

She shook her head gently, loose strands of hair swaying. "They haven't actually said anything. I'm not part of the inner council but I'm not surprised. You know, Great Bet was always very outspoken. I'm sure it must have gotten her in trouble in her job but she still did quite well here, I understand. Are you familiar with her career with the CRKA?" Willow inquired, her green eyes open wide.

"Oh, yes, we are certainly familiar with the infamous Elzabeth McGregor. She accomplished a great deal during her tenure here.

Reached Champion status, you know? She led some of our most important missions back in her day."

Willow leaned forward, her interest sparked. "Oh, I'd love to hear about her career—anything you can share with me, Agent Markel." She spoke the agent's name politely, as a child might speak to an adult.

Ramona gaped at the young girl for an instant before proceeding. "Uh, well, I'm sorry, but I'm not able to share any details of her cases with you. You may be surprised to hear that we actually brought you here to ask you questions."

She giggled, her face good-natured and calm. "I guess that's why they call it an Interrogation Room?"

"You don't seem to be taking this very seriously. Have you ever been brought here before?"

"No, never." Always obedient, Willow assumed a more somber expression.

"My questions for you, Willow, relate to two specific areas. First, we understand that you spent a great deal of time with your great-grandmother in the months before her death. Is that correct?"

"Uh, yes, that's right. We were very close."

"According to our information, that was not always the case. In fact, it seems that you had rarely visited her alone before this winter. Yet, in her final months, you spent an inordinate amount of time with her."

Willow shrugged. "She was dying. Surely, you don't have a problem with a descendant who wants to learn from a great matriarch before she passes?"

"No, of course not, it's very admirable but we are curious as to what was captivating your interest for so many visits, over so many months." Ramona moved on for the moment, remembering Sharon's words. "Secondly, and more importantly for the moment, you have access to a number of sealed and secret entries to her journal to which no one else is privy. We believe that these entries may be of great importance to the Republic, and potentially a security risk, so we would like to request that you turn these over to us."

Willow's jaw dropped open. "Are you kidding me? You want me to give you my Great Grandmother's ancestral history, her family journals? My own family hasn't even viewed them yet."

Watching the interaction from the secret viewing gallery, Sharon experienced a moment of relief at that revelation—at least no one else had read them.

"It's good news that you have honoured the secrecy that Elzabeth requested with her journals. Under these circumstances, perhaps it would be better if the family never viewed them. And," Ramona continued, "we have the matter of the security of the Republic at hand, as well."

"You can't make me give them to you. The Citizen's Contract strongly encourages everyone to maintain a journal. It's considered the property of the Family and the greatest legacy that one can leave one's ancestors."

"That is true but if the journals are considered a danger to the Republic, if the security of the peaceful society we maintain is at risk in any way, then we can."

"Don't you think you're exaggerating the importance of what can be in these journals?" Willow's voice raised a decibel higher. "How could my great grandmother's journals threaten the security of the Republic so many years after her retirement? It's ridiculous. Surely your agents enjoy the same rights as the rest of the citizens? My family takes great pride and enjoyment from our Ancestral Journals."

Ramona's tone was reassuring, calming after the outburst. "Willow, I understand your position. We do not want to interfere with your Family History. How about this? If we can work with you to remove any of the secret or sealed entries that have any reference to her career with the CRKA, then the journals can be released back to you. What do you think?"

"In other words, I would, of course, show you entries that she had deliberately sealed and left in my care?" As she spoke, Willow eyes searched the white walls of the square room, finally gazing upwards to the mirrored panels just before the high ceilings.

"Of course, but we would be very discreet."

When Willow stared up toward the secret room, it seemed as if she were looking directly at Sharon, although that was impossible. "I need to speak with you," she said.

Ramona's brown eyes bulged, her thick, dark brows raised, momentarily speechless. Finally, she spoke, "Who are you talking to?"

Before Willow could answer, the speaker in the room activated and Sharon's voice boomed into the room. "Never mind, Agent Markel. This interrogation is over. I want the girl brought to my private suite. My guards will escort her."

Chapter 29

"The universe may have a purpose, but nothing we know suggests that, if so, this purpose has any similarity to ours."

Bertrand Russell

After struggling for days with his guilt, agonizing over what he should do, Charlie finally sought Jake out, asking if they could speak privately. They both requested a time-out from their job at the information assembly plant, whispering as they walked along the corridor towards the caffeine break room.

"Jake, I'm afraid that I've breached protocol and mixed unnecessarily with one of the subjects."

"What? Who are you talking about?"

"Sophie Tyler Calloway."

"Tyler? Is she related to the Protector?"

"Yes, her cousin. We met at the Spiritual Center."

"You haven't blown your cover, have you?"

"No, no, of course not!"

"Okay, tell me what's happened."

"Well, she approached me. I did nothing to encourage it, I swear."

"Okay, so she approached you. What did she say?"

"Well, she asked me to go out with her."

Jake grinned. "Really? And, did you go?"

Charlie hung his head. "I did. She was so persistent and I didn't know how to handle it. I'm sorry."

"Okay, so what happened?"

"Well, we went to a club, we danced, and we…" He trailed off, stumbling on the next words that he knew he must confess.

Jake raised his eyebrows. "You, what?" Watching Charlie's face, the shifting eyes, his burning cheeks, he suddenly knew. "Are you trying to tell me that you messed around with her?"

Uncomfortable, Charlie raised his eyes, his expression grave. "I'm saying that we were intimate, yes. I don't know how it happened. I got, uh, carried away, I guess."

"Oh, boy." Jake whistled under his breath.

"I know we're supposed to stay in the background, watch critically and wait for instructions. I don't know what I should do. Will this jeopardize our mission in any way?"

Jake was silent as he thought through this surprising turn of events. He would not have expected this from his innocent, devout partner. "Charlie, go back to work and just keep to yourself. I'll contact the leader with this information and get instructions."

Charlie turned back towards the plant as Jake removed his portal unit, and ducked into one of the private restrooms.

It wasn't until much later, after their shift was over and they were back in their quarters that Jake received the response. He called Charlie over and they both listened to the leader's words.

"Do not fret, loyal brothers of the order. It appears that everything has transpired as it should, ordained by powers greater than either of you could possibly understand. Brother Charlie should continue to get close to this young lady, of course taking care to keep any details of his identity secure, and wait for more instructions. This could turn out to be very useful in the near future."

Chapter 30

*"Change is the law of life.
And those who look only to the past are certain to miss the future."*

John F. Kennedy

Although she'd been fairly certain of the result when she made the request, Willow was greatly relieved that she was on her way to see the woman in charge.

For a moment, she relived her shock at discovering Jericho amongst the group watching her. All along, she'd been a spy. She'd almost lost it when she connected with her, experienced her intimate memories of Aaron, and realized what she had only previously suspected, been afraid to ask. Aaron and Jericho had been lovers. She shuddered now at the images she had seen. Fortunately, she'd controlled her reaction. She'd kept it together, continuing to unobtrusively observe the group. It was obvious that Jericho was not the important person in the room and so she had focused on the situation at hand. Still, she was anxious to confront Aaron.

When the woman stated that the interrogation was over, Ramona Markel had ceased immediately and exited the room, leaving Willow alone for a time while they made their arrangements. It had given her a chance to regain her peaceful, introspective frame of mind so that when she was finally escorted through the many corridors and lifts to reach the top of the main tower—the enclave for the regional PURE Governors—she was ready—at least until she realized where she was going.

She hadn't comprehended just how important the woman was until she was on the final lift with the guards and she heard them whispering. The first one asked the other: "Are they both meeting with her?" and the second had responded, "No, just her Excellency, Governor Sharon. He's not back yet and she's waiting in her private suite." Her heart pounded loudly in her chest cavity as it registered who they were taking her to see. She understood, even without having sensed it from the guards, that this was very unusual.

The security to actually reach her private suite was astounding. Secure, password and eye-scanner protected entranceways from the elevator to the Governors' floor, then another secure passageway to get into the reception area which was still two locked doors and related security personnel away from her actual suite. By the time they had escorted Willow in and left her alone with the great woman, her serene state was shattered, her nerve-endings on high alert.

The guards pushed her forward into the room and, at the woman's dismissive hand gesture, clicked the door locked shut behind them. She was alone with World Governor Sharon.

The woman, one of the supreme members of the Council of Earth, a Governor of the Republic, stood up to greet her, extending her hand. "Willow, thanks for coming to see me. I'm Sharon. I knew your great-grandmother many years ago."

Willow gazed up at the tall woman in awe. Her features were flawless, even though she had to be well over fifty, maybe even sixty. A full, platinum, stylish halo surrounded wide, perfectly accentuated eyes. Intelligent, fine lines further highlighted the sophistication of the woman. The face was familiar—she'd seen it on the news, in public announcements, in portraits in government buildings. To say she was intimidated to be standing in the presence of this woman was an understatement. Grinning foolishly, she shook her hand. "Hi." She said.

After they were seated comfortably in the sitting area and Willow had accepted a hot drink—actually served to her by the Governor—Sharon got straight down to business.

"You surprised me back there." Her posture was straight, her eyes unflinching as she sat gracefully in her seat. "Your, uh, Vision Speak abilities are quite astounding."

Shy eyes peeped up at the older woman. "So, you are familiar with Vision Speak? I thought you seemed more aware than the others…"

"Well, I'm a little rusty, actually." Sharon raised a perfectly sculpted eyebrow. "I suspect that you know my background with it based on the message that you sent me?"

"You mean about the child?" Willow spoke softly, reluctant to say the word out loud. The room she sat in was so lush, so opulent—with leather couches, a large wall portal, the wet bar and kitchenette—it was impossible to forget where she was. Everything was accessorized and coordinated, sparkling clean: bleach white leather with chrome finishing, bright colourful lamps and tables, remote portal and communicator connections from every seat in the room. Everywhere she looked there were reminders that this was a high ranking official, one that had earned the most luxurious lifestyle possible.

The World Governor flinched at the words. "Yes." Her response was curt. She had no intention of divulging anything further until Willow explained.

"Well, it's a little hazy, actually. When we connected over there," she waved her arm in the vague direction of the Interrogation Room. "I was just trying to feel my way around, get a sense of who everyone was that seemed to be watching me."

"Uh-huh." Sharon took a sip of her iced drink, watching the girl closely.

"It was obvious you were in charge, the way the rest of the group was watchful of your presence, kind of nervous. So I focused more on you, tried to understand what you were all about." She shrugged her shoulders and reached for the mug on the table in front of her. "I didn't know exactly who you were but I tapped into some of your subconscious thoughts and fears, insecurities, I guess. I was just trying to reassure you."

"Are you telling me that you got that information from me and not from the journals?"

"Pretty much. I've recently come across a few entries and I wonder if they're related—but Great Bet wrote very little about official business in her journals. In the brief mentions that she does have, the names are changed. I'm wondering if you were an Agent Z that she referred to—you were an agent with her once, weren't you?"

"Agent Z? Well, I've never been called that." Sharon actually laughed; a nervous laugh that seemed out of character for the cool, confident woman. "Although, I did work with her in the CRKA early in my career so yes, I was an agent with her once."

"Well, that's about all I can tell you. I really don't know all the details, certainly not from the journals."

"Well, Willow, one thing you have admitted is that there are some official CRKA entries in these journals. That may be enough for us to confiscate them, I'm afraid."

"What! You can't do that!" Aghast, Willow replaced her drink on the table, almost knocking it over.

"Why do you say—we can't do that?" Sharon's face was implacable. "My dear, you really have no idea how everything works but I can assure you that there is very little that is outside the bounds of our authority. That is, if the end result is maintaining a peaceful, non-disruptive society."

"But how on earth do these journals threaten our society? That's just crazy."

"No, it's not, actually. Maintaining a peaceful society on a worldwide basis is an extremely complex business although I don't expect someone of your young years to understand."

Willow nodded, her mind scrambling to find a way out. She tried to calm her emotions, realizing that she would need to tap into all of her abilities to manage this. "Perhaps not, but I do think that much ado has been made of nothing here. These journals are not a threat to your Republic. Surely, you don't really believe that they are?"

"I do believe it, in fact. Both the journals and this emerging gift that you have demonstrated today can pose a threat." Sharon set her glass on the table, quietly, leaning back in her lounge chair. "Surely you know the story of our PURE beginnings? The world was violent and chaotic before the Republic was formed. Mankind was on the threshold of destruction. How do you think we've managed to stop this pattern from occurring again and have held it together for three and a half centuries now? The nature of mankind is to complain, to disrupt that which is running smoothly, to war with each other. For all these years, the governing bodies along with the CRKA have worked diligently to maintain a fair and just society, giving every citizen a pleasant existence with clear boundaries and goals. But, just as important, we ensure that dissident groups are kept from polluting the populace with their radical ideas. How we do this is not important. To keep this balance we must operate furtively, carefully."

"Are you saying that we are, in fact, living in a state of oppression? That you view the citizens of the Republic in the same manner that one might consider a child who is restrained from activities because he is too innocent, too ignorant, to know better?"

"Oppression is too strong of a word. No, I'm not saying that. It's more a case of careful handling. It's for your own good, the greater well-being of the people. Without our manipulation, maintaining the balance, watching for any signs of disruption, containing criminals and enemies of the state before they gain unnecessary publicity, we would quickly spiral back down into anarchy."

"But I do hear stories in the media about arrests and trials. What are these?"

"We only allow certain stories to appear. If the general population knew how busy we were, keeping the streets clean, stopping the secret societies and religious zealots who seek to disrupt the Spiritual practices of the Republic—no one would feel safe."

"So, what we see and hear—it's all propaganda? You control all the media stories?"

"That's one way to look at it. You would have to understand what came before to truly appreciate the greater good in what we do."

There was a long silence as Willow absorbed what Governor Sharon had shared. "Why do you tell me so much?" Chills coursed down her spine as it occurred to her that everything Sharon had just told her meant that they could not possibly risk having Willow go back into society with this information. Her voice shrinking, she whispered. "You are going to let me go home, back to my life, aren't you?"

Sharon nodded slowly, as she lifted the teapot, offering Willow a refill.

"You are very perceptive. It's a dilemma we must consider." She leaned back, cup in hand. "The reason that I'm telling you this is partially because I believe that with your, uh, abilities," she enunciated the last word carefully, "you will soon sense much of this, if you haven't already. In addition, you have full access to Elzabeth's journals and she was a master at this game of manipulation, invented some of our current methods, in fact. I have to assume that you will also have gleaned some of this from her. I want to make sure that you understand; that you are interpreting everything correctly."

"Okay." Willow nodded. "I understand what you are saying and I will keep what you have told me to myself."

"Will you? How can I be certain?"

Willow leaned back and closed her eyes, breathing deeply as she concentrated. She understood that should she share this information with anyone, she would be endangering not only her own existence in this society but theirs as well. She would not do that. She showed Sharon this in a way that she would have to believe her, unlike any words that she could have spoken.

Sharon reached for her temples, watched the images spinning in her head, the emotions, the promise. Finally, she spoke, "Okay, I see."

"You won't hold me here?" Willow breathed a sigh of relief.

"Not for the moment but I think," Sharon gazed across the table, "that the only solution, ultimately, is for you to join us here."

"Join you?"

"Yes, you are graduating soon, are you not?"

"Uh, yes but…"

"I know all about you Willow. I had your details in front of me before the interrogation. You have not yet been selected for your vocation. We must make you an apprentice in the administration of this office."

"What? No—no way. I have not studied for a government job."

Sharon raised her eyebrows. "Do you know how many students are vying for a vocation in this office? Only the very best are permitted to join us here."

"But, I am an artist. I'm awaiting acceptance into the Arts Community. I have dreamed of this my whole life."

"I'm sorry, Willow, but we cannot allow that to happen—not now."

Willow forgot who she was addressing. The horror of losing her lifelong dreams took over. "No, you can't do that to me! You can't!" She stood up.

Sharon rose to her feet. The two women stared across the table but were startled out of their aggressive silence when the door across the room opened revealing Craig standing in the entranceway.

Chapter 31

*"Never believe that a few caring people can't change the world.
For, indeed, that's all who ever have."*

Margaret Mead

Simon rushed out of the cleansing room before drying, water drops trailing on the floor as he ran to stop the clamour from his personal portal unit. "Simon, you have an urgent and private communiqué. Please respond immediately." The unit implored, the volume increasing with each repeat.

He silenced it as his towel dropped to the ground leaving him standing nude in the middle of his bedroom, goose pimples on his lanky, white torso gleaming with moisture, his feet leaving wet imprints on the carpet. He picked up the towel and wrapped it around his head. Turning to the closet in the corner of the small room, he pulled out an old purple robe. He was just wrapping it around himself when one of his roommates pounded on the door.

"Hey, what's with all that yelling in there? You all right?"

"I'm fine. Sorry, my unit went wacky. It's stopped now." Simon tied the sash tight around his skinny frame, cuddling into the warm, soft feel of the fabric on his goose-pimpled skin.

"Well turn the thing down next time. It woke me up." The grumbling over, Simon could hear the sound of his roommate's footsteps returning to his room and presumably back to bed.

"Yeah, whatever." Simon mumbled. He'd never received a communiqué in this fashion before so he wondered what it was. Picking up his personal unit, he plugged it into the portal screen on the wall, and opened the item. He was surprised to see that he had to go through a full security sign-on just to get at the entry. He was certain he'd left his unit open with ready access.

It was a video-mail but before Simon could open it, there was one last bit of security that required his response. It said, "This communication is intended for you only, Simon. If you're not alone with complete privacy then you must save this for a time when you are."

He responded appropriately and then settled back down in bed, his head propped up with two pillows, to watch the video message. Perhaps this is some clever, new gimmick to get one's attention for a spa or fashion product, he thought to himself.

It wasn't, though. He almost swallowed his tongue when Elzabeth's image appeared on the screen. He bolted into an upright position, his attention riveted by her words.

"Simon," she croaked.

"Yes," he whispered back, forgetting that she wouldn't really be able to hear him.

Elzabeth's face was larger than life. Simon gazed into her deep set eyes, green flecks on brown glinting from some light source, perhaps a nearby window. Wrinkles on top of wrinkles masked the beauty that had been. He remembered the images of a younger Elzabeth at the closure ceremony but the once auburn hair had turned white as the alabaster statue of Marrisha in his lobby. Still, even on her death bed—for he assumed that she had recorded this just weeks or days before her death— he discerned the magnificence in her features, the strength behind those eyes.

"When you receive this, I will be gone, and certain events should have passed. You, and the others, will have met my great granddaughter, Willow. Hopefully by now you all have recognized the great promise in her that I have." Her voice cracked as she spoke.

Simon watched her pause to take a drink from a water glass on the table by the bed as he wondered how she could have predicted future events, timed the arrival of this message. It was uncanny—they'd just met with Willow a couple of days ago.

"Something else is happening with her, Simon. She is being watched closely by the CRKA. This message has been triggered for delivery because she has just been interrogated. There are others watching too."

At her cryptic statement, he muttered, "what others, Elzabeth? How much is there that you never told us?"

Her voice boomed back, interrupting his questions. "I've known you since you were an infant, my dear boy—kept in contact the whole time you were growing up and now, as a man. You've done well with your vocation. I am proud of you. Before Willow, you progressed faster in Vision Speak than anyone else I had ever seen. This message is coming to you now because I know I can trust you implicitly."

It was true. He had known Elzabeth MacGregor for as long as he could remember. She'd been a friend of his mother's. At least, he thought that's what she was, although, remembering back, it always seemed that she mainly came to visit him. He'd never really thought much about it before but it was true. Once he'd been old enough, she had occasionally even taken him out on his own. A retired agent herself, his mother had been an admirer of Elzabeth, always regarding her with great respect. His mother had been older than most of his friends' mothers, unusually so in fact, but she'd been such a wonderfully loving woman. His father was gone before he could even remember. His mother had passed on two years ago. With Elzabeth's death, it felt like no one was left to look out for him. He missed her.

"Pay close attention to my instructions, Simon. I delayed this message until I thought it an appropriate time after my passing. You may still need to wait some period before acting. I have confidence that you will know when the time is right. I want you to listen carefully and then remember what I have told you. You should delete this communication once you have it memorized." She lifted her head from the pillow, her voice sharpening. "Do you understand me, Simon?"

He crossed his legs and straightened his spine, placing his hands in his lap. He appeared just as he had as a young boy sitting attentively in class. Leaning slightly forward towards the image on the screen, Simon paid careful attention to everything she told him before deleting the message.

Chapter 32

*"Every religion is true one way or another.
It is true when understood metaphorically. But when it gets stuck in its own
metaphors, interpreting them as facts, then you are in trouble."*

Joseph Campbell

Willow barely slept, tormented by her thoughts of the CRKA interrogation and Sharon. Even more troublesome than the events of the previous day had been the images of Aaron and Jericho. She planned to confront him about it.

Now, sitting across the table from him, she almost forgot what she had been so worried about. This is so right, she thought, this energy between us. Why spoil it with questions and accusations? After all, we have no commitment, no promises.

"Is that a shadow lurking back there?" He reached his hand over and caressed a lock of hair away from her eye. His tone teasing, he leaned forward, speaking softly into her ear. "Perhaps I need to force this secret out of you. Should we go back to my place and see how long you can resist?"

She laughed out loud, the pitch high-strung unlike her usual happy sound. Despite her determination to control her bodily impulses tonight, she felt the heat spread deep in her womb, a longing she could barely contain. She forced it down. Taking a deep breath, she responded. "Tempting, Aaron," her words were wispy as she breathed in and out again, "very tempting but you're perceptive, as always. I need to talk to you about something but first I have to be sure we're not overheard."

His eyebrows raised, he stared at her a moment before glancing around the room to observe their surroundings. They were in a small diner down the road from his apartment, their food barely touched. Their table was in the middle of the crowded room but with groups huddled into the seating all around them, each engaged in their own world. In particular, the neighbouring table was carrying on a boisterous conversation. He imagined it would be impossible for anyone to listen in on them with all the background noise, even with a sound tracking beam pointed in their direction. A large portal screen hung on the wall over the bar, across the room. He noticed his favourite sports game was viewing but, at that moment, was much more interested in Willow and what had robbed him of her usually playful mood. "I think we're safe here—too much noise around us for anyone to pick up on our conversation. Tell me what's on your mind."

She rested her elbows on the table, cupping her face in her hands, sighing. "I was interrogated."

"What! When? Why didn't you tell me?"

"Yesterday and I'm telling you now."

He gulped the drink he had been sipping, slamming the cup down. A few drops spattered on the table. "Okay, fine, now tell me what happened. What kinds of questions did they ask you?"

"The woman started to ask me questions about Great Bet, my meetings with her, Vision Speak…but she didn't finish. I reached out and connected with the interrogation team that were watching me. After what I'd discovered about them watching you—remember, Aaron?—I figured there had to be a group of them watching me, too. Sure enough, there were four of them, in addition to the person asking me the questions."

"Oh, boy." He whistled under his breath. "Willow, did they know you were connecting with them?"

"One of them did, for sure—the woman in charge, actually."

"You mean Agent Ramona Markel?"

She drew back. "You know her?"

"She was interrogating us, as well. I just figured it would be the same one."

"Oh, right." She shook her head. "She was the person interrogating me but she was not the woman in charge. It was someone much higher up, many levels her superior. Anyway, Ramona didn't have a clue but this other woman knew."

"How do you know? What happened?"

Willow leaned back in her seat, crossing her arms in front. She gazed into Aaron's eyes, her expression guarded. "A lot happened, Aaron, but I'm afraid I can't tell you everything, at least not yet." Observing the mask of indignation cloud his handsome features, she hastened to explain. "It's really for your own good—and mine. I can't take the chance." She wished more than anything that she could confide in him. She was ready to burst with everything that she had learned these past weeks—about her great grandmother, about the clandestine CRKA and their methods and even the cult. Her head was still reeling from meeting Sharon and, most particularly, from all that Sharon had admitted to her but she was also afraid. Deathly afraid of what would happen if she was not careful with all this information that was spinning around in her head. Both the veiled threats and very specific threat of her future were at the forefront. Even without them, she sensed these dangers—and more. There were days, lately, when she wondered why Great Bet had gotten her into this mess. This 'gift' that she had, that was growing, seemed a curse at times. If anything, it was leading her deeper and deeper into some kind of trap—but what exactly the trap was, she could not ascertain.

He sputtered. "What! Are you kidding me? First of all, you promised us that you would not demonstrate your abilities to anyone. Don't you remember?" She had the grace to burn guilty cheeks but remained silent. "And, what do you mean you can't tell me what happened?" When she just shook her head, he continued. "Okay, don't say anything, show me. I'm ready, just go ahead." He set his hands down on the table, starting his breathing.

"No!" At the look in his eyes, she unfolded her arms and reached across the table, placing her hand on his. "For the moment, you'll have to trust me that I can't, however…" She paused, wondering how to start.

"Yes?"

"However," she continued, "I do need to talk to you about something I discovered. It's about Jericho."

"Jericho?" He squirmed in this seat, pulling his hands back. "What about her?"

"She was there." Willow whispered softly, her words barely discernible. "She was watching the interrogation."

The squirming stopped. He froze in his seat, expressionless, while her words registered. His mind worked furiously to grasp the implications. "Are you sure?"

"Positive."

"Oh my lord, that means…" He faltered.

She finished his sentence. "It means that she's an agent, that she's been watching us the whole time."

"No. It can't be." His speech slowed as he re-examined past events. Less certain, he added, "can it?"

"Believe me, it's a fact." Willow nodded, her confidence impossible to dispute. "Even more disturbing—to me anyway," she said, "was what I saw in her." She paused for a moment, squelching down an irrational outrage. "You two are involved, have been for some time." Her tone, in the end, carried a trace of accusation. She couldn't help it.

Deep, red blotches invaded his cheeks. "Wait a minute, now." He held his hands up in defense. "Yes, we've been intimate. We've gone out. I certainly never told you I was celibate before we met." He saw from set of her jaw that her anger wasn't wavering. "But Willow, since you and I have been, uh, you know, these past weeks." He stumbled over his words. "I haven't been with her at all." Unsure of how to continue, he just stared at her and waited.

Her head pounded, the beat of her aching heart pulsating through her whole body. She stared back, incapable of speech for the moment. She felt the vibrations of him trying to reach her on that other level but she closed that outlet, refused to let him in.

Their stalemate was interrupted by the sudden silence in the crowded restaurant. They broke their painful connection, diverting their eyes to the one remaining source of sound. People were rising from their seats, everyone huddling in the bar area. All eyes were focused on the portal screen.

The sports competition had been interrupted. Instead, there was a series of messages streaming across the screen. In all her years, Willow had only ever seen such an interruption when they'd had impending bad weather or major announcements, something important that had to be quickly relayed to the general public.

The messages they saw on the world portal, now, were unprecedented, shocking even.

They claimed to be passages from some of the world's most sacred scriptures; scriptures that were studied in the Spiritual Centers worldwide for the largest, most popular religions of the ancient past.

It was unthinkable that any holy texts would be broadcast via portal, outside of the Spiritual Center. The Republic placed strict controls on when and where scriptures could be shared.

Even more shocking, however, were the bold headings which proclaimed these verses to be from holy books, quoting some of the most revered prophets from those volumes—yet the statements were inflammatory. They contradicted the basic precepts of the Citizen's Spiritual Contract. They were not recognizable as statements from those prophets. At least no one would recognize the words based on the studies that every citizen followed in their youth, that many of them continued to study at the centers. These unknown verses contradicted the exclusivity clause of the spiritual contract.

Willow watched the words roll across the screen. She remembered her conversation with Sharon, the inferences in Great Bet's journals. If it were all true then the CRKA and the Republic controlled the media centers, released only news that would maintain their peaceful existence and give the impression of a well-run, safe society. She watched the people's expressions in the diner, saw their astonishment turn to anger, their mumbling escalate to yelling. There's no way that the Republic would have released these messages—whether they were truly the long lost words of the prophets, or not. They would have suppressed them at all costs, Willow thought.

Then something happened which had never happened in her memory. The portal screen went blank. All transmission was halted.

Apparently, she was not the only one who'd never seen this happen. She sensed—even before she could hear it in their voices, see it in their faces—a group fear. Their safe, restricted, predictable life suddenly was faced with an unexpected gorge—a large gaping divide.

Before the fear converted to panic, the screen came back up. Instead of the sporting event, the familiar story of Marrisha and Kamon played. The images were soothing. They'd all seen them since childhood, narrated by the StoryTeller. There were no more streaming messages, no weather, no news in the banner. Although the uncertainty and fear were still present, she felt the room relax as they all settled back into their seats. The previous lively mood was subdued as the collective minds tried to grasp just what had happened, what it meant.

Jericho momentarily forgotten, Aaron and Willow sat down. "What on earth?" He shook his head, eyes open wider than she'd ever seen.

"Unbelievable." She murmured. She imagined Sharon and Craig, scrambling about in their opulent surroundings. There's no way they could have planned this, could have known it was even coming, she thought. "Who could have done this?" She asked the question, rhetorical though she knew it was.

"I don't know." He just shook his head.

After that, they mingled with the crowd at the bar, everyone stunned, trying to make sense out of what they had seen. It reminded Willow of childhood events where a discovery, like an unexpected glimpse into the nature of adults, had permanently changed her perspective. Somehow, this evening felt the same but it was a collective innocence that had been shattered. How would the CRKA spin this? She wondered. How could they?

Later they agreed to walk for a bit. The cool spring evening was refreshing after the crowded, emotional bar scene. They returned to their previous conversation.

"I've got to find out what she's been up to," he said.

"How do you propose to do that?" She was afraid to hear his answer.

"I'm not sure but I need to see her again. I need to observe her now that I know."

"And, if I don't want you to? What then?"

"Willow, please. Grow up. This is important to all of us. If she has been conspiring against us, I must get to the bottom of it. If she's spying on us, reporting back, I have to figure out what damage control may be required."

"So, this weekend, while I'm suffering through my Family Retreat," she spat the last words out, her disgust evident, "you'll be sacrificing yourself in Jericho's bed?"

"Don't be ridiculous!"

Even as she glared at him and then turned to march away in silence, she knew she was acting like a child. But she did it anyway. She rushed up the transportation entranceway, using her portal to summon an air taxi.

By the time she reached the sanctuary of her room at home, her anger had simmered down. In her mind's eye, she could still picture him standing quietly in the dark street, watching her as she ran away, up the staircase to the taxi.

At that moment, she felt truly surrounded, at odds with everyone, defeated. How had her life gotten so complicated?

Her family was expecting something from her this weekend. She didn't know if she could deliver, still hadn't decided how to handle it. She dreaded what would happen when she had to face them all at once. Now she had the CRKA and even the Republic leaders watching her. When Craig had arrived yesterday, Sharon had let her go unexpectedly. She'd summoned the security escort immediately—but not without another hushed warning. Willow knew now, more than ever, that they were watching her every move—they, and someone else, some other group. She sensed it but could not put her finger on who or what they were. She wondered if this group had something to do with the messages on the world portal that evening, maybe it was the cult that Elzbeth had referenced in her journal.

Even the places, the people, that she thought were safe, were now in question for her. After her session with the Vision Speak leaders, Jill had made it clear she had to keep quiet about her emerging abilities. There were moments, now, when she wanted to close that aspect of herself off forever. Thus far, it had only brought her trouble.

And, now, the one truly bright light in her world—her passion for Aaron—was in jeopardy. If she'd been more seasoned, had experienced more lovers, perhaps she would have handled it differently. But, of course, she had probably just shown him that she was too young for him. Between their age difference and whatever he shared with the stunning Jericho—it was hopeless. For the first time in her life, she felt hatred towards another human being, actually wished the woman would just vanish.

It was a mess, everything was a mess. To top it all off, now her future was at risk, the future vocation she had planned and dreamed about all her life. To live in the Arts Community, to pursue her dreams—that was more important to her than any man. To think that she might be forced to live the life of a bureaucrat or, even worse, suddenly find herself 'disappearing' from society like her great uncle Roland had—was unbearable.

As her tormented thoughts reached a pinnacle, she felt the touch. It was the touch of that other presence, the one that she had been resisting for so long. Drifting into a wakeful sleep, she succumbed, finally surrendering.

Chapter 33

"Man is nothing but contradiction; the less he knows it, the more dupe he is."

Henri-Frédéric Amiel

Willow admired Sophie's new hair colour—a lovely autumn-gold shade with subtle, shimmering highlights. It flattered her so much more than the wacky, zebra stripes. In fact, glancing at her entire ensemble, she was struck by how tastefully Sophie was dressed. She wondered what on earth had come over her cousin.

The whole family had arrived on the island and the girls were getting settled into their cabin. They were all staying in a little community of cottages circling an outdoor recreation area, with seating, nets for gameplay, and a corner wet-bar, under a terrace. It was a short ten minute walk to the beach and there were paths leading in the other direction, deeper into the woods, where they would apparently be able to find numerous walking paths. It was a great place for the family retreat. All this and there was a conference facility on the grounds. Grandma Sybil had booked it for their special event the next day, Roland's closure ceremony.

A late dinner was to be served in the lodge so she and Sophie had just changed. Claire and Triska were in the same cabin but were sharing the other bedroom.

"Sophie, you look amazing, absolutely beautiful!" Willow meant it;

she'd never seen her looking better. She sat perched on the edge of her bed, her cousin standing directly in front of her. The bedroom was small but functional. The two of them had shared worse than this on family vacations, growing up. Unexpectedly, Willow was beginning to find the celebratory mood contagious. She was actually happy to be there with her family. Maybe it would be like old times—a fun family gathering without any of the undercurrents or pressure that she had been dreading.

Sophie beamed at the compliment. "Why, thank-you so much, Willow. You really like it? I wasn't sure at first. Of all the styles I've tried, this one seemed the most radical—at least for me." She gazed uncertainly into the full-length mirror in front of her, smoothing her hair back.

Willow laughed—a heart-felt laugh deep in her belly. She poked her in the arm. "Yes, Soph, I really, really like it…but where on earth did you ever come up with this?"

"Well, actually, it's this new guy I've been seeing. He suggested it or, rather, he told me some stuff that he liked and I thought I'd try it out."

"New guy? Since when? You never mentioned him before…"

"Never mentioned him? More like you just don't listen anymore!" Sophie turned away from her reflection to fix her gaze on Willow, emphasizing her point. "I've tried to tell you but you've just been too busy lately."

Willow heard the accusatory note in her voice, like a petulant child who'd been ignored. She'd always been so attentive to Sophie, interested in everything she did. Lately, well, she'd had an awful lot going on—but Sophie didn't understand that. "I'm sorry, Soph, honestly I am but you just can't imagine all the stuff I've had to deal with lately. I wish I could tell you but…"

"Oh, never mind about all that. Just tell me what's going on with you and Mr. Suave and Sophisticated—Aaron Braxton." Sophie giggled. Her eyes were focused on her image in the mirror again so she didn't see the expression on Willow's face at mention of Aaron. If she'd been watching, even self-centered Sophie wouldn't have missed the pain in her cousin's eyes.

Willow quickly squelched down her aching heart, pretended everything was alright. "Oh, there's not too much to tell really. We've gone out a couple of times—that's all. He is a bit old for me, you know?"

Something sounded strange to Sophie so she turned to ask another question but Willow interrupted. "Anyway, you're changing the subject. So who's the guy? Where did you meet him?"

Happy to be back talking about herself, she responded. "Oh, Willow, I met him at the Centre. Remember that dreamy guy I pointed out to you?" Willow nodded distantly, not sure. Sophie was always pointing out dreamy guys. "Anyway, that night you stood me up, I…"

"I stood you up?"

"Yes, you went off with Aaron, Jill and Simon, remember? Anyway, whatever. I've gotten over it because I approached him that night for the first time and ever since then…" She put her hands on her heart, silent for once as her thoughts turned inward to Charlie.

Willow smiled. "Oh, boy. You do have it bad, don't you?" A momentary stab of jealousy shot through her. Just a few days ago, she had imagined herself as foolishly in love as Sophie did now. How quickly everything could change, she thought to herself. "I'll have to meet this guy at the next session and check him out for myself."

"Okay but—I'll be watching you." Sophie laughed, sitting down on the bed beside Willow, setting her hands on her shoulder. "Actually, coz, you're not going to believe this but he might be here this weekend."

"Here?" Outside their window, Willow heard the shuffle of creatures, probably squirrels, climbing the branches of a large oak tree that shaded their cabin. She ignored them, her attention completely focused on Sophie.

"Yes, but don't tell anyone, okay? I don't want anyone else in the family to know."

"Uh, okay…but, what's he doing here?" Willow shifted sideways, leaning back on her hands, putting some distance between them so she could gaze into her cousin's eyes. Less made-up than usual, they were as beguiling as ever. No doubt, this new young man appreciated her cousin's beauty. Sophie released Willow's shoulder and dropped her hands into her lap.

"He said he already had plans to come here to meet his father. If he can sneak away, he's going to let me know and I told him I would bring you to meet him, okay?"

"Me? What do you want me for? Three's a crowd, you know."

"Yes, well, he wants to meet you." At Willow's inquisitive look, she continued. "I've told him a lot about you."

Just then the door burst open. Claire and Triska crowded into the doorway. The two of them were stunning. Claire was adorned in a figure-hugging lemon sundress; Triska, in scarlet.

"You two ready?" Claire demanded. "Let's head over to the hall. We're late for dinner and I'm starved."

They followed the signs pointing to the dining hall along a well-lit, winding trail. Michael caught up with them on the way, teasing Sophie about her 'new look'. Claire separated herself from Triska and walked along with Willow instead. Sophie and Triska ignored Michael and were chattering, something about ideas for their next hair-coloring expedition. They were completely absorbed and Willow was completely uninterested. She hadn't even noticed that Claire was not participating in the conversation.

"Willow, is everything okay with you?" Claire blurted out.

The concern in her sister's voice caught her attention. Willow turned her head abruptly, startled eyes gazing back into her sister's sincere ones. "Y-yes, of course. Why do you ask?" They maintained intermittent eye contact while walking steadily along behind the other two.

"Well, I know you've had a lot going on lately." She continued speaking when she saw Willow's face shadow. "Don't worry, I'm not trying to pry and find out all the gory details about Great Bet's journals. We'll leave that to the older generation." They shared a smile. "I'm seriously wondering what's going on with you. You seem so distant." She glanced sideways at Willow, squinting. "Even more than usual—and, I've been worried about you."

Willow grinned. Claire had always been perfect, her parents' dream daughter. A brilliant student with amazing organizational skills, motivated to follow in their father's footsteps in the Justice Department. On top of that, she was beautiful—tall, shapely figure, flawless, honey-gold complexion, eyes wide with long lashes—with a natural fashion sense. Willow glanced at her now. As usual, she looked great. She wore her casual summer dress with an elegance all her own.

Compared to her sister, Willow typically felt like a mess—freckle-faced, unruly hair, skinny. There had never been anything dramatic or terribly noticeable about her appearance. She never put any thought into her clothes or make-up, barely looking in the mirror after she cleaned herself in the morning. But, despite all this, Willow had never been jealous of Claire. Willow couldn't compete and had long ago decided not to bother trying. They simply did not share the same interests.

They walked together in sisterly harmony. She knew that their mother glowed with approval whenever she saw her eldest daughter—but, it wasn't Claire's beauty that made their father, Arild, so proud. It was her keen mind, her work ethic, her ambitions. Already, Claire had made great strides in her job as an investigator and Willow had heard her father publicly praise Claire on many occasions, suggesting that she would go far, farther than he ever would. Her chosen career was as foreign to her younger sister as her glamorous appearance.

The comment about Willow being distant was true. She'd always been in her own world, always been a little in awe, and in recent years, a bit disdainful of Claire but now, they gazed at each other with understanding. She sensed true feelings from her sister, not the shallow absorption with surface matters that she'd often assumed.

"I have to admit that you surprise me, Claire."

"Really, how so?"

"Maybe I've been unfair but I didn't think you paid enough attention to notice how distant I might be."

"Well, I admit that I gave up trying to understand you a long, long time ago." She laughed. "But that doesn't mean I don't care about you. You're my baby sister. Until recently, I thought you were just in your artsy dream world but lately, you've been beyond that, I think."

Willow flushed, giggling self-consciously. "Artsy dream world, huh? Okay, I'll take that." She swallowed, for the first time wishing that she could confide in her sister. Claire was so knowledgeable in the laws of the Republic, so even-keeled and pragmatic, so strong and assertive—she could even handle Grandma Sybil. If she could only share what was going on and get her big sister's advice, it might take a huge weight off her shoulders. "Oh, Claire, as usual, you're right. The last few months have been, uh, huge for me, life-changing. I so wish that I could tell you..." She trailed off.

"Willow, as I said before, I don't want to pry. Honestly, I'm not trying to push you to reveal confidences that you aren't ready for. I have to say, as well, that it's not just the journal and whatever happened with Great Bet that worries me." She paused for a moment as Triska called out for them to hurry up. They'd been lagging behind the others. "We're coming." She yelled out before continuing in a quieter voice. "It's the first time I've seen you date a guy like this Aaron. It's not just that he seems older but he's so different. He's tied into this Vision Speak stuff and you seem so, I don't know, involved, so quickly. Should I be worried? Are you really okay?"

"Don't worry, sis. I'll be fine." She lied, her eyes focused steadily down on the pathway ahead. At the mention of Aaron, her heart thudded loudly, her tongue heavy as lead. As much as she wished she could confide in Claire, she knew it was impossible.

The dining hall came into sight as they rounded a bend in the trail. Sophie and Triska were waiting and interrupted their discussion so Willow was spared having to answer her sister any further.

When they entered the dining area, they saw the rest of the family just starting to take their seats. The aroma of turkey filled the air, teasing their gurgling stomachs.

There weren't four seats together so they dispersed. Willow sat sandwiched in between Michael and her father. Seated across from her were the women—the ones she'd been hoping to avoid: her Grandma Sybil and her mother, Joley.

The private dining room was lovely with cedar paneling, high ceilings and huge windows overlooking greenery and a distant view of the lake—but the Tyler women had added their touches, including two large digital portraits. There was one of Elizabeth and Evan together and one of Roland, probably taken shortly before he disappeared. They were situated side by side on the mantle of a large fireplace. To Willow, they served as a reminder of what they expected of her, a sobering reminder in an otherwise festive evening.

The husbands of the dominant Tyler women had always been kindred spirits. Although generally more reserved than their partners, not one of them was a pushover. All were successful, respected men in their chosen profession. Arild Olsen was no exception. He'd achieved advisory status in his role with the Justice Department just last year. Willow found herself wondering about her father's and Claire's responsibilities. They must know something about the strange messages on the world portal. She hadn't had a chance to talk to either of them about it.

She was enjoying a quiet conversation with her father and Michael, the rest of the table forming a boisterous cocoon around them, when she decided to ask him. "Dad, were you and mom watching last night when the alleged lost scriptures were broadcast?"

"We were." Her father's jaw set into a grim angle. "It was a terrible awakening for my team, for all citizens really. It's a reminder that we must work even harder to keep dissidents and criminals from polluting our society."

"So it was released, somehow, by a group that is against the Republic? That would mean there's some kind of rebellion going on." Her voice shook, the tremor revealing her unease. "Do you know who did it, dad?"

"Oh, my dear, there's no rebellion." He reassured her. "Nothing so dramatic as all that, I promise you. Just some sick pranksters who have already been taken into custody. I expect that we will all hear a communication about it next week, explaining what has happened."

"Pranksters? But, I don't understand. Why would they do something like this? Surely not for a joke?"

Michael supported her point. "Really, Uncle Arild, it couldn't just have been a prank."

"Okay, kids, listen." He lowered his voice a notch, tilting his neck forward. His honest eyes inspired trust. His daughter and nephew felt a special kinship with him, as they huddled together, like they were part of his wise, inner circle. "I know you're both old enough now to understand some things. You're probably hearing all kinds of wild speculation about this at school. The Republic needs level-headed, loyal citizens like you to help calm the situation. Don't let crazy rumours disrupt our peaceful life—otherwise, these criminals will have won."

Willow and Michael leaned in to listen closely to Arild Olsen's soft voice. Their expressions were like mirrors—furrowed brows, eyes open wide and focused intently on the speaker. Willow's father had never confided in them about something as serious as this. They both respected him so they listened in earnest.

He continued. "For reasons of security, I cannot tell you any details about this case; however, I will say that you are correct, this is more than a prank. The people responsible for this are fanatics. Their beliefs are dangerous to our well-being and go against everything that the Republic, our Citizen's Code, and our Spiritual Centers stand for. Their only mission is to wreak havoc on our lives and we must not tolerate it. How they got into our systems and managed to do this, is something that many great minds are working out at this very moment but the hole has been plugged." He nodded his head, eyes narrowed and distant for a moment. "Yes, it has definitely been plugged."

"But who are they? How many of them are there?" Willow whispered the words so only the three of them could hear.

"Honey, don't even worry about it. Honestly. If we were to broadcast their name and announce details of their mission and their numbers—it would only give them the publicity that they seek. They shall remain nameless. I encourage you to help spread the word that it was nothing, a criminal act that has been punished."

Michael and Willow just stared at her father, each of them speechless as they digested his words. They didn't have a chance to ask anything further because at that moment their silence was interrupted by Grandma Sybil. "My goodness, you three look awfully serious over there." They jerked away from their huddle, abruptly leaning back into their seats. They gazed across the mounds of food at Sybil and Joley who were watching them. "Is everything okay?" Grandma Sybil asked.

Arild replied, "Of course, mother Sybil, everything is great. You and your daughters have, as usual, done an outstanding job with the preparations. The meal and the setting," he waved his arm to draw their eyes around the room, "everything is absolutely fabulous."

She smiled at her son-in-law, grateful for the acknowledgement. "Thank-you, Arild." Sybil reached over and patted Joley's hand beside her, gently. "I always said you made a good choice in life mates, my dear.

He's so very observant." They both chuckled and then Sybil turned her attention to her grand-daughter. "Willow, I do hope you are prepared for tomorrow? We're all counting on you."

Why did all the conversations at the table suddenly seem to stop? Willow wondered with irritation. A hush descended as she nodded carefully. "Yes, Grandma, I have completed some preparations but I need a bit more time. Do you know if there is somewhere I can work here in privacy, later tonight?"

"Of course, my dear. I can call Robert Benson, the Guest Services Manager, and arrange this for you. He has been absolutely fabulous and so charming. Do you want some help?"

"No, thanks." Willow turned back to continue her conversation with her father but he was otherwise engaged, talking to his brother-in-law about the weekend sporting plans.

Later that evening while her cousins were making merry around the campfire by their cabins, she would have to find a quiet place to think and decide what she was going to do for Uncle Roland's memorial.

Chapter 34

"It is a man's own mind, not his enemy or foe, that lures him to evil ways."

Buddha

Willow slouched in her seat at the far side of the room. Grandma Sybil shared her memories of Roland while a succession of images flashed behind her. The family had all come to the conference room after breakfast. Grandpa Bobby sat directly in front of his wife, Sybil, his stalwart support obvious from his posture. Her mother and aunts, coordinated in sea green and violet summer dresses, all sat together with their husbands in the front row, unblinking eyes fixed on the screen, as their mother spoke. Willow's cousins and sister, Claire, were scattered in seats behind the older generation, less attentive. Sophie, in particular, was fidgeting, her eyes glazed, glancing down at the portal unit in her lap from time to time. Willow thought she seemed in a dreamy, distracted state—no doubt fantasizing about her new beau.

"He was troubled in his later years," Sybil remarked, "but I remember a wonderfully spirited child, innocent and trusting. Roland was my baby brother and I adored him from the day he was born. Towards the end of primary school, I had some awkward years. Even though he was much younger, my brother would rush to my defense with no thought to his own welfare if I was teased. When I reached my dating years, he often be famous someday. I believed it too. He had such strength, such charisma at times."

Sybil paused in her speech, leaning down to control the presentation, launching a new series of images of Roland in his younger years. He had been a tall man with striking features—thick, black eyebrows and bushy hair, eyes dark green and intense, cheekbones angular and pronounced. A short video of the young siblings, Roland and Sybil, talking about their plans for a travel journey together was charming; the affection between the two, obvious.

Roland's wedding pictures were shown. Sybil continued. "Finally, though, he settled into his job and met dear Emma. They fell in love and married. She had such a calming influence on him. For years, he seemed to settle down. We were all so relieved, so happy that he had found a woman who would help him find his way in life. My parents, especially, were ecstatic with the union." She paused for a moment, gazing down at her husband. Grandpa Bobby sat in silence—as he so often did—watching his wife, waiting for direction. She motioned for him to join her.

Grandpa Bobby limped up to the stage, squeezing his wife's hand as he stood beside her to share the podium. He showed his age more than his wife did. He'd never bothered with hair or face treatments. Still, the two looked comfortable together in their family's eyes, somehow perfectly matched—the grey-haired man with deep wrinkles and casual, creased clothes and the perfectly groomed woman with jet black hair, vibrant, stylish attire and heavy make-up camouflaging her wrinkles. Grandpa Bobby spoke, his voice subdued. "Sybil has fond memories of her brother and has chosen to focus primarily on those in her sharing. There are other memories too—some are painful and have left many of us with disturbed thoughts about Roland and the path he chose to follow in life. Sybil felt it was important that we openly share our memories of this to find closure. She has asked that I speak frankly on my perspective of what happened before Roland disappeared and then Willow can share what she has learned from the journals." He smiled at his young grand-daughter who was sitting on her own in the front corner seat, shrinking into her chair.

"The time I've spent preparing for this, in recent weeks, has left me questioned boyfriends before my father even had a chance." She laughed then, tears forming in her eyes. She used a tissue to dab elegantly at the corners of her eyes. "When my first child was born—my darling Mela." She smiled at her daughter, seated directly in front of the podium. "He came to see me. He vowed to always watch out for her.

"He'd been an artist as a child but perhaps not as gifted as some who have come after him." Sybil glanced over at Willow briefly. "He wasn't granted entrance to the artist's community. This didn't surprise my parents but it was a terrible disappointment for Roland." She sucked in air, her knuckles white as she gripped the edges of the podium. "His pattern of self-destructive behaviour started to show then, I suppose. My parents attempted to prepare him for this likely rejection, reminding him constantly of the advice his teachers had given. They'd all tried to coax Roland to consider other vocations. He never listened and so when the rejection came, he took it poorly, as if it were a personal affront. Angry outbursts, particularly directed at the Republic and anyone who celebrated their PURE-assigned vocation, became commonplace. When he started his career at the media center, he connected with people who shared his views. Late nights and carousing consumed his free time.

"At the time I was mortified, even wondered if I had caused Roland's troubles." When Mela cried out that that couldn't possibly be so, she continued. "No, no, you don't understand. I had encouraged him for so long. When we were growing up, my mother was very busy with her career. She joined the ranks of the CRKA when we were quite young and she had to go where they sent her. Sometimes she would even be away for weeks—without warning. I suppose she was on important missions or something terribly urgent for the Republic. As children, it was hard for us to understand this. Roland was five years younger so I guess I took on the role of both big sister and surrogate mother. Perhaps I babied him, spoiled him…" She shook her head, her eyes distant. "It doesn't matter now but I've often wondered if it was my fault that he had so many disappointments later in life. I always tried to protect him. I'd make up stories about his future, told him that he was destined for great things in life. When he wanted to be an artist, I told him he should follow his dreams, not understanding that he lacked the talent. I told him he would heavy-hearted. Like many who knew him in the early days, I liked Roland. When Sybil and I first married, he spent a lot of time with us, always willing to help when we were starting our home together. He was at all of our gatherings—a real party animal although at that time harmless and entertaining. It's true that he occasionally overstepped, sometimes criticizing the Republic, flaunting his careless attitude towards authority but he was within the bounds of accepted behaviour. Everyone wanted Roland at their events then." The elderly couple grinned at each other. Grandpa Bobby turned back to his family. He cleared his throat and continued. "Later, however, his bitterness brimmed over and he stepped well over those boundaries."

Willow sat hunched in her chair, listening, staring up at the likeness of Roland on the screen as her Grandpa Bobby's gruff voice resonated in the small auditorium in the woods. She saw the same man from the previous pictures but in his late thirties now, with a harder edge to his features and a heavy frown line, his gaze unflinching and unsmiling. Her grandfather was relating the now familiar story of his final years, recounting the break-up of his childless marriage, his frustration and eventual severance with his vocation, incidents of fighting and rebellious, inflammatory actions. He mentioned warnings and demerit points—constant embarrassments to his family—and some twisted views on state and religious matters.

Soon it would be Willow's turn. Her least favourite place in the world was standing on a stage in front of people. She nibbled ferociously on her nails. Today, she not only had her usual fear of speaking in a crowd, she also had her family's reaction—yet again—to concern herself with. She had decided to tell them as much as she could. The problem was that she had not been able to find any 'safe' passages from the journals to help tell the story. She knew they all wanted to see Elzbeth's journals but too many of the references involving Roland's final months were intertwined with other sealed information. And these were stories that she was not prepared to share with her family—at least not yet. She dropped her head, mentally rehearsing the words she had planned.

"Willow!" Startled, she heard her mother's voice as if from a tunnel. Jerking her head around, she realized that her grandparents had finished and were waiting for her to come up to the podium to begin her portion of the memorial service.

"Do you need to connect to the journals?" her grandmother whispered when she stood beside them. When Willow shook her head, Grandma Sybil's eyes hardened, her features held rigidly in place. Sybil and Bobby exited the stage and took their seats in the front row. Her grandmother's expression hadn't changed since she'd taken her seat, her eyes locked onto Willow as she waited.

"It's, uh, a s-sad story about Uncle Roland." Willow stuttered as her mind searched for the right place to begin. "None of us, of the youngest generation," she waved her hand to encompass her sister and cousins who were all paying close attention now, "were born yet when he disappeared but we all heard about Uncle Roland. We all felt the loss of someone in the family."

Grandma Sybil couldn't keep silent. "Willow, that is very touching but are you not going to share from my mother's journals—the sections that tell of the events leading up to Roland's death?"

"Uh, I can't really. I'm sorry but they are all mixed up with other stories, information that I can't divulge."

"What! Are you saying that you are not going to tell us what happened?"

"No, Grandma, I'm not saying that. If you will just let me finish, I will tell you what I can about Roland. It's just that there are other passages that I simply cannot talk about, though."

"And why not?" Grandma Sybil's tone was ice cold and imperious.

Willow had had enough. Glancing about the room, she saw the rest of the family sitting back, eyes wide open as they followed the interchange between the shy granddaughter and the spitfire grandmother. Her nervousness gone, her voice rose, driven by sheer anger. She'd had enough of everyone pushing her around. "Aside from Great Bet's request and the fact that these are sealed entries, I have also been interrogated by the CRKA and the regional PURE Governor herself." There was a collective gasp in the room and several voices started to speak at once. Willow put her hand up. "Please everyone just let me finish and I'll tell you what I can. I shouldn't have mentioned the interrogation, although I need to say one thing about it. Unless I'm very careful, we risk losing Great Bet's journals forever, not to mention possible, unpleasant consequences for myself and anyone that I confide in."

Her father spoke up, concern evident in his voice. "Willow, my dear, we need to talk before you say anything further. You should have shared this with me before now but I will take care of you." He turned to glance at the group. "Let's take a break, everyone, please so I can discuss this with my daughter?"

Before she could respond, Grandma Sybil interrupted, sputtering. "What? Are you crazy? This is all a smoke screen so she can avoid sharing information that I have had a right to from the beginning. I should be the Protector, not this child. Don't you dare tell her to stop!"

Willow bristled. "Grandma Sybil, you're being ridiculous." The room fell into a hush. No one had ever seen her stand up to anyone like that before, especially not to the matriarch. "No doubt the reason your mother did not bequeath her journals to you is because you have absolutely no comprehension of the enormity of the responsibility. Her life mission was not about decorating the interior of people's homes." Her grandmother's faced turned a deep tomato red. Willow experienced a reflex guilt at demeaning her grandmother's life vocation. "I'm sorry. Perhaps that didn't come out right but can we just focus on Uncle Roland for the moment?"

"Please." Grandma Sybil murmured through lips sealed tightly together.

The room was silent, finally. Willow breathed deeply in and out, closing her eyes for a moment. A pulse beat rapidly in her temple. She felt the blood rushing up her cheeks, her face flush with emotion. She needed to calm herself before she continued. Already she had blurted out more than she'd planned, had confused the message she'd wanted to deliver. She opened her eyelids abruptly to face all twelve pairs of eyes focused right back at her. She straightened her back and gazed at her family calmly. Her voice even, she began again. "As I said, I never knew Uncle Roland but I've certainly heard the stories over the years. As Grandpa has just related, the last memories of him are of an angry man, one who opposed many of the ways of life that we follow. He seemed to be getting deeper and deeper into trouble and then, suddenly, Great Bet reported that he had died in an accident. Yet, no one understood why he would have been at the location of that accident nor why his mother refused to have a closure ceremony for him."

Sybil managed to speak again without opening her mouth. "Go on." She said.

"The truth about Uncle Roland—according to Great Bet's journal," Willow responded, "is that he wasn't in that accident and didn't die that day."

Grandma Sybil rose from her seat. "What—he didn't die in that accident? How could that be? What on earth happened to him then?" Her husband and daughters rose as well, crowding around her for support.

Willow backed away from the podium as she answered. "Great Bet and her team arrested him. He was taken into custody." Her grandmother cried out, clutching her hands against her cheeks as she stared at Willow. Grandpa Bobby and Aunt Mela stood on either side of her, holding her arms for support. Watching her grandmother's stunned expression, Willow knew that questions would follow which she simply could not answer. She glanced over at the door to the side of the stage with longing.

After Sybil had absorbed Willow's words, she asked, "What happened to him? Is he still alive?"

"I don't know, Grandma. I have no idea if he is alive or dead. Great Bet was tormented by this, as you can imagine. She did manage to save his life—he would have been executed—but he was permanently removed from society and sent overseas to a prison work camp. Even she wasn't able to keep track of him once he was taken away."

She'd told them all she could—perhaps more than she should have. Before the next round of questions, she had to escape to gather her thoughts. Willow stepped sideways, inching her way towards the door.

Sophie must have sensed her need because she lunged out of her seat. She was beside Willow, pulling her towards the door. "Come on, Willow. Let's get out of here." Turning to the family, Sophie announced. "You've got what you wanted out of her. Now she needs a break so just leave her alone."

No one said a word as the two girls walked out the door. Willow followed blindly as Sophie pulled her onto a trail leading into the woods. The sun was hot as it streamed through the trees, shining down on their young, flowing hair. Birds chirped obnoxiously, beckoning them forward as they wandered down the path in the forest, the distance growing rapidly between them and the distressed family they had just left behind.

Chapter 35

"No one can conquer an enemy without coming in sight of him."

Emanuel Swedenborg

The heat was oppressive. As Willow followed Sophie down a well-worn trail, twisting amongst the lush green forest in the center of the island, they occasionally stepped onto footbridges, saving them the necessity to leap over the tiny creek that wound over their path. The trees offered welcome shade at intervals along the way but still it was hot. There was no wind, not even a light breeze, just heavy, humid sweltering heat. Summer had started early and with a vengeance.

They walked in silence for some time. Willow wasn't inclined to talk and for once, Sophie seemed to feel the same way. She was content to have Sophie lead her away, her cousin's natural bossiness taking charge. She simply followed. She didn't even ask, didn't even wonder, where they were going—at least not for a while, not until it was too late.

A steady buzz, from insects or birds, she thought, permeated the air. In the distance, her deadened senses absently noted the sounds of water, the gentle lapping of waves on the shore; yet, as they traipsed along, all she could see was the thick foliage of the forest. A bead of sweat dripped slowly from her temple down the side of her jaw. She wiped it away, triggering a sudden desire to find the lake and dive in, enclosing her face and body in cool, refreshing water. She stopped abruptly and reached for Sophie. They stood facing each other, alone in the woods. "Sophie, where on earth are we going?"

"Uh, well, I thought you'd want to get away from everyone for a bit."

"I did, I mean I do. Thanks. But, we don't need to just aimlessly wander off into the unknown forest here." She spread her arms about to showcase the greenery surrounding them. "Why don't we head back, grab our swimsuits and instead find a beach where we can hide from them, preferably underwater?" She shoved sticky, wet trendrils of hair off her forehead, forming a messy, clump of sweaty curls at the top of her head. "Man, is it hot out here."

"Sure, sounds like a great idea Willow, but first…" She peered down the path ahead of them, squinting. They were standing in the light, a small break in the tree cover, before a dark, deep section of woods. "Can we go just a bit further? Charlie told me to head out this way if we got a chance. I think we're getting very close to where they're staying."

"Charlie? You think you're going to find him in these woods? Are you kidding me?" Willow's moist, drowsy lids opened wide.

Sophie looped her arm into the crook of Willow's elbow, pulling her along companionably. "I know it sounds crazy but this is where he told me to go. Come on, let's just follow the path a little further and then if we don't find him, we'll head back."

Willow ambled alongside her cousin, pushing aside the cobwebs that had been blocking her usual perceptions. She'd been so distracted that she hadn't paid much attention to Sophie or anything else that was going on around her. On reflection, she now recognized Sophie's purposeful actions, her determined stance. It was almost as if she had planned everything in advance, even extracting Willow from the family confrontation. But how could she know that their gathering would break down the way it had? As they stepped into the deeper woods, Willow felt a minor relief from the heat and smiled. It was probably an easy bet that there was going to be some kind of scene, she thought to herself. Sophie didn't need predictive skills to figure that out.

They walked in silence, single-file when the path narrowed, for another ten minutes. The coolness of the woods was a welcome respite.

The tree growth was so heavy that Willow could no longer hear the sound of the water. Finally, they came around yet another curve, Sophie slowed down, reaching back to grab Willow's arm with her left hand as she pointed forward with the right. "Look at that."

Willow blinked. At first glance, it had appeared to simply be a mound, a small hill on the side of the path, surrounded by thick, unkempt shrubbery. Arm in arm, the girls walked carefully over to it and circled the structure. On closer inspection, it looked like a small hut. When they reached the side facing opposite to the pathway, a concealed wooden door—or a surprisingly well-engineered facsimile—opened and a grinning man with a dark complexion emerged. Willow recognized him immediately from the Center even without Sophie's enthusiastic greeting. He was the young man that she'd noticed staring at her on several occasions.

She watched as he hugged her cousin who squealed with delight. "Charlie, my goodness, this is quite a secretive little place you have here. What is this, anyway?" Sophie cupped his head with her hands and kissed him soundly on the lips, giving him no chance to reply. Willow saw the coppery brown skin of his cheeks shimmer with a blush as he returned her kiss furtively and then quickly broke their embrace. He moved to stand beside Sophie and extended his hand in greeting to Willow.

She made eye contact with the young man that Sophie was smitten with, gazing up at him. Her instincts were on alert. Something was not right. He was tall and lean, attractive in a Sophie-kind-of-way: brown skin, chiseled jaw line and square chin, soft brown eyes, round cheeks. Sophie loved to play the seductress, was often attracted to innocent young men who were less experienced. He averted his eyes from Willow's examination, apparently unnerved by her penetrating stare. In that brief moment, she sensed him. The boy was shy, nervous, uncertain—that was easy to read—but, more alarming than that, he was deceiving them. "Nice to meet you, Charlie. Sophie has been telling me about you." She shook his hand.

Before she could explore her instincts, the door below them creaked further open. An older man, short and balding, with thick, black eyebrows and piercing eyes stood in the entranceway. His stocky body was covered by a long, charcoal-grey robe. He beckoned for them to come in. "Charlie, don't be so rude. Please, invite your guests in."

Sophie smiled warmly after her initial surprise and walked forward toward the door, extending her hand in introduction to the stout man. Suddenly, he reached for her hand and yanked her inside. Willow began to back away but the man made a simple motion with his left hand and two robed figures grabbed Willow by an elbow, lifted her off the ground, carried her down the small ramp and inside the structure. She'd barely begun to struggle, fighting to break their hold on her, when the door closed firmly behind them.

Once inside and planted on the ground, she turned to escape but the two men in black hooded robes pushed her forward and stood guarding the exit door. She and Sophie darted glances at each other, almost too shocked to be frightened, as they found themselves standing in the middle of a domed entranceway, with no windows or outside light, just a dim electric bulb on the ceiling. The walls were dark plaster with no adornments and there was an open door leading to a long, downward staircase directly ahead. Charlie and his three companions stood on either side of the staircase, facing them.

"Charlie, what the hell is going on?" Sophie demanded.

This was followed swiftly by Willow's command. "Let us out of here."

The two men stood tall and straight, their faces dark masks of rigidity, as they gazed at the girls. The older, uglier man simply crossed his arms and shook his head.

Charlie glanced at Sophie, a glimmer of apology in his eyes before he closed the shutters, freezing her out. "I'm sorry but we can't do that."

Goose pimples prickled up Willow's neck. Her eyes darted back and forth between the men, realizing they could not possibly fight their way out. "Who are you? What do you want from us?" Willow demanded, struggling to keep the panic from her voice.

The ugly man focused his attention on Willow when he responded. "The leader will meet with you soon. You may get some answers then." Waving his arm towards the staircase in the manner of a concierge, he indicated that they should proceed down the stairs.

When they hesitated, the two robed men reached for them, clearly prepared to force them to comply. In unison, the girls scurried towards the dark stairs, avoiding the men's grasp but heading deeper into their prison.

Chapter 36

"Love is ever the beginning of knowledge, as fire is of light."

Thomas Carlyle

When they had exhausted the topic of Roland—for over an hour after Willow and Sophie left—the family went directly from the auditorium to the dining hall to enjoy lunch in artificially cool air before returning to their cabins. By the time they'd all changed into beach wear, the afternoon sun had reached its height. The temperature, coupled with the humidity, made any activity outside uncomfortable. They were all anxious to get to the lakefront and immerse themselves in the cool water. Even Sybil had finally dropped the subject of Roland and what might have become of him, instead expressing her longing for the crisp refreshment of the lake.

They'd half expected Sophie and Willow to join them for lunch. When there was no sign of them at the dining hall, no one was alarmed. Now, they were all gathered in the common area between their cabins after changing. For the first time, questions were voiced aloud about the girls' absence.

Joley murmured to Arild, out of earshot of her mother. "Where could she be? I know she was upset and probably needed some time on her own but it's not like her to disappear like this."

He nodded his agreement. "Yes, I've been wondering too." He motioned towards her siblings who were already on the path. "You go ahead with everyone else and I'll see if I can track her down. Send me a message if you see her at the beach."

When the rest of them were sauntering along the path leading to the beach, Arild held back and asked Claire to check the girls' room. "See if there is any evidence that they returned to change into their swimsuits." He requested.

Michael stayed behind as well. He stood silently behind his Uncle Arild, waiting to hear what Claire discovered.

Claire rushed back outside just moments after she'd entered the cabin. "Dad, their stuff is gone." Her voice wavered as she gulped in hot, stifling air. She'd barely breathed between the instant that she'd discovered her sister's belongings gone and run out to share the news.

"What?" Arild exploded. He glared at his older daughter for an instant, absorbing her words and her facial expression, before he strode into the cabin himself. The others followed and soon the three of them were sandwiched into the small room that Willow and Sophie had shared.

"We didn't even look in their room. The door was closed when we came in to get changed." Claire murmured. She lifted a pillow on one of the beds, as if expecting to find their suitcases hidden beneath.

"I can't believe they would just take off like that." Michael inclined his head to the side, his face scrunched into perplexity lines. "I mean, I know it was intense back there but to just leave…"

"It doesn't make any sense," said Claire. "It's not like Willow at all to just leave, take off." She raised a finger to her chin, a realization occurring to her. "Although, she is with Sophie, remember."

They laughed at that. Everyone knew that Sophie would leave on a moment's notice if provoked. It just wasn't what they expected from Willow.

"What do you think, Uncle Arild? Where could they have gone?" Michael gazed up at the older man. He would know what to do.

"Well, I'm stymied by this, Michael. The last thing I expected Claire to say was that they had packed all their stuff and moved out." Worry lines on his forehead deepened, shadowing an otherwise kindly, smooth face. "I don't want to over-react. I know she's been under a tremendous amount of pressure and maybe this was just the last straw." Arild Olsen shook his head. "You know, the more I think about it, I don't blame her actually. Still, I need to make sure she did leave the island and is safely on her way home."

Claire pulled out her portal unit. "Here, why don't I try to reach her? I'll just ask her what's up."

"Yes, good idea, honey." He sat down on the closest bed, the one he imagined Willow sleeping in last night. He stretched back, leaning his weight on his hands stretched behind him while he waited. "After you talk to her, pass her to me, okay?"

Claire tried to contact Willow, first by voice and then by sending a message but both attempts received the same response. She had disconnected herself from the world portal. Michael reached into his beach bag and pulled out his unit. He tried Sophie but got the same result.

"Now, that is odd." Claire remarked, sitting down on the bed opposite her father. "She's never done that before. They must really want to be left alone."

Arild stood up, his jaw square, mouth sealed tight as he decided on next steps. "Alright," he said. "You two go ahead down to the beach. I'm going to speak to the manager and see if I can find out where they went."

He was already at the door when Claire jumped up. "I'm coming with you, Dad."

"Yes, me too, Uncle Arild." Michael followed closely behind Claire.

So he waited while they pulled light clothes over their swimming attire. They proceeded out of the cabin and down the pathway to the main lodge.

When they reached the lobby, it was crowded. The attendants were occupied serving other guests of the retreat. Impatient, Arild proceeded to the manager, Robert Benson's private office down a short hallway to the left of reception. His entourage followed closely behind. He pounded on the door but received only silence in return. He reached down to try the access knob.

"Can I help you?" A small voice interrupted his attempted break-in. The man was short and skinny. He looked too old for the workforce but he was dressed in the professional uniform of the Retreat service attendants.

They surrounded the slight man. "Yes." Arild responded. "Where is Mr. Benson?"

"He's not available at the moment. Perhaps I can be of assistance, Mr. Olsen?"

Arild raised his eyebrows. "You know who I am?"

"Oh, yes, of course. We know all about your group. We were briefed on your visit and told to treat you to the absolute best care."

"Really?" He cleared his throat. "Well, then I hope you can help us find out where my daughter and niece have gone."

"Your daughter? You mean Willow?"

"Yes, and her cousin Sophie. They seem to have taken their bags and disappeared."

"Oh, yes, of course. The two young ladies left a couple of hours ago. I escorted them to the air car myself."

"You did?"

"Yes, sir, I did."

"And where were they going?"

"They said they were going home. Something had come up that required their immediate departure."

"And you didn't question this? You just sent them off on their own?"

"Uh, I understood they are both now of adult age. Is that not correct?"

"Right. Yes, they are."

"Then I had no reason to stop them."

"No, of course not." Arild paused, glancing back at the young people who were watching the interchange in silence.

Claire spoke up. "Can you tell us what time they left?"

"It was just before the lunch hour, I believe."

"We'd like to speak to the pilot. Is he here?" Arild interrupted, his voice crisp.

The assistant stammered. "Uh, I-I'm not sure." He pulled his portal unit from his hip. After a few keystrokes, he looked back up, addressing the group. "It looks like he just left the island but certainly you can speak with him. We'll arrange something as soon as he returns."

"When will that be?"

"Tomorrow."

After the old attendant had scurried away, they walked slowly back through the lobby. A large group gathered by the desk, apparently checking in. There was a loud buzz of conversation echoing between that group and some others in the corner, so they exited the building and huddled outside, deliberating on next steps.

"It's hard to believe that they just packed and left," remarked Michael.

"Unbelievable," agreed Claire.

Arild said nothing but his furrowed brow spoke volumes. He was concerned.

"What if something else really happened?" Michael's voice was low, tentative.

Arild placed his hand on Michael's shoulder. "What do you mean, son?"

"Uncle Arild, I can't help but remember what Willow said this morning. You know, about being interrogated and possible 'unpleasant circumstances' for her. You don't think she could have been taken into custody just like poor Uncle Roland, do you?" His voice quivered at the end.

Arild and his daughter Claire both jerked their heads back at the question. Matching, shrewd eyes narrowed across the group in silent communication.

Arild said, "n-no, it can't be that, Michael." He shook his head firmly, trying to convince himself as much as anyone, his gaze rooted on Claire as he spoke.

She made a quick decision. "Dad, I'll go back. I'll check at home and then go to the office to see if there's anything going on. If they've gone back, I'll find them."

Arild nodded slowly. "Yes, yes. It's a good idea. I'm sorry to cut your retreat time short, honey, but if you can do that, I'll stay here and wait for Mr. Benson to return. I have a few questions for him." His face set in grim lines, hidden wrinkles becoming prominent. He opened his portal unit. "I'll pull in a favour and get the Justice Department Copter here for you." He motioned for them to start walking. "You'd better go pack."

Chapter 37

"Holding on to anger is like grasping a hot coal with the intent of throwing it at someone else; you are the one who gets burned."

Buddha

"Sophie, you've got to calm down."

Sophie whirled from her position by the door—where she had been screaming and pounding her fists—to face her cousin. "Calm down? Are you kidding me?" Her tear-streaked, make-up smudged face and wild, bedraggled hair might have struck Willow as comical if they'd been home, safe. But they weren't and, for once, Sophie's dramatics had good cause.

"No, I'm not kidding. Believe me—I'm as upset and frightened as you are about this." They'd been trapped alone in the dark bedroom in the underground tunnel for well over an hour and still no one had told them anything or answered any of their calls. "But the only thing you're accomplishing right now is making your voice hoarse and your hands bruised." She glanced at the cuts on her cousin's knuckles and shook her head. Willow was seated on a small bed on one side of the minimally furnished room. There was another single bed on the other side and a door to a small washroom, with no windows, accessible between the two beds. A dim light shone from the ceiling.

Willow had been hunched on the bed in silence, chewing her nails while Sophie raged. Willow had been alternating between panic and reliving everything they'd said, wondering what was going on. Were they government agents? Was it because of what she'd said to her family? But, no, these people could not possibly work for the Governor's office. Could it be the cult? She smoothed the finger on her right hand where she'd cut the skin with her intense nibbling. She'd accomplished as much as Sophie had in the past hour. Nothing.

She stood up and went to her distraught cousin. "Sophie, honey, please," she reached for her hands, running soothing fingers over the battered knuckles, "please, come sit down with me and listen. If you help me, I might have a way to find out what's going on." Pulling her emotionally exhausted cousin to the bed, she propped up the pillows so they could both sit back against the wall. Their knees formed angles as they leaned toward each other so they could talk quietly.

Sophie drew a deep breath, remnants from her sobs apparent in her shuddering. "How could he do this?" She moaned. "I th-thought he loved me. How could he be so cruel?"

"Oh boy, don't go there now." Willow forced a gentle smile. "I'm sorry, Soph. Obviously, there's much more going on here than whatever went on with you and Charlie. He's probably as much a pawn in this game as you are."

"A pawn—what do you mean by that?" Even in her misery, she managed a note of indignation.

"Shh. Listen to me. Do you remember the meditation exercises that we've been doing in sessions?"

"Huh? Yeah but this is hardly the time to meditate." Sophie crossed her arms, staring at her cousin.

"Actually, it's the perfect time. Trust me. I need you to do the deep breathing." At Sophie's stubborn stare and rigid posture, Willow reached over and uncrossed the other girl's arms, holding both of her hands. "Sophie, please, you have to trust me. I might be able to reach out into the minds of those that have captured us if you will just cooperate." She ignored the disbelieving eyes. "Here, I'll breathe with you." Willow began the breathing, counting as their session leader had, and eventually Sophie followed, relaxing quickly, her emotions spent.

With Sophie's mind and voice temporarily at ease, Willow focused inward, able to move beyond, the walls no longer containing her as she sought for others who were nearby.

She sensed the presence of two guards outside their door. They were men. Both were relieved that Sophie had quieted down. One man, in particular, had imagined performing violent acts on her if she had not stopped. His anger was still simmering. The other was calm and peaceful. He was reciting a prayer, of sorts, in his mind. She sensed a deep piety in this man. He believed intensely that what he was doing served a higher purpose. And, there was something else. He was excited, practically in rapture. Capturing them—no, it was really just Willow that concerned them—capturing Willow, signified the beginning of some glorious event for him. Actually, it seemed to be an odd combination of glorious and foreboding—for there was something dangerous, something that could mean disaster for many, in his imaginings of what would come next.

His adulation was primarily centered on two individuals, she saw the hazy images—an older man, cloaked in flowing robes and a young man, practically a boy. She was sure it was the boy she'd been dreaming about, the one she'd sketched. She had felt his presence before but not now. Where was he?

Moving away from the guards, she concentrated still more, seeking others who dwelt in their underground world. She found four others, with similar emotions to the pious guard, who were together. One of them was Sophie's Charlie and she sensed the depth of his commitment, his beliefs. He had thoughts of Sophie, fleeting sensations of guilt, remorse, even desire but none would overcome his intense belief that what he had done was right; that the future they were fighting for was the ultimate goal, the righteous end.

She shuddered. How could a group of people all believe so completely in such a hideous fate? It was twisted and frightening. Yes, this must be the cult.

Based on the rhythm of their minds, she assumed Charlie and the three men were discoursing quietly amongst themselves, waiting for direction. It was clear that none of them were in charge. None had ordered that Willow and Sophie be captured. None would be the ones to make decisions about their fate. Although Charlie was the most idealistic, all of them had similar revered images of their leader—and of their messiah, the man-boy. They would follow them both to their death. This she sensed strongly, shivering as she realized that no amount of sympathy for Willow or her cousin would help them with this group.

Breathing deeply, in and out, she calmed herself, preparing to find the ones who held her captive. She checked on Sophie first. Her cousin was in a semi-conscious state which Willow had coaxed her into. She was safe and relaxed for the moment.

It took her some time. She floated in the space she had found most effective for seeking gently outwards. She floated past the others again, and another group who were insignificant, meditating in another area. She'd picked up from them that there was an important meeting in progress, with the High Priest and his council.

It did not take her long to find them. They were apparently even applying Vision Speak in their meeting. Some of their communications were non-verbal but they managed it in a way that she could not easily read them. Willow thought that they must have developed techniques for secure interactions.

Her gentle probing yielded no results. These men were masters in Vision Speak, apparently knew how to guard themselves. She would have to push harder. She had to find out their plans, what they were going to do to her and Sophie, why they had imprisoned them. Gulping down the panic that lay on the other side of consciousness, she sought her inner resources. Great Bet had told her, over and over, that no matter what went on in her physical existence, she could always return to this inner peaceful world. From there she could launch out to anywhere. From this place, she had found unknown reserves of strength. She still did not understand why it was so easy for her to reach this haven and so elusive for others but she had gradually been realizing her gift, gaining confidence.

She lost track of her physical surroundings, delving deeper, preparing to mentally force herself into their meeting, regardless of the risk. She knew now that it would be impossible to surreptitiously access their inner images. She had to push her limits, beyond anywhere she had ever been before, or she and Sophie would be at the mercy of this fanatical group and their insane mission.

Chapter 38

"You can kill a thousand; you can bring an end to life; you cannot kill an idea."

Shimon Peres

People were streaming into the Square from all directions, drawn to the sounds and growing crowd. In the center of the square, down in the pit where the festival would begin in a few short days, there stood a group of four. They were in vivid orange costumes. The four stood in the center, their backs forming a square so they could face the crowd on all sides. Their faces were painted white, eyes ringed in black. They spoke in unison, repeating themselves, chanting, almost a song.

"What is the truth?
How can we continue?—until we know the truth,
We are spoon fed our religions,
told what we can and cannot do,
how we can and cannot practice, believe, think
What is the truth?
What are these long-buried words of the prophets?
What more has been hidden?
We must band together, we must seek the truth,
Or will you behave like sheep,

blindly do their bidding
Believe their lies?
What is the truth?"

They were mesmerizing—their still vibrant figures, white faces, the circular verse, the melodic chanting. Somehow their words were broadcast to the crowd via the speakers on the four corners so that anyone could hear them once they entered the amphitheatre-like square. After a time, some people joined them in the center, chanting with them. A few left in fear or disgust, but many stayed and watched. The crowd continued to grow.

Finally, the PURE security team arrived. They descended from all four sides of the square in synchronized motion. The speaker system stopped broadcasting the chant. Instead there was a single voice. "Clear the area and return to your homes or face charges."

The security team nudged the outer crowds away, telling them to go home, threatening demerits. Most of the outer group left quietly. As the team descended, there was more reluctance. Some scurried down, hiding deep amongst the people huddled around the chanting four at the bottom. The four did not move or stop their words, seemingly oblivious to the activity around them. Many followed their lead and chanted, even louder. The sounds of the chanting voices echoed eerily in the square.

Sharon and Craig watched the proceedings in the Square on the large screen in their office, rooted to their seats, speechless for minutes that seemed like hours.

"Craig, this is unacceptable. We have been forced into heavy-handed actions in a public forum." She gripped her fingers together, forming a bridge to cradle her distraught face, elbows on the desk supporting the weight of her head. Her mind was racing but her words came out quietly. "We've maintained the balance for so long. How can this be happening now, so fast?"

Craig shook his head, his eyes echoing her concern. "Who could be responsible for this? Could it be the cult?"

"The CRKA is still investigating but there has been activity similar to this in four other cities." She replied. "They're sure it's related to the hijacking of the world portal."

"Yes. It's too coincidental otherwise but I suspect we'll get as much out of these four," he waved his hand toward the screen in disgust, "as we did out of the others we captured in that incident. The two remaining prisoners from the portal incident, who we prevented from suicide wouldn't divulge anything, even under extreme torture."

"We must make them talk." Sharon insisted. "We have to get to the bottom of this quickly or who knows how it will escalate."

"Yes, I agree, but how?"

"Perhaps it's time to pull in all the imposters. We know that there are hundreds in our city alone who have registered with the Spiritual Center under an assumed identity. We allow them to register falsely so we can secretly keep track of their activities but, with everything happening now, we must not be tracking them well enough. If we arrest all current imposters, we could perhaps do a clean sweep of the dissidents in our region." Her voice trailed off at the end. The suggestion was weak and she knew it.

"Sharon, if we did something that drastic right now with all the attention they've generated—it could be disastrous." He waved his arm towards the window, disgust evident in his eyes. "These people may not even be the imposters. They could be accredited citizens of this region. There have been similar incidents in other regions but our remote colleagues are also stymied—although, everyone is beginning to come to the same conclusion."

"That the Cult of Armageddon is responsible?"

"Yes."

She nodded, her face grim yet suddenly thoughtful. Sharon released her hands and rose from her chair, pacing the room, as they both watched the security team finally disperse the crowd. Before it was over, they had arrested over twenty people. This was an unheard of number to bring into custody in one day, let alone one instance. The four had been successful in rousing the crowd. Unbelievably successful.

"Craig." She said his name, stopping in her tracks, her eyes steady on him. His steely gray hair and lined face usually gave him the appearance of granite strength. At that moment, she only noticed that he was aging.

"Sharon," he replied, smiling for the first time that day.

"I just thought of something." She swallowed before continuing. "There might be a way to get information from these people even if they won't say a word."

"Really? Do tell."

"It just occurred to me that, well, I know someone who can get inside their heads."

"Inside their heads?"

She sighed and returned to her seat. Decisively, before she could change her mind, she reached for his hand. Her grip was firm. Her eyes captured his. "I have some things to tell you, Craig. I see now that there may be a relationship to my past."

He raised his eyebrows, silent, waiting.

"Please listen to everything before you respond. Craig, I hope you understand why I've kept this secret for so long." She took a deep breath, watching his reaction, before she began.

Craig released his hand from Sharon's tight grip, squeezing it into a fist. With his lips pressed together, he stared at his partner in life and politics; the platinum blonde dynamo he had joined with so many years ago. He pounded his fist on the table and glared at her.

"Just tell me, Sharon. You've already waited too long. There's a lot more at stake here than keeping your precious secrets."

Chapter 39

"Those who fear the dissident are those who have a vested interest in the maintenance of that order."

Jean Vanier

From their vantage point on the couch, Simon and Jill watched Aaron pace back and forth across the room, his feet thudding on the floor pads. His living area was small and sparsely furnished with a large window to the right of the couch-dwellers. The size of the room necessitated sharp turns every few seconds. Aaron's rapid pacing in the small room might later be considered ridiculous, comical even, but at that moment the two on the couch remained silent, sensing his need to sort through his muddled thoughts.

Oblivious to his audience, he thought about his date with Jericho, frustrated with his unsuccessful attempt to probe her for answers. At the end of the evening, he had rebuffed her sexual advances, miserably wondering what Willow was doing.

He'd decided to leave Willow alone for the weekend, to give her a chance to be with her family and to think, hopefully to come to her senses. Of course his assumption had been that she'd realize her foolishness and come home remorseful by the end of the weekend. His confidence had begun to wane. He'd expected some message from her by now, anything to indicate she was sorry and wanted to see him when she got back. But, there'd been nothing. Even before Simon's call, he'd been on the verge of calling her. It wasn't just that he craved her physically—although he certainly did that. It was also that her abandonment, her anger at him, had left him disoriented and more alone than he'd ever felt.

He'd spent most of the day paralyzed, uncertain of what to do. Before he knew how the time had passed, it had been late afternoon, the hot sun beating down outside. Rather than buzzing about the city in the glorious sunshine, seeking luxury items that his earned credits might acquire, he'd been absorbed with thoughts of Willow. He expected she would return that evening. Finally, Simon interrupted his obsessive thoughts with an urgent call requesting to speak with both him and Jill.

When the three of them gathered in Aaron's small living area, Simon told them about Elizabeth's time-delayed message including the possibility that Willow might need protection. Simon had been meditating for days on what to do. Last night, a growing certainty that the time to act was upon them had caused him to request this meeting.

The news had literally knocked Aaron in the gut. Thus far, he'd been unable to utter anything intelligent while his companions helplessly watched him, sensing his distress. He was rethinking everything that had occurred with her in this new light.

He stopped mid-stride, facing the couch. He opened his mouth to speak but had barely uttered the first syllable—"Wha"—when the automated greeter in his building announced a visitor.

"A young lady, Ms. Olsen, is on her way up to see you, Mr. Braxton." The robotic voice spoke in a clipped, nasal tone.

The three locked eyes for seconds before rushing towards the entrance. Aaron's pulse sped up, beating hard. She was here to see him. The attendant's words had a heavenly quality to them: "Ms. Olsen is on her way." He pressed the keypad by the door so that it slid open. They stood in the doorway waiting for her arrival.

It seemed an eternity. In fact, it was less than a minute but to Aaron and his hammering pulse, time froze while he waited to catch sight of her long, wavy golden hair. Already he was pondering how he would get rid of Simon and his mother after she arrived. His plans for her required no speech and no audience. Everything else could wait.

They heard her soft footsteps walking along the perpendicular corridor before she came into view. When she turned the corner, they all drew in a breath.

The raven-haired beauty might have attracted him a month ago—but not now. His heart dropped to his knees as he murmured, "It's not Willow."

Simon leaned into him from behind, whispering in his ear. "Who is that?" Before Aaron could respond, she was standing directly in front of them. They stood crowded in the doorway, staring at her, blocking her entrance.

"Well, this is quite a welcoming committee," she said, irony dripping from her smooth voice. "Are you going to invite me in and introduce me to your guests, Aaron?"

Aaron recovered quickly. "Of course, Claire." They stepped back so she could enter. He introduced them. "Claire—this is my mother, Jill, and Simon LaChance." He motioned from Claire to each of them in turn. "Mother, Simon, this is Willow's sister, Claire."

They held each other's arms, crossed in greeting. Simon's eyes remained steadfast on Claire. She ignored his unwavering stare. Perhaps she was used to men watching her. "You're really her sister?" Simon asked the question, as if he doubted Aaron's words.

"Yes, I'm her sister." She nodded, thick, stylish red hair bobbing. "Do you know Willow?"

Aaron suggested they should all come into the living area where they could talk more comfortably. As they moved into the room, he answered for Simon. "Yes, Claire. Both Jill and Simon are well acquainted with your sister. They, along with me, are the council representatives for Vision Speak."

"Really?" She murmured, choosing to sit in a solitary chair to the side rather than huddle too closely with them on the sofa.

"Yes, in fact, we thought you were Willow when they announced Ms. Olsen." Simon spoke up as he sat heavily down on the couch, sitting on the side closest to Claire whose back was now to the window.

Aaron grabbed a small, portable stool from the corner and pulled it up against the table so he could face them all at eye level.

"Are you expecting her?" Claire's voice raised a decibel. For the first time, she betrayed a glimmer of emotion. "Have you heard from her?"

Aaron's head snapped back. His brow folded in puzzlement as he gazed first at her and then at his companions.

At their silence, she spoke again. "Well? Have you heard from her?"

Aaron responded. "Claire—I don't understand. What are you doing here? I thought your whole family was away for the weekend at the Island Retreat?"

"Y-yes, we were. I mean, we are or rather, they are." She stuttered. It struck Aaron as unusual for the confident, self-possessed, bronze beauty.

"Well, why aren't you there? Isn't Willow at the Island Retreat?"

"She was." Claire nodded. "But, hey, you said you thought I was Willow so have you heard from her? Do you know where she is?"

Aaron gulped down his frustration. "I haven't talked to her in a couple of days." He said. "What's going on, Claire? What do you mean she was there? Did she come back?" As he fired out the questions, it occurred to him for the first time, that it was rather odd that Claire had stopped by. How did she even know where he lived? He'd been so surprised to see her at first that he hadn't thought much about it.

"Well, yes, I think she did. I was hoping you would know where she is, actually."

"You think she did? In the name of Marrisha, what is going on?" Aaron demanded.

Aaron, Simon and Jill were staring at Claire, disbelief evident in their eyes, concern forming on their brows. She could see that they spoke the truth. They had not heard from her sister but what now? Should she confide in them, enlist their help? She hesitated as she considered her next move.

At her silence, Aaron exploded. "Claire. Tell me what's going on. Now!" He stood up abruptly, his small stool making an irritating clatter as he knocked it over.

Claire's eyes widened, her lips pursed, as she watched Aaron's violent reaction.

Jill intervened. "Aaron, my dear, sit down." She spoke softly, watching as her son obeyed, quietly sitting after lifting the fallen stool. She turned to Claire. "My dear, I apologize for my son's outburst but as you can see, he has grown to care for your sister." She swept her hand to include Simon. "In fact, we all have—although we've known her a relatively short time. She is a remarkable young woman."

Claire smiled at Jill, relieved to focus on the reasonable, older woman and away from her sister's tempestuous boyfriend. "Yes, I think she is, too. Thank-you, Jill."

Jill continued. "And, before we met Willow, we knew your great-grandmother—Elzabeth—for many years. We were all great admirers of your late matriarch." She swallowed, speaking slowly. "It has been, uh, rather complicated for us since her passing."

Claire lifted her left eyebrow. "Complicated?"

Simon giggled like a small boy. "Yes, that's it. Complicated."

Jill placed a quieting hand on his knee. "Claire, we need to trust each other. Perhaps you can go first. Is this an official investigation with the Justice Department?"

"No, of course not." Claire snapped back. "I'll be honest with you all. I'm very worried about her." She made a quick decision. She didn't know what else to do. "I'll tell you what's happened if I can trust you?"

They all leaned in closer, nodding. "Of course, Claire, please tell us what's going on." Aaron urged.

"Okay, but when I'm finished, I expect the same from you. I need to know anything that might help me find her."

Aaron's face set in grim lines. He ignored his mother's cautious eyes. "I give you my word, Claire. Nothing is more important to me than Willow, right now."

"Without delving too deeply into our family skeletons, I'll just tell you that Willow has been pressured by the family ever since she was named the Protector. They've wanted her to share information from Elzabeth's journals."

Jill's eyes narrowed. "What kind of information?" She asked.

"Mostly some family history. Uncle Roland—Elzabeth's son—disappeared many years ago. We thought he was dead."

"Thought?" Simon piped up.

Claire continued with the story, sharing as little as she could. "Finally yesterday, after my Grandmother Sybil insisted, Willow told everyone that he hadn't really died, that he'd been taken away to a prison camp overseas. It was quite a shock."

"I bet." Jill murmured. "Do you know what became of him?"

"No, we've never heard anything." Claire shook her head. "Anyway, after she made that dramatic announcement, Willow and Sophie—she's our cousin—took off."

"Took off? Where did they go?" Aaron leaned forward further, his elbows on his knees, hands cupped around his face. His eyes were locked onto Claire.

"That's just it. We don't know. We assumed they just went back to the cabins, had an early lunch and went swimming at the beach." Claire looked up, her eyes distant. "But, they were gone. After lunch, we realized they had packed their stuff up from the cabin and left."

"They just packed their bags and left?" Aaron leaned back, crossing his arms. "But, where did they go? You were on an island, for Kamon's sake. Are you saying you found no trace of them?"

"No, not really. We inquired at the administrative offices, of course. We were told they'd taken a taxi off the island." Claire touched her portal unit on her belt. "When we tried to contact them to find out where they had gone, both of them had disconnected from the world portal. Can you believe that? Willow's never done anything like this." Her head cocked to the side, she raised her eyeballs in reflection. "No, she's never done anything like this at all. It's not like her—although, she is with Sophie…"

Aaron and Simon interrupted her in unison.

"Who is Sophie? Is she that crazy-dressed girl?" Simon asked.

"Have you checked if she's at home? What about Sophie's place?" Aaron's questions overpowered Simon's.

Claire nodded. "I came back late yesterday. The rest of the family stayed. My dad figured they might still turn up back there. We were trying not to panic at first. We thought maybe she and Sophie just wanted to get off on their own somewhere." She turned to Simon briefly and responded to his question. "And, yes, Sophie does generally dress kind of crazy but

I wouldn't talk if I were you—not with that weird purple garb you're wearing."

Simon looked down at his fashionable purple tunic. "Huh?"

She turned away and focused on Aaron again, extending her manicured hands, palms open. "I'm really starting to get nervous. I've checked everywhere I can think of. In fact, I even came looking for you, last night, Aaron—just in time to see you being picked up by another woman." Her tone turned accusatory. "At that point, I figured she wouldn't be around you. Now, I'm wondering if she ran off because of you."

"Now, hold on for a minute." Aaron sputtered. "Okay, you've got me. I was out with someone last night but Willow knew about it and why I was doing it. She didn't like it—and I was hoping we'd have a chance to talk about it tonight—but she wouldn't have disappeared over it." He clasped his hands, sitting up straighter. "Honestly, Claire, my motives for last night were to find out about, uh, something that Willow had confided in me."

"Uh-huh." Claire didn't sound convinced. "Well, that's about it really. I can't imagine where she could be but if she's just gone off cavorting with Sophie, I'm going to murder her when she returns." Her glib warning of sisterly abuse was delivered with a lightness she did not feel. Her tone changed quickly. "On the other hand, after hearing the story of Uncle Roland, this left us with frightening, perhaps paranoid, thoughts of something similar happening to the girls."

Aaron, Jill, and Simon exchanged glances. Claire watched them closely. Although she'd had no Vision Speak exposure, she was perceptive and had been trained to read non-verbal communications. In her line of work, she often had to interrogate suspects. What they didn't say was just as important as what they did say. Aaron was clearly concerned whereas his mother seemed reticent, guarded. There was a warning in her eyes, meant to keep Aaron and Simon from talking. Simon was easiest to read of all. She watched his bulging eyes and twitching fingers, the way he nervously glanced back and forth from Aaron to Jill, looking for direction. They knew something that they were reluctant to share. That much was obvious to Claire and she wasn't going anywhere until they told her everything they knew.

Jill cleared her throat. It was a loud grunt meant to focus attention on her and away from the men. "Claire, it's certainly odd the way that Willow and Sophie left your family gathering. Very odd." She continued slowly, as if thinking out loud, her eyes calm and direct. "But, really, I can't imagine why anyone would think they'd be taken into custody. Isn't that a little paranoid? I mean, what on earth could these girls have done to warrant this?"

Claire watched the other woman. Yes, she'd definitely underestimated her at first impression. Raising her eyebrows a margin, she ignored the question. "Enough. I'm not here to play games. I've told you everything. Now, it's your turn." She returned her attention to Aaron. "If you do care about my sister, you'll tell me what you know. Anything—no matter how unimportant it may seem. She's in over her head and I plan to help so let's work together on this." When Aaron did not immediately respond, she raised her voice. "Aaron, talk to me."

Aaron nodded. "Okay, you win."

Jill interjected. "Aaron."

"I'm sorry, mother, but I can't risk it. She may be in trouble." Aaron's voice was earnest when he turned back to Claire. "We need to be able to trust you, as well. Some of the information I will share with you could be used against us by the Justice Department."

"I have no intention of using anything against you or your spiritual offering. My only interest is finding Willow."

"Okay, Claire. I believe you, partly because if you harm us, you'll ultimately harm your sister." He made the point succinctly but it seemed to be more for Jill's benefit. "I think the first thing you should know is that your sister is very special." At Claire's uninterested nod, he emphasized. "I don't think you understand. Willow is, well, like a prodigy. She is able connect to others at a level of consciousness that you can't imagine. Your great grandmother realized this and trained her well."

"Huh? I mean I guess she's smart enough but she was never a genius or anything."

"She is in Vision Speak, Claire but our current academic system would not have noticed this ability." He nodded. "Yes, and because of this, and probably also because of Elzabeth's journals, there seems to be, uh, a lot of interest in her." Aaron placed his hands on his knees, glancing sideways, absently noticing the setting sun in the window, wondering where she was at that moment. Could Willow see the orange glow of the sun? He hoped so. "We know agents have been following her." He used his hands to tabulate the incidents as he recounted, pulling down one finger at time. "We know she's been interrogated and even met with the World Governor, Sharon. We also suspect that there is some other group with a mysterious cult leader—that may be watching her. And, to top it all off," he glanced over at Simon, "it seems as though Elzabeth expected much of this to happen and has left instructions for Simon to go to World Governor Sharon if there was any trouble."

Simon concurred. "It's true." He spoke directly to Claire. "And this seems like trouble to me."

Claire leaned back in her chair, crossing her arms under shapely breasts, her mouth agape. Her eyes darted back and forth between the two men. "Are you kidding me?"

"I'm afraid not." Aaron and Simon both shook their heads firmly. Jill was silent.

Simon voiced his concern. "In her instructions, Elzabeth said I would know when to act. I've been so confused, not sure how I would know. But, now, I think it's time—and she told me exactly what I must say so that the World Governor will see me." He paused. "But, if this message will grant me an entrance, how can I be sure she'll actually get it? Surely, they won't let just anyone who shows up at the PURE Administrative Center send a message through to the World Governor. Will they?"

"No, they probably won't." She concurred. "But if what you say is true then I will help you. Between my father and I, we should be able to make sure the message gets through to her." Claire continued with purpose. "But, first, start at the beginning, please." She breathed out deeply, her sigh echoing in the room. "I need to hear all the details and then we'll figure out how best to handle this—together."

Chapter 40

*"Truth is always present; it only needs to lift
the iron lids of the mind's eye to read its oracles."*

Ralph Waldo Emerson

    The ruling priests of the cult were situated in their position at the three ends of the unusually-shaped stone table. The table itself almost formed a triangle, except the corners were removed and inverted curves cut into the stone, providing a comfortable place for each man. The men's chairs fit perfectly into these slots with jutted handles pointing outwards behind their backs, thus completing the triangle that was formed when they sat together at their inner council.
    Intricate carvings in the stone illustrated a story. There were images of death and destruction—bombs and fires—with ruby gemstones interlaced among the carvings. Scenes of human suffering led to man coming together in unison. There were gold and silver filaments, used in more profusion as the story progressed. It showed the unified human race banded together in one glorified burst that sent them all sailing upwards to heavenly bliss. The table was old yet well-preserved over the centuries. The artistic detail was exquisite. According to legend, the artist had spent painstaking years, actually destroying the first one just before completion. In a trance, guided by the spirits, he had hammered

the original work to pieces in a destructive frenzy before beginning again.

The three men wore the distinctive robes of the high council—long flowing black robes with bright orange bands down the front and in the lining of the hoods. Their hoods lay on their backs, their faces exposed in this inner sanctum. No person would enter without invitation. They could speak without fear of intrusion.

"The steps we've taken are drastic. I have grave concerns." The man's face was white, his slanted eyes glowing blue in the dim light. "Our only possible escape is to destroy the girls and leave their bodies in the city. If they are traced here, we will be exposed. Everything we have worked for centuries to build here—our secrecy, our underground community, our sacred temple—will be uncovered. The Republic will find us and obliterate everything if we do not quickly take measures to protect ourselves. At a minimum, we must now begin evacuation procedures to leave this location."

The leader spoke firmly. "But you are forgetting our goals, our holy mission—the completion of God's plans. The ultimate goal is the end—not only of our communities but of theirs as well. Only then can we reach our nirvana." He paused, speaking deliberately. "We led her here for a reason. Do not forget that. She is part of the prophecy."

"It's too soon. We aren't ready. How do you know she is the one?" The man leaned forward, his elbows on the table, the blue gleaming bright in his ghostly face. He stretched out his arms, hands open as he spoke. "You don't understand the power they wield. I do. I see it everyday. They will wipe us out and ensure that no one ever knows anything of what we were, what we have accomplished."

The third man listened to the debate as he gently caressed the scar along his jawline with his thumb. "Remember that we are not alone." He said. "The other regions are aligned, ready to move, are they not?"

"Yes, it is time." The leader insisted. "We were so close. In our ancient past, the world came to the edge but the voice of reason won out. The ones they worship, that they consider saviours of the planet—Marrisha and Kamon. They may have saved the planet but they damaged our souls. They stopped the destruction before the messiah could come and lead us into glory. But not this time. As Samuel predicted in the Holy Journals of our Trial, this time the messiah will come first, a young man from over the seas born centuries after the first Cataclysmic event." He pounded his fist on the table. "And, I found him. I found him. The journey has begun."

"Yes, but what about the second part of the prophecy? The woman who will join him; the power they will wield together? If she fights us; if she does not succumb, what then?"

"Well, then, we will consider your original suggestion."

The three men snickered, their dark humour echoing in the chamber. Suddenly, almost simultaneously, they reach for their heads, eyes frantically seeking each other. A full fifteen minutes passes where they cannot speak, rooted to their seats, their brains linked unwillingly to another.

"What was that? Was that Kalesh?"

"What is he doing? I thought you told him to never…"

"It was not Kalesh." The leader responded slowly. Putting words together was a challenge after the onslaught to his psyche. "It was her."

"The girl?"

"Yes. Couldn't you tell by the clumsy, juvenile way that she invaded us? She is like a toddler, knocking about."

"Clumsy? Maybe, but my goodness, the power. If she can do that now, without any training…"

"Hush! We were not prepared. Next time we will be. And next time, we will ensure Kalesh is here to protect us. He is in solitude now. He needed time before he was ready for her." He leaned forward, his voice a whisper, almost as if he thought she could now hear them. "She is desperate, seeking about blindly for answers. Her desperation has fueled her, given her an unexpected strength. She will tire soon."

"Well," the man with the scar added, a sardonic tone to his voice, "at least it seems as if we'll be able to see her coming a mile away."

Chapter 41

"When good is in danger, only a coward would not defend it."

Confucius

Simon and Aaron approached the guard desk. Simon greeted the robot on duty with relief. He imagined a human guard would surely have laughed at his request, glared at them haughtily and refused their admittance. He searched for the name of the World Governor on the electronic sign-in sheet. It was surreal. In his craziest dreams, he would never have done this but Elzabeth had insisted that Sharon would see him if he sent the message. And Willow was missing. Claire would be working behind the scenes to ensure his message got through. This knowledge didn't settle his churning stomach but it kept him focused on the goal.

Glancing at his reflection in the mirrored glass behind the guard desk, he was suddenly embarrassed about the purple highlights that he'd always loved. He noticed too that his clothing was garish and worn-out, the pleasing violet of his shirt starting to fade. Why hadn't he pulled out his new outfit this morning? Saving it for that perfect occasion was never going to happen.

Shaking himself, he concentrated on their mission. He found her name and selected it. It must have set off an alert because the robot stood up immediately and directed his attention on Simon. "What is your business?"

"Um, I want to see the Honourable World Governor Sharon."

"Follow me." The robot left his desk without a backward glance and led them both to the elevators. Out of the corner of his eye, Simon noticed another robot exit the closet at the back of the guard desk, replacing his escort at the front counter.

They knew it would not be this easy to see her. Aaron and Simon exchanged sideways glances, remembering Claire's words. She'd explained the process to them the previous evening. "When you announce your request to see the World Governor, they will immediately sequester you. Be careful of what you say aloud. You will be under surveillance from that point on. Your request will trigger a bulletin to our department, as well as the CRKA. This will enable us to intervene."

On the third floor, the robot escorted them into a meeting room and then closed the door behind him, leaving Simon and Aaron alone. A news viewer on the wall portal cycled through the day's headlines. Simon scanned the news items, wondering if there were any official releases about the riots in the city that weekend: "The Leaders of the World continue to collaborate on peaceful solutions for humanity"; "The last devastated region of the world is in the process of being saved."; "The artist showcase of the week"; "Preparations for the Spiritual Center's Summer Solstice Festival are underway." No, there didn't appear to be news of the riots—just a typical news day.

Since Elzabeth's death, Simon's nerves had been aflutter. She'd been a godmother to him as well as a mentor and a friend. He'd grown to rely on her wisdom, her advice—especially after his mother had died. On top of that, she'd left them with the enigma of Willow. Ever since the time when the four of them had joined and they'd seen her power, he hadn't been able to stop thinking about it. On his own, outside of the Center, he'd found himself venturing further, his mind and spirit open for adventure, able to see more, feel more. He had wanted to seek her out, ask her to teach him but he was reluctant. Simon was supposed to be the experienced one, the senior representative, not Willow. And then he'd gotten Elzabeth's secret communiqué and he'd been paralyzed, afraid to approach her until he understood what he was to do.

Now, they were trapped inside the PURE waiting room. It was too late to turn back. After the same news items had cycled around the screen for the third time, the door finally opened. A tall, broad-shouldered official strolled to the head of the table where they sat. He wore a black uniform with a gold striped band down the arm. The crest on his chest labeled him Security Chief Jones, Squadron 5.

Aaron and Simon rose. Aaron smiled and extended his hand. "Hello," he said.

"Hello," the Security Chief muttered. "Sit down." He pulled out a chair across from them, his beady black eyes scanning them as if they were statues. Simon forced himself not to flinch. He waited for the examination to end, again berating himself for not wearing his new outfit.

Chief Jones' voice boomed in the small room. "I understand that you've requested an audience with World Governor Sharon?"

"Yes, sir." Simon nodded politely, respectful gaze trained on the security chief. Aaron remained silent, allowing Simon to be the focal point.

"Is she expecting you?"

"No, sir."

"Are you Mr. LaChance or Mr. Braxton?"

"LaChance, sir."

The man grunted, reviewing the portal unit in his hand. "What possible business could you have with the World Governor, Mr. LaChance? We've done a review of your vocation and I see that you work at the Media Center?"

"That's true but this is not a professional visit. Actually, sir, it's of a rather personal nature. I really need to speak with her directly."

"Is that right? And, if I were to give her your name, would she know you?"

"Uh, no, probably not, sir…"

"Well, then, I'm afraid…"

Simon interrupted before he could dismiss them. "However, sir, she knows the person that sent me. Could you possibly tell her that Elzabeth MacGregor has sent me? If you can please give her a message for me, I'm sure that she will want to see us."

"You want me to give her a message for you?"

Simon nodded gravely. "Yes, it's very important."

Security Chief Jones just stared back.

As the silence dragged on, Simon began again. "Please, I'm not insane, really. If you could just send my message and see if she would see me, I'd be forever grateful, and I'm sure she will be as well." Simon's bravado was diminishing but he couldn't give up.

"Okay then, let's hear the message our World Governor will be grateful to hear?"

"Tell her: Elzabeth MacGregor sent us. The Lost Orphan is seeking World Governor Sharon's assistance in an emergency."

The chief glared at Simon before he abruptly stood up, his chair screeching as he pushed it back. Aaron sat still, watching. Simon began to rise but Chief Jones extended his right hand, motioning him down. "Just wait here," he said. "I'll be back shortly."

He did not return shortly. Aaron and Simon remained in their seats, afraid to speak, mindlessly watching the portal screen. Fifteen minutes passed, then thirty, finally after an hour of silently waiting, Aaron spoke. "What on earth is going on? Perhaps, I should go out and ask someone."

"No, we have to just wait." Simon responded in hushed tones.

"Maybe we could..." Aaron's sentence trailed off when the security chief returned, the panel-door swishing open.

The man's expression had undergone a transformation. He no longer seemed to consider them lunatics. He smiled, revealing oddly crooked teeth, an unusual flaw in a society where citizens invested heavily in their visual appearance. "Please come with me." He said. "You will be escorted to the Governor's Tower."

When they reached the atrium, he passed them into the care of two official women who stood waiting, an incongruent pair in appearance. The fashionably dressed figure of Claire was a welcome sight but her companion, the robust Ramona Markel, was an ominous reminder that they were embarking on a risky course of action.

If the World Governor was angered by their intrusion, the possible repercussions were unthinkable.

Chapter 42

"Man does not know in what rank to place himself. He has plainly gone astray, and fallen from his true place, without being able to find it again. He seeks it anxiously and unsuccessfully, everywhere in impenetrable darkness."

Blaise Pascal

They'd fallen asleep huddled together on the small bed after whispering frantically half the night. Their limbs were tangled, their anxious minds at complete rest finally, taking comfort in each other. On the edge of consciousness, Willow inhaled the scent of her cousin's sweaty arm draped over her head. It brought back memories of summer camps and family reunions—times when they'd been inseparable. But in those days, Sophie had been the leader; Willow had happily followed her wherever she wanted to go. Something unexpected would always happen on Sophie's adventures.

Everything was different now. Willow knew she had to lead the way. The little girl who'd shied away from confrontation, from strangers, who'd lived in her own dream world—had to step aside. Sophie's life and her own depended on her drawing on reserves of strength she'd probably never tapped into.

The room in the tunnel, their prison, was deathly dark. The single dim light above had been extinguished early in the evening. Consequently, with no windows to the outside world, and their portal units confiscated, they had no sense of the time when the creak of their prison door opening catapulted them into wakefulness.

They sat up slowly, rubbing the sleep from their eyes, adjusting to the meager light that was switched back on. Sophie smoothed her hair back. Willow watched the woman enter the room.

She wore a long, flowing black robe. Her arms were full with garments, while she rolled a cart laden with breakfast food towards them. Behind her, at the open door, there were two guards blocking the exit. Willow knew it would be pointless to attempt escape even if they could get into the passage. There were too many cult disciples within the underground tunnel system.

The woman carefully gazed away from the girls, avoiding eye contact. She left the cart in the middle of the room. Proceeding to the empty bed, she removed a basket from the lower shelf of the cart and set it down, along with two robes—one black, one white.

"After you've eaten, you must remove your dirty clothing and cleanse yourselves," she motioned towards the washroom between the beds. There was a small shower within. "And then dress in these clean garments. The white one is for you." She pointed towards Willow. "The black one is for your companion." Her mission complete, she turned away and was out of the room before the question forming on Sophie's lips could be spoken aloud.

Sophie expressed her frustration by jumping out of bed, grabbing a bun from their breakfast tray and hurling it at the closed door. "Who the hell are you?" She screamed.

Willow giggled softly behind her. "I hope you realize that was your bun." She said. When Sophie whirled about, her eyes still burning, Willow continued. "Come on, Soph. Calm down. Don't you remember everything we talked about last night? We might as well follow their instructions for now. I'm hungry and I could use a shower. We'll be better able to function afterwards."

Sophie sighed as the memories came back to her. "Okay, you're right." Willow had never seen her cousin in such a disheveled state. Sophie's hair stuck out at odd angles. She had teary make-up streaks all down her cheeks. Her eyes were red and swollen from her hysterics during the previous afternoon and night. Sophie sauntered meekly over to the food. It did look appetizing. "I'm hungry too but, how do we know this isn't poisoned?"

"Don't worry. I know it's not."

"How do you know? Is it the advanced Vision Speak stuff you showed me last night?" The thought seemed to cheer her up some. Her eyes opened wider as she smiled at her wavy-haired cousin. Willow had shared a lot with her in the early hours of the morning. Since they were both in the same predicament, it seemed only fair to try and help Sophie to understand what was going on.

"Yes, something like that." She pulled the cart towards the bed. "Let's eat."

When their appetites had been sated, they used the supplies in the basket to clean their sweat, grime, and tears in the shower. Once they were finished and dressed in the robes, they again huddled closely together on the corner bed, whispering while they waited for their captors to make the next move.

"Do you know what's going to happen now? Can you sense anything?"

"A little. I think they'll be coming for us soon. They're going to take us to see the leader. He's one of the men that I found last night in that council."

"Will we see them all—all of those council men—wherever they're taking us?"

"No, not now. I don't think the other two are close." She murmured.

"What about that younger guy, the one that you sketched, the one that you say is so powerful—is he here?"

"It's strange. I haven't sensed him at all and yet I know they plan for me to meet him soon."

"Are they going to hurt us, Willow?" Sophie's voice quivered. She swallowed down her tears.

"Soph, as I explained last night, there is danger here. I can't lie to you." Squelching down the tremor in her voice, she reached over to smooth her cousin's hair, attempting to calm them both. "We have to proceed very carefully. What they do next—to us—may depend on how we handle ourselves today." She reached her arm around her cousin's back, pressed her face against her cheek and whispered closer, quieter. "I don't have all the answers but I hope to figure this out as we go on. You have to trust me. Don't let your nerves get you. Remember to breathe evenly, just concentrate on your breathing when they take us. Keep your mind calm and open, the way we practiced. If you do that, I can reach you. If you get hysterical again, it could be disastrous. And keep quiet about everything I've told you. Do you understand?" Sophie nodded but Willow persisted, hissing in her ear. "Don't forget Sophie. Keep calm and quiet. Let me handle everything, okay?"

"Okay, whatever you say, boss." Sophie's quip lightened the mood. Willow pinched her cheek and they smiled together for the first time since their capture.

Eventually, they settled back on the beds, drowsy, calm for the moment and thoughtful. Willow pictured Aaron's expression the evening she'd walked away from him. How foolish she'd been. Her jealousy over Jericho had been ridiculous, juvenile. Did he know she was gone? She prayed for the chance to apologize, to hold him again. The images of their nights together were too tantalizing, too torturous to think of now.

Also haunting her were the faces of her family when she'd told them about Uncle Roland. She could still see the fiery splotches on Grandma Sybil's cheeks just before she left. She'd focused her anger on her granddaughter—and it hurt—even though Willow understood that it was misplaced. She'd wracked her brain during the long hours of the night, questioning if she could have dealt with the situation better. In the end, she hadn't come up with an answer. By now, they must all realize that she and Sophie were missing. Surely, they would be looking for them. She knew her father would be, at least. But who would ever think to look for them underground? This group had plans, imminent plans. She realized she couldn't count on being rescued. She and Sophie could be history if she waited for that.

Glancing over at Sophie, she saw fresh tears running down her cheeks. Poor Sophie, she'd fallen hard for that boy. True, she'd unwittingly led them both into this trap but if Willow hadn't been so self-absorbed, she would have realized in time. Guilt burned in her gut. It was Willow they wanted. Sophie had been unlucky to get caught in the middle, used as a pawn to get at her cousin.

Her agonizing thoughts reached a pitch of self-recrimination before the door finally creaked opened again and they were told to follow the guards. It was a wake-up call for her. The last hour had been unproductive, detrimental even. She had to be strong. Her inner abilities and her mind were her only weapons.

Willow's heart hammered in her chest. She'd told Sophie to breathe evenly, stay calm and yet she suddenly found herself panicking. Where were they taking them? What was going to happen? She remembered with a jolt that one of the leaders wanted them killed.

They were led along narrow passageways, single-file, passing alcoves and entrances, with occasional glimpses of groups within small chambers, meditating or chanting. She sensed them all. It was suffocating, depressing, frightening—for they all felt deeply about, believed unequivocally in, their leader, their messiah, and the dismal end they viewed as glorious.

She took her own advice and breathed deeply, in and out, in and out. She had a momentary inclination to scream for help. It would be useless. She squelched it.

The hallway was bleak. No windows, not even a glimmer of the brilliant sunshine that Willow vaguely remembered now. Would she ever see the sun again? Shuddering, she forced herself to stop. Her mind could be her enemy or her ally. It was up to her.

They halted before a large floor-to-ceiling door. It was more impressive than the others, with old wood carvings in four sectioned panels. The guards opened the door, ushering the young robed girls—one in white and one in black—inside. Their escorts stayed back, pushing the girls forward before they closed the door firmly behind them.

The room was enormous, much larger than they had expected to find in this underground maze. They faced an elaborately decorated platform with a podium and a large stone altar. It was surrounded by faded imagery of fiery war on the left, transforming into heavenly splendor on the right. A darkly-robed man with a black and orange lined hood hiding his features, stood at the back of the platform watching them. There were other robed figures in the shadows of the room, along the walls. Two men held treacherous sword-like weapons—sharp gleaming silver instruments of death. They were cloaked in black, situated on either side of the shrine, by the wall. They stood so still that they almost blended with the stone sculptures along the edge of the platform. There was a large, stone altar to the left center stage, silent and foreboding. Willow thought there may have been another ten people in the room but she focused on the hooded man in the center, with the piercing eyes, familiar in their intensity.

"Step forward girls." His voice boomed in the silent room. "You must kneel before the high priest of the Cult of Armageddon."

She walked slowly towards him, holding Sophie's hand. Sophie inched forward, keeping a step behind Willow. When they stopped at the lower railing, just in front of the platform, he stepped forward, dropping his hood.

A light shone brightly on his face from above. His hair was white; his face, deeply lined. Piercing dark green eyes and bushy brows glared at them, the intensity of his stare intimidating.

The girls stared back, both of them speechless, unable to utter a sound. As they watched the man who glared at them, Willow became aware that the face was familiar. Something hauntingly familiar lurked behind the bitter lines of his face, the unsettling stare. Just as the realization leapt into her consciousness and she stepped back in astonishment, she heard Sophie suck in her breath.

She turned to her cousin, about to warn her to hold her tongue.

Before Willow could stop her, Sophie exclaimed. "Oh my god. It's Uncle Roland! Willow, look at him. He looks just like the pictures." Her eyes darted from Willow and then back to the man on stage. "Well, he looks a lot older, of course, but you can tell it's him." She placed her hands on her hips. Raising her voice, she spoke to him directly, insistent. "You're our Great-Uncle Roland."

The craggy face did not greet them warmly as one might expect from a long lost relative. On the contrary, his lips pursed firmly together, his brow furrowed and he glared at Sophie even more intensely than before.

He said nothing—neither confirming nor denying her assertion. Willow's breathing was shallow and soundless, contrasting with her rapid, painful heartbeat—while they both waited for him to respond.

Finally, he stepped forward to the edge of the stage, standing tall. His right arm swung forward to point at them. "Kneel!" He bellowed. "Kneel before the high priest of Armageddon or face the consequences." The guards with the gleaming blades lunged forward in unison, the lethal edges within arms reach of the quivering girls.

Sophie cried out. Willow wrapped her arm around her cousin, silencing her as they dropped to their knees before the commanding figure of the high priest.

Chapter 43

*"The significant problems we have cannot be solved
at the same level of thinking with which we created them."*

Albert Einstein

After the long wait, Simon and Aaron were on their way to meet the regional World Governor Sharon. They were escorted through a series of buildings—up an elevator to a secure area of the twentieth floor within the Central Tower where they then followed a connecting bridge to the World Governor's Tower and accessed an even more secure bank of elevators. Finally, they were seated in a small conference room on the 99th floor. The marble table was complemented by padded white leather swivel chairs, enormous moving art along one wall, and a floor to ceiling retractable screen at the front of the room. The current setting was exponentially more luxurious in furnishings, amenities, and artwork than the lobby waiting room. Even more impressive than the accoutrements, however, was the fabulous view, on display via enormous windows along the wall opposite the artwork. The cityscape, on that glaringly bright morning in June, was a magnificent setting for an otherwise nerve-wrenching situation.

Claire had never been to the executive floors of the Governor's Tower. Ramona had led the way. Aaron thought that nothing—except her sister's well-being—would have prompted Claire to risk her career by finagling this audience with the World Governor. After everything they'd endured to get here—the various checkpoints and security personnel, the physical search, and intense questioning—he realized anew just how impossible it would be for the average citizen to gain access. How important had Elzabeth been to have this influence? What was the Lost Orphan? Was it a code word of some kind?

Now, sitting, waiting again, the men were silent, lips sealed tight until the World Governor arrived. Claire tried to make small talk with Ramona, her usual smooth, confident voice betraying signs of shakiness. She asked Ramona about her studies at the institute, discovering some similar courses they'd taken. It was her subtle way of reminding the CRKA officer that they were colleagues. Ramona was reserved, her answers short, although Claire did manage to draw her into brief conversational spurts.

Aaron and Simon stared out the window, barely hearing the women's chatter, their minds absorbed. Where could Willow be? Aaron wondered. What if he never saw her again, never had the chance to apologize, to hold her? He shuddered, gaining control of his random, panic thoughts. These mind pathways would not serve anyone. He glanced over at Simon, surprised to realize the other man was in a deep trance, concentrating on his inward visions.

When the door finally slid open, they all shot upwards, standing at attention, eyes riveted to the entranceway. Two burly security guards stepped in first, eying. Ramona assured them that the visitors were clean. They stepped back out into the hallway, taking positions on either side.

World Governor Sharon entered the room. They all recognized her. Her platinum hair was an enormous halo surrounding a stately, chiseled face. Eyebrows shaped and accented to perfection; eyes deep set with gentle maturity lines, enhanced expertly with shades of violet; her suit tailored and fashionable. She was a tall, shapely woman who would be admired anywhere, even if her picture did not appear on the news portal regularly. World Governor Craig entered next. He was several inches taller than his companion, his hair steel grey, the lines around his eyes more pronounced. He was a man who emanated power, someone who would always seem virile and ageless. Together, they were a formidable, striking pair.

Following closely behind the governing couple, was an unusual man. His face was in shadow, beneath a dark hood. Even so, slanted, glowing blue eyes pierced outward surrounded by pale, glowing white skin. He closed the door behind him.

The seven people in the room remained standing. Sharon, Craig, and Burton scanned the four individuals at the table, their curious eyes primarily focused on Aaron and Simon. Aaron, Simon, and Claire surreptitiously glanced at the newcomers, respect battling with curiosity, their eyes slightly averted.

Sharon broke the silence. "Which one of you has come with this message about a Lost Orphan, from Elzabeth?"

Simon raised his hand. "The message was given to me, your Excellency."

"How did you receive this message? Before Elzabeth passed on?"

"No, I received this communiqué, recorded before she died, very recently. It was time-delayed. She said in an emergency situation, this message would get us an audience with you."

"Right. Your message indicated an emergency." Sharon and Craig exchanged glances. Sharon asked. "What is the emergency?"

Aaron's deep voice interjected before Simon could respond. "Willow, Elzabeth's Protector, and her cousin are missing. We fear they have been abducted." He cleared his throat. "Unless, uh, you know where they are…"

Craig inclined his head forward, peering at Aaron through deep slits. "I beg your pardon. Did you say unless we know where they are?"

Aaron flinched under the piercing stare of the World Governor. "I, uh, I'm sorry. We know you brought her in for questioning. We, uh, just wondered if maybe she was here?"

Sharon reached out and touched Craig's arm, her gentle restraint sending a silent message to her partner. They glanced at each other, locked in soundless communication while the room waited. Finally, Sharon spoke. "She is not here." Turning to Ramona, her voice became authoritative. "Agent Markel, see what you can find out about Willow

Tyler Olsen and her cousin. Report back as soon as you have any information on their whereabouts." She waved her hand in Claire's direction. "Perhaps this representative from the Justice Department can assist you while we meet with our visitors?"

Agent Markel picked up her bag and glanced at Claire before exiting, expecting her to follow.

"Excuse me, your Honours." Claire spoke clearly, her voice resonating in the small room. Sharon and Craig regarded her for the first time, surprised to be addressed by this junior official from the Justice Department. "I must tell you that I am not here on business, exactly. This is personal for me." Sharon raised her left eyebrow, waiting to hear more. "Willow is my sister. My family is very concerned. I would like to stay, please."

Burton shuffled from his position behind the world governors to direct his gleaming eyes at Claire. Claire broke her eye contact with the world governors, unnerved by Burton's gaze. She smiled tentatively in his direction. "Have we met before?" She asked.

Startled, he shuffled back. "No," he said, his tone low.

Sharon recovered from the unexpected news that Willow's sister was with them. "Okay, you can stay." She decided, pointing at Claire. Speaking to Burton and Ramona, she continued. "Burton, Agent Markel—we will speak with these three in private; however, first they must be sworn in as clandestine agents of the state."

Everyone in the room, except Craig, reacted to her request. Claire spoke up first. "You want us sworn in as agents? But, there's a rigorous screening and training process before anyone would achieve such a position."

"We don't have time for that." Sharon responded.

Agent Markel found her lips. "Your Excellence, I don't understand. You want to certify these people—all three of them—as CRKA agents?"

"They will maintain their current occupations but be sworn in as agents, highly classified, to be mobilized only when absolutely necessary. They will pledge to abide by the Secrecy Clause."

"Ahhh—I see." Agent Markel nodded, a slight uplift in the corners of her lips.

"The Secrecy Clause." Claire murmured, searching her memory. "That means that divulgence of information deemed government classified—to anyone—is treated as treason?"

"Exactly." Craig nodded. "We cannot possibly speak with any private citizens unless they are governed by these principles which everyone in this building has pledged."

"And treason is punishable by death?" Aaron asked.

"Precisely." Craig responded.

Aaron and Simon glanced at each other and then at Claire. Simon's eyes were bulging. Aaron's temple beat a visible pulse. Claire's elegant profile was thoughtful, serious. She directed her gaze back to the world governors. "I understand your reasoning. Of course, we would be discrete with anything that is discussed here—but do you really think this is necessary? Having us pledge such an oath, on such short notice—how can we be sure what is considered classified without the full training?"

"For starters, everything that is spoken within this room today will be classified unless we otherwise instruct you." Sharon responded. "You will be pledged to share our life mission to protect the Republic at all costs."

"My father is in the Justice Department as well as I. We are both committed to the Republic. We have pledged our life and careers to upholding the PURE laws." Claire demonstrated her skills as a litigator with her direct speech. "However, my family is very worried about my sister's safety. Couldn't I even tell my father anything?"

"Absolutely not," Craig insisted, "unless we specifically grant permission."

Claire had a talent for reading people. What she saw in both Sharon and Craig's eyes convinced her that there was no other way. She turned back to Aaron and Simon. "Do you understand what this means?"

Aaron wondered how he would be able to face his mother without telling her anything but he knew better than to echo Claire's concern. "Right now," he responded, "I don't totally understand but I don't care either. We are wasting precious time. If making this pledge will allow us to get closer to finding Willow, then let's do it."

Simon swallowed down a painful lump, nodding his assent.

"Okay then," Claire responded. "Let's please just get this done so we can move on to the purpose for our visit."

Craig motioned to the door. "Burton, Agent Markel—on your way out, please send in the PURE officials who are waiting outside the door."

Burton turned to Craig. "Your Excellence, I should remain here so that I will be able to later advise you more effectively on these matters."

Craig shook his head firmly. "I'm sorry, Burton, but this time, we will not need your assistance."

The cloaked albino paused momentarily, his mouth ajar as if about to say something. He must have realized the futility of protesting. He obediently turned for the exit without a word, followed by Agent Markel. The angry flash in his bright blue eyes was witnessed only by Aaron as he lowered his head to follow orders.

Chapter 44

"Spiritual force is stronger than material; thoughts rule the world."

Ralph Waldo Emerson

Willow's knees ached, her constant shifting starting to chafe the skin around the bone. How long had they been kneeling before this man, encircled by these chanting, hidden faces? It seemed forever, had to be at least an hour. At first, she'd been terrified, had barely grasped the words he preached. Then she'd begun to listen intently, searching for meaning. Finally, she used her abilities to search deeper.

Gradually, understanding of their situation was growing in her mind. Her cousin, by contrast, was in shock and didn't seem to be absorbing much. When the chanting first began, Sophie had become hysterical, screaming for release. Violent prodding by the guards had quieted her. The two girls had their backs to each other, facing outward, but she sensed her cousin. She was terrified, stunned into silence.

At that moment, Willow couldn't help Sophie. She had to expend all her energy to figure out what was going on. Some of the chanting was unintelligible but much of it was repetitive. The thirteen people in the room with them were some of the highest order within this cult. They were in a trance-like state; their chanted lyrics were only part of their ritual. The circle they formed around the two girls was linked by hands;

the leader towering above everyone from his pedestal, directing activity—occasionally with sharp words but primarily with a mind-link, unlike anything Willow had ever experienced.

Their minds were brainwashed with repetitive, frightening phrases which flowed mentally and verbally around the circle. Shared images fueled the emotions of the words, made them more real. Images of death and destruction, cities hollowed out by atomics, mutilated bodies and limbs along roadsides, children screaming—the images were horrific but somehow bathed in a holy, golden light. She saw how these people revered the Great Annihilation. They desperately strove for a repeat of that horrendous period in human history. They believed it was coming. They would risk their lives to ensure it did. The twists in logic which led them to believe it would be glorious, would ultimately save the human soul—was impossible to follow. For Willow, who had grown up in the sheltered world of the Republic and a loving family, always trusting blindly in the system, optimistic about her future, it was impossible to understand, deplorable to see. Yet, she could not deny it. To these people, the Republic and everything it stood for was evil. Mass murder, death and destruction for the human race were preferable.

"Samuel, we are ready. The messiah is here. Judgment is coming. This time we will face the day. We will lead the people to their glory." The priest repeated the words they'd chanted, his voice booming above them. Willow had not yet built up the courage to try to delve beyond his pious, repetitive mind stream but she was inching closer. He was leading the group with his mind as well as his voice.

At the mention of the messiah, she felt the group's reverence. She saw what they saw. It was the boy with the deep, dark eyes, the face she'd seen in her dreams. He was their messiah. She shivered, remembering his power. Still, she hadn't sensed him at all since their capture. She refocused on the group and especially on the priest who stood above them all—her long lost Great-Uncle Roland.

"The woman-child is here. The prophecy has come true. She is the catalyst. It will all begin now." His voice rose even higher as he spoke, yelling by the final sentence. These words silenced them. They all stood still, their eyes piercing into Willow.

The abrupt end to the chanting was a jolt. Both girls flinched and gazed about them. The leader's final words echoed in Willow's head. He'd said 'she is the catalyst' and they were all staring at her. She read it in their minds; she saw it on their faces. She was part of their prophecy, their plan—their absurd, twisted, deadly plan.

Willow lunged off the floor and faced the leader. "You're insane." She screamed. With all the force within her, she mentally launched her attack. Gripping his mind, she felt the initial resistance. He had more power than she'd expected but it was not enough.

From a distance, she heard his feeble protest. "No, stop." He gripped his head with both hands.

Willow ignored his protests and drove forward, forcing her way into his thoughts and feelings, memories and dreams, as she'd never done before to anyone, never would have done if she weren't desperate. It was rapid-fire and confusing—like watching ten movies at once. She knew she was causing pain, experienced it even, but she continued.

She knew his bitterness, his hatred as if it were her own. She saw the squalor he'd lived in when he'd been sent away, relived his vengeful determination to do what he now planned. Although he believed in the cult's mission, as the rest of the group did, his drive was fueled by animosity and a need for power. It wasn't love or devotion for the future of humanity. He was, in fact, their Great Uncle Roland but it would not buy them any favours. He hated his mother, her great-grandmother, and all she stood for—even in death. He hated her with a passion that overshadowed all else.

Sophie's shrieks tore her away from her probing. "Let go of me. Stop it!"

Willow hadn't even noticed that she was being physically restrained. The two guards held her tight from either side. Her cousin had been grabbed by two of the other robed figures. She felt the pain in her arms, where they were gripped in an iron vice, as she relinquished her mental control over Roland. He staggered backwards, his gnarly hands massaging his temples.

His voice hoarse and noticeably weakened, he commanded. "Lock them up and make sure that one," he slowly raised his hand, pointing at

Willow, "is sedated until my son is ready for her." Switching his attention to Sophie, he moved his arm to specify his next order. "This one should be prepared for the indoctrination ceremony." His orders delivered, he turned abruptly and exited the room through a hidden doorway behind the stage. The robed worshippers backed up against the walls, their heads down in prayer.

The guards pulled roughly on the girls' arms, dragging them out of the great room and into the tunnel hallway. They walked rapidly down the passageways, encountering no one on their way back. The guards pushed the girls back in to their cell room.

As soon as the door thudded closed behind the guards, leaving them alone, Sophie turned to Willow grasping her arm, staring at her cousin as a young child does with her mother, looking for answers. "You must tell me. What have you figured out? What is their plan? Why have they captured us?"

"I don't completely know yet, Sophie. I'm learning a lot, though. They've taught mind control techniques for centuries and, as a group, are much more advanced than our small group at the center. Still, none of these people have been able to resist my probing." Willow murmured with a note of surprise in her voice. "From what I can glean, their purpose in pursuing what we call Vision Speak has always been to further their mission."

"But, what is their mission?"

"Ultimately, it's Armageddon." Willow responded. "They want a repeat of the Great Annihilation."

"Oh my god, that's what those ridiculous verses were about that they were chanting." Sophie gasped. "How could anyone want that? It was the worst thing that ever happened in the history of the human race. Millions died. The planet was almost destroyed."

"To them, it was the most holy of times. It was glorious." Willow shook her head. "It's impossible to understand but it's real, Sophie. I felt it. I saw it. They actually believe this. They want to make it happen again."

"But, it's so warped. How can they really want that?" She moaned. "And, he's our Uncle Roland, Willow." Sophie's voice broke. "Doesn't he care about us?"

Sighing, Willow responded as best she could. Sophie had never encountered evil like this. To her, family members loved each other. They helped each other. "He hates us, Soph." She reached out her hand to touch her cousin, to try and soften the pain. "You heard the stories at the ceremony. He was very twisted by the time he disappeared and when his mother arrested him, it went beyond anything rational. He was—is—mentally ill, I think."

"Great Bet was actually the one that arrested him?"

"Yes, Great Bet was undercover in the cult at the same time that Roland was rising up the ranks. She didn't realize his involvement until it was too late. That's also when Great Bet first learned about Vision Speak."

Sophie's brow furrowed. "Is that why you didn't want to read from the journals about Uncle Roland?"

"Exactly, I couldn't find a clear passage that didn't involve the whole convoluted story. Even though she despised the Cult and everything they stood for, when she learned the Sacred Trance, she grew spiritually and glimpsed the potential for humanity, if only it could be followed without the Cult's twisted control. Once they'd successfully arrested or disbanded the cult, Elizabeth focused on the good she had learned. She renamed it Vision Speak and started the offering at the Spiritual Center so that citizens of the Republic could begin to explore the possibilities."

"I can't believe she arrested her own son and told the whole family he was dead."

"Yes, she…" Willow stopped her speech abruptly and put up her hand. Focusing intently beyond their four walls, she was silent for several minutes. "They're coming, we don't have much time." She announced. Realizing she had to take advantage of the brief time remaining, she grabbed Sophie's head, whispering frantically in her ear. "Listen to me." She hissed. "They're going to separate us and you will have one chance, and only one chance soon, to escape. I cannot bear what might happen if you do not take advantage of this chance."

"What?" Sophie's voice rose in alarm. "What is this indoctrination? Is that what you mean?"

"It's something that they do to new female initiates. I don't want to frighten you but I know of another female who was forced to go through this, many years ago. If you don't comply, it will be even worse than what she went through." At Sophie's panic-stricken eyes, she quickly continued. "No, Sophie, stop. You mustn't panic. I can see one way out for you and you've got to take it."

Sophie started to cry. "How? Will you be with me?"

"Shh!" Willow put her finger on Sophie's lips. "Please, Sophie, your only chance is to be calm. Listen to me. We don't have much time. They're going to separate us and make me unconscious for a while." She waited a brief second, mentally relaxing her cousin. When her tears had stopped, she continued. "You're a strong swimmer, aren't you Soph?"

Sophie gazed up at her cousin, nodding gently, her eyes filled with trust.

"Okay, then breathe easy, in and out, concentrate deep inside and let me show you what to do. Don't worry about me. You won't be able to look back. Once you've reached safety then you can send help for me, okay?" Willow took a deep breath, watching Sophie nod obediently. "Now, stay focused, memorize my instructions. It might be your only chance. You must be brave. I know you can do this. Do you understand?"

They heard shuffling outside their door. The guards were preparing to open it. Willow ignored it and focused on Sophie.

Sophie's cheeks burned bright, mottled red with worry, her pupils dilated as she breathed loudly in and out. Again, she nodded at Willow, silently acknowledging her understanding, her earnest gaze indicating she was ready.

Willow directed her full attention on Sophie, showing her what she needed to know. The two stood huddled together against the back wall, deep in trance, when the door burst open.

Chapter 45

"In the great moments of life, when a man decides upon an important step, his action is directed not so much by any clear knowledge of the right thing to do, as by an inner impulse—you may almost call it intuition— proceeding from the deepest foundations of his being."

Arthur Shopenhauer

Aaron sat between Simon and Claire, his gaze locked on the imposing figures of the governors who now sat across from them. Finally, they were alone and ready to begin their conversation. He rubbed his left underarm where it still stung from the small chip that had been implanted there. That was only one of the details they'd neglected to mention about the CRKA pledge. Although trying to gain his equilibrium with so much happening, he was nevertheless single-minded in his intent. There would be time later to dwell on his pledge and what it meant. Presently, he had only one concern and that was Willow. For Sharon and Craig to have granted them a private meeting and to have forced their commitment in such an unorthodox, rushed fashion could only mean that they had information to impart. They must have a significant interest in Willow and whatever happened to her.

Before he could begin to ask the questions that were burning in the back of his throat, Sharon took control of the meeting. She wanted to know how and when Willow had gone missing. After Claire detailed the weekend events leading up to the girls' disappearance, Sharon turned to Craig, saying simply. "The Island Retreat. I wonder…"

Craig pulled out his portal unit and fired instructions into it, commanding a unit to search the Island Retreat.

Once Craig had finished, Aaron broke the ensuing silence. "So now you understand why we're here. We're terrified that something might have happened to her, I mean—to them."

Claire quickly added. "Yes, and Willow mentioned her visit with you and so we naturally assumed that you would, uh, share our concern."

Sharon, her eyes bright with comprehension, nodded. "Of course, we are concerned but, I suspect that what you're really saying is you assumed that we may have abducted her?"

"N-no."

"Shush, of course you wondered. Now that you are pledged to uphold our directives in utter secrecy, I will admit to you that she was endangering her freedom by telling you of her visit here. It is because of this that we had to take more decisive measures with you. If only we'd done the same with her, at least she would have the tracking device implanted." Sharon sighed. "Unfortunately, we don't know anything about her disappearance. Now, I wish we had kept her here. We actually had been considering asking for her assistance today, before you came."

"Her assistance?" Claire queried.

"Yes, her abilities are needed right now—to investigate, er, help contain a situation." She cleared her throat. "Ironically, we want her help to track down those that have probably captured her."

Claire's brow furrowed over shrewd eyes. "Your Honours, please, can we be very straight with each other? All I care about right now is finding my sister and ensuring her safety."

"Of course." Sharon smiled.

"I assume the situation—that you need Willow's help to investigate—relates to the recent protests and the hijacking of the world portal. Is that correct?"

After glancing at each other, Craig responded. "Correct."

"How do you think she can help with that?"

"We're not certain, of course, but with her special abilities, it occurred to me, to us, that is." Sharon quickly corrected herself. "That she may be able to extract information from our prisoners where we have failed—such as the identity and location of the rest of their group."

The group was silent for a moment as they considered Sharon's statement. Simon sat up straight with a little cough as he prepared to speak for the first time since they'd sat across from the leaders. "I agree with you that Willow probably could have found out what you needed to know." He began with a soft, tentative voice. "We are not as strong as Willow and I'm not sure if we can help or not," he glanced over at Aaron, "but I've been able to go deeper and connect at new levels since experiencing Willow." His face flushed, uncomfortable with everyone's attention on him while he spoke. "I'm not sure but if you want my help, I could try to access these prisoners." Simon dropped his head, embarrassed to make further eye contact with the World Governors. "Aaron, I might need you too." He muttered. Aaron didn't respond, his lips sealed tight while he gazed thoughtfully at his companion's profile.

"Interesting." Sharon murmured, her eyes shifting sideways to gage her partner's reaction. "What do you think?" She asked Craig. He shrugged.

Before Craig could respond, Claire redirected the conversation back to the cult. "So you believe that all of the recent incidents have been orchestrated by the same dissident group?" At Sharon's nod, Claire continued. "And, you also believe that this same group may have kidnapped Willow and Sophie?"

"We do not have any hard evidence about the disappearance of these girls." Craig responded. "But, that would be our suspicion."

"Who is this group? Why would they want Willow?" Aaron interjected, his impatience barely masked in his voice.

"They call themselves the Cult of Armageddon." Sharon answered him directly. "We will tell you what we know but it is highly classified."

"Isn't everything classified that we discuss here today?" Aaron bit out the question before he could stop.

"Absolutely." Craig's voice was curt.

Sharon continued with her explanation. "This group, as with many of these modern-age doomsday cults, sprouted in the aftermath of The Great Annihilation. Unlike some of the others who have come and gone, this one is highly organized and large in numbers, with divisions worldwide."

"Are they sanctioned by the Spiritual Center?" Simon's soft innocent question was more startling than the louder voices of the rest of the group.

"Certainly not." Sharon insisted. "Never would a group like this, with such radical, harmful beliefs, be sanctioned. They worship the end of times. They believe The Great Annihilation was holy. They strive to achieve it again. They have no tolerance for other traditions and faiths. They believe the Republic is evil for maintaining peace in the world." She shook her head to emphasize her point. She glanced in Claire's direction. "We thought we'd disbanded them under your great-grandmother's direction, decades ago."

Claire's eyes popped open wider. "Do you think they've taken Willow and Sophie for revenge because of Great Bet?"

"I doubt it's that simple." Sharon was quick to respond. "We have no idea what, if any, interest they may have in your cousin Sophie but Willow is another story. If they have any knowledge of her abilities, we suspect that is their motivation."

"These abilities that you all reference—I can't fathom how my little sister could have some special powers and we've never noticed anything." Claire shook her head. "And how would this group know anything about her?"

"She shocked us too." Aaron was quick to interject. "She did mention sensing some others, outside of our group. There was someone very strong that she encountered, as did Elzabeth. Is it possible that they also have been trained in Vision Speak?"

"Definitely." Sharon concurred. "They began these practices centuries ago, although they called it something else—Sacred Trance. Elzabeth first discovered this on her mission. It was after that that she extracted this part of their practices and created the sanctioned offering."

"You seem to know a lot about my great-grandmother and this mission." Claire commented. "Is that why Elzabeth left a message for us to come to you?"

Sharon was unprepared for Claire's direct question but she recovered quickly. She cleared her throat. "Yes, I was involved. It was a long time ago when I was an agent with the CRKA. I'm sure that's why she sent you to me."

"But why did she send the message to Simon and what is the Lost Orphan?" Claire persisted.

All eyes turned to the slight young man with the bulging eyes. He stared back at them in astonishment. "I, uh, I'm n-not exactly sure." He stuttered. "Um, Elzabeth said that she trusted me and she said World Governor Sharon, w-would understand."

At his words, inquisitive eyes rolled across to Sharon who was staring at Simon, her posture rigid. She seemed to be assessing his features while she ruminated on her next words. "Simon LaChance." She said. "I understand you were adopted. Do you know who your birth parents were, Simon?"

He fidgeted in his seat. "No, I, uh, don't know anything about my birth parents."

"According to your records, I understand that you are turning thirty this year?" When he just nodded dumbly, she continued. "And, how long have you known Elzabeth?"

He sat still, his eyes gazing ahead, yet backwards in time. "I've known Elzabeth my whole life, I think. She was a close friend of my adopted mother."

Sharon breathed out loudly, turning to look at her partner. Craig inclined his head forward, imperceptibly giving his approval. Finally, she turned to Aaron. "I understand that your vocation is with the Health Investigation Labs?"

"Uh, yeah," he concurred at her unexpected question. "That's right."

"I need you to run a confidential DNA test for me."

"A DNA Test?" Aaron's startled expression mirrored his companions'.

"Yes, I've brought a kit." With calm deliberation, she reached under the table, and pulled out a package from her bag, passing it across the table to Aaron.

Chapter 46

"Human life is thus only an endless illusion. Men deceive and flatter each other. No one speaks of us in our presence as he does when we are gone. Society is based on mutual hypocrisy."

Blaise Pascal

Kalesh glanced down at his quivering hands. He clasped them together briefly, before moving them back down by his side. Showing an outwardly peaceful demeanor was critical. If these disciples sensed the state of his nerves; if, for one moment they thought that their 'messiah' was uncertain of the future, of next steps, it would be terrifying for them. To these people, he represented all that they lived for, that they believed in so fervently. He must lead them to the destiny that they, all of them—his father, the council, the priests of the order—had preached for generations. From the time of his youth, he'd been raised to believe in his duty for this mission.

Even so, his heart was racing because finally now, it was time for him to see her, to be face to face with the girl.

They were all evacuating his island, his home. The High Priests had been the first to arrive at their secret destination. It was no longer safe on the retreat. He had known peaceful meditation and security in the years they'd lived on the island. It saddened him that he could not return. The beginning of their divine trial was now in motion. There should be joy in knowing that it had begun. He felt jubilation emanating from the disciples who lead him down the hallways to the council room but he did not share their emotions. His features were set, almost grim. He strode purposefully, slowly, towards the grand door at the end of the dark hallway.

She sat now before the council of three. She was draped in a white, voluminous robe, her face pale with a determined set to her chin, her lips sealed tight. He saw her through the eyes of his father. The high priest of the cult, the man he called father, harbored strong, angry, deeply personal feelings towards this girl—he felt it as intensely as if it were in his own heart. He did not understand it, had hitherto missed this. Regardless, there was no time to explore his father's emotions now.

They stood before the door.

It was time to see her through his own eyes for the first time.

His companions swung the door open. He stood in the doorway, observing the scene before him. She resembled his visions except more beautiful, more vulnerable, more intimidating. The girl with the pale face and flowing, golden waves of hair sat alone at one end of the old stone conference table in the center of the room. She was to his left and the others were to his right. The single light source in the room had been directed to shine toward her, bathing her gentle face in brilliance. Rather than huddling away from the spotlight, she sat erect. She held her head up and forward, shoulders back. Frightened green eyes remained steady, staring at her captors. The three men, cloaked in black with the orange bands of the high council, sat together at the opposite end of the table. Their hoods covered their heads. With the light source diverted from them, their features were in shadow—gloomy and foreboding profiles protruding from the loose hoods.

Kalesh stepped into the room, his simple black robe swishing about his legs. The door closed firmly behind him, leaving him alone with the four occupants.

She moved her head deliberately, slowly to look into his dark, soulful eyes, shadowed by his deep set eyebrows. Their gaze locked for brief moments before his father drew Kalesh's attention away.

"Sit down, my son." He pointed toward the empty chair to the right middle on the long side of the rectangular table. It brought him closer to the council members and further from her.

Kalesh sat down, his tongue frozen as he gazed at the delicate girl in the light.

Into the anxious silence, she spoke softly, her eyes directed at the boy. "Who are you? What is your name?"

"Do you not know me?" He asked her, a hint of surprise in his voice.

"I, uh, recognize you." She responded. "I've seen you but I don't know your name."

"I am Kalesh." He said simply. "I have seen you, too, Willow."

"Kalesh is our chosen one." Roland's voice boomed after their quiet words. "He will lead us on our path. For you, Willow," he leaned forward, pointing at her in a menacing fashion, "he will either be your future or your end. It will be decided today."

Willow felt a painful flush down her neck when she changed her gaze from the gentle boy to the dark, twisted stare of her great-uncle.

She kept her eyes on her great-uncle. "Why do you do this?" She demanded. "Why do you have such hatred in your heart—for the Republic, for your family, for life itself?"

"Hatred is not what drives us forward in our mission." He denied it flatly. "We believe that where we take mankind is for the greater good. The Republic has manipulated everything. Nothing about your life is true. The Spiritual Centers are a sham."

"How are they a sham? We live peaceful, fulfilling lives. We want for nothing. Our religions join us together without dividing us. What is so terrible about this?"

"It's all fabricated. You are like idiotic children who are not being allowed to grow up, who are being trapped in your playpen for life. And yet you smile and happily take your nightly bottle from the hands of the Republic who dictates and manipulates every aspect of your life. You have no free will. Your minds are becoming more and more simple. Your society is killing that which is human in all of us, every day, in slow, painful fashion." His upper lip twisted in disgust at the end of his speech.

"Surely you exaggerate." She responded calmly. "In what way is the

Republic killing humanity? Are you talking about those ridiculous verses that were released on the world portal last week?"

"That was the beginning, the first step." He said.

She gazed at him, her brow creased in inquiry. "But what on earth do you think you've accomplished by releasing these words? You say they've been suppressed? So what—how could they possibly have that much impact?"

"Every great religion, the books you have studied and worshipped, even thousands of years worth of literature—all of these great works have been tampered with. The words that we released were merely samplings. When citizens start to realize how manipulated they have been; how the very spiritual paths that they have been told to follow are a hoax—surely they will begin to question PURE. They have been fed on half-truths, the most glorious, god-fearing sections of these texts removed." He paused, taking a deep breath before he continued. His companions sat silently on either side of him, their shadowed faces steady as granite. "The Republic controls your beliefs, your vocation, your family structure—everything about your life. They forbid exclusivity claims and private religious rituals. If any citizen steps out of line, they may just disappear—in silence. No one knows what happens; no one questions it. You are like rats in a cage." The two men on either side of Roland nodded their heads in agreement. "The world portal serves as their propaganda machine and you all listen, follow it blindly. And, even worse, they smear one of the greatest events in our history, the most holy time ever—The Great Annihilation."

As he ranted, Willow turned inward, searching for answers. Kalesh, sensing her quest, connected with her easily. She felt him instantly. It was a strong bond, cleansing her of her deep feeling of isolation.

Roland continued. "Almost every holy book in history proclaimed the answer, announced their way as the only way. Those that have been following their great traditions, mandated by the state to attend, will be shocked when they see the true words, the intended message of their prophets." She heard his words from afar, her psyche escaping the mundane limitations of mere verbal language. "Many of these great religions prophesied our future—the end of times, the destiny that we now follow for the benefit of mankind."

Kalesh showed her what Roland tried to explain in words. He showed her in a way that she could never have seen on her own—the manipulations, the cover-ups, the hushed sentences pronounced in secret and executed without public knowledge. As a protected child of the Republic, she may not have believed it—had not wanted to face it. Even her brief experience with Sharon had shown her only a glimmer of the harsh reality of how they ruled; how they maintained peace. To Kalesh and the others, they had always been outsiders. They had kept themselves separate. They took from the Republic what they needed to survive and scorned the rest. Some of them lived on the edge, assuming false identities, moving from city to city, organizing movements, secretly recruiting dissatisfied citizens. For them, they found deeper meaning in the righteousness of this cult, the brotherhood—their secret rituals and the holy mission that they pursued.

They knew of injustices that she had never imagined, loved ones who had been tortured and executed. In seeing this, she finally understood some of Great Bet's passages from her journals. Her great-grandmother's disillusionment with her career flooded back into her consciousness. Without a doubt, Great Bet had carried out many of these injustices, the clandestine arrests. It had all been in the name of maintaining the PURE balance.

Willow began to feel that disillusionment. It became her own. She found herself no longer able to defend the Republic—the life that she had happily lived for nineteen years. As these thoughts grew, an unexpected anger fuelled her. How dare they operate that way—playing god, making judgments, abandoning free will for the masses? She remembered Sharon commanding her—insisting that her future, her dream of a life in the Arts community was now impossible, could never be. Red-hot fury blinded her thoughts—suddenly, intensely. As the bitterness twisted in her gut, she suddenly realized that Kalesh was manipulating her. He'd seen the beginnings of her disillusionment. He'd planted more seeds. He'd nudged them deeper. With a start, she broke free, gazing at him in wide-eyed bewilderment. Breathing deeply, she released the negative emotions, pushed him away.

His head pulled back in visible surprise. No one had ever been able to push him away like that before.

With a clear mind, she focused her thoughts back to her own

experiences, her deeply ingrained beliefs. She instinctively understood that the original premise behind PURE was for the greater good of the populace, for the peace and well-being of the people. She remembered the words that had hung on Sharon's wall in her private suite. "Our mission: Protect Mankind from himself. Never again. Never again."

Perhaps they had gone too far. Perhaps it was time for a change; time for mankind to wake up and take control of his destiny. She saw the truth in that. But did that destiny mean the end of life for masses, the destruction of everything that had been built over the centuries? Anarchy, chaos, human suffering—this is what the cult wanted. They believed it was the only way to break free, to bring the enlightened ones forward to ultimate nirvana. They believed they had been on that path, in Samuel's day, when PURE was formed, when they were first forced to go underground. Their ancestors had been secretly plotting against the Republic for centuries, following the prophecies and beliefs documented during a traumatic, post-atomic age. She projected her beliefs, her thoughts outward—hoping to show Kalesh another view.

The three men at the end of the table concentrated, sensing the interplay between the two young people. Roland was able to follow the strong emotions, the confusion, a power play of sorts between the two gifted ones—but only from a distant, hazy place. The other two men saw much less, were even more distant.

Finally, the council member on Roland's right spoke. "We do not have time to waste." As he turned to face the high priest, his hood fell back slightly, exposing glowing white skin and slanted, hidden eyes. He pulled the hood forward to cover his features. "The ceremony is tomorrow night. We must be ready to set everything in motion then." He inclined his head toward Willow. "She must either succumb, become one of us—or we must dispose of her before the festival."

Roland nodded his head slowly. "Yes, it will be decided by morning." He turned to Kalesh. "You have until day break to tame your intended—or we will take care of her for you."

Kalesh directed solemn, deep-dark eyes to his father. "Yes, I understand." He stood up, his head bowed in respect. "Please leave us now. We will be together through the night."

Chapter 47

"The journey of a thousand miles begins with one step."

Lao-Tse

After being trapped underground with no windows to the outside world, it took Sophie's eyes several minutes to adjust to the brilliance of the June afternoon in the forest. Moisture-speckled leaves hinted at the rain that must have fallen during the night. The oppressive heat that she remembered from two days before had been replaced by glorious late spring warmth without the claustrophobic humidity that the rains had swept away.

Sophie was alert, glancing sideways at her companions. Two female escorts held her arms on either side, leading her forward along a path. They were flanked by big, burly guards. If she tried to make a run for it now, they'd have her flattened in seconds.

She breathed the fresh air deeply into her lungs, remembering Willow's direction. Be calm. Stay focused. Wait until the moment and the circumstances are aligned to give you the best chance. Do nothing before to arouse suspicion.

The silence played on her nerves. Finally, she broke it, deciding no harm could come from trying to talk to these insane people. "Where are we going, anyway?" She glanced over at the women—one appeared old enough to be her mother but the other was younger, maybe in her middle twenties. Both had their hair pulled back tightly, with gray tunics and loose fitting pants. They had covered Sophie in a white robe, similar to the one that Willow had worn. They'd taken all of her other clothes, including her undergarments.

The older woman smiled vacantly at Sophie. "We are going to the water, my dear, where you will be cleansed."

"Cleansed?" Sophie queried. "But, I already had a shower."

"You must be cleansed in the great waters." The older woman responded. "You are to become a woman of the order. We must prepare you for your indoctrination."

"What is this indoctrination?" Sophie had an idea but she wanted to hear them say it.

"Shush! That is enough." The younger woman intervened. "When it's time for you to know, you will be told. Now move along."

Sophie was quiet after that. She breathed in and out, steadily, just as Willow had instructed. At one point, she heard the guards murmuring behind her but could not catch their words.

It was a long and winding walk through the woods, gradually leading to a secluded area on the water with a small, sandy beach surrounded by forest. The beach area was so small that the five of them were crowded, brushing against each other, when they all stood in the sunshine on the sand.

The larger of the burly guards spoke. "We will move into the dark of the forest and wait for you. It would not be proper for us to watch your cleansing ritual but we will be within hearing distance. Call when you are ready for us to return and escort you back."

The women nodded in agreement.

Before they turned away, the other guard spoke. "Remember, sisters, the evacuation has begun so we do not have very much time."

"We understand, my brother." The older woman spoke quietly. "You may leave us now so that we can begin."

As soon as the men were at a safe distance into the woods, the women of the cult removed their garments. Both revealed slender, nude forms with small breasts. The older woman had silvery stretch marks along her belly with loose, empty skin. Sophie had little time to inspect their bodies. As soon as they'd discarded their garments, the younger woman reached over to remove Sophie's robe so that she, too, stood nude on the beach. Her large breasts pointed mockingly at the meager breasts of the younger woman. Sophie's hair had been pulled back by a clasp. The older woman removed it and let her hair fall gently around her face and shoulders.

Sophie squinted behind the women into the woods to determine the position of the guards but she could not see them in the shadows.

The women turned her away from the woods and pulled her gently towards the water.

"Come into the great waters, my child."

"We will cleanse the sin from your body so that you will be purified."

Sophie obediently walked into the water with the two women. It was cool, a minor shock to her warm skin. Still, she barely hesitated at the feel of the water on her feet. She eagerly continued into the water, her heartbeat thumping loudly in her chest.

"You will be ready for them tonight."

The lake was just past her knees now. The women on either side of her were beginning to slow. The younger woman reached down to cup some water in her hands and pour it on her backside. She shivered in shock at the cold water on her back but kept walking. They followed alongside her until the water was just below their buttocks.

"This is enough, my dear child." The older woman murmured. "We must join hands now and meditate before the cleansing."

Sophie's heart rattled hard against her chest. She tried to hide her ragged breathing, afraid they would guess her intent. "A little deeper." She murmured, continuing to walk forward even once the two women had stopped, preparing to join hands. After a long walk forward in shallow waters, the sandy ground was beginning to drop off quickly.

"No." The older woman responded, gently. "This is far enough."

Sophie continued to walk forward, pretending not to hear them. She was just beyond their arm's length now.

The younger woman spoke louder. "Stop." She commanded. "Come back here, we're not going any deeper." Instead of complying, Sophie lunged forward, diving deep into the waters ahead, swimming underwater as fast and as strong as she could. When she finally came up for air, continuing to swim away, she glanced back. She saw that the older woman had not moved from her position in the water. She was waving her hands, screaming frantically. The guards had just come running from the woods to see what the commotion was. They stood on the beach, staring out in confusion.

The younger woman was in pursuit of her, swimming directly towards her. Sophie had a good lead. She felt strong and confident. Focusing all her energy and strength on swimming away from them, she continued forward towards the middle of the lake. She had no direction at the moment except away.

Finally the younger woman gave up. She couldn't catch Sophie and had to turn back.

Once Sophie was safely out of their clutches, she treaded water and looked back at the shore. The four of them stood on the beach, staring out at her in frustration. After a heated debate, they picked up their garments, dressed and rushed back into the woods. Sophie assumed they would go back for help, or even worse, a boat. She had to move quickly. She swam out deeper still before she turned and began to parallel the island's shoreline, hoping to find the beach crowded with people on the retreat side. The cold water invigorated her, propelling her forward in her mission to find safety.

Chapter 48

"Three things cannot be long hidden: the sun, the moon, and the truth."

Buddha

"Well, do you have the results?" Sharon turned to Aaron again, barking out the question. She was standing, along with Craig, on the other side of the table, her regal appearance even more pronounced than when she'd been sitting. "What does it say?"

Aaron was intent on the task in front of him. His busy work complete, he stared at the small screen as the results crystallized before his eyes. Finally, he glanced up at the anxious face of the authoritative woman. Aaron's two companions had also risen, turning to admire the magnificent view by the window while he worked in silence.

Aaron leaned back in his chair and closed down the small testing apparatus, the decisive click gaining everyone's immediate attention. Claire and Simon returned from the window and took their seats on either side of him. The world leaders slid back into their chairs, their eyes never leaving his face.

"Well?" Sharon's clipped voice demonstrated someone who was used to having her questions, and orders, answered immediately.

"Aaron?" Simon's soft, tentative voice contrasted sharply with the woman across the table. "What did you find out?"

Aaron turned sideways to look at Simon and then at Sharon, finally returning his gaze to the visibly shaken Simon before he spoke. "She is your biological mother, Simon." He turned back to face Sharon. "There is absolutely no doubt."

Claire watched the dramatic interplay before her eyes. Although the room was silent for a full minute after Aaron's pronouncement, the visual array of facial expressions was entertaining.

Craig's lips pursed together tightly, the colour draining from his granite face. He gazed outward while his mind quietly absorbed the news, calculating damage control. Sharon's face deepened with emotion, her white coiffure framing shiny red cheeks, tiny droplets of water forming in the corners of her eyes. For once, she ignored Craig's concern and focused instead on another. She stared across the table at Simon.

Simon's eyes widened even further than they had been, shock evident in his frozen expression. "My birth mother? You?" He shook his head in bewilderment. "But how can that be?"

Sharon sighed deeply, her usual confident demeanor shaken. "Simon, I'm sorry. I didn't know. I had absolutely no idea that Elzabeth knew who you were or where you were." She placed her palms down on the table in front of her, as if physically reaching outward with her explanation. "It was a long time ago, before Craig and I met, before I began my pursuit of the leadership program."

Simon laughed nervously. "Well, yeah, I guess it was just over thirty years ago."

"Elzabeth helped me at the time. I thought she had placed you in the system, in the manner that it's usually done—anonymously, with no traces. It was a difficult time for me. When I moved ahead with my life, my career, I never looked back." She swallowed down a painful lump in her throat. "I always imagined you with a good family, a happy life."

"But why was Elzabeth involved? Who was my birth father?" Simon could barely breathe as he waited for her answers.

"Well, it's, uh, complicated." Sharon responded, choosing her words carefully. "It relates back to the mission we were just talking about. Elzabeth and I were both undercover agents, assigned to infiltrate the cult."

"Simon was conceived during that mission?" Claire interjected.

Sharon nodded slowly. "They have some unusual practices, particularly for women who are being elevated to the higher levels." Her composure was faltering, red cheeks glowing brighter. "I was", she paused, struggling with her next words, "indoctrinated as they call it, in a ceremony involving several, uh, brothers as they called them."

"Several?" Simon squeaked out the word.

Sharon gazed sightlessly out the window, avoiding eye contact with her biological son. Her voice was quieter than it had been before but she finally answered him. "Yes, I'm afraid so. By the time I realized the plans, it was too late." The hazy images from decades past invaded her memory for a moment. She shuddered. "Their faces were covered. Drugs are involved with the ceremony." She visibly swallowed down the lump again. "Simon, what I'm trying to tell you is that I don't know who your birth father is." She turned to him, stretching her arms out on the table in his direction. "I'm just going to give it to you straight. From the cult's perspective, they would say you were a Son of Samuel, that your conception was holy."

"Oh my god." He moaned. "This can't be happening to me. I just can't believe this." He reached up to bury his crimson face, hiding his visible emotions from the group. His muffled voice carried on. His elbows were propped on the table in front of him, his hands covering his tormented face. "First, I'm the illegitimate son of a World Governor. Now, I'm the result of some sick ritual of group rape? I'm the son of this insane cult that has taken Willow?" He shook his head in denial, swaying his arms as he did so. "No, this can't be true."

"Simon," Sharon began, her voice soft. "Please, don't dwell on the conception. There is some good news here. With Elzabeth's help, I was able to escape before you were born, otherwise they would have kept you, raised you to be one of their disciples."

Claire cleared her throat. It was a lot to absorb but, like everything else, there'd be time for that later. "That is quite a revelation, Sharon. I'm sorry for Simon—I'm sure it's quite a shock—and for what you must have gone through. Please know that we certainly understand that this is, uh sensitive information that you have shared." Glancing sideways at Aaron and then at Simon who peeked out at her from behind his hands, she noted that they were both willing to have her lead the conversation forward. "I guess we'd better focus on the practical knowledge we have now so we can use this to find my sister and cousin."

Sharon nodded, relieved to move back to solid ground. "Absolutely."

Craig rejoined the conversation, his grim expression relaxing slightly. "You should know that our team has arrived at the Island Retreat. We expect to hear some news soon. They will question everyone there and do a more extensive search."

Claire smiled. "That is good news. Thank you."

Aaron added. "Yes, it is but do you really think they're still there? Didn't they leave on the air taxi?"

Craig shook his head. "We're fairly certain that they never left on an air taxi but we should have more details shortly. With what has just happened, we are now beginning to suspect that there might be a connection between the cult and this retreat."

"Oh." Claire exclaimed. "It just occurred to me that, if they're connected, maybe Great Bet didn't arrange for our family retreat as my Grandma Sybil was told. Perhaps this was a set-up all along?"

Craig and Sharon nodded in unison. "Yes, that's what we suspect." Sharon said.

Just then, the ringer sounded on the door and it swished open.

Ramona Markel stood in the doorway. "Requesting permission to enter."

"Yes, come in." Craig barked. As the door closed behind her, he asked. "Where is Burton? I assume he permitted you to return?"

"We could not find Burton, your excellence." Ramona responded, inclining her head in respect. "However, we have news that we thought you would want to hear immediately."

"What is it?" Sharon asked, her voice smooth and unruffled.

Ramona glanced over at Claire, Simon, and Aaron. "Do you want to speak privately first?"

"No, just tell us what has occurred, Agent Markel." Sharon insisted. "They've all been sworn to secrecy." She waved her hand dismissively at their three guests.

"Okay. One of the girls washed up ashore in the middle of the public beach. She gave a few of the occupants quite a shock."

"Oh my god, was she, uh, are you saying she was dead?" Claire's throat constricted in fear, her last word barely squeaking out.

"No, no. She's very much alive." Ramona shook her head, her lips curving upward in amusement. "She was naked as the day she was born, though. Came staggering out of the water and gave everyone a good display before she started screaming for help. Sounded pretty healthy, apparently."

The clouds in Aaron's sapphire eyes cleared; his heart thudded painfully in his chest. "Was it Willow?" He dared to hope.

"No. It was the other one—Sophie. They're bringing her back now. She should be here within the hour."

Chapter 49

"I now understand that my welfare is only possible if I acknowledge my unity with all the people of the world without exception."

Leo Tolstoy

They were connected in every way except by physical touch. He'd brought her to his meditation garden where they sat alone under an enormous oak tree, shaded from the gradually departing sun. She knew there were guards nearby but they were unobtrusive, hidden from view.

The late afternoon sunshine was still radiant, heightening the brilliant array of colours in the flower beds and surrounding shrubbery. The aromas from the garden floated gently under her nose, delivered by the warm spring breeze. The sound of innocent life was musical: squirrels rustling in the trees, birds chirping. After spending days sequestered in dark, underground rooms and tunnels, the beauty of the garden uplifted her soul. She felt strength returning to her bones.

They'd walked freely together on the upper floors of the secluded mansion where they were now staying. No one bothered her while she was with Kalesh but they watched. At every move, she felt their eyes on her. After consuming a light lunch, they'd come to this place to be alone.

But now, he was steadfast, focused on his mission in earnest. She saw it in his expression; she felt it deep inside. Already, their connection was a steady hum at the edge of her consciousness. Their eyes locked together.

Something was happening tomorrow night, they'd said, on the evening of the summer solstice. If she didn't cooperate, didn't come around to their way, they said they would kill her in the morning. These thoughts coursed icily through her veins, paralyzing her whenever she faced the reality of her situation. She knew she couldn't fool this manchild who sat before her. She could not pretend to believe with them. She either had to truly be with them—heart and soul—or she was doomed.

Unless Sophie could somehow get help, she thought, a dim hope in the back of her mind. She knew Sophie had escaped but, unfortunately, they were no longer on the island. Willow had been unconscious during the move. She didn't even know where she was now and neither would Sophie.

What about the rest of her family? Her father and Claire—surely, they would be looking for her, would use their resources in the DEFJ. And she wondered about Aaron. She'd been dreaming of both him and Kalesh again. Her body yearned for Aaron when she'd lain in her dark, lonely bed. The dreams had been repetitive. Always she'd faced that fork in the path, seeing Aaron down the easy, sunlit path—his physical beauty shining in the light, a draw to her libido. Yet, she could never go there, always lunged into the dark, twisted forest with Kalesh, Aaron lost to her forever. Her heart skipped a beat as she remembered Aaron on the last night she'd seen him. How foolish she'd been, how insignificant her anger over something so silly, she thought now. Her physical being longed for him. But would she ever see him again? Even if she did, would she still be able to love him after Kalesh finished with her?

She gazed into the boy's deep, dark eyes now and experienced raw fear. He was powerful beyond anything she had encountered before. He was determined, raised to be fanatical in his beliefs, needed her to share those beliefs, to follow him—and even more, it seemed. He wanted her to lead his fellow fanatics along with him, join with him as his partner. Could she withstand him? Should she even try?

He watched her, followed her thought patterns and waited. Finally, he took hold.

They left the vivid, physical world of the garden, soaring to heights that Kalesh alone knew. She followed him blindly, willingly. The pull was too strong to resist. Her fear left behind, she felt only deep, inner peace at their joining. She sensed great beauty. She saw it now, wanted to be part of it.

They were on a journey. He wanted to share with her everything he'd seen.

He showed her a view of humanity she could never have imagined. It gave her a sense of mankind's struggle for life, for depth and meaning, beyond her personal experiences. He was uniquely gifted, able to tap into some all-seeing, ageless, eye—a connection that few others in the history of mankind had experienced in mortal life.

She saw the birth of the human species, the millennia of struggles, two races of man—one highly spiritual and intuitive—the other more focused on their logical, intelligent side, physically adept yet out of balance. Ultimately, the physically strong, logically innovative race gained supremacy, overcame the other in the vicious struggle for survival in an untamed world. The stronger species multiplied rapidly, spreading throughout the planet.

All this she saw, as if from a great height, like a series of swiftly moving images. It would all be nonsensical without the inner feelings, the insight, the knowing. She watched and she felt a part of what he showed her. It was holier than anything she had ever experienced.

Their race was brilliant in so many ways. Watching the rapid progress was illuminating but the other side, the aggression, the anger, the murderous inclinations—this was unbearable. It was like watching your own children perform heinous acts.

As they passed through history, they witnessed places in time and space that were fertile training ground for the evolving mind of man—the areas where climate and large hunting animals led necessarily to innovations. The people formed civilizations, created inventions which made life easier, established hierarchical societies, divided labour and multiplied—again and again.

These societies grew stronger and larger; building tools that gave them a mastery over the Earth and its creatures. More advanced civilizations stormed into other areas, conquering, enslaving, destroying.

Too often, the peoples that were annihilated or diminished had grown in other senses. Some had the gifts that were blossoming now in the world but, too often, they were squashed. She saw visionaries who built monolithic monuments, inspired by visions, dreams, shared collective ideas from peoples that they would never encounter in the physical realm. Their artistry expressed subconscious ideas they could not explain.

Repeatedly, the human themes played out—birth and rebirth; brilliance, creativity, innovation; coupled with intolerance, aggression and cruelty, death and destruction. With each age of man, the destructive capabilities increased. They saw the devastation increase exponentially as they moved forward in time. She felt his heartbreak. It was the pain of the entire race, a pain shared by some greater indefinable life force connecting everyone. Finally, they witnessed the pinnacle of man's evil, the terror and mass murder that culminated in the Century of Despair. Pain gripped her chest. How could they do this? How could it happen? They anguished together over the terrible past of their ancestors. A self-inflicted disease had taken root.

But even while they experienced the human suffering of this devastation, he showed her something else that came out of the ashes. It was a spirituality that transcended the physical hardships, the loss of human life. Even while so many lost all faith, there arose a new devotional faith among others. Their deep belief in something more, something beyond life, joined them in their suffering. She experienced their conviction. Severing the chains of their physical existence to soar beyond, was the ultimate path. They separated themselves from the old institutional belief systems and the bureaucratic rule that was growing. She saw the good in what the cult had built together in the early times. There were communities, like communes, that supported the weak and dying, gave them hope and the early prophets were inspirational—Samuel and his parents, and many others that followed.

Although she had only followed his lead thus far, she kept up with him at each step. She knew he reveled in the connection they shared. It was a first for her but their sharing was also new for him. Their spirits were linked in a unique and awe-inspiring way. She dared to hope she could persuade him but he felt the same way. The determination was still with him.

Encouraged by her empathy, he showed her how his people had progressed with the early ventures into Sacred Trance, their non-verbal connections, the spiritual searching that she and Kalesh had now ventured so far beyond.

She saw how large and far-reaching the cult was. All the major cities, branches in the countryside, high-ranking officials secretly sworn to loyalty—they had built up an infrastructure that would be formidable to the Republic. The CRKA and PURE officials had no idea how powerful the cult had actually become.

Again he demonstrated the machinations of the Republic, their persecution of devout cult members, their manipulation of the populations. She saw through the eyes of those who had suffered at their hands. She felt the frustration, the rage.

She gazed inwardly with him. She hated the PURE methods with him. She touched him, caressed him through the pain. He felt her warmth, her sympathy but knew that she didn't understand, not totally. Finally, she asked him why. Why must we return to anarchy and murder? Why is it the only way?

Don't you see? Images of warfare, of evil-doing flashed again. He fired the devastation back into her psyche, the terrible experiences.

No, no, please. I don't want to go there again. Not then and not now. Neither do you. I feel your pain. I know it hurts you as it does me. Why do you want to lead your people—all the people of the world—back down those paths of misery again?

It is the only way. It is inevitable anyway. Would you rather a slow, painful death? When we leave our physical bodies, we can abandon the hell on this world forever. Let me show you. He took hold of her and brought her to a peaceful place, high above the world.

It was as if her entire body sighed, releasing all tension, floating aimlessly with him for an immeasurable time. They glided along together, reveling in their freedom, the blinding beauty of the light before them. In this place, there was only peace, the end of suffering—yes, she wanted this. Everyone would want this, she realized.

They lost all track of time, wandering blissfully in the otherworldly haven until they were shaken out of their deep trance. Blinking, Willow slowly became aware of the physical world around her. The leader, Roland, towered above them where they lay side by side on the grass, their hands clenched together. Behind him were three guards and a trolley of food. Glancing upwards, she saw the sun had gone down. It was dusk. Although they must have joined together for hours, it seemed like mere moments.

Slowly they stood to face the severe, old man in the long, dark robe.

"Well?" His unspoken question was directed at Kalesh. He barely glanced at Willow.

"We are making progress, father."

"Time is ticking by, my son. We must make our plans."

"Where we go, father, there are no clocks. Make whatever plans you must but for now, you must leave us."

A visible pulse pounded in Roland's temple. He pursed his lips, his aging face set in grim lines. The boy and the man were silent for moments, staring into each other's eyes. Willow sensed the interchange, the tension.

Finally, Roland responded. "Very well, eat your dinner and then you will be left in peace—but the next time I come to you, she is either with us or she is not. If she is not, the matter will be dealt with swiftly." His pronouncement complete, he retreated from the garden, the guards following on his heel.

Chapter 50

"Politics have no relation to morals."

Niccolo Machiavelli

Gazing intently at her partner, she detected deeper, more severe grooves running down his granite face. Sharon gulped back her old insecurities. Recent events had certainly added tension to their already high-stress lives. She watched the pulse beat in his temple, admiring the strength of his profile as he stared out the window of their private suite. This was the man she had joined with to ascend to leadership just over a decade ago. They had chosen him to lead with her and—despite the arranged nature of their union—he was the first man with whom she had fallen deeply in love.

But, he was angry with her now. She sensed this as surely as she discerned, glancing over at the view of the horizon, that the sun was setting in the west.

"Craig," she moistened her lips, the applied color long since dissipated. "I don't know what to say except I'm sorry. I'm sorry it happened. I'm sorry I didn't tell you about it sooner."

He turned his head abruptly to lock his gaze on her. Accusatory glints of slate connected with her softer, apologetic eyes. "Sorry? How could you withhold information like this from me for all these years?" He shook his head angrily. "In fact, I can't fathom how this information wasn't a deterrent to your ascension to world leadership in the first place."

"I know. At the time, I fully expected it to come out, to end my career but Elzabeth was good. That's all I can figure. She sequestered me for the months I carried. She took care of everything, explained my absence as a continuation of the mission. She told me to move on, that she would take care of it, that I should never mention this to another living soul." She inhaled deeply. "I was happy to follow her direction at the time. It was a devastating period for me, personally, but I put it behind me and focused on my career, on my devotion to the Republic."

"Touching." Sarcasm reverberated in his voice.

She ignored the jab. "And ultimately, Craig, I fell in love with you. Perhaps that has blinded me in some ways to my duty to share anything like this, anything potentially damaging, with you. I can only apologize again and say that I honestly thought this was dead and buried."

Sighing, he strode across the luxurious carpeting to the window. They were alone in their private quarters which were situated between each of their own suites and directly above their official offices. Everything about their life and business was intertwined. Except now this. She had a son. That knowledge, if it escaped, would jeopardize both of their careers. World leaders were not supposed to breed. It affected their judgment. They had both been sterilized when they had taken their oath.

Finally he spoke. "I'm sorry too. We've gone over this already and it serves no purpose for me to continue with recriminations. It's just that the reality of it really hit me with the DNA results, you know?"

Her voice was soft. "I know but I hope you understand that I had to find out the truth, as dangerous as that is for us."

"I'm trying to understand, Sharon."

She went to him. Leaning into his solid frame, she folded her arms about his waist from behind, leaning her head against his shoulder blade. "I know." She said and waited, the sound of his steady heartbeat reassuring her tense nerves.

When he moved, she released her grip on his waist so he could turn gently around to face her. He kissed her then, steely grey head leaning into the platinum blonde halo of his partner, and they held each other tight, each building back their strength from the other. They both knew their time alone together was limited, moving apart after brief moments in their embrace. He held her hand and led her back to their soft, leather armchairs, facing each other.

"Okay, my dear, enough said about that." He released her hand and switched the portal unit on. After viewing the update alerts, he scanned the reports, made contacts, barked out questions and orders, and finally set it aside. She watched him, listening intently. For this one time, she was content to let him take complete control.

Once his calls were complete, his attention returned to Sharon, she asked. "So, the girl, Sophie, has been interrogated?"

"Yes—and her information, together with what your son."

"Don't say it." She warned. "Not ever again. His name is Simon."

Craig took a deep breath. "Of course." When he continued, his voice was even and professional. "Simon, with Aaron's assistance, was able to extract information out of our prisoners from the incident in the square. They are all members of the Cult."

"The Cult of Armageddon?"

"Mm-hmm. Apparently, their network is more far-reaching, and threatening, than we'd realized. They seem to be as powerful as ever. There've been other accounts, too. Five major regions across the globe have reported similar public disturbances."

"We documented the portal hijacking and the disturbance in the public square." Sharon stated. "But do you think we should report anything about Willow to the PURE Security Council?"

"I'm afraid we'll have to. In fact, I think we should call an emergency meeting," Craig responded, "based on what we've learned from both Sophie and the latest interrogation of the prisoners."

"You were discussing tomorrow night, the summer solstice, in your calls?"

"The Cult has big plans for the summer solstice, apparently. It's bigger than just our region and I fear we'll be forced to mobilize a red alert security force. No matter what we do, the risks to our peaceful balance appear to be enormous right now."

"Bloody Annihilation!" Sharon cursed. "How did those fanatics manage to advance to this stage? What have the CRKA been doing all this time, sitting on their thumbs? And where is Burton?"

Craig nodded gravely, the grim set to his jaw indicating he wondered the same things. "These are questions that someone will have to answer to." He concurred. "As for Burton, he is back and anxious to meet with us."

"Where was he?" She demanded.

Craig shrugged. He reached for her hands. "Sharon, we must proceed cautiously. At this point, the only people we can trust absolutely are each other. Understood?"

She grasped his hands tightly. "Understood, Craig. No more secrets."

"And, we cannot release our new team of agents." Craig pronounced. "Your, uh, Simon, Aaron Braxton, and Willow's sister, Claire, even this young girl Sophie—we will lodge them in quarters here tonight."

She swallowed down the lump in her throat, nodding mutely.

He continued. "I'm afraid until this crisis is averted, they must all stay within our grasp; out of touch with society, the media, and their families. Once it is averted, I am not at all sure what we should do with them—or with Willow if we find her in time. I don't see how we can allow them all to return to their lives in the community."

"We'll have to cross that bridge when we come to it." She agreed. "In the meantime, let's allow them each a brief, monitored communication with their families so that no one panics."

"Yes, and then we can continue to keep a tight leash on them."

Chapter 51

"Life is a process of becoming, a combination of states we have to go through. Where people fail is that they wish to elect a state and remain in it. This is a kind of death."

Anais Nin

They ate dinner in silence, disconnected, each brooding in their own world. In the end it was Willow, gazing across at the boy with whom she'd experienced immense intimacy a short time ago, who broke the silence. She addressed him by name for the first time. "Kalesh, what's going to happen tomorrow night? Why is it so important?"

He glanced at her furtively, deep set eyes shifting between her and the dark, vine-covered wall of the house beyond. After experiencing his inner confidence, she was surprised to see how shy he behaved. His voice was soft. She had to strain to catch all his words. "Tomorrow is the summer solstice. Every spiritual center in the world will celebrate with the Festival of all Festivals. It's a fitting time for us to launch the tribulation upon the leaders of PURE, to focus our order towards the future. I am of age now and we have found you. All the prophecies are in line. We have one year to accomplish our goals." His quiet voice was calm and sure.

"What do you mean launch the tribulation? What's going to happen?"

"I cannot say."

She reached out tentatively, connected to him, asked again in a way that he could not lie. He didn't try to hide his visions. She saw angry people, riots, violence—assassinations at public events. She saw explosions. She saw the Spiritual Centers being destroyed, trashed. Shuddering, she pulled back. "Again, I ask you." She said aloud. "Why do you want this? Surely you know that just as many of your people will die in this fanatical mission as anyone else. What possible good can come from violence and the senseless death of thousands, perhaps millions, possibly leading to anarchy?"

"The violence and human suffering is unfortunate." He agreed. "But the deaths will not be senseless. They will lead us all forward to a better place, to our destiny."

"Kalesh, I know your intentions and beliefs are pure but your logic is flawed." Impulsively, she reached out and touched his hand across the table, her eyes locking into his. He flinched at her unexpected touch. She gripped his hand anyway. "Kalesh, everyone must find their way to that better place in their own time, in their own manner. It's the human way."

"The human condition—the limitations, the ego, the temperament of man," he responded, "this cage we are trapped inside," he waved his hands downward to indicate his body, "is hell. Surely you see that?"

She shivered, all of a sudden aware of her physical surroundings and the vulnerable casing that held her spirit. She desperately wanted to protect her corporeal existence even though she'd glimpsed exquisite possibilities beyond this life. It was the survival instincts of her race. Why didn't he feel the same way?

Darkness was approaching with a full moon blossoming on the horizon. The warm breeze had turned chilly. She wore a short, mid-calf length, white tunic with short sleeves, the long robe abandoned in her small room.

She rubbed the goose-pimples from her arms as she pondered the situation. They'd reached a level of understanding. He'd shown her what he believed and why. She even sympathized, could share his emotions as if they were her own—yet, she still had her own feelings, her own beliefs. She had to show him the other side but how? She didn't possess his ability to traverse time and space, to see humanity's ebb and flow, the patterns of their race.

"I have seen what you see, Kalesh. I even feel your pain but you've been conditioned to find the suffering, the cruelty, the weakness of man. You've been reared on the impossibility of man's future trapped as we have been in our solitary egos. Don't you see that you've been manipulated to only look for these signs? There is more that you must see, that you must experience, before we can join together to carry out any plans with such far-reaching consequences for so many. I am beginning to believe this is a responsibility that we must own together—but, we can't operate under rules or mandates dictated by others."

"Willow," he spoke her name aloud, his urgent whisper circling, echoing strangely, in the breeze. She both heard and felt his inner panic. "We have very little time. You must join with me." He leaned forward, his body rigid. "You can't question the path we've chosen. It's too late. This has been ordained for centuries. Don't you understand what will happen if you don't completely acquiesce?" He glanced about them furtively, his shaggy, dark head still while his eyes darted from side to side rapidly. No one was close enough to hear their words.

"I do." Willow nodded gravely, her pupils large, darkening the green in her eyes to match the foliage surrounding them. She shivered again. "Kalesh, I'm getting cold. Is there anywhere we can go inside?"

Nodding he rose and reached out a hand to lead her.

As she followed him into the mansion, hand in hand, she squelched down her own panic, bracing herself. It was all up to her now. She had to find a way out of this and she had to convince him—of what exactly, she was not sure. At this point, the chance of being rescued was unlikely.

She knew she wouldn't be able to pledge allegiance to their bloody plan although she had no idea what the alternative was. The Republic's way, PURE, was flawed, unforgivably flawed. Without believing to the point of knowing—as he did—she wasn't sure how she could alter his conviction, lead him to another path. But it was the only approach she could come up with.

There was no room for self-doubt. Roland would return soon and it could be all over.

Chapter 52

"If there is no meditation, then you are like a blind man in a world of great beauty, light and colour."

Krishnamurti

"I still don't understand why we're here." Sophie asked, not for the first time. "Why can't I go home?"

They were gathered around the counter of the open, common area of the executive suites, housed deep within the government towers where they had been lodged. There were nine bed and bath suites with the shared living, dining and kitchen area in the middle. With only four of them staying, it was overly large and luxurious for their needs. Two guards were stationed outside the door but otherwise, they had been left alone with a well-stocked kitchen and a prepared meal on the table. They had all the amenities they could possibly require for a comfortable stay although their portal units and any other means of communicating with the outside world had been confiscated.

Aaron pushed away from the counter to pace the living area. "Sophie, for the tenth time, we don't know exactly why—but it's probably because they don't want you to contaminate the community with stories about the Cult." He shrugged. "At least until they have contained the situation."

"They barely let me speak to my parents. They wouldn't let me tell them anything about what happened," she moaned.

"No kidding," Aaron responded. "You can't imagine how inquisitive my mother was when I spoke to her via portal earlier. It was very hard to hold back but I think she realized that I couldn't tell her anything. She wanted to come and join us but they wouldn't let her."

Simon's eye's bulged in his thin, pale face. "I don't understand. We helped them, didn't we?" He folded his arms, wrapping them tightly about his chest. "How could my, uh, my m…" He stumbled in his sentence, stopping himself from using the word. "How could she—how could they both—just lock us up here like this? I was able to read the prisoners. I told them everything. I thought we were working together." He whined.

"Everyone, listen." Claire hissed. She motioned to Aaron who was at the other end of the room, having just strutted back in their direction. "That includes you, Aaron, come back here."

Aaron flinched, visibly jolted out of his miserable self-absorption by her command. "Yes, boss, on my way." He drawled and returned to the counter, pulling out a stool to lean on.

When all three of them were silently grouped around the counter and focused on her, Claire continued. "The three of us have been pledged to abide by the PURE Secrecy Clause." Simon and Aaron nodded solemnly. "Sophie, I don't know what transpired during your interrogation but I suspect that they requested discretion from you in terms of sharing information about your experiences?"

"Uh, yeah, they said that I was not to tell anyone what happened." She concurred. "But, that doesn't make any sense to me and anyway, why shouldn't I? I didn't do anything wrong."

"Well, you did lead my sister into a trap, after all." Claire snapped back. "So, I'm not sure that you're quite so innocent in all this."

"Claire, how could you?" Sophie exclaimed, pushing back her stool to stand erect in her indignation. "You know I would never do anything to hurt Willow. I was tricked. P-ul-lease. It was horrifying. I'll probably never recover from the trauma."

Claire took a deep breath. There was nothing to be gained by this, she reminded herself. When she'd found out how Sophie had blindly led Willow into the hands of the cult, she'd been infuriated. But her cousin was just self-centered, oblivious Sophie. It wouldn't do any good to point fingers right now. "Yeah, okay, Sophie. Whatever. Just calm down and take a seat, will you?"

Sophie's stool scraped loudly as she shoved it back in place and planted herself down. Aaron cleared his throat and spoke directly to Claire. "What were you going to tell us? Do you think we're in danger here, even within the ruling walls of the Republic?"

"I'm going to tell you what I know," Claire responded, "and then I'll tell you what I think." With her elbows leaning on the counter, she tabulated with her fingers as she spoke. "First, the Republic and the CRKA take these oaths very seriously. I know you heard it earlier today but I want to remind you that breaking the Secrecy Pledge is considered treason and can be punishable by death." She gazed calmly at the wide, silent eyes of her companions as she spoke. "Even inadvertently speaking about certain, classified details amongst ourselves could qualify."

Simon nodded obediently. "Okay, Claire, I understand what you're saying."

Sophie glanced over at him, her perky face scrunched into a question mark. "What, in the name of Marrisha, are you hiding?" She asked. "Punishable by death—are you kidding me?"

"Sophie, shush." Claire insisted. "The less you say, the better off we'll all be. The other thing that I can pretty much guarantee is that everything we say in this room, in fact anywhere in these buildings, will be recorded and analyzed by the CRKA."

"Yes, of course, you're right." Aaron agreed. His soft brown hair was a mess, tangled curls protruding in various directions. He brushed the loose hair off his forehead and leaned forward on his hands to listen closely.

"I hope they understand that we're all concerned, committed citizens of the Republic." Claire stated succinctly for the record. "I hope they understand how desperately we want to help bring this cult down and save my sister but," she paused significantly, "unfortunately, there is nothing we, nor anyone else including my father, can do to change our situation until they decide to take us out of here and involve us further."

"So, we're prisoners?" Sophie groaned. "I thought I'd just been rescued."

"Let's just say we're honoured guests of the state. It could be worse." Claire waved her arm about the beautifully, decorated rooms. "We have everything we need."

"So, what do you suggest we do?" Aaron asked, his voice low and ominous.

"Well, I think we should, uh, meditate," Claire responded, "and verbalize as little as possible."

"Meditate?" Simon squeaked.

"I wonder if you could all teach me how you do it?" Claire asked. "You know, go into that trance-like, relaxed state? It occurs to me that if Willow has reached out to others who were not physically in her presence before, well, uh."

Aaron's face brightened. "Aaahh. You're a genius, Claire."

Even Sophie was nodding in agreement. "Oh yes, you're right Claire. She could find us, I think. You can't imagine what she can do unless you've experienced it before."

Simon smiled. He stood up, pushing his stool back with deliberation, suddenly taking command. "Yes, of course, it's the only sensible thing for us to do now. I don't know why I didn't think of it." He marched to the edge of the living area, inspecting the blue leather and chrome lounge chairs and soft, furry couches. "Okay, let's move the furniture around so we can all get comfortable and hold hands at the beginning." He glanced over at Claire. "With your family connections, I bet you'll be a natural. You just need to relax, get yourself into a drowsy, dreamy state and we'll lead you the rest of the way."

Chapter 53

"We don't realize that the gods are not out there somewhere. They live in us all. They are the energies of life itself."

Joseph Campbell

They lay together on soft, white sheets draped over the enormous bed in the dark, silent room—hands clutched together, heads touching softly, blonde and black hair intertwined on the shared pillow. He'd taken her swiftly back to the peaceful, joyous place where they could rest and be together as one. She felt the presence of others, of the whole world at once, and yet of no one but the two of them. The others weren't really separate entities; it was as if they were part of her. It was as if everyone she had ever loved was there, sharing her bliss. A lifetime of her parents' loving guidance, Great Bet somehow watching over her, her passion for Aaron—although not able to take hold in this place—the pure ecstasy of their loving experience lingered nevertheless. All of this floated along and contributed to the beauty and serenity. Shimmering sights and sounds, fragrances and touches—all the senses flowed along in the heavenly space. Only the glorious good, the wonderfully peaceful, exquisite feelings existed together all at once and yet not all—for there was an immense emptiness that supported everything.

They lingered, floating, loving each other, connected in a unique and binding way. They did not exist in time or space. Their love was timeless. It was as if they had always been that way. Finally, reluctantly, he pulled her back. They faced each other in a deep, dark void. She sensed what he wanted. He waited for her commitment, her promise to join him on his path, to believe what he believed, to follow blindly. She drifted, reluctant to relinquish her peaceful state. He reached for her, gently, pulling her along until they faced the twisted pathways from her dreams. She felt his need, his yearning for her to join with him, his belief in the holy mission he had been raised on.

This time, he showed her the pathways of the future: events, causes and effects. She watched in amazement as various futures played out in their collective dream state. At first, she wondered if it could be his imagination, so vivid that he was simply laying out scenes in his fantasy world but then she felt a connection, understood more deeply what was happening.

He answered her unspoken doubts, somehow missing that she had actually started to click. She already saw the truth in what he'd shown—but something more as well.

"It is real." His words echoed in her mind. "I have seen reality exacted according to my visions before. You can see the variations, the small changes that can trigger enormous consequences—it's impossible to know, to control everything."

She learned as she followed him, comprehending in an innate, non-literal, non-logical sense, why this was possible, even how he could see it.

The chances of his brotherhood actually succeeding with their end goals—with the complete destruction of the Republic, the cult assuming power and ultimately the mass devastation of Armageddon—she felt, were slim. If they did succeed, however, if they were able to move us along this path, she shuddered, inwardly shocked, it would be holy wars all over again, death and suffering to countless human beings, and ultimately the end of the blossoming gifts that they both were experiencing.

She saw the anguish as it spread from his heart, understanding, truly knowing, in that instant what it was to be him, to have these abilities, to have grown up as he did, used as he had been—yet driven by loyalty and devotion to his father and brotherhood. Conversely, she was coming into her gifts later, after a stable and loving upbringing. Perhaps she was not at the same level as he—yet—but she hoped that if only she could guide him along other paths, she might have some influence.

Even while she empathized with him, she glimpsed, in that moment, something that was missing—that he lacked something that she possessed. He saw the patterns, he traversed time but he didn't see inside the heart of humanity, even deep within an individual, not the way she could. She had to show him, make him understand—for it was her only chance to demonstrate the possibilities, to negate the futility that he believed demanded a dark destiny. The loss of this new state of consciousness—for humanity—made the slight chance of the cult succeeding even more devastating. She was beginning to perceive a possibility, a glimmer of a wondrous possibility. He'd shown it to her and yet he didn't see. She felt they had to strive for this impossible dream for humanity. They had to try before admitting defeat.

She reached for him, holding him as he'd never been held, loving him as he'd never been loved. Come deeper, be with me, she encouraged. Irresistible though his desire was, he held back, uncertain. You have shown me so much. Let me show you what I see, she coaxed. He relented, his hold relaxing as he trusted her to take him.

She brought him on her personal journey, the journey of her life. He felt what she felt, grew along with her. He saw her family as they are. He saw their flaws as she did but she took him deeper. She showed him the heart and soul of people who struggled to be their best in life, to raise their families, to be good citizens. She showed him a mother's love and devotion, the generations of mothers in her family. They traversed time to experience his mother. Willow encouraged him. He found the woman who had nurtured him as a boy. Together, they felt her heart, experienced her love.

They reached outwards and found others. They saw the failings, the human emotions and egos that often ended in anger, sometimes even in tragedy, but also in passion and love, in acts of charity, in expressions of great beauty. She revealed the possibilities if they could all experience their life with this new sense that they had developed, if they could be one.

Together they envisioned a new path. They saw a narrow, hidden way, a hidden exit from the midst of the twisted path, into the most beautiful section of woods. Fragrant blossoms dangled from trees, sunshine streamed between branches. This path was hard to find but it led to a new world, a new existence. At the end of the path, so far out in the distant, they saw an end to humanity but not a violent devastating end—rather a rebirth, a new beginning, a metamorphosis. It was glorious, it was right. Suffering was minimal. It was a much different end than he had been raised to instigate. It was an evolution—not only of life on this planet but of the universal life force, of something much greater than they even yet comprehended.

As they gazed together, as one, at the pathways, the possible futures, she felt a tug, another presence calling, desperate. Together they turned to the beaconing source, felt the primitive reaching. After her experiences with Kalesh, she reached them easily. They circled the four, shared their presence. She wrapped them in their loving spirit, pulling Kalesh in. She saw where they were, understood they were safe. When Kalesh began to back away, seeing their past connections, feeling alienated, she held him tighter, loved him openly, made him part of their circle. He felt them all. In that instant, he knew them all intimately, as she did.

But then an inner voice shrieked. He recoiled. No, he insisted. It is not the way. You must join us. We don't have time for this. Again, he showed her the plan, the path they must follow. This time, they all saw. The others were horrified. It was too much for them. Willow soothed Kalesh, leaving Claire and Aaron, Sophie and Simon. They saw that they could not follow where she must go. They radiated their love. They were gone.

Again, Willow and Kalesh faced each other in the void.

Chapter 54

"The god of the cannibals will be a cannibal, of the crusaders a crusader, and of the merchants a merchant."

Ralph Waldo Emerson

The golden light streamed in from the east-facing window, absent of coverings. They awoke in unison, rising slowly, each moving to opposite sides of the bed, locked in their own thoughts. The longest day of the year was beginning. It was the day that had been anticipated by so many and that now each of them, in their own way, dreaded.

Alone, jolted into the physical realm, disconnected for the first time since evening, Willow began to tremble. The danger to herself and to so many others was real. In their connected state, with the power they'd discovered together, she'd believed anything was possible but this morning, she was vulnerable and afraid. He was not convinced. She knew this. Without his support, without their joining and becoming true soul mates, she was doomed. Even with their shared visions, he seemed to be as stuck in his beliefs and loyalty to the cult as she was in her aversion to it. Still, there had been moments when he'd seen, felt, experienced as she had. In those moments, they'd bonded together on the brink of a magnificent future. She thought they'd made progress, found a hidden crevice where they could forge a new path. She thought he'd been ready to march forward with her—but then she'd lost him, again.

She remembered their encounter with Aaron and Claire, Sophie and Simon. How she'd wanted to stay with them longer but couldn't. To do so might have risked the intense yet tenuous connection that she and Kalesh were forming. Still, she'd shown them what she could.

Goose pimples rose on her bare arms as she relived her brief experience with Aaron, glimpsing the pain in his heart, the longing. In another time, another place, she would've soothed him with body and soul, loved him back the way she now knew he loved her. Even in her present crisis, she was haunted by memories of their love-making, the ecstasy in just staring, touching, stroking, running her hands through his shiny, soft brown hair. But this physical, self-indulgent, passion was no longer for her, might never be hers again. Deep inside she sensed that no matter what happened today, even if she lived to see the sunset, there were too many obstacles for them, too many conflicts in their future paths. Still, the blossoming young woman, the sensual creature that he'd awakened, prayed for a return to her previous life, somehow, someway.

She was escorted back to her chambers where she cleaned and dressed into the virginal white, kimono-style robe laid out for her. After picking at breakfast left on a tray, she was whisked away again, this time to a large library in another wing of the mansion.

She recognized the young man who stood guard at the entrance, opening the door wide for her entry. It was Charlie, the object of Sophie's foolish infatuation, the one who'd coerced them into the trap. Willow stood erect and paused in the doorway to stare at him, searching within to find the evil lurking. The dark-skinned young man flushed and looked away. She ravaged his inner being, surprised to find love and kindness within. Another one, she thought, another pure heart led astray by a fanatical belief in this cult. He suffered for his betrayal to Sophie but nothing could take precedence over their holy mission. Just as she began to probe deeper, seeking the source of his loyalty, she was abruptly pushed into the room from behind. The door closed firmly. Releasing her mental hold on Charlie, she gazed forward to face her judge and jury.

They sat in comfortable chairs, turned away from an old stone fireplace to face the doorway. An ornate desk across the room, under the windows, was clean and uncluttered. There were air-locked shelves of well-preserved old books and large open windows facing the back garden.

Roland sat in the middle. He was flanked on either side by his priests. In the bright morning sunlight, even with their hoods, she could see them more clearly. Her attention was drawn to the mysterious man with the odd colouring. His skin was so white that it glowed, his eyes, slanted and bright blue. An Asian albino, she thought to herself, surprised. Usually one with such an abnormality at birth would be sent away. His piercing stare was grim, unrelenting.

The other man was familiar. She'd encountered him on the Island Retreat. Benson was the name, she recalled. He watched her closely, stroking the scar along his left cheek, more tentative than the others, his eyes wary.

Kalesh stood slightly behind and to the right of the regal, burgundy stuffed chair where his white-haired father sat. His posture was rigid. Willow glanced past Roland, ignoring the family resemblance to her Grandma Sybil, twisted into ugliness, and found the boy's soulful, black eyes. He resisted her mildly, finally making eye contact, letting her touch him as only she could. Their connection snapped back into place, both feeling the steady hum of their peaceful coexistence. In the early morning hours of their dream state, she thought they'd found a way—a way forward for all, a wonderful future. It would require careful planning, manipulation, a ruthless loyalty to each other and to the narrow pathway of their dream. It was her lifeline, the one chance she had left but, apparently, it was not his. She'd lost him. His years of loyalty to the cult, to Roland, to Armageddon—death and destruction, anarchy—had pulled him back.

"Today is a sacred day. The holy events of our prophecy will begin." Roland pronounced, watching her closely.

"The summer solstice." She murmured.

"Yes, since the beginning of time, the solstice has been a day revered." Roland agreed. "Today will mark the most memorable solstice ever. The world will see us for the first time. They will follow us when we lead them forward."

"Forward? Don't you mean downward?" Her sarcasm was revealing.

"Hasn't my son shown you the way?" Roland spoke quietly, his voice dangerously soft.

"We've visited many places together." Willow concurred. "Many places, many times. I understand what you want, what you're planning."

The three men jerked their heads back in unison, glancing sharply at Kalesh. "How much does she know?"

Deep colour rose from his neck up into his cheeks. The boy, their messiah, shrugged. "She knows essentially what I know. It couldn't be helped." Kalesh moved from behind Roland to stand in front of the three, closer to Willow. They all faced one another, in a tense pentagon of diverse features, the white robed figure of the fair-haired girl and the black robed figure of the dark-haired boy contrasting with the elderly council before them.

"But has she pledged herself to our path?" Roland glanced over at the two guards standing inside the doorway, prepared to call them into action. "Kalesh, there is no more time. Either she becomes your wife today, to worship you, to follow you, to help lead our people—or she must be obliterated. She represents a danger to us all unless she pledges to follow the mission of the Cult of Armageddon."

Kalesh turned to face Willow. She stared back, absorbing the set of his jaw, the deep sadness shimmering in his eyes. He held his lips firm, not yet ready to speak, not yet ready to pronounce the truth which would be the end of her—and of their precious, newly formed, union.

An idea, just the barest glimmer of an idea, occurred to her. Maybe there was one chance, one last revelation which could make him see. "Kalesh," she whispered. "Follow me." She pleaded. She took hold of him and dove deep into the heart of the man he loved, the man he called father. He'd never looked, perhaps had been too afraid to really see what lay there. She had to show him.

Roland froze in his seat, closing his eyes tightly, attempting to resist. It was futile. He grasped his head with both hands. "No." He whimpered but it was already too late. The three relived his life experiences and his deepest desires, in a flash. Kalesh understood the family connections to Willow. He experienced his father's disillusion with society, his feud with his family and the ultimate bitterness that had long since twisted into hatred. The fuel that drove him, the need for vengeance, was impossible to miss. How had Kalesh overlooked, neglected to see, his father's real motivation for all these years? He'd sensed glimmers of his father's dark side but hadn't wanted to face it. Even Roland's devotion to Kalesh wasn't truly spawned by love but by a desire to use his powers, his abilities. He experienced anew his father's elation when he'd advanced so rapidly as a child. Roland married Kalesh's mother afterwards, not before that, he realized. His kind-hearted mother had loved Roland—this he knew—but even her sweet devotion had only been a pawn in the high priest's plans. Roland had never mourned his mother's passing the way Kalesh thought. In many ways, it had simply made his plans easier, his control of her son more absolute.

"Enough!" Kalesh shrieked. The sharp pain in his heart was a throbbing, living organism. Willow relented immediately, experienced his pain as if it were her own. The three separated and remained still, panting, eyes wide open. The guards at the door continued their steadfast watch, expressions implacable but the two priests on either side of Roland had sensed the inner turmoil. They'd both arisen in alarm, leaning over the high priest's chair.

"Your Worship." The albino's voice was clipped. "We must end this now. Give the order."

The other man, Benson, shook visibly at the recommendation while his head bobbed nervously in agreement. "Y-yes, it is time."

Roland required only a moment to collect his wayward emotions. "Guards." He bellowed. The two at the door sprang to action, taking position on either side of Willow. The burly man on her left was careful not to brush up against Kalesh who stood close by, his respect for the boy evident. "Take her now and follow the instructions you were given earlier. Do it swiftly." He waved his hand towards the garden doors, indicating they should take her outside. He turned to Kalesh. "My son, you must ensure that she doesn't interfere. Hold her mind."

Willow screamed as the guards each yanked her by an arm and dragged her towards the garden doors, the brilliant morning sun blinding her as her head was thrown backwards. She fought violently, trying to wrestle herself free, applying all her physical strength. She soon realized the complete futility of her actions. They could crush her with their bare hands. Finally, she forced herself to be still as they pulled her along, focusing her mental strength. Even that was futile, she discovered. Kalesh encircled her, his mind as solid as a fortress. She was trapped.

"Everyone stop!" Kalesh roared, the unprecedented insistence of his voice was accompanied by a mental command that no one could ignore. They all froze. He kicked a small table out of his way, causing it to ricochet across the room, smashing a large vase in the corner. The explosive crash assaulted their ears. He stepped back to the doorway, glaring at them all. "Put her at my feet where she belongs." He motioned to the guards. "She will follow my orders." They complied without hesitation, ruthlessly pushing the slight young woman in their grasp onto the floor before him. When she began to rise, the boy pushed her back down. "Stay in your place." He growled. "Or suffer the consequences." Willow remained down.

Roland swallowed through a dry mouth. "Kalesh," he began.

"No, I'm ready now, father." Kalesh interrupted him. "I have seen the way. It's time for me to take control." He pointed at his three elders. "We must be more aggressive than planned in our next steps. I will tell you what to do, from this point forward." At their silence, he seized their minds again, watching as they all reached for their temples. "Do you understand?"

Mutely, the three men nodded, their facial expressions stunned into acquiescence, wondering how the shy, unassuming boy had undergone such a transformation. Willow gazed up at Kalesh from the floor, fear pulsing through her veins, no longer able to recognize the gentle, young man she thought she'd known from the inside, out—even though they'd only just met. Now, his dark eyes gleamed astonishingly in the light. His intentions were closed to her.

Chapter 55

"It's no measure of health to be well adjusted to a profoundly sick society."

Krishnamurti

After Claire's brief communication with her parents late in the morning, she waited smugly for the summons. By mentioning that she'd heard from Willow, she expected to get their attention.

Finally, as anticipated, Ramona Markel came to escort her alone to meet with the World Governors. Her three roommates had been dismayed when Ramona called only for Claire. Aaron, in particular, insisted that he accompany Claire to the meeting but Ramona ignored his request.

Claire squeezed Aaron's hand as she prepared to leave. "Don't worry. We have the same goal here: to get Willow home safely. I'll be back soon." She waved good-bye to them all and exited the suite, following Agent Markel into the bright corridor.

"So, how are you this morning, Ramona?" Her friendly question was greeted with a silent sideways glance so she continued. "Okay, I guess you must be having a bad morning. Going to the Solstice Festival tonight?"

After scanning her hand to gain access to the lift, Ramona led Claire into the cubicle. She turned towards her prisoner as they ascended to the upper levels. "Miss Olsen, perhaps you haven't noticed but this is hardly a social stroll we're taking."

Claire's return laughter was infectious. Even the overly intense Agent Markel couldn't hold back a smirk. "I wish we'd met under other circumstances but surely you're not going to treat me as a suspect or a criminal in one of your cases, Ramona?"

Her famous charm seemed to finally hit its target. Ramona grinned, her somber, square features transformed. "Okay, Miss, uh, I mean Claire. You're right. These are unusual circumstances. In another situation, we could be colleagues. Not that I'm a huge fan of you uptight, law-frenzied Justice types." Her smile took the edge out of her comment. The lift pulled to a smooth halt on the top floor. The doors slid open. Ramona reached her arm forward to direct Claire out first. "As for the Solstice Festival, it looks like I'm working tonight. We all are. Personal plans have been cancelled."

So they were concerned about the Solstice Festival, Claire thought, wondering what their intelligence had discovered. Her ruminations halted abruptly when she realized where they were. They'd passed yet another security entrance and were marching through the exalted Governor's suite of offices. She'd dreamed of this. Even under the current circumstances, her heart beat a touch faster as she stepped into their suite, excitement flushing her cheeks.

The World Governors' shared office was opulent and enormous. Two separate seating areas, decorated in earthy tones—shades of beige, brown, greens were situated at opposite ends of the room. Wall to ceiling windows spread across the entire back wall, with a breathtaking view of the city.

Sharon and Craig were waiting for her.

They led her towards a glass conference table in the back corner of the room, with the largest portal screen Claire had ever seen at one end. Sharon abruptly excused Ramona and then the three of them were alone in the magnificent office suite, Claire facing the two leaders who sat side by side across from her.

"You'll have to excuse me for gawking." Claire smiled. "This is absolutely fabulous. I've often wondered what it would look like."

Sharon smiled. "No problem. You seem to have more interest in the Republic and its inner workings than your sister did."

"Ha Ha." Claire laughed aloud. "That would be an understatement. You've probably never seen two sisters more different than we." Her expression sobered quickly. "But that doesn't mean we aren't close. I'm very anxious to get her home. My parents are becoming quite anxious."

"We're also anxious." Craig concurred. "Which is why we called you in. I'm sure you're aware that your conversations are being monitored?" At Claire's sardonic nod, he continued. "In the early hours of the morning and then again in your call with your parents, you referenced being in contact with Willow. Is this true?"

"Yes, I believe it's true but it was most unusual, unlike anything I've ever experienced."

"You must tell us everything. We can only help if we know what we're dealing with." Sharon interjected.

Claire nodded agreeably but her lashes lowered, eyes focused inward as she considered her next move. "I will try to tell you. It's hard to put it all into words." She licked dry lips, wishing she had her gloss. "However, I'm concerned. If I share everything I know, how can I be certain that you won't just lock me away again? I too can help here. I'm a qualified investigator. I've taken more than one oath of loyalty and secrecy to PURE. Plus, this is my sister. Why can't I be part of the team? Why do you lock me away as if I'm a danger to the state?"

The leaders glanced at each other, considering her words. They nodded in silent agreement. "Okay, Claire." Craig agreed. "You have our word that we will keep you on this team as long as your actions continue to be consistent with your pledge. But, you have to remember that your first loyalty is to us, to the PURE principles—above even that of your sister's life. Do you understand?"

Her throat was dry, her face frozen as she considered their words. She'd never expected it would come to this when she'd pledged her allegiance. There was no choice but to accept their terms. "Of course, your Honours, of course. I understand my commitment to the state. It has always come first with me."

Sharon reached across the table and shook Claire's hand. "We have a deal then. Effective immediately, you will join our staff here." She activated the portal, giving rapid fire instructions to grant Claire access to their floor and provide her with a working space. "Okay?"

"Wow, that was fast." Claire nodded. "I'm excited to be joining your team or at least I will be when we get through this current crisis."

"I'm sure you won't disappoint." Craig remarked dryly. "Now what did you learn about Willow?"

Claire sat up straighter, assuming her professional demeanor as she reported crisply. "We joined together to meditate, to reach a state where we might be able to connect with her. I had no previous experience with Vision Speak so I simply followed their lead. When it happened, it was almost like I was sleeping, dreaming but it was real. It was her, and she was with another. Her companion was powerful, experienced in this inner way of communicating. Yet he was immature, youthful in other ways. I know that doesn't make a lot of sense." She shrugged.

"No, it makes more sense than you know." Sharon responded. "There are reports of a messiah within this cult—a young devotee who has great spiritual abilities and will lead them to their Armageddon. We suspect that is the boy you encountered. Our intelligence now indicates that they want your sister to join with him, to mate for life. They have a prophecy about two gifted ones."

"Oh." Claire said, thinking of Aaron, remembering her sister's infatuation for him, her dreams of her future in the Arts Community. "What will happen when she refuses?"

"We hope for that, in the end, of course." Sharon answered. "However, her refusal could mean a death sentence if we cannot get to her in time." Claire was silent as she began to understand her sister's predicament.

"Tell us what else you learned." Craig veered the conversation back to a productive area. "Do you know where they are?"

"She shared so much with us, so fast. I'm still processing, discovering that there is new information up here." She tapped her finger against her temple. "It's astounding. Willow doesn't know where she is but I saw some of her visions. She's in an enormous old mansion with beautiful gardens. They are watching her constantly. She will not have the opportunity to escape like Sophie did."

"Do you know what they're planning?"

Claire winced, the question triggering terrible visions inside her mind. "They want chaos, anarchy. They will sacrifice many lives to take us back to the same state as the Century of Despair. To them, it's holy. I know you told us this but now I've experienced it. I've seen what they want. They have many plans but I don't know the details. I don't think Willow knew the details. They have some weaponry which can cause death and destruction to many, some kind of bombs. They have enormous connections in every region of the world. Their reach, their power is much more of a threat than anyone has realized."

"In the name of Marrisha." Sharon exclaimed. "How are we to contain all this? If we don't stop them in time, it will be impossible to prevent this from leaking out to the general populace."

Claire's gaze sharpened. "It already is too late."

"What do you mean?"

"Surely you know that these last two incidents—the messages on the world portal and the riot in the square—have already been talked about widely?"

"Yes, it can't be helped but we've provided explanations. We've kept the name of the Cult from the news, dismissed them as isolated, criminal incidents. People will forget."

"It's gone too far now. More will happen, possibly tonight or in the coming days and weeks, I fear." Claire spoke confidently, realizing that her words, this message, also came from Willow. "Don't you see that they expect you to suppress this information, as you have for so long? They will use this against you, to show how you have been manipulating the good citizens for centuries. They will expose your methods. PURE citizens will see the propaganda for what it is. They will become outraged at the lies, the deception, the injustice."

"No." Sharon whispered, her face ashen. "No, it has all been for their own good, to preserve peace. We must continue to maintain the balance."

"The scales have tipped too far." Claire insisted. "Everything will unravel and the Cult will win without ever having fought a battle. Anarchy will follow. Perhaps it is time to carve out a new way while you still have your hands on the controls."

"What are you suggesting?" Craig barked.

"I don't have all the answers. Perhaps if we can survive this present crisis, there are those who will have the vision to show us the way." Seeing the alarm in the leaders' eyes, Claire moved on. "I'm merely sharing with you what I learned. I haven't had time to think it all through. In the short term, I believe the best course of action is to advise the People of the United Republic of Earth of the impending threat. Tell them the truth about the Cult and their machinations. Warn them of the possible terrorist attacks. Tell them we are on a high security alert. You may even have to cancel the Solstice Festival tonight."

"But they will panic. What you suggest will cause chaos in our society." Sharon objected. "It goes against our guiding principles. And, we absolutely would never announce the name or details of a dissident group such as this. It gives them too much recognition. We must manage the situation, bring them down and work to hide this harmful information from the citizens. It's the only way to maintain the PURE balance. The World Leaders stand united on this. Otherwise, the questions that follow will have enormous impact."

"I know it is your way, has always been the way that peace has been manipulated with the Republic. In the early days, it was necessary. I know this but I'm telling you that, now, it's too late. With everything that's happened and will happen, the repercussions are real. You won't succeed in suppressing this. In fact, it will probably backfire. Continue to manipulate people, smother the truth and you will be playing right into the Cult's hands. It's what they expect you to do."

"How can you know all this?" Craig demanded.

"I, uh, I'm not sure." Before Claire could continue, an urgent request for entry was announced. At Craig's verbal command, the doors swished open and their Executive Aide, Burton, rushed into the room. His pale white cheeks were flushed with pink excitement. The hood of his cape had fallen back, exposing his unusual features in the light. An albino, thought Claire, how unusual, particularly in a high-ranking government job.

"I'm sorry to interrupt your meeting but we've just received a communiqué from the Cult, an ultimatum of sorts, directed to you personally." He blurted. "We have only two hours to comply or they'll kill the girl, Willow."

Chapter 56

"The important thing is not to stop questioning."

Albert Einstein

Willow had been trapped for hours. Physically she was restricted to her quarters with guards posted outside the door but, even worse, Kalesh still held her inner consciousness. She was amazed that he'd managed to maintain his hold for so long and still function in other areas but that appeared to be what he was doing.

She had no idea what he was intending or what was going on. He'd spared her life—for the moment—but she couldn't read him at all. Still, even in the tyrannical mood he'd demonstrated earlier, she'd prefer to be at his mercy than at the mercy of Great Uncle Roland.

Roland was insane. She'd be in a deep, dark hole by now if it was up to him.

It was inconceivable to her that Kalesh would harm her, not after their intimacies, not after how deeply they'd bonded together. And, not after she'd seen the beauty deep inside his soul. It was this belief that kept her together while she waited—for what, she did not know.

She let out an involuntary scream when the door burst open, startling her out of her reverie. The guards motioned for her to follow.

They led her back to the library. They pulled open the double doors and pushed her inside. She heard the loud thud as the doors closed firmly behind her.

She was alone with Kalesh who was perched on the desk. As they faced each other from across the room, she felt the release. He no longer held her mind.

"We will be leaving soon." He said, rubbing his temple. His unlined skin was so young and yet the way he carried himself, something in his demeanor suddenly seemed so old.

"Where are we going?" She inched forward to stand closer, tentatively reaching outwards. He was exhausted. She sensed it.

"To meet your leaders. To see your people." He responded. "To end this."

Chapter 57

"Everything you are against weakens you. Everything you are for empowers you."

Dr. Wayne Dyer

The wrinkled face, surrounded by ancient white, unruly hair was overpowered by his wild, intense, jade-green eyes. The man's head was enormous on the portal screen in the World Governors' office. Sharon and Craig, Claire and Burton sat riveted on either side of the conference table as they watched the fanatical man, who claimed to be the High Priest of the Cult of Armageddon, deliver his message. He'd been ranting since they began the video feed several minutes earlier.

"Your Marrisha and Kamon—they are the most colossal hoax ever hoisted upon a population. You say they saved humanity. I tell you they have desecrated our souls. You force your people, the PURE citizens," he spat out the words with disdain, "to take their religious training, to attend your centers. They have no free will. They are lambs led to the slaughter—the slaughter of their creativity, of their minds, of their very souls."

He paused to take a breath. Sharon and Craig exchanged a glance. He covered her hand with his and they returned their attention to the crazed man on the screen.

"You pretend to be peaceful, kind, benevolent—and you commit cold-blooded murder everyday to maintain the pretense. The people will know the truth. We will flood them with the truth."

"Three and a half centuries ago, our people were ready to face a new destiny but your PURE power play prevented it. You manipulated the world then, delaying the messiah and our ultimate journey. But now we are ready again. The miracle has occurred. As Samuel predicted in the Holy Journals of our Trial, the messiah is here. We are poised and ready to begin our attack, to lead the people to glory.

"It will begin tonight. First, with the sacrifice of the young girl and then with widespread destruction. We give you one chance to prevent her public execution, for all to see, on the world portal. You—the leaders—will meet with us today, in person, to discuss terms."

When the video ended, they all remained still. The room echoed their stunned silence.

Sharon spoke first. "I think I recognize that man. The lunatic."

All eyes centered on the ashen face of the World Governor. Claire responded first. "I do too." She said. "I can't believe it but I know who he is—or who he was, rather."

"You both know him?" Craig's tone was disgusted, incredulous.

Sharon locked eyes with Claire. "You know him too?"

Nodding solemnly, she swallowed through a tight throat. "I believe he is my long-lost, Great Uncle Roland." She said.

"Your great uncle? But that means that he's Elzbeth's."

"Son." Claire finished her sentence.

"Elzbeth's son." Sharon repeated. She continued to stare at Claire as she absorbed this information.

"How do you know him?" Craig demanded an answer.

Visibly shaking herself, she gazed at Craig. "He was part of the Cult back when I was an agent, when I was undercover. He was ascending to the upper levels, fast, at the time. It's just that, well, he was captured."

"Was he part of the indoctrination ceremony?" Craig's question was razor sharp.

"Uh, he might have been. I'm not sure." Her face glowed red. "But, that is not my point. The point is that I thought he was executed at the time. I know he was scheduled for it just after I went into seclusion."

Burton was silent during their interchange but he listened attentively, his expression masked.

Claire told them about the revelation during Roland's closure ceremony just before Willow disappeared. "Apparently Great Bet saved him from that execution and arranged for him to be sent overseas to a work camp." She concluded. "We didn't know if he was dead or alive after all these years. I guess now we know."

"Your great grandmother manipulated a lot in her day." Craig remarked, his tone laced with sarcasm.

"I'm afraid so." Claire agreed. "It's what made her such a good CRKA agent, I guess."

"Yes, she was a master." Sharon concurred. "Could this somehow explain why she took care of Simon? Because she wondered if her son…" She couldn't finish the sentence.

"Hmm." Craig's eyes silenced her. Claire exchanged eye contact with them and they all stopped speculating.

"Simon?" Burton spoke up. "What does that bizarre young man have to do with this?"

"Just another game of manipulation for Elzbeth, I suspect Burton." Sharon responded quickly. "Regardless of any past affiliations with this madman, we have a decision to make. What do we do? I don't doubt the validity of his threat. Do we dare try to meet with them?"

"We can't do it." Craig stated flatly. "It's too risky."

"But my sister," Claire pleaded, "is at risk if you don't meet with them. Surely you can't take that chance. And what about his threat of the public execution? If you don't care about her life, I know you care about the world watching them do this. A public showing such as this will blow everything that you are trying desperately to contain, out of the water."

"She's right, Craig." Sharon said. "Have we covered up the security holes since the last incident with the portal? Do you think they can do this?" Craig shifted his gaze to Burton, his eyebrow lifted in inquiry.

"I think they can do this." Burton answered tonelessly.

The chiseled face of his superior winced, as if in pain. "Burton, what do you recommend?" He asked. "Do you think you can you put together a security plan for this meeting so that we are covered?"

"It will be a challenge but I can do it." Burton agreed. "We don't have much time."

"His instructions were clear." Sharon remarked. "He wants us to use the Hover Council Ship. How does he know so much about its operation? He even instructed us to dismantle the tracking device."

"It's like I said earlier. They have resources within all of our organizations that you cannot imagine." Claire responded.

"I'm afraid it must be so." Burton nodded, his pale face glowing in the bright room. "We can follow the instructions but secure the ship in such a way that we will be safe. He said no weapons and we could bring interested parties or family members but only one, unarmed guard."

"The girl must board with them or no deal." Sharon insisted.

"Agreed. We will send word." The Albino replied. He shuffled to his feet abruptly. "Do you want me to proceed with preparations?"

Sharon and Craig exchanged a long, lingering glance before the steely grey head nodded affirmatively. "Yes, we'll do it. Proceed."

Chapter 58

"Great talents are the most lovely and often the most dangerous fruits on the tree of humanity. They hang upon the most slender twigs that are easily snapped off."

Carl Jung

The interior of the hover council ship was spacious and functional, suitable for traveling dignitaries to conduct meetings while travelling. The large conference room in the center consumed most of the space with four small private rooms—an office, washroom and two bedrooms. The pilot was separated from the rest of the group in an enclosed area in the upper front section. Holographic walls in the meeting room harmonized with the view of the sky from the windows, with fluffy white clouds on a gentle blue background.

The directions had led them on a zigzag pattern, arriving at two false coordinates first. Presumably the cult wanted to ensure they weren't followed. Finally, they'd landed on an old farmer's field at the edge of a small forest, about 100 km northwest of the city, with instructions to wait.

Almost half an hour had passed. Craig was like a caged beast. He pushed back his chair in frustration and walked to the window. "We have to get back." He complained. "Today, of all days, we have personal responsibilities with the festival tonight—especially with all the security concerns. And, hardly anyone knows where we are. We were very secretive about this meeting."

"I know, Craig. This is intolerable." She turned to Burton. "Is everything in place as planned?" Sharon asked him for the third time. Uncharacteristically, she was twisting her silk scarf into knots in her hands.

"Our people have been able to keep track of our location, I assume. And, you're sure they won't be able to get on the ship with any weapons, right?" Craig added.

"Correct. They will be scanned to ensure they are unarmed before entry. Once we have them onboard, with the girl, the pilot has instructions to lift off and return to base on our signal. First, we need to manipulate them so they are on this side of the room." Burton pointed towards the back corner. "I'll then be able to activate a force field so they'll be trapped until we have safely returned."

"I think I see them." Claire interrupted from her perch by the window. "An air cargo van is approaching." They all crowded around the windows on the side of the ship where Claire was standing to get a glimpse. It was a much smaller vessel than the one they were in. Aaron, Simon, and Sophie had been given seats against the back wall with instructions to remain there and stay quiet. Thus far, they had obeyed but now all rushed to the window to see. There was a nervous energy bouncing about the room. Even Ramona Markel, who had stood stoically on guard by the entranceway, now scurried over to get a better view.

The vehicle had landed and five robed figures emerged, standing on the grassy field in the sunlight, the wind whipping their robes about their legs. Willow stood in the middle in a shiny white robe surrounded by the four men in black.

"I will take care of this, Agent Markel." Burton declared when she turned towards the embarkation area. "Stay at your post by the entrance to this room while I scan them and bring them on board."

The conference room door swished closed behind the World Governors' Aide, leaving the seven remaining perched by the window. They saw the five guests walk towards the doorway around the front of the ship and just out of sight.

"Okay, Burton will bring them in. There's nothing to see now so let's return to our positions. Everyone stay calm and let us handle this." Sharon's steady voice belied the ball of nerves in her abdomen. They all obeyed her in silence, moving to stand by their chairs.

The blaring of an alarm assaulted their ear drums and catapulted the nervous energy to a new level. Simon's eyes bulged and he twitched visibly, his glance darting to Sharon. Aaron spoke aloud. "What on earth is that?" He demanded. The alarm stopped abruptly but left the question hanging in the air.

Ramona bolted into action. "That was the automatic weapon scanner at the embarkation entry doors. I'd better assist Burton." As she stepped forward, the door swished open and Burton led their guests into the room. Ramona backed away to the side of the room, her stance wary as a stalked panther.

Burton and the five visitors fanned out by the entrance to face the others. Sophie gasped from the back of the room when she saw Charlie, his innocent, swarthy face grim and determined, enter and move to stand opposite Ramona. He kept his back to a front, side window, facing the agent squarely. He gripped a weapon in his hand.

Willow stood closest to Ramona, just inside the doorway, a lean, dark-skinned boy close beside her. Her pale, freckled face; pure, white robe; and soft, long, waves of golden hair contrasted with her odd companions. Claire made a start of rushing towards her but Willow's eyes warned her away. Claire stepped back to her place behind her chair towards the other end of conference table.

She heard Aaron whisper her name and their eyes met from across the crowded room. The anguish and longing he'd suffered was all there. For brief seconds, they locked together while she soothed him, loved him. Everything she sent to him darted sharply into his chest, the physical pain reaching an agonizing pitch when she deliberately glanced away, forcing the connection to end. She blinked away the wetness in the corner of her eyes; gulped down her lingering emotions; and, reached for Kalesh's hand, gripping it tightly. Kalesh watched the interchange in silence, his dark eyes deep and brooding.

Sharon and Craig were frozen as statues at the head of the conference table on the other end of the room, with Sophie, Simon, and Aaron directly behind them. They stood erect, staring at the men in the entranceway. The fanatic from the video, Roland, was flanked by two men. The man on his right, who stood slightly in front of their younger companions, had a long scar down his cheek. Burton stood to his left, close to their armed guard, and now, disturbingly was cloaked in the same dark robe as the other two.

Craig spoke into the tension, his voice crisp and confident. "Burton, what's going on? Why did you allow this man to enter?" He pointed towards Charlie. "We heard the alarm."

Roland reached his left hand to touch Burton, silencing him before he could respond. "You will address all questions to me." He glared into Craig's granite features. "I am the high priest of the Cult of Armageddon. The man you call Burton is my bishop, a member of the high council. He does not answer to you."

Sharon and Craig's gaze flew to Burton, their eyes refusing to believe the truth of the statement. They watched the queer smile on the albino's face confirm it. "Burton, how could you?" She gasped.

"Traitor!" Ramona bellowed. "You are a traitor to the Republic. I will personally oversee your execution before the day is out." She stepped forward in a menacing stance, glaring at the man who had been her superior. Across from her, Charlie also stepped forward, pointing his gun at the security agent, warning her to stay back with his movement.

"Do you really think you can get away with this, Burton?" Craig continued, ignoring Roland's command. "If we don't return soon, a fleet will arrive here. Remember, we are scheduled to preside over the festival tonight."

Roland smirked, inclining his head towards Burton, apparently permitting him to respond. "No one will be looking for you." The white face of the albino asserted. "You aren't expected back today at all. I left instructions that you were on a retreat and would televise your message via the World Portal this evening, from a remote location." He nodded toward the video conferencing cabinet enclosed within the back wall. "We will all deliver our message to the world from here."

Roland finished his sentence. "Once everyone understands what that message is, of course. Those that don't may not survive to see the nightfall." His sinister words left an uncertain chill in the room. Sharon and Craig gazed at each other in silent communication, measuring the situation. Roland scanned the room, his eyes flitting over the occupants, disregarding the three at the back, barely acknowledging their presence. Finally his gaze settled on Claire. "My goodness." He proclaimed. "I certainly can see the family resemblance. You look just like my dear sister Sybil in her youth."

When he mentioned their family connection, Claire's anger boiled over, obliterating her fear for a moment. She took a step towards him, surreptitiously eying Charlie who was now pointing the gun in her direction. Claire was on the same side of the table as Charlie and now only about two paces away. "Stay back." He growled.

Claire stopped in her tracks. She faced Roland. "You are completely mad." She accused. "I can't imagine why your mother helped you, why she saved your life. She should have let them execute you thirty years ago." She took another step forward, mesmerized in her hate. Charlie stepped away from the window and towards her. He pointed the gun directly at her heart.

"My mother never helped me." The old man roared, his face red with fury. "She was the insane one. Her dedication to the Republic, to the CRKA, was more important to her than her family. Never speak to me of her again!"

"She was an icon, a hero. We all owe her a great debt for her service to the Republic and to our family. I'm sure she died regretting the day that you were born." Claire spoke brazenly as she inched forward again. Her heart was hammering in her chest. Her facial skin burned. She was directly in front of Charlie and his gun now and only two steps away from Roland. Her head was buzzing, uncertain of her plan of attack but committed, nonetheless.

"Enough!" Roland screamed. Turning to Charlie, he commanded him. "Shoot her. Kill her now and let this be a lesson for everyone." His bloodcurdling order triggered a group state of panic, a moment of mortal, paralyzing fear that could be felt collectively. And yet no one moved. Hardly anyone breathed.

Charlie leaned backwards, his eyes focused on his target, taking aim. His trembling finger curled around the trigger, preparing to fire it at Claire.

Chapter 59

"Our truest life is when we are in dreams awake."

Henry David Thoreau

Charlie hesitated. Roland took a step forward. "Shoot her, I said." His commanding voice boomed in the silent, dread-ridden room.

"Stop!" Willow and Kalesh cried out together, stepping forward in unison. Their collective focus was concentrated on Charlie who froze momentarily. It was if the room were filled with statues. Everyone was completely still, their eyes on the gun. Charlie's finger moved off the trigger. His eyes darted from Claire to his messiah and the man who had always been leader.

"What are you doing?" Roland glared at his son. "Do not dare to interfere with my orders, Kalesh." Charlie watched the interchange, his soft brow furrowed in confusion.

Ignoring Roland's outburst, Willow turned to Sharon. "Where is the incinerator chute?" Sharon expelled the breath she'd been holding, mutely pointing to a concealed hatch in the back.

"Charlie, shoot this disgusting representative of the Republic, now!" Roland demanded again. "Listen to me." Roland ordered, an edge of panic in his voice this time. "Don't let them manipulate you." Roland stepped forward as if to physically intervene but it was too late.

Willow and Kalesh directed their full attention on Charlie. His grip on the gun loosened and it hung limply from his hand. Claire pounced. Before anyone knew what had happened, she wrenched the weapon from Charlie's hands.

Claire gripped the gun and pointed it at Roland.

"Claire, no." Willow's soft voice resonated in the still, silent room. "Claire, you must trust me. There cannot be any violence here, in this room today. Please, put the weapon in the incinerator."

Claire turned to stare at her sister. She heard sounds of protest from Craig behind her. Before anyone could utter another word, she backed away steadily to the area Sharon had indicated. She deposited the gun into the incinerator with a loud clang before returning to stand by her seat.

"What do you think you are doing?" Craig demanded, his attention on Claire, his voice solid ice.

"You complete and utter fool." Roland's eyes rolled about frantically. He stepped towards to his son. "You stopped him from executing my order. Why?"

"Violence is not necessary." Kalesh responded quietly. At the back of the room, they strained to hear his words. "Please, let's all sit down." A stunned silence, like a momentary calm, descended upon the room. No one moved for seconds, frozen after the rapid turn of events. Finally Claire pulled her chair back and sat down.

Everyone else followed, finally obeying Kalesh's quiet command. Chairs squeaked loudly as they were pushed into position around the table. Ramona circled the conference table to stand protectively behind the world leaders. Claire, visibly shaken, her eyes wide with shock, took her seat beside them. Willow and Kalesh sat side by side in the center of the long table. The three huddled at the back—Aaron, Sophie, and Simon—moved their seats to the opposite middle side of the table facing the two.

Roland, Burton, and Benson sat at one end of the mahogany conference table, facing the World Governors at the extreme other end. Charlie moved to stand behind the cult leaders, shaking his head in perplexity as he gazed at his empty hands. He glanced surreptitiously at the young messiah and Willow, awestruck, quickly averting his eyes as if blinded by their holy presence.

The outwardly reserved youths, contrasts in white and black, were the center of everyone's attention. They sat side by side, angled towards each other, their focus locked together. The room was silent. To some present, it was eerie, for they sensed a steady interaction. Yet, most of them could barely discern anything. They felt sensations, saw shadowy images if they closed their eyes, but it was a haze, disjointed and indistinct. There were two in the room who could follow them at a distance: Roland and Simon.

Craig, who typically would have taken control of the meeting remained tight-lipped. He gripped Sharon's hand under the table while they both waited. Everyone waited to see where the teenagers who had quietly taken control would now lead. They wielded a power that could be sensed but not verbalized.

The priests of the Cult, with Roland crimson-faced in the middle, waited too but their anxiety was palpable. They all directed piercing stares at Kalesh whose head was down, leaning towards Willow.

Willow was completely focused on Kalesh as well. She barely concerned herself with the others in the room; she was so consumed with him, making sure he didn't waver from their shared vision. Most of all, he needed support so that he didn't succumb to pressure from his father.

The necessity for mass destruction, obliterating the Republic, striving for the end of times in a series of dismal, catastrophic events—all this, Kalesh had been raised to believe imperative for the betterment of mankind, the spirit of humanity. His loyalty to the brotherhood but, above all, his devotion to his father—had compelled him to follow this path. He'd seen a glimmer of Willow's dream but he felt the odds were stacked against them, her youthful optimism stoked by an easy life. His abhorrence for the Republic and their ways was too deeply ingrained in him to change. Keeping him committed to their middle path was critical.

They both sensed his father who was applying all his psychic energy to reach Kalesh. He was growing impatient, insisting it was time to bring the woman under control. He berated his son for letting her get to him and radiated reminders of their mission, of the necessity for what they must do. They sensed another presence who watched them intently, steadily. Willow glanced over at Simon with a startled expression.

Finally, Roland broke the silence. "Enough!" He bellowed, attempting to break their connection with the force of his voice where he had failed inwardly. "Kalesh, you must not let this girl lead you into the arms of these soul-sucking leaders of the Republic. Have you forgotten everything we've planned?"

Kalesh breathed in deeply and turned to face the glowering eyes of the man who had raised him. "I have not forgotten anything, father. We, together," he motioned towards Willow, "have seen the necessity for the end of this Republic."

Craig made a start as if to interject but Sharon silenced him with a gentle tug and a murmur. "Just wait," she whispered.

Roland leaned forward, grasping his hands together eagerly. "Then we will continue as planned? Tonight, the world will see the beginning at the Solstice Festival. Our people will be watching from the hypocenters. They are expecting you."

"We're making some changes to the plan." At the angry burn running up his father's neck, Kalesh continued. "I'm sorry, father, but the end as planned by the Cult is wrong. Too many people would suffer and die. We would miss a magnificent possibility for all people. There is a better way—one that you couldn't possibly have envisioned."

"You have let this, this," the old man sputtered, struggling for words in his outrage, "ridiculous, little bitch change everything. How could you have let her undo everything that we've worked towards for centuries?"

Kalesh turned to look at Willow again. They'd struggled first against each other and then together to find an answer, a way forward in this quandary. He'd been so certain at first and almost forced her. His sheer power, experience and mental energy were all stronger than hers. She could not possibly win in a straight battle. And, yet he needed her. Together they were so much greater than apart. Her gift was more empathetic, more nurturing—it was rooted in love. Ultimately, it could not be measured by force but in influence and insight; a deep, gentle understanding that led gradually to persuasion—and, she was still blossoming.

"Together we are able to see what we cannot see alone. This is what changed for me, father, but she didn't trick me. Truthfully, the turning point for me was when I looked deep inside and saw your motives." Kalesh sat up taller, his confidence growing. "You have been my mentor, my guide for many years. I loved you. I worshipped you. I believed everything you told me, everything you showed me. But now I know that it was all lies. Your motives are not pure. You do not care about the future of your fellow man. You care only for revenge, to feed this twisted hatred that you have bred all these years." Kalesh reached his hands in the direction of his father. "I love you still, father, but I will not follow blindly. You have raised me to be a leader and now I am ready to lead the way."

Burton spoke up. "You deceived us." He snarled. "When you stopped us from killing her, when you locked her up and we made our final plans: were you lying to us the whole time?"

"There was no other way."

At the stunned silence of the cult leaders, Craig finally interjected. "See here, uh, Kalesh. We appreciate whatever it is you just did to stop these maniacs," he glared at Roland, "from murdering Claire. But, some of your statements are well, out of line, and in other circumstances you could be in serious trouble."

Kalesh and Willow exchanged a glance. There was now between them, a wonderful lightness, now that a dark, uncertain cloud had invisibly been removed. United, they could face anything. Their lips upturned slightly, in unison, before they turned their focus to the world leaders at the other end of the table.

At their silent watchfulness, Craig continued. "If you cooperate and help us get back to our home base, I give you my personal assurance that you'll be treated fairly."

"We're not going anywhere, right now. Your pilot is asleep." Kalesh responded. "We have a great deal to do here first."

"I beg your pardon?" Craig's indignation rose in his throat. "Who exactly do you think you are to give me orders?"

"Craig." Sharon spoke softly, watching the two gifted teenagers with cautious attention. "We need to hear them out."

Instead of responding verbally, together, they captured the minds of everyone in the room, shared with them in a forceful manner—the only way to reach them all—the inner conflict that had raged between them all night. It had been a battle between alternate destinies: the path of the Republic which led to a life of mediocrity, avoidance of potential, suppression of creativity, and manipulation, lies, a precarious balancing act—the slow road to spiritual death, and the next great apocalyptic age that Kalesh had wished for, believed to be the saviour for the human spirit, but Willow had fought against this. Ultimately, it was another potentiality for the human race that Willow saw, believed in desperately, but Kalesh had been afraid to consider, afraid to even face. In the end, these visions had sown the seeds of a solution. For so long, he'd been conditioned to the path of Armageddon and to believe that any allegiance with the Republic was sinful, evil. When they had finished sharing their vision, they waited while everyone's awareness returned to the physical, some of them massaging temples, blinking rapidly.

"Kalesh. You've just shown us the evil ways of the Republic." Roland had to try again. "Their lies and manipulation, their only goal is keep their power intact, to control the people. What are you doing? You must stay with us. We will still win."

"No, father, there is no winning. I fight for you, although you do not see it, although you do not agree. I fight for humanity. I fight for the future."

Roland's face dropped. "Are you saying that you follow the lead of the Republic? That road is dismal. We have seen it!"

"No! I did not say that. I do not follow the Republic. We must forge a new path."

"What new path?" Sharon sputtered. The leaders at each end of the table began to murmur, each raising their objections. The others continued to watch in fascination.

"Everyone, just listen." Willow spoke softly. Her voice was barely discernible and yet it had the desired effect. The table hushed. "No matter what we do now, changes have been set in motion." She turned to Sharon and Craig. "You cannot go back. The Republic's carefully constructed façade, the spiritual life with no conflicts, the citizen's contract—all of it will start to unravel, questions will be asked increasingly. Already you see the cracks begin to form, the protests, the unrest. They," she pointed towards Roland and Burton, "have toppled the first dominoes. You cannot make everything that's happened disappear and just go back." She reached her arm sideways to touch Kalesh's, demonstrating their unity. "We will not let that happen."

The beginnings of an evil smile upturned the corners of Roland's mouth. "A-ha," he said. His two hands clapped together on the table.

"Not so fast, Uncle," she emphasized the word, "Roland. The end of the Republic, as we know it, will not necessarily mean the end of the world. You can forget your sick ideas for Armageddon." Willow shook her head, her eyes glancing over at Kalesh who gazed intently at his father. "Your plans for violence tonight will be unraveled just as your intended murder of my sister was."

"Father, can't you see now that your plans would cause misery and death, possibly for millions, which would solve nothing? The world would continue, in more chaos than before, living conditions deteriorated. The progress we've made with our minds, our spirits, would die, perhaps forever. A new republic would likely form—this one more controlling, more evil than the one before us."

"I see nothing of the sort." Roland's voice was clipped. He held his head high as he stared at Kalesh, his presence commanding. "What has she done to you?" He flicked his hand in Willow's direction. "You and I have seen the future together. We have seen the path that led to the glorious end. Have you forgotten?"

"I have forgotten nothing, Father." Kalesh stood up as he spoke. All eyes followed him. Although a slight figure at just sixteen years of age, his presence was that of a much older, more experienced man. No one could doubt his words when he spoke with such authority. He possessed wisdom beyond the combined age of the table. "You trained me in this art, the one they call Vision Speak. In the early days, you led me along your vision. The past and present mingled. I saw what you wanted me to see."

"It's not true." Roland interrupted, indignant. "She has manipulated you."

"Father, I'm sorry but you are the only one that has manipulated me. I had begun to see other visions before Willow came into my life, before I ever encountered her. They confused me at first." His eyes moved away from the table, gazing both upward and inward. "More and more in the past year, when I followed your path, I saw devastation and loss but not the glorious end of your dreams. When Willow and I joined, it changed everything—for both of us. We were freed. We've been places together that you can't go."

Willow nodded. "There are no words to describe it but we have seen a glorious future. It can happen."

"Exactly. We don't have to perish. We can grow and flourish as a race, evolve to a new level but only with drastic change—now. We can't let this opportunity be ignored. We will do everything in our power to make it happen."

Sharon cleared her throat loudly, ignoring Roland's clenched fists and hostile glare. "Assuming that we were to cooperate," she squeezed Craig's hand, "what kind of changes are you proposing?"

Willow responded to her. "We can outline the first steps for you but the plan will evolve. We'll need more time, more intense study." A solemn shadow covered her face at these words. She swallowed hard and gazed at Kalesh. "We must be sequestered, in a safe and secluded environment, where we will be able to spend our days in deep meditation so we can provide counsel." She felt, rather than heard, Aaron's reaction at her words. He was already her past. "You must listen to our counsel and follow it if you are to remain in your positions."

Kalesh nodded. "Yes but first, you'll have to change the spiritual contract. You will have to introduce Vision Speak to the world, particularly the young people. They must all be trained at an early age."

"What?" Craig interrupted. "This is preposterous. How can we possibly do this? That contradicts the basic tenets of the citizen's contract. It will be a free-for-all. Any religious fanatics, such as these doomsday types, will be free to espouse their ideas. Chaos could reign. It would be the world before the bombs all over again and these lunatics would win after all."

"It will not be that way," insisted Willow, her voice low yet firm. "Change is in progress. As we've stated, you cannot stop it. You must not stop it. And, you will have to allow this cult, and many others who have been refused, a spiritual offering and free speech, as well. Suppression of information, secret trials and manipulation will come to an end tonight.

The ancient myths, the scriptures and gospels that you have censored will be released." Her gentle face became forceful. "What must happen now is the truth—a slow, unraveling of the true state of our planet, of our humanity, for public consumption. We are ready."

"How can you know? What will prevent history from repeating itself over and over and over again? These ancient myths and scriptures have been the source of bloody warfare and destruction for thousands of years."

Kalesh answered Craig. "And the source of love and devotion, brotherhoods, morality laws, and the cultural centers. There is good and bad."

"Yes, and in building the Spiritual Centers, we kept the good parts, the safe parts. We allowed people to practice these faiths in a controlled, respectful manner. In essence, we saved them from themselves. We stopped the bloody history from repeating itself."

"Perhaps there was a time when the subterfuge and controls were necessary but that time is over." Willow maintained. "The citizens have grown up. This new awareness will change everything. It's time for the nursemaid to move on."

"Oh, is that what we are? Nursemaids?" Craig's sarcasm had a bitter ring.

"Perhaps." She responded wryly. "But if we were young children then, we are now about to reach adulthood. What's happened to us is already spreading rapidly." Willow rose to stand beside Kalesh, holding his hand in hers as she continued. "Together, we will continue to meditate, to make sure we stay on the path. We must embark on a psychic journey that has some risks." Across the table, Claire squeaked out a sound as if to protest but Willow smiled at her, held her hand up in reassurance. She continued. "But the risks are minor compared to the ultimate rewards for all of us, for our children and the children of the future."

"No." Roland pounded his fist on the table. "I cannot allow this."

"You cannot stop it. The events have already been set in place. You can't possibly halt what is already in progress. A psychic energy has been unleashed. Already there are changes happening that the affected people do not yet understand. Look at Simon, for example." All eyes turned to

Simon who shrunk into his seat with the sudden attention. "Simon has taken a leap forward and has grown more in this past week than in the previous years before this. Isn't that so?"

Simon's purple streaks jumped out of his skull in the sunlight from the window. He nodded in agreement, his gaze locked with Willow's. "It's true. I couldn't fathom how it happened at first but I believe it's just as you say. Ever since we connected that day…" He trailed off, his quiet voice full of wonder.

"Without training and guidance, it will be a rocky road. We must provide this. We'll also need to engage members from both the Cult and Vision Speak to help. Kalesh and I will provide leadership on this new path but we require your cooperation." She glanced at Sharon who appeared intrigued but Craig was less convinced.

"This is crazy. How can you tell us that we must change the PURE laws and our way of governance? How can you, who are little more than children yourselves, be so certain of this? Even if we agreed, we couldn't possibly convince the other world leaders." Craig spoke firmly.

"You will not have to convince them." Kalesh asserted. "There are others, like us, all over the world. Many of the other leaders have already seen this now, are being influenced as we speak. Regardless, we will show them today. Before we leave here, you will call an emergency world council. We'll join you in this meeting—and then we'll join you again tonight to address the citizens of the Republic at their festivals." He glanced at his father, "and we can reach the cult members at their meeting as you'd planned to do." Roland's return stare still burned but defeat was there too. Kalesh turned away from the man who had raised him, instead locking his gaze with Willow. "We must show them the future. Tonight, we'll send out a beacon that will touch many. It's the only way." She nodded her agreement. "We'll show you now, the possibilities. Follow us. Give us your trust. We'll share our vision of the future." Kalesh's voice was pacifying, a gentle hush. "Close your eyes, breathe deeply in and out."

Craig crossed his arms, glaring across the table at Kalesh while the others followed his direction. Willow smiled at Kalesh. Gently, quietly, she worked on Craig. His eyes closed; his arms relaxed by his side. They waited for everyone to be relaxed and connected. This time they were not forcibly led. Within minutes, the only sound in the room was the heavy in and out sounds of their collective breathing.

Willow and Kalesh united as one. Together they were strong. They instinctively knew how to coalesce, how to share their visions with the group, how to lead as a unit.

When it was over, they released them. The two returned to their seats, watching the others. Willow and Claire exchanged glances. There was love in their gaze, unlike they'd ever openly demonstrated before. For the first time, Claire looked at Willow and didn't think of her as her baby sister. She was a powerhouse.

Sharon and Craig sat in silence, the dream in their eyes still alive as they gazed at each other, the connection they'd always shared suddenly stronger than ever before. But it was all different now. How could they set aside their convictions for this new way?

Roland was the first to recover. "No, I can't believe it. This can't be happening." He wailed.

"It is so, father, and it will be good." Kalesh answered gently. He sent soothing waves to the man who'd raised him. "Take comfort in the knowledge that our actions, your actions, however misguided, have actually helped to move the world forward to this point. It will someday mean the end of human existence as we have lived for thousands of years—but the birth of a new and glorious species."

Chapter 60

"Even a happy life cannot be without a measure of darkness, and the word happy would lose its meaning if it were not balanced by sadness."

Carl Jung

Her eyes traced his profile, admiring his rugged jaw and cheekbones, the slight bump on the bridge of his nose, his auburn eyebrows. He turned as she approached, watching her steadily. After rising to greet her, he pulled her into an embrace, holding tight. He kissed her on the cheek, lingering, inhaling her scent.

Together they sat down on the green leather couch in the suite. They were alone for the first time since she'd left for the retreat. It had only been a week but it seemed like a lifetime. They only had a few minutes.

They clicked as they always had. She felt the heat rising inside her just as it had before—before everything changed. Her face burned. She touched her hands to her cheeks, stroking the blush away. Finally, she giggled like the school girl she'd been just a week ago. "Oh, Aaron, you always did have such an effect on me."

He smiled through the heartache. "And you, on me, Willow. I've never experienced anything like what we've shared." He reached for her hand, caressing it gently. "Do you have to leave? I mean, I know you have a new life, a new mission. But, I don't understand why we can't still spend time together." He tried to keep the desperation out of his voice. He grinned. "I'll work around your schedule."

"Aaron, if only we could. If I had two lives to live, oh, how I wish… But I can't." She gripped his hand tighter. "Like so many before me who have been called to a spiritual life, there are sacrifices."

"But, Willow, why do you have to sacrifice love and passion?" His whisper was earnest.

"Where I must go now, you cannot follow, Aaron." Regret was deep in her voice. "I must be with Kalesh. It's the only way. So much is at stake for so many. I've seen the consequences if I don't do this." She shuddered, pulling away from his hand so she could wrap her arms around herself. "He is my soul mate in so many ways. We belong together."

He sighed deeply, his hand suddenly cold where she had warmed it moments before. The heaviness in his heart was a physical pain. He knew what he wanted was selfish. How could he push her when she was so selfless and so sure? He swallowed his desires, forcing his thoughts away. Acceptance would come later. "Part of me is still in shock over everything that's taken place these past couple of days. It seems like years." He shook his head, remembering the broadcast that she and Kalesh had made with the World Leaders.

"It can't be measured in physical time. The transformation is incredible." Willow agreed. "So much has taken place. So much is changing and yet it all seems so natural somehow, so peaceful."

"I still can't believe it, how you reached out to so many. You've already made an impact. There's a new hum, like a collective shift in consciousness. I can actually feel it without being in deep trance." His face lit up as he spoke. "I never imagined anything like this. Everyone is working in harmony. It's like the same melody is playing in everyone's mind."

"It's wonderful…and it's only the beginning." Willow smiled, her eyes caressing the soft waves, memorizing the way he looked in the afternoon light. "So, much for your Guiding Principles, huh?"

His laughter was light and musical. "Oh, yeah. I guess they're right out the window. Surprisingly, my mother hasn't protested at all." His face sobered before asking: "Where will you go?"

"We'll live within the Artist's Community. I have one last night to see my family before we leave tomorrow." Her wise, young eyes were wistful. "We'll have a private residence within the most secluded area. We may not be seen in public for some time."

He reached over, clasping a long lock of her soft blonde hair between his fingers, pulling on it gently. "Be safe, Willow. Take my love with you." His gaze was earnest but she felt it without looking. "I can't just let this feeling between us disappear... You know that I will think of you often?"

"I know." Tears almost filled her eyes. She blinked hard, smiling at him as she rose. "Goodbye Aaron." Just before she turned for the door, she whispered. "I'll see you again soon, maybe even in your dreams."